DEKLAN

USA TODAY BESTSELLING AUTHOR

SHAY SAVAGE

D1401136

Table of Contents

DEKLAN

Prologue

When someone saves your life, you owe them.

When someone saves the life of your only child, you owe them big time.

My kidnapping at the age of fifteen and my father's inability to come up with the ransom money left him no other choice but to turn to the only person who could help him—mafia kingpin Fergus Foley.

I don't remember much of the kidnapping itself or the four days I was held in captivity. I've got a therapist who says it's my mind's way of coping with the trauma. Sometimes there are flashes of memory, but I usually try to push those out of my head.

The outcome, I remember.

See, my father was a small-time money launderer with a big gambling problem. He was already in serious debt to the Foley family. Without any tangible money to pay his debts, let alone a demand for ransom, my father paid with the only thing he could offer for one successful rescue mission—my hand in marriage to Fergus Foley's son and heir, Sean.

I'm supposed to become a princess in a vast criminal organization, but arrangements can change, and I'm facing a future quite different from the one I had anticipated.

DEKLAN

Chapter 1

I've always considered myself the pragmatic type. Even as a child, I realized that wanting chocolate chips in your pancakes didn't mean that the restaurant you are in served them that way. When it was picture day at school, but no one had bothered to do laundry the day before, you couldn't always wear your favorite shirt. When you outgrew that favorite shirt, and Dad had a fistful of cash from last night's poker tournament at the River Casino, you'd get a new one that was even prettier than the last—complete with sequins or ruffles or whatever you were into that year. When Dad lost the game, you got smacked for even asking about a shopping trip.

Sometimes, when you are walking home from school in the ninth grade, two men grab you and drag you into a windowless van. They tie you up and say they are going to kill you if your father doesn't deliver some ridiculous amount of money to them, but your dad has been on a losing streak and in more debt than the government.

What else can your dad do but make a deal with the biggest crime lord he can find to make sure you're brought home safely?

Pragmatism brings me to where I am now—on a long, winding country road leading to a new life.

This is the moment I've been waiting for, but I can't concentrate on the scenery as my father cruises his older-model BMW around curved roads and up steep hills. I barely slept last night, and I doze with my head against the window.

I'm on a boat. I can feel the rocking motion, but I can't see. There's a blindfold around my eyes and ropes bound tightly around my wrists, holding them at the center of my back. My temple throbs, but I'm not sure if it's because of the punch I took to the face or the pressure of the floor where I lie, curled up in a ball.

"It's past the deadline. He ain't gonna make it."

"What now?"

"Kill her, that's what."

I'm gonna die. I'm gonna die. I'm gonna die.

I feel hands lifting me from the floor, and I try to scream. Nothing comes out. I thrash against the hands grappling with me, but I'm overwhelmed. There are gunshots. I fall to the ground...

I come out of semiconsciousness with a jerk, hitting my head on the car window in the process. I can't remember the dream, but I know what it was about. Mom glances back at me and scowls.

"Get yourself together," she says. "We're almost there."

"The big day is almost here, princess," Dad says. "You've got to be at your best."

"I will be." The answer is automatic. When Dad tells someone to do something, it gets done. That's just the way it is. It doesn't matter if he's instructing one of the people who works for him, his wife, or his daughter—we all obey.

Any other action is dangerous.

I lick my lips, anticipating the view as we come around the corner, and try to forget the nightmare. My father makes one last turn to the right and heads up the long, brick driveway toward the gate and buildings behind a line of willow trees.

This is it. Starting tomorrow, this will be my new home.

The house—if it can even be called that—is insanely huge. A tall, iron security gate with spikes on the top surrounds it. Only two of the house's wings are visible from the front, but I know from my last visit that there is another wing jutting out from the back. There's also a pool, a fountain, and a paved path leading to another house that isn't nearly as big, but still impressive, and the stables where the Foley family keep their horses.

Sean likes to race horses.

Sean Foley is older than I, and he has blond hair and dark brown eyes. The first day I met him, I remember thinking it was a strange combination. We were introduced in this same house. No, not house—*mansion*—the same huge, ridiculous building that encompasses the horizon in front of me, complete with a wing for the servants. A wing! For servants! The house I grew up in was a posh Tudor with five bedrooms, but it was nothing compared to the Foley family home. From the Greek statues at the entryway to the horse-shaped topiary in the garden, I had been in awe from the first moment I laid eyes on it.

"It will all be yours someday," my mother had said.

"I'll live here? With him?"

"When you're old enough."

"When will that be?"

"Not until you're nineteen, dear. You have to finish high school first."

It didn't quite happen that way.

I finished high school way before the age of eighteen; I'm no one's idiot. However, the wedding had been delayed without explanation until this summer, a full year after the agreed-upon time. Then last week, Fergus Foley fell ill. There was talk of postponing the wedding until he was out of the hospital, except he never came out.

The patriarch is dead. I've had the final fitting for my dress, and the wedding is supposed to be tomorrow afternoon. But now, my family has been called to the Foley home to discuss the arrangements.

Arrangements.

Arranged marriage.

What century is this anyway?

I swallow hard and steel myself. I try not to think this way. The idea of marrying a man I hardly know is frightening, but I've known it was going to happen for five years, three months, and four days. My future was sealed in an agreement between my father and Fergus Foley—an agreement that saved me from a horrible fate.

I owe the Foleys my life, so I guess I'm going to give it to them.

To him.

Sean Foley.

Dad drives up to the gates of the property, and the security guard gives him a nod as the gates are opened, and we drive through. The driveway is long and paved with sand-colored bricks, complete with inlaid designs in red, gold, and green. It makes me think of the eighties music Mom always listens to in the car, and I wonder what kind of karma a family like ours collects.

Marrying Sean Foley doesn't upset me. Forced marriage isn't my preference, but I've had a long time to think about it, and I'm comfortable with the idea. I don't know the man well, but we've exchanged emails and have met in person a few times. Our fathers have always been present when we have been together. Nothing has ever happened between us—not even hand-holding or a kiss.

Every time I have been in his presence, Sean has been polite. He shakes hands, makes eye contact, and smiles a lot. We have similar tastes in music. We are likely better off than a lot of other couples. At least, that's what I keep telling myself.

As we come around to the front of the estate, I think to myself, *One thing is for sure—I could get used to living like this.*

Even if Sean and I don't end up getting along, I'll have plenty of other people in the house to keep me company and plenty of activities on the estate to keep me occupied. I've been home-schooled since my ordeal, so I'm used to a solitary life. I can continue my education online. I have friendships with people I've met through social media book clubs and baking websites. Through the internet, I can keep in contact with them, and my life won't be drastically different than it is now. I'll be fine living here. I'm excited to try horseback riding.

Who am I trying to convince?

Dad pulls up and puts the car in park. He reaches up and runs his hands through his thinning, grey hair. Whenever the Foley family is involved, Dad displays this nervous tick even if he is just on the phone with one of them. He isn't like that with other people.

Cormick O'Conner, my father, has a collection of small businesses: four convenience stores, six gas stations, two nail salons, and a small bookstore. Though none of them do much business, they all bring in money.

A lot of money.

I know they're all fronts. The people who come to talk business with my father range from the seedy, creepy types to the far too well-dressed. Crates of goods that never make it onto the shelves of the stores are always coming in and out of the warehouses and are always moved in the dead of night.

I don't know what might be in them, but I have my suspicions.

"Mind your manners," my mother says for the umpteenth time.

"I will."

"And don't talk too much. You get so chatty sometimes. Sean Foley doesn't want to hear all your chatter."

"I won't." Truth be told, there's a lump in my throat. I'm not sure I could talk even if I knew what to say.

I rub my left wrist. It's a nervous habit. Miss Jolly, my therapist, tries to get me to remember why I started massaging my wrist whenever I was uncomfortable with a situation, but I won't talk about it. There might not be any permanent marks anywhere, but I know I was tied up. That's just a part of being kidnapped and held for ransom. I remember being grabbed on my way home from school, and I remember thinking that I was going to die. Sometimes, if Miss Jolly tries to force it out of me, I remember the sound of gunshots, followed by my body being lifted off the floor, presumably by my rescuer. Everything in between is blank, and I'm all right with that. I don't need to remember the details.

It's the outcome that has my attention now.

I understood the basics of the deal my father had made for my safe release though I didn't really understand the why of it. Why me? Why would the head of such a powerful family bother with rescuing the daughter of a gambling addict in the first place, and why would Mr. Fergus Foley want me as his son's wife? No one seemed to be able to give me a decent answer. Even at fifteen, I had been able to comprehend what was going on around me. My mother's babble about Irish family bloodlines was just that— babble. Our families had all been here since before the Civil War. Our genetics had melted in the pot along with everyone else's, and I didn't even know anyone in Ireland. Mom said to just go along with whatever the Foleys wanted without question, but that didn't clarify why I was eligible to be a wife of a Foley.

I still don't know why. All I know is that I'm about to be married to a man I barely know and that he is now the head of one of the wealthiest families in the country. I try not to think too much about what must have been done to amass such wealth. I don't know exactly what the Foley family is involved in, but I know it's no more legitimate than my father's businesses. Drugs? Weapons? Something worse? Whatever it is, they're good at it.

A valet comes around to open my mom's door then mine.

"Welcome, Mr. and Mrs. O'Conner," the valet says as he tips his navy blue hat. "Miss O'Conner, it's a pleasure to see you again."

"Hello, John," my mother says politely. She nudges me with her elbow and gives me a harsh look as she straightens her skirt with slightly shaky hands.

"It's good to see you, too, John," I say quickly. I try to smile, but my stomach is turning flip-flops. The face of the valet isn't one I remember. I have no idea if I have met him before or not. I probably won't remember him later, either.

It doesn't matter how long I've known about the arrangement my parents made with Sean Foley's father or how much I've tried to prepare; I'm still nervous. The obvious discomfort of my parents doesn't help at all. Being called to the Foley family home the day before the wedding has left us all on edge. The meeting is unexpected—just as unexpected as the massive stroke that took Fergus Foley's life two days ago.

"Martha! Cormick! I'm so glad you've made it safely!" Sean Foley himself opens the door and carefully traverses the steps as the valet takes off with the car. Sean approaches with one of his henchmen—a huge monster of a man—just behind him. "And Kera, of course"—Sean takes my hand and kisses my knuckles—"so good of you to come."

I look into Sean's dark eyes. They sparkle, making his smile appear genuine. I feel heat rising to my face as I glance from Sean to the stern face of the tall man behind him.

Every muscle in my body tenses, and I quickly look to the ground. Sean Foley's henchman embodies the phrase "If looks could kill." I don't know if he's angry or not, but his presence alone is unnerving. I suppose that's why he's around.

"I hope the weather holds out," Mom says as she glances at the clear blue sky. "I hear a storm is headed our way. It would be a shame if we had to hold the ceremony inside."

My father glares in her direction, and I have to stop myself from rolling my eyes. Fergus Foley is dead; we've been called to a spontaneous meeting, and she's talking about the weather. It's nothing more than a hopeful hint that the wedding hasn't been called off entirely.

I rather hope it has been.

"No worries about that." Sean's voice is soft. I'm not sure if my mother even hears him—she's looking nervously at my father, probably wondering if he'd slap her right in front of Sean—but Dad hears the tone of Sean's words. He glances at my fiancé with slightly narrowed eyes.

Sean Foley is tall and very easy on the eyes. I have a picture of him on my nightstand at my parents' house, and I look at it all the time. His smile is quick and reassuring as he continues to hold my hand to lead me up the steps and through the huge double doors to the marble-tiled foyer beyond.

Sean pulls his hand away from mine as soon as we're inside, and a woman in a severe black suit takes our coats and disappears off to the left as the rest of us head to the right with Sean in the lead. The henchman behind him sticks to his left shoulder as we head down a long hallway to a spacious, open room lined with bookshelves. There's a desk, several comfortable chairs and couches, and one of those globe-shaped stands for holding expensive liquor without having it on display. Sean moves to sit in a large, wingback chair. All the other seats in the room are angled toward him, rendering him the center of attention.

As soon as he sits down, his whole demeanor changes. A crooked smile crosses his face as he looks from my father to my mother and back again. There is still a sparkle in his eyes, but it's no longer reassuring or friendly. It's more like static electricity—as if there is lightning flashing around in his brain. He never looks at me. For a long moment, there is silence as I glance around the room.

The henchman stands just behind his boss. I remember seeing him before when I was invited to dine at the country club with the Foley family and my parents. He's a foreboding man, and his size alone makes him memorable though I don't recall his name. He's taller than Sean by a good three inches, and he's so big, his shoulders brushed the sides of doorway as he entered the room. I can understand why he's acting as a bodyguard for the mafia kingpin. No one in his right mind would go up against him. Even though he's an attractive, dark-haired man, I can't even look at his face for more than a second.

There are three others in the room, and despite my nervousness, I recognize them all. Neil Foley, Sean's older cousin, is standing by the globe with a glass of something dark in his hand. He's haggard and gaunt, and his gaze doesn't leave the ground as we all sit on the couches surrounding Sean. Teagan Foley, Sean's sister, leans against a bookcase with her phone in her hand. She's a beautiful woman with golden hair and a lot of eye makeup. From what I have gathered, she is a math genius, and she handles the family's bookkeeping.

Leaning back against the couch, opposite where I sit between my mother and father, is Lucas Elliot. I have no idea what he does in the organization, but I know he was a very important advisor to Fergus Foley. I suppose he's Sean's advisor now.

"I hope you received the flowers I sent to the funeral home," my mother says, breaking the silence.

"I did," Sean replies. He snickers through his nose as he takes a cigar from a box on the side table near his chair. "Thank you for your condolences. My father will be greatly missed by some, I'm sure."

Sean rolls his eyes and grins. He pats his front pocket, glances at the table, and then turns toward his bodyguard.

"Deklan, do you have a light?"

13

I nod to myself, hearing the name of Sean's strongman. With so many people in the Foley family's organization, I was going to have to focus on memorizing names.

"Yes, sir," Deklan responds.

"Have you decided on a date for the services?" my father asks.

"The services will be private," Sean says curtly. He holds the flaming end of Deklan's lighter to the tip of his cigar, but it won't light. He scowls at the end. "Family only. We won't be publishing the time."

"Of course," Dad replies. I watch his lips twitch and wonder what else he wants to say. He's obviously holding something back.

"Will we have to push back the wedding?" My mother's voice is quiet and timid. She doesn't even look up from her hands as she speaks. "We can, of course. Whatever you need to do."

This is her fear. If the wedding doesn't occur, they are still in the Foley family's debt, and it's a debt my parents have no other way of paying. Money laundering might be a lucrative business, but my father has a serious issue with Texas Hold'em, a game he claims to be good at but constantly loses.

"The wedding will still be tomorrow," Sean says, and my mother lets out a sigh of relief. Sean tilts his head and grins. "However, there will be a slight change."

My father lifts his head with a jerk, staring straight at Sean. I can see his shoulders tense, and my own anxiety is an automatic response. When my father gets angry, someone usually gets hurt. Most of the time that's Mom, but sometimes it's just whoever happens to be closest, and I'm sitting right next to him.

"What change?" my father asks. I can see his throat bob up and down, and he grips his thighs with his fingers, making the knuckles go white.

"The venue, for one," Sean says. "With the funeral plans, there's just no time to set up the garden outside. We'll hold the ceremony here with a justice of the peace." He pauses as he taps his cigar into an ashtray, stares at the tip, and tries to light it again. This time, he is successful, and the tip glows briefly as he puffs. "Oh yes"—he uses the cigar to point toward the ceiling—"and the groom. The groom is going to change."

DEKLAN

Chapter 2

My whole body goes cold. I realize my mouth is hanging open, and I close it quickly. Dad straightens in his seat, and my mother places her hand over her mouth.

"But, the arrangement with your father—" Dad starts to speak before he's interrupted.

"You mean the dead guy?" Sean's hollow laugh fills the room as his eyes dance around with their electric flashes. "It's null and void, Mr. O'Conner. Nevertheless, out of the slim respect I had for the man, I won't leave you or little Kera here out in the cold, but I have no intention of marrying her myself."

I rub at my wrist as a thousand thoughts and emotions run through me. There's dread—how else will my father pay his debt? There's relief—I don't have to marry this man. There's terror— who does he want me to marry instead?

"That...that wasn't the arrangement," Dad says. "Kera is supposed to become a Foley, not be sold off."

"No," Sean says with a shake of his head, "she's payment for everything you owe my family." He leans forward and places his elbows on his knees. He stares at my father and grins, showing his teeth. "I already have her in my wallet. How I choose to spend her is completely up to me."

I stop breathing. I keep my eyes down, refusing to look up at Sean Foley's insane, laughing face. I'm reminded of Jack Nicholson in *The Shining*. My heart is pounding, and my palms are clammy. I shove one hand between my leg and the cushion of the couch and grab my wrist with my other hand, trying to stop them both from trembling.

In this day and age, it's one thing to know I've been betrothed to someone, but to be referred to as property—not even property, but currency—is another thing entirely. I want to speak up and tell Sean to go fuck himself. I want to say that I'm not on the gold standard, but I can't. I can't say anything. The debt is still owed, and there is no way my father can pay it in actual cash. If my father won't offer me as payment, Sean will take it out on him in some other way. Without funds, my father can only pay in blood.

Whose? His? Mom's? Mine?

When someone else controls the distribution of the cards, you can't argue the hand you're dealt. They're already holding all the aces, and bluffing is futile.

My gambling father should know that.

"It's okay," I say quietly. Without looking up, I pull my hand from under my thigh and place it on my Dad's arm. "Really, Dad. It's okay with me."

My father glances at me, and I try to keep my expression in check. I swallow hard and blink to keep the burning in my eyes from turning into tears.

"Smart girl," Sean says. I glance up briefly, and he winks at me.

I shudder and look away.

"Who...who will she marry?" My mother's voice is barely audible.

"I haven't decided yet." Sean leans back in the chair and puffs on the cigar as he looks around the room. "Neil won't work out. I'm pretty sure he'd be caught cheating on her—probably with the pool boy."

Sean laughs in his cousin's direction, and Neil snorts as he shakes his head slowly before taking a big gulp from his glass, draining it. He places the glass on a nearby table, crosses his arms, and taps a shiny brown loafer against the floor. Teagan finally looks up from her phone, staring at Sean with raised eyebrows.

"How old are you, Lucas?" Sean asks abruptly.

Lucas takes a step away from the couch where he's been leaning and tilts his head to one side as he frowns. His mouth opens and closes a couple of times before he answers.

"Forty-eight."

"How much Viagra would you need to keep up with this young, hot piece of ass on the couch, huh?"

Lucas grins and then leers at me.

"I might need a few," he says, "just in case."

My father stands before my mother can grab him, and his shoulders tense as he points a finger at Sean Foley.

"Wait just a minute!" Dad yells. "This is not the deal! This is not what Fergus and I talked about at all! Kera is supposed to be set up for life—a *good* life—not just paired up randomly! She was supposed to be treated like a princess, and you're talking about her like she's a whore!"

Dad takes a step toward Sean and his chair, and everything happens so quickly that when it's over, I have to run through it again in my head to make sure I didn't miss anything.

Sean doesn't move as Deklan comes around the wingback chair, grabs my father by his outstretched arm, and spins him around. With one leg, the henchman catches my father near the ankles and takes him to the ground. I hear a click and see a gun in Deklan's hand, the muzzle pointed at the back of my father's head.

My mother lets out a high-pitched squeak and squeezes her eyes shut.

I'm the opposite. I can't look away as Sean stands slowly and then crouches down next to my father. Sean tilts his head and smiles broadly at him. Deklan leans forward, smashing my father's face against the expensive woven rug.

"Let's get something crystal clear between us," Sean says, still smiling. "If it wasn't for my family, your daughter would be either dead or being passed around some rich sultan's household as a fuck toy. Instead, she's a pristine little virgin"—he stops speaking to my father and looks up at me—"You are a virgin, right? I mean, you wouldn't dare present yourself to me if you'd let some high school boy get up in there before I got the chance, would you?"

I can't speak. All I can do is stare at the gun now pressed against my father's neck.

"Kera? I'm going to need an answer."

I finally manage to switch my gaze to Sean's face, see his raised eyebrows, and then nod quickly.

"Speak up!" he commands.

"Yes!" The word comes out as a sob. "I never even went back to high school after...after..."—I take a shuddering breath— "I'm a virgin. I swear!"

"I thought so." He turns back to my father. "As I was saying, instead of dead or fucked senseless by a hundred different guys, she's here, safe and sound, hymen intact, and just waiting to become my bride and absolve you of your debt. The fact that I've decided to make a slight change to this deal doesn't really have an impact on you, so stop your bitching."

Sean stands and motions toward Deklan, who releases my father's arm and pulls him back to his feet. The gun disappears somewhere inside Deklan's jacket, and he takes his place behind his boss.

"Now, let's speak reasonably, shall we?" Sean slides nonchalantly back into his chair, and my father sits heavily on the couch next to Mom. "Your debt will still be paid with the hand of young Kera here. I just need to figure out who the best fit for her might be."

Sean rubs his chin in thought, and Dad sits, red-faced and rubbing his shoulder. Mom isn't even trying to stop the tears running down her face. Though my heart is pounding, I try to keep myself composed. If I have to marry a guy twenty-eight years older than I am, I will. It's not like I have any real choice.

If I refuse, my father will probably kill me. If he doesn't, Sean will. Or rather, he'd have Deklan do it.

"I don't think I'll be able to afford all those little blue pills, Lucas." Sean snickers, and Lucas shakes his head. He shrugs his shoulders and looks back at me. He licks his lips slowly as Sean continues. "I'm going to have to come up with another option."

Mom and Dad both look at their hands clasped between them. I sit still, but I keep my eyes on Sean's smiling face as he looks around the room once more and then looks over his shoulder at the buff man behind him.

"What are you, Dek? Thirty or so?"

"Thirty-two, sir." Deklan narrows his eyes slightly.

"That's not too bad. Do you own a tux?"

"Yes, sir."

"What are your plans for tomorrow?"

Deklan glances at his boss. I can see his forearms tense and his tongue dart out to wet his lips before he responds.

"Whatever you need, boss," he says.

"Well," Sean says as he stands and reaches up to place his arm over Deklan's broad shoulders, "I need you to marry that young lady over there."

Using his cigar as a pointer again, Sean aims the lit end in my direction as he grins up at his henchman. I hear Deklan mutter something under his breath, but I can't make out the words.

"Of course I am," Sean says softly. "How often do I make jokes?"

Deklan's throat bobs as he stares intently at his boss. There is a silent battle going on between them, but Sean's expression never wavers. Deklan clenches his fingers into a fist but only briefly.

"If that's what you need, boss."

"That is what I need." Sean sits back in his seat and smiles at each one in turn around the room. He may be trying to appear friendly with his grin, but his eyes dare anyone to question his decision.

Deklan nods and glances at the floor. He tightens his hand into a fist again and then crosses his arms in front of his chest. I can see the muscles in his forearm tense through his shirt. He looks up, meets my gaze briefly, and then looks back at his boss.

"My daughter," Dad says with a growl, "is not marrying some brute."

"Your daughter isn't yours," Sean replies with a smile. "Her life belongs to me. Did I not make that clear? She'll marry who I say she'll marry, or I'll have the groom put a bullet between her eyes. Would you prefer that?"

I watch Deklan shift his eyes toward his boss as he uncrosses his arms and moves his hand closer to his waist.

Near his gun.

"Cormick," Mom whispers as she puts her hand on my father's arm. With her other hand, she reaches out and clasps my fingers.

"It's okay, Dad," I say again. "Really, it's fine. I'm fine with it."

If I keep saying it, maybe it will be true. Deklan looks at me again, but his face holds no expression. I have no idea what he's thinking.

"It's not," Dad says softly, but there's no fight in his tone. "You were supposed to live in prosperity, here, not marry some random…"

22

Dad's voice trails off as Mom grips his arm tightly. He looks at me, his eyes filled with terror, and his mouth slightly open, but I have no words to comfort him. I smile gently, hoping the gesture will reassure him.

Inside, numbness and shock conflict with panic.

"Mr. O'Conner has mistaken you for some commoner, Dek." Sean clicks his tongue on the roof of his mouth. "Let's hope he doesn't make any more mistakes."

My father clasps his hands in his lap and bows his head, defeated. I'm all too familiar with the look. It's the same look he often has when returning from Vegas or Atlantic City.

"Aww, don't look so sad!" Sean grins again and calls to Neil, telling him to pour everyone a drink. Neil passes out glasses of Irish whiskey to everyone but me, and Sean continues. "How about this? You hand me the money you owed my father at the time of your little girl's ordeal, plus interest, in cash, right now, and we'll forget the whole thing."

I glance at Dad. I have no idea what kind of money he owes to the Foleys, only that it is substantial.

"Teagan"—Sean turns toward his sister, the math wiz—"starting with the original amount and calculating the interest at the usual thirty-five percent, going back five years, what does Mr. O'Conner owe today?"

Teagan stares into space for only a few moments.

"Four hundred twenty-three thousand, six hundred and fifty-four dollars. Rounded."

"Quite a chunk." Sean whistles low and loud. "You got that in your pocket, Mr. O'Conner?"

Dad doesn't respond.

"Then I guess we'll be having a wedding."

My mind is racing, but I can't make sense of any of my thoughts. Sean doesn't seem like the same man I had met in the past. He's not temperate and friendly. In the past, he had seemed nearly submissive at his father's side. Not anymore. It's like something in his brain switched on when his father died, and he is now a completely different person.

A maniacal, insane person.

"Cheers!" Sean holds up his glass for a second and then quickly downs it with another snicker.

This can't be happening.

Chapter 3

Flowers lining the path leading up to a white trellis covered in roses, hundreds of guests dressed in their finest as the sun begins to set in the distance, and a huge champagne fountain decorating the vast garden behind the Foley estate—that's the image I had in my head.

It's far from the reality of the day.

Inside the Foley home is, of course, beautiful, but the sky is overcast outside, and the hallway where I stand with my father is dim and bleak.

The expression "giving the bride away" keeps running through my head.

Since the fateful meeting yesterday, I knew this wasn't going to be a normal wedding, but I figured we'd all at least go through the motions. From ceremony to reception, we would pretend we were enjoying the whole thing. I thought my father would still kiss me on the cheek and tell me how happy he is, but he doesn't.

There isn't even any music as we walk into the Foley family study, the same room we were in the day before. I'm decked out in a shining white dress with a long train, my father dressed in his finest, holding my arm, and my mother sitting in the same place she sat yesterday while my father had a gun held to his head.

She's wearing the dress she had picked out when I was going to marry Sean. This morning, she came downstairs wearing the black dress she reserves for funerals, but Dad made her change. She initially refused, but the idea of going to the wedding with a busted lip didn't appeal to her, so she changed her clothes, if not her attitude. The dress was very expensive, and Dad wasn't going to let her waste it.

I don't look at Deklan, but I know he's in a tux. I wonder if he has to have them custom made, considering his size. I suppose he can afford it, seeing who he works for and what he does.

Just what does he do?

Sean is standing up as Deklan's best man. Teagan is holding a bouquet of flowers in one hand as she stands on the other side of the judge. In her other hand, she's tapping on her phone.

Neil and Lucas are here. There are two other men I don't recognize, but that's it for the guest list. Those two aren't even dressed up. Not "wedding" dressed up anyway. They are wearing Dockers and fairly nice shirts but no ties. One of them is wearing dark tennis shoes.

I'm starting to feel overdressed.

Dad leads me up to the small group and stands between me and Deklan as the judge speaks, asking who gives this woman to this man. I hear my father mumble an answer, and then he places my hand in Deklan's.

His hand is huge, encompassing mine completely as his fingers wrap around it. He rubs his thumb across my knuckles as my head swims. I realize my knees are locked and try to relax my stance before I faint.

It's all too surreal. I can't think. I can't comprehend that this is actually happening to me. This was supposed to be a fairy tale although a bit of a twisted one. I was supposed to live in the castle with the prince, not one of the prince's guards.

Deklan grips my hand, and I glance up at him. He's so tall, I have to tilt my head just to meet his eyes. He's looking at me out of the corner of his eye, but I don't understand his expression or why he is lightly squeezing my hand. Is he trying to reassure me? Are his look and gesture telling me everything will be all right or something else? Maybe it's possessive. Maybe it's his way of showing me that I'm his now, and he can do whatever he wants.

I have no idea. I know nothing about this man.

As soon as I knew I was supposed to marry Sean Foley, I studied him. I paid attention to him on the few occasions when we were together. I researched as much as I could about him and his family. Everything I found was more rumor than anything else, but I listened closely when my father had people at the house. I heard what they talked about. I knew the Foley family.

About Deklan, I know nothing.

Holy shit—I don't even know his last name.

I look down, and my chest tightens along with my throat. I can hear the justice of the peace droning on, but I don't listen to the words. I stare at the ground and try to concentrate on what's going on around me, but I can't. I'm only aware of the sensation of Deklan's hand clasping mine and the sound of my mother sniffling, somewhere behind me.

It's taking all my willpower not to let the tears fall.

"Kera Margaret O'Conner, do you take this man, Deklan Darius Kearney, to be your lawfully wedded husband?"

Kearney. His last name is Kearney. Kera Kearney. My name will be Kera Kearney.

"Kera, answer the man so we can get on with this." Sean's voice startles me. For a long moment, I have no idea what I'm supposed to do. Sean is staring at me, his lips pressed together and his electric eyes glaring. He taps his finger against the face of the watch on his wrist.

Oh, yeah—answer the judge.

"I will." I manage to say the two simple, damning words without my voice breaking.

Deklan turns toward me, and Sean hands him a ring. I hold out my left hand, and Deklan reaches for me. He takes me by the hand for a moment, his long fingers moving up to the top of my wrist. For a moment, he uses his thumb to rub the skin right above my wrist bones.

A tremor runs up my arm. I close my eyes briefly and take in a long breath. The touch against my wrist is identical to the way I often rub at the same spot and has a similar calming effect on my body.

Deklan slides a giant rock in a bright platinum setting over my ring finger. I stare at it in disbelief for a moment until I feel Teagan smacking my arm. She hands me a similar, much larger platinum band, and I place it on Deklan's finger with shaking hands.

"I now pronounce you husband and wife. You may kiss the bride."

I stand completely still, my stomach churning, as Deklan places one hand at the back of my neck and tilts my head toward his. He has to lean over quite a bit to reach me, and I wonder if I should try to stand on my toes to make it easier for him. I don't. I can't move. I stare into his eyes as he closes the gap between us. They're pale blue and surrounded by long, black lashes. Cold. His intense look makes me shiver, and I close my eyes as he presses his mouth to mine.

His lips are warm, and he kisses me gently, lingering for a bit before he shifts to the side of my mouth and then runs his nose over my cheek.

"I'm going to take care of you," he whispers into my ear.

His words echo through my head.

He's going to take care of me.

Take *care* of me.

What does that mean?

"Take care" as in be there for me physically and emotionally? Provide and protect and all the other shit the judge said? Or does he mean something more sinister? Did Sean instruct him to "take care of me"?

Would Sean do that? Would he go through this ceremony just to set my father up and then have his henchman-groom kill me on the wedding night? Is he that sadistic?

I look over to him, and there's a half-grin of self-satisfaction on his face. The lightning in his eyes flashes, and a single tear falls down my cheek.

Yes. Yes, he is.

Deklan turns to face the rest of the room, and I follow suit. Neil, Lucas, and the two unknown men clap slowly without actually looking at us, and the wedding is over.

The reception, if you can even call it that, consists of drinks from the globe-bar and a couple of trays of hors d'oeuvres. I spend the time at my new husband's side as quiet panic builds up inside of me.

None of it feels real. There is no photographer, no dinner, no music or dancing. There's no champagne. No one comes up and congratulates us. My mother is still in the same seat, staring blankly at the floor. Dad is helping himself to multiple glasses of whiskey.

Deklan doesn't drink anything, and neither do I. I'm not sure if anyone cares that my twenty-first birthday is still a few months away or not, but I don't even try to acquire any alcohol. Maybe I should. Maybe getting drunk would make all this more bearable.

It seems to work for my father.

One of the unnamed men that has been here since the start of the wedding beckons Deklan, and he walks away from me without a word. I watch him lean close to the man as they begin talking softly and then startle when Sean appears behind me.

"Well, isn't this all just lovely?"

I stare at him, wondering what he expects me to say.

"I did go through some minor effort to pull this together," Sean says. "Don't you think you should thank me?"

"Thank you," I reply quietly. I quickly look away from his eyes. They're wide with stormy flashes inside the irises.

"I was pretty damn generous, really," he says, continuing. "Neil definitely prefers cock over pussy, and I'm pretty sure Lucas has herpes. I could have done anything I wanted with you, even sold you off to the highest bidder. Yeah, I'd say you should definitely be thanking me"—he grabs my chin and tilts my head to look at him—"and mean it."

"Thank you, Sean," I say quickly. He narrows his eyes at me. "Really, thank you. I'm sure being married to you would have been better, but I'm certain you're only doing what's best for everyone."

He looks shocked at my response for a moment, then smiles again.

"I know this is not what you were expecting, but you seem to be taking it all pretty well."

"I'm fine," I tell him. Forcing myself to breathe slowly, I look straight at him. I hope he can't hear my heart beating. I don't want him to know how terrified I am. "Deklan seems…nice."

Sean snorts.

"For a killer."

I swallow hard. I've conditioned myself not to think about such things.

"You realize there was no way I was ever going to marry you," Sean says, grinning his maniacal grin. "You were my punishment, you know. Got some slut knocked up and had to send her away so no one would know the kid was mine. My father thought he could teach me a lesson—control me—by making me marry some small-time fuck-up's daughter, but he couldn't. I'd say next time, he'll know better than to drink anything I've mixed for him, but it's kinda late for that."

He laughs loudly as my eyes widen, and I process his words.

Did he…did he kill his own father? Is that what he is telling me?

Sean leans in close to me.

"You didn't lie about being a virgin, did you?"

"No," I whisper back.

"Have you seen your husband?" I stare at him, not knowing how to answer. Sean grabs my arm and points toward Deklan. "Just look at those size-fifteen shoes. You know his cock has got to be a monster. You're going to get ripped open tonight."

I freeze, inside and out, and Sean walks away from me, still laughing.

I have intentionally not thought about what is going to happen on my wedding night. Even when I thought I was going to marry Sean, I didn't let myself think about it. In my mother's words, "It's just something you have to put up with."

I know her thinking is old-fashioned. I know there are plenty of women out there who enjoy sex. I know there are men out there who want to make sure the women they are with enjoy it, too. I've masturbated. I know what an orgasm feels like. I've also known such things were off the table, considering my betrothal, and so—like most things I can't control—I have pushed thoughts of sex out of my mind.

I've never seen an actual penis. Pictures, sure, but those were all in the name of online health classes. I've heard rumors that the size of a man's dick corresponds to the size of his feet…or his hands…or his nose…or the gap between his teeth…or a dozen other random body parts. Is there any truth to any of it?

Every part of Deklan is oversized.

You're going to get ripped open tonight.

Is that a real possibility?

I had given the act of sex very little thought, but now I can't get it out of my head.

Chapter 4

"This is my place." Deklan passes by me and walks over to the kitchen where he grabs a coffee cup from the sink. He tilts his head to one side. "*Our* place, I guess I should say."

The apartment is only a few minutes from the Foley estate. Before leaving, my mother had grasped my hands without looking into my eyes and then started crying as Dad hauled her off, and I got into Deklan's car, scooping the train of my dress up and piling it on my lap as I sat in the low seat of the car.

It's a flashy sports car, but I don't know what kind.

There was silence the whole drive over here. Deklan didn't even turn on the radio, and I opted to stare out the window instead of watching him shift gears with his huge hands.

I swallow hard and look around the sparse apartment, clutching the little bag my mother had packed for me.

If those home and garden magazines had a special edition for "typical bachelor pad," this place would fit nicely on the cover. The television is huge. Underneath it is a Blu-ray player and some kind of gaming console. There's a couch, a recliner, and a coffee table, but that's it for furniture. The walls are bare. There's a short hallway that I assume leads to the bathroom and bedroom.

Bedroom.

I swallow again.

The kitchen is big enough to be the eat-in sort, but there is no kitchen table. I watch as Deklan washes out the coffee cup and places it on the top shelf in the cabinet. His shoulders rise and fall as he takes a deep breath before turning around.

"Do you want anything?" he asks.

Yes. I want to go home.

I shake my head slowly.

"You sure? I've got bottled water in the fridge."

"I'm sure." My voice sounds small and meek. I *feel* small just being in this man's presence. I tense my fingers around the handle of the overnight bag. My palms are sweating, and my grip keeps faltering.

Deklan lets out a breath and mumbles something I can't understand. He looks nervous as he runs his hand through his short, dark hair and glances at me.

"I wasn't expecting this either," he says.

"I know."

"I've never even had a woman in here before."

"You a virgin, too?" The words pop out of my mouth before I have a chance to stop them, and I feel my ears go red.

"No." He offers me a wry smile, but his pale eyes remain cold. "I just don't bring anyone here."

"Why not?"

"I don't want people knowing where I live."

"Why?"

"Because someone would try to come here and kill me."

"Oh." I don't know how else to respond to a statement like that. His answer makes sense, but this isn't something I'm used to. Talk of illegal activities, shoving piles of money into safety deposit boxes, and the occasional, loose threat, yes, but not murder.

Of course, when you're married to a killer—a mafia-backed hitman—there are going to be people out there who want your husband dead. You should have thought about that before you said those two magic words that tied yourself to him.

I'm married to a murderer.

I force the thought from my head. I can't think about such things. There are more pressing matters on the near horizon.

I'm married, and my non-virginal husband is going to want to make me his non-virginal wife. Sean's words echo in my head.

You're going to get ripped open tonight.

I close my eyes for a moment and then pretend to look around the room some more.

"Are you hungry?" Deklan asks.

"No."

Out of the corner of my eye, I see him run his hand over his head again. He's nervous, and it's making me even more nervous.

When presented with an unpleasant task that you have to accomplish, it's best for you to just get it over with.

"Can I use the bathroom?"

"Yeah," he says as he points down the hall, "it's on the left."

I grip the handle of the bag again and head down the hall. The bathroom is pretty big. There's a huge walk-in shower and a large cabinet under the sink. I lock the door behind me and then lean against it, finally letting the tears flow. I let myself cry for a few minutes, trying to keep from sobbing out loud.

Get a grip.

I clench and unclench my hands a couple of times to center myself. I can't just stay in here forever—Deklan will come looking for me. If Mom ever kept Dad waiting, and she didn't often, there was always hell to pay. My father isn't a huge man like Deklan is, but his temper is big. I don't want to find out what Deklan's anger is like on my wedding night. With a handful of toilet paper, I wipe my nose and eyes. I really want to wash my face and brush my teeth, so I open the bag to look for some toiletries.

Mom didn't pack much.

In fact, she packed almost nothing. The bag contains only the box for my wedding jewelry and one other item. At the bottom of the bag is a flat pink box. I pull it out and open it, wondering why she would put toiletries in a pink box.

It's not toiletries. It's white lingerie.

It's sheer silk and feels soft on my fingers. Mom must have purchased it when she still thought I was marrying Sean. It's my wedding night attire, and Deklan is probably out there, waiting for me to emerge in such an outfit, and I don't even have any way of cleaning my teeth.

Maybe Deklan has an extra toothbrush somewhere.

Glancing back at the locked door, I start opening drawers in cabinets. I find the toothpaste but no extra brush. No hairbrushes either, just a comb. Under the sink, there are boxes of gauze, first-aid tape, and three bottles of rubbing alcohol.

I take a deep breath and wash my face with the liquid hand soap. At least my cheeks aren't all red and blotchy now. I toy with the idea of using Deklan's toothbrush, but considering we had only kissed once, the act seems a little too intimate and a little bit gross.

I settle for rubbing my teeth with a washcloth and borrowing a bit of mouthwash.

Looking back at the pink box, I wonder if I should just put it on. The wedding dress is cumbersome, and I certainly can't wear it to bed. There isn't a change of clothes in the bag, either.

Why the hell did she even bother packing me anything?

I stare at myself in the small mirror that doubles as a medicine cabinet and think about the man in the other room. He said he was going to take care of me. Maybe that means just what I feared.

It explains Mom's excessive crying. It also explains why she didn't pack anything for tomorrow. Maybe she knew I wouldn't need it.

But she did pack the sexy nightie.

This must be the plan then. He's going to fuck me and then kill me. He's going to rip me open, and then I'm going to die in his bed.

The violent thought has a strange, calming effect on me. At least it will be over soon. It's already very late, well past midnight, and I don't have to worry about what I'm going to wear in the morning. If I can manage to make Deklan happy, maybe he will at least kill me quickly.

I clear my mind as I reach down and remove my shoes. I pull the garter along with the sheer pantyhose from my thigh and shove all of it in the bag. I stand up and reach behind my neck to loosen the dress. The first couple of hooks release easily, but I have to contort myself to get to the next one. I can't reach the one below it at all.

"Dammit." I mutter as I twist around, trying to get the hook with my other hand. It doesn't work, so I attempt to pull the tight dress up from the waist, but it won't move.

Maybe if I get some of the lower hooks first.

The lower hooks are covered with a long satin ribbon, which laces all the way back to the top. I can't reach the ties or get to the hooks underneath them. In the mirror, I can see where I need to be, but I can't reach the right spot.

My eyes burn as I stare at the little pink box and the contents within. How am I supposed to put that on when I can't get out of what I'm wearing? I want to scream, but I cover my mouth with my hand and clench my teeth. I reach behind myself to try again, but now my hand is shaking, and I can't grip the hooks at all.

The knock at the door startles me enough that I should have popped right out of the dress, but that doesn't happen.

"You okay?" Deklan's voice is muffled through the door.

"Um…yes?" I immediately turn the water on at the sink to muffle any sounds I might make. "I'm fine."

Apparently, the water isn't enough to hide my panic.

"Convincing." His sarcastic tone isn't lost on me.

"I just need a minute."

"You've been in there almost an hour."

I have?

With no other option, I admit my problem.

"I can't get my dress off." I hear the doorknob rattle.

"Open the door."

I look in the mirror again. The blotches on my cheeks have returned. I close my eyes, grip the sink, and take one long breath.

"Open the fucking door, Kera." His voice isn't raised, but his words are harsh enough that I jump to his command and unlock the door.

He stands in the doorway for a moment. He looks angry, and I brace myself for whatever that might mean.

"Do you want help," he asks, "or do you prefer to keep struggling with it?"

"Help," I say quietly. I close my eyes as I turn away so he can reach my back, wondering if he can hear my heart pounding.

I feel his hands at the hooks between my shoulder blades, and I wonder if he can even release the tiny clasps with his big fingers. I glance sideways at the mirror, but it's small, and the angle is wrong. I can't see what he's doing.

I close my eyes again and try to feel what he's doing instead. There's a slight tug as the satin ribbon is untied, and then the dress begins to loosen from top to bottom as he works each hook in turn. The shoulders of the dress sag down my arms a bit, and Deklan places his hand at the back of my neck.

I don't move. I don't even breathe. Maybe I was wrong, and he's not going to fuck me first. Maybe he doesn't like me, and he's just going to snap my neck right now.

He rubs the back of my neck for a moment, and then I feel him trail his finger down my bare back, stopping at my waist, just above the curve of my ass. I think his finger is right at the edge of my lacy, white panties, and I can hear his breath becoming heavier.

"Is that better?" he asks. His voice is soft and gruff.

"Yes." I can feel the heat from his body at my bare back, but he's still only touching me with his finger.

"Do you want more help?"

"I think I can manage."

"I'll be close by if you need anything else."

"Okay."

He walks out, closing the door behind him while I wonder why I didn't ask him for a toothbrush. I rummage through the bag again, but there isn't a little zippered pocket or anything like that inside of it, and my dress is trying to fall right off of me as I move.

With a deep breath, I stand and slip the dress from my body. Behind the bathroom door is a hook, and I hang the dress there, smoothing it slightly before stepping away and grabbing the lingerie from its box.

Ditching my bra and panties, I replace them with the white silk. Though it covers me from the top of my breasts to the top of my thighs, it's practically see-though.

I squeeze my eyes shut, but when I open them, I'm staring into the mirror again. My dark hair is piled on top of my head with a ton of pins and another ribbon. Should I take them all out?

If I do, my hair will be a disaster, and I have no hairbrush. There's no way Deklan's simple comb will leave me with anything other than frizz, so I decide to just leave it as it is.

With a final, deep breath, I open the bathroom door. Deklan isn't in the hallway, but I hear him in the next room. The door is open, so I walk in.

Much like the rest of the apartment, Deklan's bedroom is plain and undecorated. The only thing of note—and it's a big note—is the bed. It's huge. It's bigger than any king-size bed I have ever seen. It's covered with a duvet, and there are six pillows on it. It looks like he just went into a nice department store and bought the display.

Maybe he did.

Deklan is standing by the dresser, depositing his watch and wallet onto a small tray. His gun is in its holster sitting next to the tray. He's ditched his bowtie and cummerbund, and his shirt is untucked. Deklan has his back to me, and I watch him for a moment as he stares at his left hand, silently rotating the platinum band around his finger.

I take another step into the room, and he turns.

"Sweet Jesus." Deklan's eyes go wide as he gawks, and I feel my face go red. His gaze travels from my face to my bare feet and then back again. Deklan licks his lips as he takes a predatory step toward me.

I stiffen and keep my eyes focused on the floor in front of me.

He looks like he's about to say something, but he doesn't. Instead, he leans down and presses his lips against mine. I close my eyes and tilt my head up as I feel his hand move around the back of my neck. He puts more pressure against my lips as I place my hands tentatively on his waist.

I open my mouth, allowing his tongue access to mine. His hand grips my head and neck as he deepens the kiss. I stay still, not returning the kiss. I can't move. All I can think about is the lack of a toothbrush.

Deklan pulls back, and I open my eyes. His eyes are narrowed as he looks me over and sighs again.

"Kera, we don't have to do this tonight."

"Yes, we do."

"Why?"

"Because Sean wants it."

"He isn't here," Deklan says, "and I've got the weekend off. He isn't expecting to see me until Monday. There is plenty of time."

How long will it take for you to dispose of my body?

Will my body ever be found? Do my parents already know, or will they look for me? Will the police get involved or

40

look the other way like they usually do when it comes to the Foley's activities? Will some hiker come by my remains accidentally? What will I look like?

I don't have any clothes to wear tomorrow. I don't even have a hairbrush here.

Without warning, I burst into tears. I'm not crying over my impending wedding night and subsequent death. I'm crying because I'm going to be buried in a shallow grave with unbrushed teeth.

"Kera? What's wrong?" Deklan grips my upper arms and tilts his head to look me in the eye.

"Nothing." I sob as I turn away from him.

"Would you stop that?" Deklan lets out a long sigh. "Just tell me, all right?"

He's staring at my face, his expression intense—worried. Why would he be worried? Didn't he expect me to cry when he held a gun to my head—or would a gunshot be too loud, and he plans to use a knife? Maybe he'll smother me with a pillow.

"What are you thinking?" he asks quietly. "Please, Kera, tell me what's wrong."

"It's just…just…I don't have anything to wear tomorrow. My mom didn't pack me a toothbrush or a change of clothes. I don't have any deodorant or socks or anything, and I know why!"

I put my hands over my face. I sound ridiculous, and he's going to think I'm a whiny child. I brace myself, waiting for him to smack me for being so obnoxious and needy. When Mom whines about not having what she wants, dad always backhands her to shut her up.

"What do you mean, you 'know why'?" Deklan takes my wrists and pulls them from my face.

"Never mind," I whisper as I turn my head so I don't have to look at him. "It's nothing. Mom's just…forgetful. Dad's always saying that. It's fine. I'm fine."

"You don't look fine. You look…terrified."

He takes my chin in his hand and won't let me look away, keeping his grip firm as he stares at me. There's no avoiding this. There is no point in prolonging the inevitable. It's best to just let it all out now. I take a deep breath.

"I know what you meant when you said you were going to take care of me," I say.

Deklan frowns and looks confused.

"I can take it," I say softly. "If you're going to kill me, can we just get it over with?"

"Kill you?"

I let out a long breath. I'm officially tired of the charade.

"I know that's what you're going to do," I tell him. "You don't have to pretend anymore. It's not like I'm going to fight you or anything."

"Why do you think I'm going to kill you?"

I stare at him as I try to figure out his tone. He's not asking out of curiosity, as if to ask "How did you figure out the plan?" He's not acting surprised that I know what he's going to do. He seems more…horrified.

"You…you said…" I pull back from him, confused.

"What did I say?"

"You said you were going to 'take care of me,'" I whisper.

"What?"

"At the end of the ceremony," I say, reminding him. "After you kissed me, you said that."

His eyes go wide for a moment.

"No…I-I…" Deklan shakes his head sharply. "I didn't mean it like that. I mean, I'm really going to take care of you. I was…I was trying to reassure you."

He lets go of me for a moment and takes a step away from me. He looks at me with a furrowed brow for a long moment before he reaches over and takes one of my hands in his. He pulls me to the edge of the bed and sits me down beside him. He leans slightly, putting our heads closer to the same level.

"I wasn't expecting this to happen. Sean didn't give me any kind of heads up, and I'm not any more prepared for this than you are. You might actually have the advantage—at least you knew you were going to get married. I didn't expect this, but I'm going to do right by you."

I'm skeptical, to say the least. I stare into his eyes, trying to figure out if he's telling me the truth. I have no idea. I'm not a great judge of character, and I don't know his expressions well enough to determine if he's lying or not.

"I work a lot," he says as he strokes the side of my hand with his thumb, "but I'll be here with you whenever I can. I'll always protect you. I'll never fuck around on you."

Deklan pauses, and I realize he's giving me his own version of marital vows. I feel my heart beating in my chest even faster as he wraps his hand around my left wrist, rubbing my skin with his thumb. My brain flickers with brief, uncertain memory. The touch feels familiar, and I realize he's rubbing my wrist again—the same way he did before he put the ring on my finger and the same way I do when I'm anxious. I stare at his hand and feel myself relax slightly.

"I've got a temper," Deklan says. He presses his lips together for a moment before he continues. "You're bound to see that at some point, but I'll never lay a hand on you in anger. If you want anything—anything at all—I'll get it for you if I can."

I stare at him, open-mouthed and in complete shock. He seems completely serious. There's no reason for him to tell me any of this, not if he's planning to kill me.

"I'm from a traditional Catholic family," Deklan says. "We take marriage pretty seriously. This isn't about the piece of paper we signed—not to me. I'm serious about this, Kera."

"Sean didn't tell you to kill me?" I can barely hear my own voice.

"Jesus, no!" Deklan shakes his head rapidly. "He told me to be your husband, and that's what I intend to be. I'd never hurt you."

I stare at his face, trying to find some lie in his eyes, except there's nothing but sincerity. We are here alone. I can think of no reason to lie about killing me now. In fact, he is completely serious about being a husband to me.

A *real* husband.

What does that even mean?

Chapter 5

"I'm going to go get you a few things for tomorrow," Deklan says. He stands up and goes to the dresser for his keys.

"It's two in the morning," I say as I glance at the clock on the nightstand.

"There's a twenty-four hour place at the end of the block. They should at least have a few things you'll need. I'll be back soon."

In a flash, he's gone from the bedroom. I hear the front door open and close again as he leaves, and I sit on the edge of the bed, alone.

I narrow my eyes at the bedroom doorway, trying to comprehend Deklan's words and actions, and I don't know how I should react. Is he really going to the corner store to get me supplies, or is it a ruse? He wouldn't take the time to set up such a ruse if he's just going to kill me, would he?

Maybe he wants me compliant. Maybe he wants to catch me off guard just to make it easier on him. He probably just doesn't want me crying and whining on our wedding night. He wants me calm until he's ready to kill me.

But everything he said, and the way he said it, sounded completely true. He has no reason to lie to me at this point, and going out to buy stuff would be a total waste of time and effort.

Money, too. Based on the sparse nature of his apartment, Deklan obviously doesn't live like the Foleys do.

He's not going to kill me.

I let the thought sink in for a moment as I rub at my left wrist. I remember his fingers there, rubbing my skin in the same circular motion. Just the thought of his hand on me brings a moment of peace deep inside of me.

Why did he do that? Is he so observant that he remembered me rubbing my wrist yesterday when Sean was announcing the change of plans? Does he realize that sort of touch calms me?

I wrap my arms around myself and try to rethink everything I assumed since the moment Deklan kissed me in front of the justice of the peace. If half of what he told me is true, maybe this will work out better than I expected.

I'm still lost in thought when Deklan returns with a plastic shopping bag. I take the bag and look through it. He's done a decent job of finding me the necessities though the only clothing is a three-pack of store-brand, bikini underwear and a pair of white socks. At least I will finally get to brush my teeth.

"Sorry I couldn't get any real clothes," Deklan says. "We can go get your things later or even go shopping if you want."

I stare at him as my mind plays with the idea of Deklan taking me to a mall and buying me clothing and makeup. The image of him holding up dresses for me to try on doesn't suit him. Maybe he'd wait outside the dressing room, guarding me with his watchful eyes.

"Why are you doing this?" I can't quite swallow past the lump in my throat.

"Doing what?"

"Getting this stuff. Talking about shopping. Being nice to me."

Deklan takes a half step backward and stares at me.

"You said you needed that stuff."

I stare back at him. He looks genuinely confused, and his expression mirrors my own. Everything that has happened over the last day is just too much, and the pressure behind my eyes is threatening to give way.

"Kera, what is it?"

"Nothing," I say. "Sorry, I'm just a little tired."

I take the plastic bag from the corner store and return to the bathroom to brush my teeth. The simple act calms me slightly. I check myself in the mirror one last time before returning to the bedroom.

Deklan is standing near the dresser. His feet are bare, and his dress shirt is draped over a chair along with his belt. I can see the sharp outline of his back muscles through his white T-shirt. He looks me over as I enter the room. His eyes darken, and he quickly wets his lips.

"Maybe you should just go to bed."

I glance over at the monstrosity covered in pillows and blankets. If I were to get into it now, which side would I be on?

"I mean to sleep," Deklan says, clarifying. "You said you were tired. I could even stay on the couch if you want."

"No." There's no point in prolonging this any longer. "This is our wedding night, after all."

Our wedding night.

I swallow hard.

"We don't have to, Kera. Not unless you're ready."

"You said you were Catholic."

"I am."

"Well, marriage doesn't even count until...until it's consummated."

"I'm Catholic," Deklan says, "not living in the fourteenth century."

"It still doesn't count," I say again. "The marriage can still be annulled. I bet Sean will ask, too. Would you lie to him?"

"No." Deklan shakes his head slowly. "My loyalty is with the Foley family. I would not lie to him or go against him in any way."

"Then we should do this."

"I can refrain from answering for a while," Deklan says. "I don't have to lie to him to protect you. I could just keep my phone off. Problem solved."

"I wouldn't want to put you in that position."

He takes a deep breath and exhales slowly. His gaze drops for a second as he takes in the sheer white lingerie I'm wearing. My skin tingles and a shiver runs down my spine. No one has ever looked at me in such a way, and I can only assume the look on his face is pure lust. He quickly looks back to my eyes.

"Are you sure," he asks, "or are you still worrying that Sean will find out?"

"I'm sure."

He looks at me doubtfully. He clenches his fingers slightly, and I wonder what he's thinking. Is he imagining his hands on me? Is he thinking about laying me down on that gigantic bed and making me his wife in that final, undeniable way? The image runs through my head, and my thighs clench.

Deklan presses his lips together and starts to shake his head. He's going to refuse, and I suddenly don't want that to happen.

"Really," I say quickly, hoping to sound more convincing, "I'm sure. Please. I…I want to."

Deklan glances away and closes his eyes for a moment. His body goes tense. I don't understand his frustrated look.

"Come here," he says softly as he reaches toward me.

He takes my hand and leads me over to the bed. We both sit at the end, and he turns to look at me. I can't meet his eyes, so I look at my hands instead. He won't have any of that, though. He places his hand under my chin and turns me to look at him.

"You know what I am…what I do." It's a statement, not a question. I don't know the specifics of the job, but the image of Deklan holding a gun to my father's head flashes through my mind. I nod quickly, and Deklan's eyes soften slightly. "I'm not gonna hurt you."

Deklan stares into my eyes with intensity, his pupils dilated. I have no idea how to respond to his statement; I don't even know what he means. He won't hurt me right this second? He won't hurt me when he fucks me? Or does he actually mean he's going to be merciful and wait to kill me in my sleep so I won't feel anything?

"I know you're scared," he says.

"I'm not." I don't even sound convincing to myself.

"I know you are," he says again. He releases my chin and sighs. "You have every right to be scared. This whole situation is…is…fucked up."

I can't argue with the sentiment.

"But I'm not going to hurt you."

I nod though I'm still not sure I believe it. Deklan looks back at me.

"Stand up," he says as he takes my hand in his and pulls lightly.

I do as he asks, and he pulls me around until I'm standing in front of him. With him sitting on the bed and me standing, we are just about at eye level. He watches me as he reaches to his waistline and pulls off the plain white T-shirt, and I'm staring at his naked chest.

Every muscle is outlined. He's got an eight-pack for abs instead of the usual six. His shoulders and arms are huge. They look like they could crush a man without any effort at all. There's a long, thin scar near his shoulder.

I look back to his face, and his blue eyes have a softer look about them. For the first time, I find myself really looking at him. His cheekbones are high, his jaw strong, and his nose perfectly straight. His dark hair is cut short, nearly military style, and contrasts sharply with his skin. The calm displayed in his eyes has changed his appearance completely, and I feel some of my fear slip away.

I watch as he drops his gaze from my face to my body, feeling heat rise to my skin as he looks down to my feet and then back to my eyes.

"You're a beautiful girl," he says, and I glance away, embarrassed by his words. Deklan reaches up and touches my shoulder before slowly tracing his fingers down my arm and gripping my hand until I look back at him.

He takes my hand and places it on his chest, right above his heart, never taking his eyes off mine. I take in a long breath, wondering why my heart is beating so quickly. He doesn't speak. He just holds my hand against his skin until I move my thumb back and forth, running it along the curve of his pectoral, and a shiver courses through my body.

He's so warm. I can't believe how soft his skin is, considering the hard, external appearance he's displayed before. I can feel his heart beating under my palm, and my head swims.

Deklan reaches up to my hips and steadies me. I didn't even realize I was swaying. He moves his hands up and down my sides, and I tense.

"Relax," he says quietly.

"I don't know what I'm supposed to do."

"You can do whatever you want, as far as I'm concerned."

"But...what am I *supposed* to do?"

He smiles gently.

"Touch me," he says.

"Where?"

"Anywhere."

The reality of what we are about to do floods my brain. I'm so nervous I can barely stand. My hands are shaking as I copy his earlier motion, and trace his shoulder and arm with a single finger. When he doesn't move, I run back up his arm with my whole hand, stopping at his bicep. He flexes, and I push back against the firm muscle.

"How much can you bench press?" I know almost nothing about weightlifting, but it sounds like the kind of question someone might ask a body builder.

"Four hundred or so," Deklan responds with a slight shrug, "if I have a spotter."

I nod as if I know what he's talking about, but I have no clue what a "spotter" is. Four hundred pounds is a lot.

Deklan stands, and my hands fall from his shoulders as he towers over me. He reaches down and releases the button on his pants and then lowers the zipper. As his pants fall to the floor, I notice scarring on his lower leg, but it's not a thin line like the one on his shoulder. His skin looks mottled, like the kind of scar left from a burn. As I try to be subtle about looking at the scars, Deklan hooks his thumbs into the waistline of his boxer-briefs, slowly pulls them down, and my eyes go wide.

I don't know if it's huge; I have no basis for comparison. It *looks* big, jutting out from his body like a tentacle attached to a bizarre underwater alien in a monster movie.

It also looks…weird.

From the pictures I remember from health classes, I'm expecting a ridge and a bulbous tip at the end, but there isn't one. Instead, his whole shaft runs smoothly together, all the way to the end.

"I was never cut." Deklan's voice startles me from my ogling.

"Cut?"

"Circumcised."

"Oh." I don't know how else to respond. I know from my online classes that some men have a foreskin and some do not, but apparently, I've only seen pictures of men without one.

I realize I'm still staring at it and quickly look away. I hear Deklan chuckle softly, and I wonder what is so funny.

"You're laughing at me." I sound like a petulant child, and I don't care. This is all bad enough as it is. I don't need him mocking me as well.

"I'm not."

"Yes, you are."

"You're just…young," Deklan says. "It's not what I'm used to."

I consider asking just what sort of woman he is used to but think better of it. I'm pretty sure I don't want to know the answer.

"It's all right." Deklan takes my face in his hands. "Touch it. Feel it. Do whatever is going to make you more comfortable with this."

My heart beats faster. I'm not sure I want to touch it, and I don't know how I'm supposed to touch it. Should I caress it softly or grip it hard? My inexperience is leading to panic, and I can't even bring myself to move.

"You really don't want to do this."

"Yes, I do." I want it over with. I want it done— completed.

Consummated.

I also just want it. I want to feel his hands on me. I want to know what it's like to have something like that inside of me. I want him on top of me, looking down at me with that lust-filled stare. I shiver at the thought, and my breath catches audibly in my throat.

Deklan suddenly takes a step away from me.

"I can't do this," he says. "I'm not a rapist. I'm not going to do this."

My stomach drops with his words, and I'm suddenly aware of the chill in the room as he backs away from me, denying me the heat of his body as his words chill my bones.

"Maybe this is all a big mistake."

Chapter 6

I blink a few times as I try to process his words. Mistake? Rape? What happens if he goes back to Sean and tells him this isn't going to work out? What if he tells him he doesn't want me? Who gets me then?

Sean could—and would—do anything he wanted with me then. He made it clear he never intended to marry me, and God knows what he did to his father to keep that from happening. Would he give me to Lucas, that lecherous older man, or would there be some other, worse fate in store for me?

Deklan may have been unexpected, but so far, he has been kind. He said he would take care of me like a husband should, that he wouldn't hurt me, and that he isn't going to kill me. Right now, he is the best option I have, and I can't let it slide.

My throat tightens for a moment, and I have to force air into my lungs before I can respond.

"You're my husband. You can't rape me."

"Jesus." Deklan breathes the curse sharply. "Who the fuck told you that?"

"My father."

"Your father is an asshole."

I bite my lip as I stare at Deklan's harsh eyes, and memories of shouts from my parents' bedroom drown out any sounds in the room. I remember the sound of Mom's crying and Dad's angry growls telling her to "just take it" as rhythmic thumps against the wall rattled the house.

"I want you to," I say again. My voice sounds small, and I have to clear my throat.

"It's all right if we wait," Deklan says again.

"I don't want to wait." I manage to sound definitive this time. "This is our wedding night, and we're supposed to do this now. I'm not resisting. I…I want you to do it to me."

"What do you want me to do?" Deklan asks.

"Um…make love to me?"

"Jesus." He closes his eyes and takes a long, slow breath. I can see tension in his jaw, and he presses his lips together tightly. I dare to glance down just in time to see his cock twitch. "Kera…"

As his voice fades, I take a step closer to him and then hesitate. If I move any nearer, I'll bump into his dick. Maybe I should. Maybe he would like that. Maybe I'm supposed to do that, but still, I falter. I reach out for him instead, wrapping my fingers around his forearms.

"I want to," I say again. I look up into his eyes, holding his gaze as best I can. My heart is pounding in my ears. I recall his remark about how young I am. I *feel* young. Young, inexperienced, insecure, and desperate.

Deklan moves his hand to my cheek and rubs his thumb across my skin as he stares into my eyes. He leans down and brushes his lips over mine. Instant relief washes over me, and I raise myself up onto my toes and push back against his lips until he opens his mouth. This time, I don't wait for him, but push my tongue into his mouth.

He moans and pulls me closer for a moment before breaking the kiss.

"We'll go slow," Deklan says. He swallows hard and places his hands on my hips as I slide my fingers up to his biceps.

I can't get my fingers even halfway around them, and the distance between us reminds me of grade school dances.

Deklan takes one of my hands and guides it to his shaft, using his hands to wrap my fingers around it. I move my hand with his, stroking him up and down. It's hard and thick, but the skin is surprisingly soft. I can feel the edge of a long vein running along the underside, and Deklan moans when I run my finger over it.

"Go ahead," he says as he lets go of my hand. "Touch me some more."

I stare down at my fingers as I continue to stroke over the skin. I tighten my fingers around the shaft to see how far they will reach, and Deklan hums. When I glance at his face, there's a slight smile and a sparkle in his eye. I loosen my grip and reach beneath to touch that vein again. Deklan seems to like that as well, and I run my hand up to the base of his scrotum. The skin of his balls isn't as soft as his cock, and I can feel a harder lump inside the sack. I give it a little squeeze just to see how hard it is.

"Careful!" Deklan lets out a hiss. "Those are kind of sensitive."

"I'm sorry!" I start to pull my hand back, but he grabs my wrist.

"It's all right," he says. "Just a little softer touch."

I bite my lip, now terrified of doing something else wrong. I start to touch him again, but I hesitate.

"Really, Kera, it's all right."

I look down again, but whatever boldness I had acquired is abruptly gone. I don't know where I should put my hand, and my thighs keep clenching in the most distracting way.

"Please," I whisper, "will you just do whatever you want? I have no idea what I'm doing."

Deklan stares at my face for a long moment, licks his lips, and brushes his knuckles across my cheek.

"Would that make it easier for you?"

"Yes."

He kisses me gently—lips only. He lingers for a moment before I feel his hands at the hem of the sheer white lingerie top. I swallow hard and raise my arms so he can lift it off of me. I turn my head to the side, my face warming with embarrassment as he stares at me.

"You are so fucking beautiful," he says quietly.

"So are you." I quickly close my mouth but not before the words come out. Deklan is a big man and unmistakably masculine. I can't believe I just called him beautiful.

He gives me a half grin as he slides his hands down my sides. When he brings them back up again, his thumbs brush the sides of my breasts, and I shiver.

Without warning, he lifts me up, turns around, and tosses me onto the bed. He leans over and grabs the edge of my panties, slowly peeling them off me. His eyes go dark as he looks me over and places his hands on my ankles. Slowly, he runs his hands all the way up my legs, and I feel my muscles tighten as he gets close to the top. He doesn't touch me though—not *there*. Instead, he caresses my hips as he crawls on top of me.

He balances with one hand on the mattress as he uses the other to explore my body. My shoulders, my arms, my sides, and then finally my breasts. I gasp as he leans down to take a nipple in his mouth, sucking and licking gently. I press my thighs together, suddenly needing friction.

"Do you like that?" he whispers as he runs his tongue over one nipple and then the other.

"Yes," I whisper back.

He kisses me as his hands roam over my body. I try to copy his movements, running my hands over his back and shoulders. I'm continually amazed at how his body can be both soft and hard all at the same time. I slide my hands a little lower down his back and reach the curve of his ass. I feel him flex, and his cock presses against my leg as he grips my hip. The more he touches me, the more I don't care about whether or not I'm doing it right.

"You're clenching." He reaches for my thigh and pushes my legs apart. "Leave your legs open for me."

I gasp again as his words affect me more than his touch. I squirm a little, and he puts pressure on my leg to hold me still. He maneuvers one of his legs in between mine and pushes my knees farther apart. I feel his hand on the inside of my thigh, creeping slowly up until he finally reaches the top, and I moan as his fingers find me.

He slides one inside, and I close my eyes as I push the back of my head against the pillow. He adds another finger, slowly moving in and out of me. I rock my hips to the motion, and when his thumb brushes my clit, I yelp. I reach for him, grabbing his shoulders with both hands as I start to rise up.

Deklan places a hand against the middle of my chest, between my breasts, pushing me back against the bed.

"Stay right there," he says. He moves his fingers again, thumbs my clit, and covers my mouth with his own. I moan against his lips and feel his mouth turn up in a smile as his tongue glides over mine.

I'm so close, I can almost taste it.

I push harder with my hips, trying to reach that last bit of friction, but Deklan abruptly removes his fingers. He places another gentle kiss on my lips as I moan in protest. He snickers softly and then sits up, reaching one of his long arms over to grab something from the nightstand drawer.

"What is that?" I ask.

"Lube," he says simply. He tilts the small bottle into his palm before he runs his hand along his shaft. "You're pretty wet already, but a little more won't hurt."

I swallow hard, recalling the emphasis my health class placed on using protection. I have no idea how many women Deklan has been with before or if he could be carrying any STDs.

I bite my lip. This man is my husband. He's also Catholic. There's no way I'm going to ask him to put on a condom.

Once he's done coating himself, he rubs his fingers between my legs again. I can feel how slippery the lube makes me, but I'm still nervous. Glancing down at his cock so close to the entrance of my pussy makes it look huge.

Deklan leans over me again, pressing his lips to the side of my neck, near my ear.

"It will fit," he says softly. "I promise."

"Are you sure?"

"Positive."

"Will it hurt?" I close my eyes. I'm not sure I want to know the answer.

"It shouldn't. Not much anyway. That's where the lube comes in handy." Deklan kisses me again, slides his fingers in and out once more, and then sits up. "It will be easier if you're on top."

"It will?" I look at him dubiously. Everything about him makes me think he isn't normally a bottom kind of guy, and his suggestion surprises me.

"Trust me."

I don't trust him—not in the least. Still, I follow his directions, and when he lies on his back, he pulls me over the top of him until I am straddling his waist. I don't know where to put my hands. On his chest? His shoulders? To the sides of his body, my palms against the mattress?

"Just use me for balance." Deklan takes both of my wrists and guides my hands to his sternum. Once I have myself positioned how he wants me, he lets go of my wrists and reaches down between us.

I look down, watching his fingers as he wraps them around his cock and holds it up, pointing at me. With a deep breath, I position my body over the tip, and Deklan slides it back and forth across my opening, spreading the lube around my folds. He steadies himself as I drop my hips until I feel the head of his cock push inside of me. I'm expecting pain, but all I feel is pressure. Deklan doesn't move. He just watches me and waits until I push down a little more, allowing him entrance to the very core of my being.

It's a strange feeling, this stretching of my body. The lube makes everything slippery, and even with the stretching feeling, it doesn't hurt as I slowly lower myself a little more, and his cock begins to disappear.

"Keep breathing," Deklan says softly.

I didn't realize I was holding my breath. I inhale deeply, adjust my hands on his chest, and push down again. The pressure increases as his cock goes in deeper, and Deklan strokes my wrists, arms, and shoulders. My skin tingles everywhere he touches me, bringing out the goosebumps though my flesh feels warm.

I watch his face as he strokes his fingers from my shoulders, across my breasts, and down to my waist. He grips my hips, encouraging me to move the rest of the way down. With a deep breath, I lower myself as much as I can and feel a trickle of sweat run between my shoulder blades. Deklan's eyes close, and he lets out a quiet groan.

I'm all the way down, and I think he's completely inside of me. I gasp as I feel him flex, pushing himself just a tiny fraction deeper until he is buried.

"Oh, fuck," he whispers, eyes still closed. His chest rises and falls quickly with his breaths, and he grips my hips a little tighter before he runs his hands up my back and pulls me down to press his lips against mine. I meet his tongue with my own, daring to rub it against his as his fingers tangle in my hair.

He breaks the kiss and stares at me intently.

"You okay?"

I nod, licking my lips. I can still taste him.

"Ready for more?"

"What should I do?"

"Raise yourself up a little, baby," he says. "Up on your knees and then back down again. Go slow until you're used to it."

I do as he says, closing my eyes to the feeling of his cock sliding in and out. The recent, unresolved tension begins to build again as my clit presses rhythmically against his pubic bone. Deklan places his hand on my shoulder, pushing me backward until I have to put my hands behind me to keep from falling right off of him. The pressure changes, and Deklan and I groan together.

He sits up, wrapping one of his arms around my lower back. He holds me tightly against his chest for a moment as he squeezes his eyes shut and hisses through his teeth.

"I can't hold back, Kera. I can't. You feel so damn good…Sweet Jesus, I can't hold back anymore."

"It's ok." I reach up and wrap my arms around his shoulders. "I'm ready."

He angles his hips as he raises my body and then brings it back down again, meeting every stroke. His breath is hot against my shoulder, and the new position puts a lot more pressure on my sensitive flesh, rubbing up and down as my breath catches in my throat.

"Oh, yeah! Sweet Jesus, you feel so good!" His words are grunts against my skin. He briefly covers my mouth with his before he groans again, increasing his speed.

"Oh, Kera…Fuck! So good…"

"Deklan! I'm going to…going to…"

"You're going to come all over my cock." His voice is deep, and his teeth are clenched. "That's what you're going to do, baby—come on!"

He lifts my body, impaling me as I squeeze my eyes shut and cry out. A wave of sensation courses through my body as I tighten my legs around his waist and let go. I dig my fingers into Deklan's back, just trying to keep myself from collapsing as the intensity of the orgasm hits me full force.

Deklan's muscles tense under my fingers. His pace is furious as he growls my name and slams my body onto his cock again and again. I feel warmth spreading inside of me as he grunts and leans his head back to face the ceiling.

"Ahhh! Yeah!" He's panting as he tightens his grip on me, holding me fast against his chest. A moment later, he drops on his back to the mattress, taking me with him.

My head is spinning. That was nothing like the times I'd pleasured myself. Not at all. I play through the whole scene in my head again, trying to remember exactly how it all felt, and find myself reflexively clenching his cock, still pulsating inside of me.

"Oh, fuck," Deklan says with a moan. "Don't do that."

"I'm sorry," I whisper against his chest.

"No reason to be sorry. It's just a little too intense right now. Feels good just being inside you like this."

"It does?" I raise my head up to get a good look at his face.

"It does." He reaches for my face and strokes my cheek. He closes his eyes and pulls me back against his chest. I lay there with my cheek pressed against his beating heart, listening to it slowly return to its normal rate. As it does, Deklan shifts his weight, and I feel his cock slip out of me.

I tense, not sure if I have done something wrong or not. He sighs but doesn't say anything or open his eyes. He moves his hand down, slowly rubbing my lower back in small circles. I relax slightly and close my own eyes as my mind continues to race.

My previous fears return. Now that he's fucked me, will he kill me? Did he lie just long enough to get the sex out of the way first? Take what he could from me before the bloodshed has to occur?

I remember the sensations he brought from me, and I wonder if it might have been worth it.

Still, the panic that was there before we began is back again. My eyes start to burn as I wonder how quickly the end will come and if he'll be as kind about killing me as he was about taking my virginity.

Deklan rolls us to our sides and places his hand on my cheek again, turning me towards him. My eyes burn as I try to look away, not wanting him to see me cry.

"Kera? You okay?"

I clench my eyes shut and nod. I start to shake as the tears fall against my will, and Deklan tightens his arms around me.

"Tell me you won't kill me," I say though tears.

"Jesus, no!" Deklan hugs me to him for a moment before backing off and wiping tears from my cheeks. "I'd never hurt you. Never."

My chest tightens and I cry even harder. I have no idea if my tears are due to fear or relief. Deklan grabs a handful of tissues from the nightstand and gives them to me before he pulls me back on top of him and holds me tightly.

"Shh," he whispers against my ear. "It's all right, baby." He kisses the top of my head over and over again. "You're mine now. My wife—now and forever. I will always protect you and keep you safe. No one will ever hurt you as long as I'm alive."

I sob into his shoulder as he holds me against him and continues to reassure me that everything will be all right. Eventually, my tears subside, and I lay limp against his chest, surrounded by his strong arms.

The warmth of Deklan's body beneath me and the exhaustion of my own body and mind from the ordeals of the day converge, and I can't keep my eyes open any longer. With Deklan's arms wrapped tightly around me, I succumb to sleep.

Chapter 7

Despite the late hour Deklan and I finally fell asleep, I wake at the crack of dawn. For a brief moment, I don't know where I am, but there is a tiny sliver of light from the edge of the blackout curtains over the bedroom window, and I can see the outline of Deklan on the bed beside me.

I remember falling asleep on top of him, but now I'm on my side, up close to Deklan's warm body. I've got an arm and a leg wrapped around him, and one of his arms is under my shoulders. His other arm is stretched out across the bed with his hand hanging over the edge. His head is turned slightly away from me, and there's dark stubble on his cheek and chin.

He looks peaceful, and I take a few minutes just to stare at him.

He has dark brows, and his long eyelashes nearly touch his cheek when his eyes are closed and flutter slightly as he sleeps.

I lick my lips as I think back to the night before, my memories focused on the image of Deklan's face as he came inside of me; head tilted back, eyes clenched shut, and his mouth open slightly as he groaned. A shiver runs through my body, and my nipples contract.

Deklan lets out a long breath as he turns toward me in his sleep, tossing his formerly outstretched arm over my body. My leg is still wrapped around his waist, and I can feel his cock lying between my thighs. He mumbles and tilts his hips, pushing against my core.

Abruptly, I understand the phrase "morning wood."

I look up at Deklan's face, but his eyes are still closed. His lips part, and he breathes heavily again as his arms tighten around me. His hips flex, pressing his hardening cock against my leg. A moment later, he opens his eyes and meets my gaze. He looks confused for a second, then smiles gently. He reaches for my cheek and strokes his thumb over my skin.

"How sore are you?" he asks.

I stare into his eyes for a moment before I realize what he means.

"Just a little."

"Not too much?"

"No."

"Good."

A second later, he's on top of me. I gasp as he guides his fingers between my legs and works one of them inside of me. He thumbs my clit until I moan, then quickly replaces his finger with the head of his cock.

"Hold on." I barely have enough time to hear his words before he braces himself, one hand against the mattress and the other on my hip, and slams into me.

"Ah!" I cry out and arch my back as I wrap my arms around his shoulders. All I can do is hold on as he moves in and out slowly, pulling almost all the way out before thrusting back home, grunting with each penetration.

My eyes go wide as I realize something very, very important. I realize I shouldn't have worried about waking him up. I should have extracted myself from his arms just long enough to go to the bathroom, but it's too late now. I don't think I could have stopped him even if I would have wanted him to.

With each thrust, Deklan puts pressure against my bladder as well as my clit. It's slightly painful but also amplifies the sensations between my legs and inside my body as he moves. It's all I can do to use every muscle in the general vicinity to keep from losing control.

As I flex, Deklan moans loudly.

"Oh, Jesus…that's so good. Keep doing that."

I can't answer him. I clench my teeth, squeeze my eyes shut, and keep holding on. The full feeling of my bladder, combined with flexing my internal muscles and Deklan's increasing movements, intensifies every sensation. I'm already close to orgasm, but I'm terrified I'll pee on him if I do and can't speak coherently enough to tell him to stop.

Instead, I wrap my legs around him as tightly as I can, brace myself, and pray I don't lose control of my bladder as waves cascade through my body. The sound that comes from my throat is a high-pitched squeak as Deklan fills me with a scream of his own.

He collapses on top of me, and I shove at his hips, trying to get his heavy body off of my stomach.

"Please! Please get off!" I cry out.

"Kera, what's wrong?" Deklan looks horrified as he pushes himself off to the side, allowing me to jump up from the bed.

"I have to pee!" I yell as I run to the bathroom with Deklan's laughter following behind me. I barely make it to the toilet in time and sit there with my head in my hands.

When I return, embarrassed and barely able to look Deklan in the face, he's reclining against the pillows with his arms behind his head and a big grin on his face. The smile lights up his eyes and gives him a completely different appearance than his usual, forbidding demeanor.

"Sorry," I say softly.

"No reason to be." He shakes his head as he tosses his legs over the side of the bed and kisses me briefly on the forehead before making his own way to the bathroom.

I climb back into the bed and pull the sheet up around me. I can hear him peeing, and I can see into the hallway well enough to know he didn't even bother to shut the bathroom door. When he returns, I still can't look at him when he gets into the bed beside me.

"Stop looking so embarrassed," he says. "Besides, it's best for women to go to the bathroom after sex. Avoids UTIs."

"UTIs?"

"Urinary tract infections."

"Oh." I make a mental note to look that up later.

He stretches out beside me on his side with one arm under his head. He uses the other arm to grab my hand and pull it to his lips. He kisses my knuckles before holding my hand to his chest, rubbing my wrist.

I relax with my head close to his on the pillow, suddenly quite sleepy again. I watch Deklan's face as he looks down at our hands on his chest.

"I'm surprised there aren't any permanent marks."

"From what?" I tilt my head and look at him quizzically.

"The rope."

I freeze, overcome by a sudden, sinking feeling in my chest. I pull my hand away from his and tuck it between our bodies.

"Sorry," Deklan says quietly. "I didn't mean to bring back bad memories."

"I don't really remember any of it." I lick my lips and try to keep my breathing steady. I stare at a shadow on the wall to keep my mind focused outside of my head. I try to find a discernible shape in the shadow, but it's nothing more than a blob.

"What do you mean?" Deklan asks, and I have to take a moment before I can answer him.

"I assume you mean when I was kidnapped. I don't remember much of it."

"What do you remember?"

I tense again as memories of therapy sessions rattle through my head. I steel myself against any actual memory, and when I speak, my voice is monotone—rehearsed.

"I remember getting off the bus and starting to walk home. I remember someone grabbing me and throwing me in a van. There weren't any windows in the back. All I remember after that is waking up in the hospital."

Deklan also goes still and doesn't say anything else for a couple of minutes.

"You lost four days?"

"I guess so." I shrug. This is not a topic I care to discuss with anyone, and questions make it difficult not to trigger the few memories I have. "That's what they tell me anyway."

"You don't remember anything at all?"

I don't know why he's harping on this, but it's very uncomfortable. I squirm a little, trying to put some distance between us, but he's holding me tightly. I fall back on more rehearsed lines.

"I get a few flashes every once in a while, sometimes dreams, but I never remember the details when I wake up. I remember being kidnapped. I remember being scared and thinking I was going to die."

"What about…what about when you were found? Do you remember anything about that?"

"Not really." I shake my head. "A vague recollection of being picked up off the ground, but that's it."

Deklan leans his head back against the pillow and stares at the ceiling. He looks frustrated, and I feel guilty for not being able to tell him more.

"I don't like thinking about it." Admitting this doesn't appear to alleviate his frustration, but he does hug me close to him for a moment.

"It's all right," he says. He looks closely at my eyes, and I think he's going to say something else, but he stays quiet. Shuffling a little, he lays flat on his back, and I place my head on his shoulder.

He's warm, and I'm still sleepy. At some point, I doze off again. When I wake, I'm on my back with Deklan still beside me, his arm under my shoulders and one leg tossed over mine. I stare at his peaceful, sleeping face for a moment before carefully pulling my legs out from under him and heading to the bathroom.

I'm fully awake now, and I'm not sure if I should go back to bed and wait for him to get up or just go ahead and find myself some breakfast. The rumbling in my stomach makes the decision easier. Trying to stay as silent as possible to keep from waking Deklan, I pull on a pair of the panties he bought me, grab his white T-shirt off the floor, and pull it on over my head. It hangs almost to my knees, which is actually quite perfect.

It smells like him.

I find very little in the refrigerator that counts as either fresh or breakfast food. There's a box of cereal in the pantry but no milk. I see bread and cold cuts, so I place the bread in the toaster to make it at least feel breakfast-like.

I feel strange. Not bad, just different. I silently ponder the possible reasons: I'm married now. I'm no longer a virgin. I'm in a completely different kitchen and no longer live in my parents' house. Deklan really isn't planning on taking my life and throwing my body into a ditch. In fact, he seems rather...*nice*.

I think about how it felt to have his hands on me, and I realize I'm smiling.

Most importantly, I did *not* marry Sean Foley.

After seeing his behavior the last couple of days, I find myself relieved. I don't know Deklan, but he is at least trying to make the best of all this. What he said last night made sense: he wasn't any more prepared for this marriage than I was, and it puts us on similar ground.

Though the act of poking around in someone else's kitchen is a little nerve-racking, I look through the cabinets until I find a plate for my toast. I also locate a coffee pot and get it going. The coffee mugs are on the very top shelf, and even on my tiptoes, I can barely reach. I glance around for a stepladder and almost laugh out loud.

Of course there isn't a stepladder around. When would Deklan ever need one?

There are two barstools pushed up against the kitchen island. Without another viable option, I pull one of the stools next to the counter. The top spins slightly as I try to steady it so I can stand and reach the top cabinet. It still swivels, and I have to grab the cabinet door to keep my balance.

I should have realized how stupid my actions were before I ever started.

Just as I get my fingers wrapped around a mug, the top of the barstool spins to the left, and I lose my balance completely. In a fraction of a second, I'm horrified that I might drop the coffee cup or pull the cabinet door off its hinges, breaking the first things I've touched in Deklan's apartment. It doesn't occur to me at first that I'm about to hit the floor.

I scream. At least, I think I scream. I wave my hands around in the air, trying to keep a hold of the cup, but I lose track of it completely as my legs fly out from under me, and the cold linoleum floor is abruptly next to my face.

Blue and white sparks dance around in my vision, and my head throbs painfully. I reach back to touch the spot on my head, and there's already a good-sized goose-egg forming. I moan—partially from pain, partially from my own stupidity—and roll to my side. I get up on my knees, and everything swims as I fall back to the floor.

DEKLAN

Chapter 8

"Kera? Kera!" Deklan appears from the bedroom, still naked. He's crouched at my side a second later, cradling my head in his hand and holding it up off the floor. "Don't try to move."

"I'm okay," I mumble, more embarrassed now than hurt. "Did the cup break?"

"Fuck the cup," Deklan says with a growl. "You hit your head."

He lays my head down gently and uses a flashlight from the kitchen drawer to look into my eyes one at a time as I try to assure him I'm fine. He's not having any of that though.

"We need to get you checked out," Deklan says. "You probably have a concussion."

"I'm okay, really."

"We're going to the hospital."

Arguing is obviously pointless. A few minutes later, Deklan has me dressed in a pair of his sweatpants, and we're in his sports car on our way to the emergency room. I look ridiculous in the way-too-big pants and T-shirt. I feel ridiculous, too.

In the ER, the receptionist is giving me the side-eye. I'm pretty sure everyone is looking at me funny as I sit in the waiting room with a bag of ice against my head and Deklan glaring at anyone who looks in our direction. Thankfully, we don't wait long.

Deklan fills out some paperwork for me. He has to lean over a couple of times to whisper into my ear to get my health history. The nurse is staring at me, and I don't like the look on her face. Deklan tells her we don't have insurance but that he'll pay in cash.

The last name he puts down on the form isn't Kearney. I swallow hard and say nothing when he pulls out a driver's license with the name Kera Malone on it. The birthday is wrong, and the address is not one I recognize.

Once we're in an exam room, the nurse tries to get rid of Deklan.

"We'll need to see the patient on her own," she tells him.

Deklan stands up straight, towering over the poor woman.

"That's my wife," he says with a snarl. "She isn't going anywhere without me."

"It's standard procedure to—"

"Fuck your procedures!" he yells. "She's my wife!"

"It's okay!" I step in between them and place a hand on Deklan's arm. "I want him to stay with me. Please."

The nurse glares at Deklan, and he glares back. Finally, she relents and walks away.

Deklan calms immediately, taking my hand and helping me sit on the exam table. When the doctor checks me out, he says I'll be all right—no concussion—and just to watch me for a few hours. As long as I don't experience vision problems or start to vomit, there is no real concern.

"How did this happen?" he asks.

"I fell," I tell him. "It was just a stupid mistake. I was trying to reach something up high."

"Oh, really?" The doctor glances at Deklan. "What were you trying to reach?"

"A coffee cup."

"Hmm." He looks me over again. "I think you'll be fine. You don't have any signs of a concussion, but I'm sure that smarts. You're good to go. Just take some ibuprofen for the pain."

Deklan disagrees, and I think he's going to insist I get admitted, but he finally takes the doctor at his word after insisting on a script for painkillers and a follow-up appointment for the next day.

"That's an interesting outfit." The doctor comments on my apparel with a smile.

"Um…my clothes were all in the wash." It's such a ridiculous lie, and the look on the doctor's face says that he knows it. He glances at Deklan again before handing me a card.

"Well, if you need anything at all, please feel free to call my office."

I don't know what else he thinks I might need, but I don't miss the look he and Deklan exchange. The doctor's eyes are narrowed, and Deklan is staring him down. I reach for Deklan's hand, and we head back to the car.

I'm beyond embarrassed, especially when we get home. The smell of burned toast fills the air, and the coffee has gone cold.

"How's your head?" Deklan asks for the tenth time since we left the ER. He hands me my prescription pills, some fresh toast, and a glass of the orange juice he grabbed from the corner store where we picked up the painkillers.

"It's still throbbing a little," I tell him, "but it's really not that bad. I probably don't even need the pills. I just feel ridiculous."

"Take the pills." He doesn't leave room for argument, so I comply. My head does hurt but not as much as the embarrassment of Deklan having to take me to the hospital within the first twenty-four hours of our marriage.

Deklan opens up a couple of the kitchen cabinets and glances at the items on the top shelves.

"I guess I need to rearrange some things, shorty."

I glare at him, and he winks back at me.

"I'm perfectly average," I say. "You are a monster."

He raises an eyebrow at me, and I realize my choice of words might not have been the best. I cringe, but he doesn't appear to be angry as he directs me to the couch and hands me the remote control for the television.

"I'm going to go find you some actual clothes," he says. "Nothing fancy, just something to get you by for a day or two until we can do some proper shopping."

"I could just call my mom and have her bring some."

"No." Deklan's eyes darken. "I don't bring anyone here. I could go get your things, or you can go back to your folks' place when you're up to it."

I find my purse and pull out my phone. I have a few social media messages, but I don't want to check them with Deklan there in the room. I send my mom a quick text about needing to pick up some clothes and set the phone aside. Deklan stares at it as he rubs his thumb over his bottom lip. The phone chimes with a new message a few seconds later, and his eyes narrow.

Mom: Foley bought you. Tell him to get you some fucking clothes.

I tense at the tone of the message. My mother didn't write this—I know that. These are Dad's words.

I glance at Deklan, and he's staring at me. I look away and try to think of something to say.

"How about we just go shopping?" Deklan says.

He's perceptive. I have to give him that.

"That might be best."

He reaches over and takes the phone from my hand, turns it completely off, and sets it on the table next to the couch.

"I can still run out and get you some things, at least something to get you through the next couple of days until you're healed up."

74

"I could just do some online shopping," I say. "Then you don't have to bother."

"No online shopping." Deklan shakes his head and then crouches down to look me in the eye. "You are never to do anything that may compromise this address. No online shopping. No pizza delivery. We're going to have to discuss the security of that phone of yours as well."

"What's wrong with my phone?"

"GPS tracking. When it's on, you can be located. I can't have that here."

"Don't you have a phone?"

"Several. They're all prepaid burner phones. I'll get you one as well."

"Those don't have GPS?"

"All phones can be tracked if you know what you're doing," Deklan says. "Even with mine, I have to be careful about when it's on and when I use it."

"You have a computer."

"I rarely use it, and there's no internet connection here. If I need it, I use it somewhere else."

I chew my lip, wondering if Deklan is smart or paranoid. Either way, it's the end of the discussion. On Deklan's insistence, I jot down my clothing sizes and he heads out to find me something more suitable to wear.

While he's gone, I consider the differences between Deklan and my father.

On the surface, my father's businesses seem perfectly legitimate. The Foley family also has plenty of legitimate businesses as well, but anyone close to them knows there's a lot more going on, and none of it legal.

Deklan though...Deklan is completely different.

As far as I know, he doesn't own a lawful company or work at any legitimate job. Maybe on paper somewhere, he's considered "executive security" or something like that, but no one would believe it. I wonder if he even files taxes.

The medication is making my head swimmy, and I lie back on the couch to really think about whom I married.

He's a killer.

All my life, I've been exposed to the criminal underworld but not at this level. My father was content with threats, which usually got him what he wanted. The Foley empire is completely different, and Deklan's role is that of enforcer of the empire's will, and that puts me in a confusing situation.

Deklan doesn't want anyone to know where he lives. Why? Because someone might come after him. Someone might come here and try to hurt him. Where does that leave me? Am I now a potential target?

I can't keep my eyes open anymore, and the next thing I hear is Deklan's voice.

"Wake up. You need to eat."

"Hmm?" I blink a few times. The lamp on the side table is lit, compensating for the dim light coming through the window. I've slept most of the day.

"How are you feeling?" Deklan asks after I've eaten the sandwich and soup he's prepared for me.

"Better." I lean my head side to side, stretching my neck. "A little sore."

"I should have moved you to the bed."

"It's all right."

"I'll fix it." Deklan stands and heads down the hallway.

I rinse the dishes and put them in the dishwasher. Using a sponge I find under the sink, I wipe down the counters and the stove. Deklan returns as I'm finishing up.

"Come on," he says.

"Where are we going?"

"Bath." Deklan takes my hand and pulls me down the hallway and into the bathroom.

I can hardly believe what he's done.

The lights are off, and there are a handful of candles next to the sink, providing just enough light to see the bathtub full of bubbles.

"What is all this?" I normally despise when people ask questions with obvious answers, but I'm in shock. When I look at Deklan, he's grinning.

"What the hell does it look like?" He pulls his shirt over his head, ditches his jeans, and then quickly removes my clothes before he steps into the tub and sits down, knees bent. He takes my hand again.

"Careful—it's hot," he says as he helps me into the water. "Also don't want you falling again."

"No, no more of that, thanks." He's right—the water is pretty hot. It takes me a second to let my feet adjust. As I start to sit down, the heat hits all my lady-parts, and I yelp.

"Just give it a second," Deklan says. "Once you're used to it, it will feel good."

Eventually, I lower myself into the water, and Deklan holds me in his lap. He pulls my back against his chest and wraps his arms around me. I have to admit, once I adjust to the temperature, the water feels great.

"Just what you needed?" Deklan asks.

"Yes," I say with a nod. "Thank you."

"Just relax now." I tense for a second, then quickly relax against him.

I'm surprised we both fit in the tub together though there isn't a lot of extra room left. The tub is deep, but Deklan's strong arm around me keeps my head above the water, and I have no fear of sinking too low.

The heat feels fantastic on my body, alleviating some of the soreness from last night's activities. I lean my head to one side, melting into Deklan's body and nearly falling back asleep. I feel the tip of his nose run along my neck and shoulder and hear him inhale as he holds me against him.

"Tell me about your family," Deklan says suddenly.

"Not much to tell," I say with a shrug. "It's just me and my parents. No extended family except a great aunt and a cousin I've only met once when we went to my grandfather's funeral. Aunt Mabel lives in Kansas, or at least she did. Her daughter Marie is a couple years older than I am. I kind of remember playing with her after the service, but that was the only time I ever met them."

"I know your father." Deklan runs the washcloth up and down my arms. "I know what he's like. What about your mom?"

"She does what my father tells her to do."

"Are you close?"

"We were."

"Something changed?"

I shift against his chest, and Deklan wraps an arm around my stomach, just under my breasts. He hugs me to him, and I relax again.

"It was okay before Dad's debts got bad," I tell him. "The more money he lost, the more time he spent trying to win it back. When he won, everything would be great for a while, but then he would lose again, and…well, things weren't so good then."

"He hits your mom a lot, doesn't he?"

"I don't know." I shrug again. "How much is a lot?"

"I shouldn't even have to answer that." Deklan's words are mumbled, and I only barely catch them.

"Just when he's angry or drinking," I say. "Most of the time, he's fine. He just has a bit of a temper."

"Not here." Deklan sighs and hugs me again. "That won't happen with me, you understand? I don't do that shit."

I shrug again. Inside, I feel myself go numb. How many times did Dad tell Mom that it wouldn't happen again? Eventually, he just stopped saying it, and she stopped asking for an apology.

"What about you?" I ask as I turn my head to look at his face.

"I never had a family," Deklan says. "I mean, I had parents and whatever…but not really. Not since I was young."

"Who raised you?"

"Foster care from age four to twelve. Group homes for a couple of years after that. By the time I was fourteen, I was on my own."

"What happened to your parents?"

"Hand me the shampoo over there," Deklan says as he points to a bottle on the far side of the tub, near my feet.

He's distracting me on purpose, and it's working. I debate asking him about his parents again, but I don't want to push. If he doesn't want to talk about them, asking again isn't going to get me anywhere.

He washes my hair, and the feeling of his long fingers combing through the strands is enough to set the rest of my body on fire, irrespective of the water's heat. He tilts my head back, rinses me, and then gets a handful of shower gel. He washes my shoulders, my arms, my breasts, and then moves lower to wash my thighs. He reaches for my knee and holds my leg up out of the water as he runs his sudsy hands over my skin.

He slides his hand up my thigh, stroking between my legs, and I tense.

"Shh…" His breath is hot against my ear. "Relax, baby."

He strokes me slowly, fingers dancing along my sensitive skin. Each breath is a gasp as I begin to writhe on top of him, but he has his arm still wrapped around my leg, holding me open and leaving me nearly immobile as his fingers enter me.

"Oh! Deklan!" I try to arch my back, but he keeps me in place as he works his fingers in and out. His thumb circles my clit, massaging it until I'm struggling for breath. My body tries to curl in on itself as the tension builds.

My pulse rings in my ears as I sit partway up and grab Deklan's wrist, squeezing it as a shudder runs through my body, and I cry out. A moment later, I collapse backward against his chest, panting.

I've splashed water right onto the bathroom floor, but Deklan doesn't seem to care. He slowly pulls his fingers from me and goes back to rubbing my legs and arms as I try to regain my senses.

I feel his cock pressing against my ass. The bath and Deklan's erotic massage have helped the soreness between my legs though it's definitely still present. Nevertheless, I'm pretty sure I shouldn't leave him hanging, so I shift my weight and reach for his dick.

Deklan takes my wrist in his hand and pulls it away.

"Not this time. You're still sore. This one was just for you."

"Shouldn't I…give you a hand job or something?"

Deklan's body shakes with his chuckles.

"You want to know a secret?" he asks.

"Okay." I have no idea what he might reveal, and I turn my head to hear him better.

"Last night," he whispers into my ear, "was full of firsts for me, too. First time I'd ever had a woman in my own bed. This morning was the first time I'd ever woken up with a woman before."

He trails kisses down my neck while I think about this for a minute. I want to believe him. I want to think that there is something special about being his wife, but I'm not so sure. I don't know how to determine if he is telling the truth, and something doesn't quite fit.

"And," he whispers softly into my ear, "last night was the first time I'd ever come inside a woman."

"You used condoms? I thought you were from a *traditional* Catholic family."

"I am." Deklan raises an eyebrow at me. "Traditional, not living in the dark ages. If a woman wants to be a priest, she can do it as far as I'm concerned. If two dudes want to get married, I really don't care. And if I have no intention of procreating, I'm not going to be stupid enough to chance it."

He runs his hands over my skin, and I relax against him. The warmth of the water and the security of his embrace threaten to lull me to sleep. When Deklan speaks again, and his voice is so soft, I'm not sure if I really hear the words or if they are only in my imagination.

"So, last night was a first for me, too." Deklan runs his nose along my neck. "You know what? I rather liked it." He presses his lips to the edge of my jaw. "I liked it a lot." I feel his hands run over the top of my thighs and then to my hips. "That feeling…coming inside of my wife. Sweet Jesus…It's never felt like that before." He hugs me against his chest and presses his lips to my temple. "So no, I don't need a hand job. I'm going to take care of you, my wife, and when you're ready, I'm going to give you a proper fucking, followed by filling you up with my cum as often as humanly possible."

DEKLAN

Chapter 9

I feel like I've been sleeping for days.

My head is still a little sore but much better than it was yesterday. I roll to my back, but Deklan isn't on his side of the bed. The sheets aren't cold yet, so he hasn't been up long. I stretch my arms above my head and yawn and lean my body over enough to see the bathroom door, but Deklan isn't in there.

The smell of coffee drags me from bed and toward the kitchen. I can see Deklan as he leans one hand on the kitchen island and holds one of his disposable phones in the other. He's speaking so softly, I can't make out what he's saying, so I hesitantly move closer. Suddenly, Deklan raises his voice loud enough for me to hear the words.

"I don't give a shit, you motherfucking maggot! You've got an hour—one hour—to get it all, or you and I will be having more than just a little chat. After that, the only conversation we will be having is my fist finding its way into your brain through that big mouth of yours!"

I place my hand over my mouth and take a step backward into the hallway, closer to the bedroom door.

"Don't even think about running. I always find runners. When I do, the only thing left to recover is pieces."

Deklan flips the phone closed, opens a kitchen drawer, and tosses it inside. He slams the drawer shut and leans against the counter for a moment, breathing deeply enough that I can see his shoulders rise and fall. He stands up straight, and I run back to the bed. I climb in quickly as I hear his footsteps in the hallway, pull the sheet up to my neck, and close my eyes.

I will my heart to stop pounding so hard as Deklan approaches the side of the bed.

"Babe? You awake?"

"Hmm?" I feign sleep as best I can as I open my eyes and see him crouch beside the bed.

"How's the head?"

"It's all right." I reach back and rub the spot. "Just a little tender."

"Good." He reaches out and runs his hand over my cheek. "I have to run off for a little while."

"Where are you going?"

"Business."

"I thought you had the weekend off." I pull the sheet up to my chest as I sit up.

"Shouldn't be long." He leans over and kisses my forehead. "There's coffee ready. Make a grocery list and we'll go shopping when I get back."

"Where are you going?" I shouldn't press. I know I shouldn't, but his harsh words on the phone are rattling around in my head.

Deklan takes my chin in his hand and stares intently into my eyes.

"I don't want to ever have to lie to you," he says, his voice dark and his eyes even darker. "Sometimes, it's best to not ask questions." He places a finger between my eyes and slowly draws it down to the tip of my nose. "I just want to keep you safe."

I nod slowly, and Deklan taps the tip of my nose before he smiles and stands back up.

"I won't be long," he says again.

I nod once more, and he's gone a moment later. I have no idea what else I should do, so I get up, take a quick shower, and put on some of the clothing Deklan brought me.

Candle wax from last night's festivities covers the bathroom counter. The wax is white and hard, so it comes up easily. I clean up the rest of the bathroom and head to the kitchen for coffee and toast.

While I nibble, I dig through the freezer and cupboards until I find enough ingredients to make a simple casserole and get it in the oven for later.

After I've eaten, I stand in the middle of the apartment, wondering what the hell I should do with myself between now and when Deklan returns. I'd really like to check my phone, but I know I'm not supposed to use it. Though I've been out of school for some time, there are a few friends I've stayed in contact with, and one of my online book clubs is supposed to be discussing the latest C.D. Reiss book.

I glance at the television, but I've never been much of a TV watcher. I'm antsy, and I feel the need to do something physical. I glance at the dishes in the sink, rinse them off, and get the dishwasher going.

Should I clean the rest of the place?

Under the kitchen sink, I find some all-purpose cleaner and sponges.

"I shall embrace my role as apartment wife!" I say out loud, and I hold the cleaning supplies up high. I giggle, covering my mouth with my forearm and then have a sudden moment of dread. Is this place monitored? Are there hidden cameras and microphones around the room where Deklan can see what I'm doing?

I check the ceiling corners and under the shade of the table lamp in the living room, but I can't find any monitoring devices. Without any other ideas, I start to clean.

Though Deklan's place has the bachelor-pad feel, it really isn't very dirty at all. The baseboards have a lot of dust on them, as do the blinds that cover the window, but nothing else is too bad. The surfaces of the kitchen and bathroom are still shinier when I'm done, and everything smells like pine. With only four rooms to clean, I'm done quickly. Again, I stand and stare at the space around me, wondering what I should do next.

I find myself looking through the books on Deklan's bookshelf, but nothing catches my interest. It's mostly non-fiction and manuals for various high-powered rifles. Though I have studied many topics, I know nothing about guns, and the manuals are way over my head.

The timer on the stove goes off, and I check the casserole. It's done, but I'm not sure when Deklan will return, so I put the oven on low, cover the dish, and leave it inside to stay warm.

A few minutes later, I hear a sound at the door, and Deklan enters. He stops in the doorway and looks at me for a moment before coming inside and closing the door behind him.

"Hey," he says. His jacket is unbuttoned and slightly open, but instead of taking it off and hanging it on a hook, he pulls it around his body a little tighter.

"Hey," I say back. He looks ill at ease, and I wonder if, during the brief time he was out, he had completely forgotten that he has a wife now.

I find it comforting that he feels awkward. At least we have that in common.

"Did you clean?" he asks suddenly, tilting his nose in the air.

"Yes."

"You don't have to do that." He narrows his eyes at me. "I have a service that comes in."

"You trust someone to come and clean?"

"She's in the family," he says with a shrug. "One of Foley's distant cousins."

"Tell her she's been missing the baseboards."

Deklan grins and shakes his head.

"I cooked, too. Trying to be the proper wife here." Maybe if I use the term, he'll remember that we're married.

"I'd better clean up, then," Deklan says with a smile. He excuses himself, and I lay the food out on the kitchen island. I hear the water running in the bathroom sink for a few minutes before Deklan returns to the kitchen, sans jacket and in a fresh shirt. He comes up behind me, wraps his arms around my waist, and kisses my neck.

"I could get used to this coming home to hot food thing." He hugs me tight enough to lift me off the floor and then sets me down gently. "Makes me feel like Ward Cleaver."

"Who's that?"

He rolls his eyes and doesn't answer.

I sit down on the barstool that tried to kill me, and Deklan drops down beside me. He digs into the casserole like a starving man, occasionally pausing just long enough to moan in appreciation.

"You really didn't have to do all this," Deklan says as he finishes up the last of the food on his plate. "It's fantastic though. I almost never cook for myself."

"I wasn't really sure what else I should do," I tell him.

"Well, let's finish up so I can take you shopping for whatever else you need."

I feel weird spending Deklan's money. I try to just keep to the basics, but he pushes me to buy something at every store in the mall. He pays for everything with cash and declines any offers for store credit cards or discount programs. I end up with a huge pile of clothes, including quite a stack of slinky underwear and bras.

"Thank you," I say for the hundredth time as we get into the car and head back to the apartment. "Really, you don't have to do all this."

"I want to." Deklan shrugs. "I don't really spend a lot of money on myself. It's kinda nice to have someone to use it on."

He reaches over and grips my thigh. He glances at me out of the corner of his eye as he drives down the freeway. I place my hand over his and then lean over, gently kissing his cheek. Deklan turns his hand palm up and rubs the inside of my wrist as he continues to drive, and I start to babble.

"My dad would go through stages of buying me anything and everything," I say. "It depended on his mood and what was going on at the time. Mom used to shop a lot, but he would make her return things when money was tight. It embarrassed her."

I don't know why I'm going on like this. I must be on some kind of shopping high, and it's reminding me of times my mother would take me on similar sprees. I smile out the window. The sun is shining. Deklan seems to be in a good mood, and I'm relaxed, feeling safe in his presence.

"Do you actually like to shop?" I ask him.

"I don't mind it," Deklan says. He grins over at me. "I don't think I like it quite as much as you do."

I'm pretty sure I'm blushing like a schoolgirl. Despite Deklan's short and concise manner of speaking, he's easy to talk to.

"I think I've always liked it," I say, "even as a kid. I loved going to toy stores and playing with all the stuffed animals. I had quite a collection of them. I'd line them up on my bed and sleep with a different one each night so none of them would feel jealous."

I laugh at the memory, and Deklan shakes his head at me.

"Did you have stuffed animals as a kid?" I ask him.

"I had a teddy bear," he says quietly. He takes his hand away from my wrist to he can shift into a lower gear and take the exit off the freeway.

"Did your parents give it to you?" I remember his reluctance to talk about his family and try to tread softly. It's been a good day, and I don't want to ruin it by asking too much.

"I guess so," he says. "I don't remember exactly. I just remember having one."

"Did you still have it later?" I pause, trying to choose my words carefully. "I mean, when you lived with foster parents?"

"Yeah." He goes quiet.

I want to press him for more information. I want to know how he got that scar on his shoulder and the burn marks on his leg. I want to ask him what happened to his biological parents, but he's focused on the twists and turns of the road and offers no additional clarification.

It takes three trips from the car to the apartment to get all the packages inside. While I take everything out of the bags, Deklan makes space for my clothes in the closet and clears out a couple of dresser drawers for me. He also makes room in the medicine cabinet and empties a drawer in the bathroom for me.

After the clothes in the bedroom are organized, I start finding places for my toiletries in the bathroom. New toiletries mean a lot of packaging to disposes of, and when I'm done, I try to shove it all in the bathroom trash, but the small bin is already full. There's something made of blue cloth taking up most of the room, and I pull it out of the trash to see what it is.

It's the shirt Deklan was wearing when he left the apartment this morning, and I wonder if it fell in there by mistake. I pull it out the rest of the way, intending to ask Deklan if he meant to discard it, when I see the dark, red-brown stain on the front of it.

Blood.

I swallow hard.

The shirt isn't soaked in it, but there is enough to know it isn't from a small cut or a scrape. Deklan hasn't been acting like he's hurt, so I can only assume that the blood is not his.

What did he do?

My hands are shaking as I silently shove the shirt back in the bottom of the trashcan. I place a few of my empty boxes on top of it, arranging them carefully to make them look like they'd been casually tossed in. I can't risk him realizing I've seen the shirt, which he has obviously shoved in here so I wouldn't notice it.

I take a step back and clasp my hand over my mouth as the abject idea of Deklan being a killer and the reality of what he does slam together like two MMA fighters dueling for the championship. The burn of bile fills my throat, and I can no longer breathe.

My back hits the wall before I realize my feet are moving. I squeeze my eyes shut, praying that the whole idea will simply fade from my mind as the light fades from my eyes, but it doesn't work. Even with my eyes closed, I can see the dark stain. I can still smell the acrid odor that threatens to bring my dinner back up.

While I was casually cleaning and making dinner, my husband was out killing someone.

I barely have time to turn the water on to cover the noise as I grab the sides of the toilet, my dinner suddenly wasted.

Chapter 10

The next morning, I sit on the couch with my cup of coffee, dressed in the sleek purple robe Deklan bought during our shopping spree. The night before, Deklan had insisted that I looked pale, questioned me continuously about my head, and threatened to take me back to the doctor. I convinced him that I just needed a good night's sleep, and he cradled me in his arms as I thought about all that blood.

In the end, I'd barely slept at all.

This morning I'm focused on my options, of which there are really only two: stay or go.

If I were to leave, I know I couldn't go back to my parents' house. They would just force me back here. The only other option would be to make a run for it—flee the city and never look back.

I have no cash, no credit card, and no bank account. I have no transportation or friends who would be able to help me. Even if I did, I have no doubt that Deklan would manage to find me, and what happens then? What would happen to my mother and father if I were to run? What would life with Deklan be like if he had to drag me back here, kicking and screaming?

I seriously doubt he would continue to be as pleasant as he has been so far.

Running is not a viable option. Besides, I've already heard how Deklan deals with runners.

So I stay, and staying means coming to terms with what Deklan does when he's not around me. I need to concentrate on how he is when he is with me, and thus far, that has been wonderful. He's been kind, gentle, and generous. That's who Deklan is to me. That is *my* Deklan. I will just have to forget about who he is when he's not here. If there is one thing I am good at, I'm good at suppressing thoughts that cause me grief.

My Deklan isn't violent. My Deklan is not a killer. He treats me well. He makes me feel fantastic. He is going to keep me safe and be a good husband to me—a real husband—just like he said on our wedding night. Whatever he does when I'm not around doesn't matter.

I swallow down the lie I have told myself just in time to catch sight of Deklan out of the corner of my eye. I turn to face him, smiling broadly.

"Good morning!" I say cheerily.

"Feeling better?" he asks.

"Much. There's coffee if you want some."

"I do. Thank you." Deklan pours himself a cup and comes to sit next to me, and I watch his gaze move up and down my body. He places the cup on the coffee table before he reaches over and takes the edge of my robe between his fingers.

My heart starts to pound as he moves his finger slowly down the opening. He reaches the halfway point and stops. My robe is partway open now but still not showing much. He runs his tongue over his lips as he continues down until he reaches my leg. He stops again and lets his hand rest on my thigh with just his thumb inside, rubbing back and forth on my bare skin.

"Sleep well?" he asks.

It takes me a second to catch my breath and answer him.

"Well enough."

"What would you like to do today?"

"Well," I say as I try to ignore the clenching of my thighs, "I'd like to do a little more cooking, but your refrigerator is rather bare."

"Our refrigerator," Deklan says as he taps my chin with his finger. "You're right though. I rather like your cooking, so we'll get whatever you like. Ready to go now?"

"Can I get dressed first?" I glance down at my robe and then back at Deklan.

"I suppose." Deklan runs his hand over my thigh. "We could just go back to bed."

"I think we might starve if we do."

"Possible." Deklan shrugs. I'm not sure he cares.

Deklan drives us to a large supermarket, and I collect everything I'll need to prepare some of my favorite dishes. Just as we're leaving the store, Deklan's pocket buzzes, and he takes out one of his prepaid, hard-to-trace phones.

"Yeah, boss?" Deklan glances at me as he takes the last bag out of the cart and shoves it into the trunk. He nods toward the passenger side door, and I head in that direction. "They were supposed to send you an email, right? Uh…yeah, sure. We can stop by. Yeah, we're out doing some shopping…"

Deklan gives me a hard look, and I quickly drop into the car and shut the door. A moment later, he gets in beside me, his call ended.

"We need to stop by the Foley place," he says. "It should only take a minute."

I'm not eager to see Sean Foley again, but I also know I won't be able to avoid him forever. I feel better knowing I'll be at Deklan's side.

We pull up to the mansion, and John the valet takes Deklan's car without a word to either of us. I guess the pleasantries are no longer needed. Deklan places his hand on my lower back as we pass through the doorway where Sean greets us.

"You can still walk," Sean says as we enter. "I have to admit, I'm surprised."

I drop my gaze to the floor. I hear Deklan let out a short sigh, but Sean doesn't let up.

"Seriously, I'm surprised you can even stand, let alone walk straight. I thought by now you'd be curled up in a ball, whimpering in the corner." He laughs loudly, but I keep my eyes on my feet. "Aw, come on, Dek! Just having a little fun."

"You wanted me to check on the details of that shipment," Deklan says, his voice monotone.

"Yeah, yeah," Sean says quickly. "Everyone's in the office."

We follow Sean through the halls to a closed door. When he opens it, I see his sister Teagan and another young man I don't recognize.

"Hey, Dek!" the young man says.

"Brian, how are ya?" Deklan reaches out and shakes the young man's hand.

"Better," he says. "Sorry I couldn't make the festivities. Is this O'Conner's girl?"

"Kera"—Deklan tilts his head in my direction—"this is Brian."

"Good to meet you," I say quietly.

"You, too." Brian says as we shake hands briefly. "I would have been at the wedding, but I had a little…mishap."

He motions to the floor, and I notice the odd way he's standing and the crutch leaning up against the chair behind him.

"What happened?" I ask.

"Someone needs to do a better job of covering his tracks so he doesn't get followed," Sean says. "Next time, instead of a hairline fracture, Dek here can introduce him to Melissa, the Angel of Death."

Sean laughs, Brian looks nervous, and Deklan stands motionless and unreadable.

"Melissa?" I ask quietly.

"Don't worry about it," Deklan says. "Teagan, what do you have?"

Teagan spins the desk chair around to face the group and gestures toward the screen of the laptop.

"Morons," she says. "That's what I have."

"Something wrong with the pickup point?" Deklan takes a step toward Teagan, and I stay close behind him as I keep Sean in my peripheral vision.

"If you can figure out what it is from this message, be my guest."

"What's the problem?"

"Well, for starters, they think the wingdings font is the same as encryption," Teagan says with a huff. "Seriously, these people are idiots."

"So, what's in the email?" Deklan asks.

"I have no idea." Teagan turns the laptop to face everyone, and I lean around Deklan just enough to see a bit of the screen. "I don't want to just throw it into an online translator. That shit can be tracked."

"Is that Spanish or something?" Brian asks as he peers at the screen. "Don't these fuckers know we're in America?"

"They aren't in America," Teagan says, "and this isn't Spanish."

"It's Portuguese," I say.

Deklan snaps his head in my direction and narrows his eyes. I look back to the floor and position myself behind him again.

"We can wait for Jesus," Brian says.

"He's not coming." Deklan's voice is sharp and his words are clipped.

"Not unless it's a second coming," Sean says with a laugh. He slaps his hand on his thigh. "Get it? Jesus"—he pronounces the hard J—"second coming?"

He laughs long and loud. Teagan raises an eyebrow at Deklan, who shakes his head slightly and says nothing.

"Can you read it?" Teagan asks as she turns toward me.

"Maybe," I say. "I think so. My Spanish is better, but I know a little."

Sean stands up, wiping tears from his eyes, and gestures toward the screen.

I look up at Deklan, and he nods at me. I approach the laptop and peer at the email.

"Do you want me to just read it?"

"No, write a fucking dissertation on it." Sean's no longer laughing.

"Just read what you can," Deklan says softly as he places his hand on the small of my back.

"Okay." I take a deep breath and move a little closer. The email isn't written in sentences, just short phrases and numbers. "It says 'the ice cream man is coming,' then there's a bunch of numbers spelled out. Three-slash-two and four hundred. The next line says 'friend' and 'green,' but I don't know the verb. I could google it."

"I've got it," Teagan says. "It means collect or collection."

"Then it's just that line of numbers at the end," I say.

"Three-two?" Sean turns to Brian and glares. If that's a date, that's a fucking month away!"

"I think it's February third," Teagan says. "Three days."

"They're delivering the snow February third, four in the morning," Deklan says. "The numbers at the end have to be the coordinates."

Snow. He means cocaine. I glance at Deklan, but he doesn't meet my eyes.

"And a friend is going to collect it." I try to smile at Deklan, but he just narrows his eyes.

"Well, aren't you full of surprises?" Sean says as he grins at me. "Maybe we should just send you out to pick it up, huh?"

I look at the floor as I take a slight step closer to Deklan.

"She on the payroll now?" Brian asks.

"She is not." Deklan takes my arm and pulls me back away from the computer. He glares at Brian, who looks at the floor and doesn't make any further remarks.

"Brian, make sure the cargo in the shipping containers is unloaded by tomorrow," Sean says. "Gotta be ready for the new supplier."

"I'm digging into these guys a bit more," Teagan says. "I know they've been vetted by Lucas, but something isn't right here. They can't really be this stupid."

"Check it out," Sean says. "If you find something hinky, we'll let Dek deal with it."

"Kera," Dek says softly, "go wait in the hallway. I'll be out in a minute."

"Okay." I back away from him slowly, and I don't miss the smirk on Sean's face as he watches me leave the room.

I'm perfectly happy to be out of Sean Foley's presence. I walk halfway down the hall to put a little more distance between us. The walls are lined with expensive-looking paintings of people, but I have no idea who they are.

I don't wait long before the office door opens, and Sean and Teagan walk out.

"Give me two hours," Teagan says. "I should have something by then."

"It's a plan, baby sister."

Teagan rolls her eyes, gives me a nod, and heads off down the hallway, leaving me alone with Sean.

I'm instantly on edge, even before he takes a step closer to me, invading my personal space. My back is to the wall, and I can't move away from him without being extremely obvious. I glance at the door, but it's closed again with Deklan on the other side.

"Little Kera." Sean smiles and inches nearer. "I have to say, marriage seems to agree with you. You are positively glowing, as they say. Kinda like one of those monkeys that hold their bright red asses in the air, begging to be fucked."

I don't respond. I can't even look at his face. I just keep glancing at the door, praying for Deklan to come out. I can feel sweat collecting at the back of my neck, and I'm positive my heart has stopped beating.

Sean places his hand on the wall beside my head, and I turn away from him, still focused on the door to the office. He leans in until his mouth is right next to my ear.

"You know, back in feudal days, lords would take a turn at commoner brides on the wedding night, hoping to spread a little noble cum around. Maybe I should have done that. Maybe you'd like a taste of my noble cock, huh?"

"Come on, bitch. Lick my balls!"

"We ain't supposed to touch her."

"Who's gonna know?"

I swallow hard, forcing the unknown, menacing voices from my head along with the smell of grease and old sweat.

"The wedding night's over," I say softly, trying to keep my nerve. "I'm…I'm Deklan's now."

"And who do you think owns Dek?"

Voices on the other side of the door get closer, and the doorknob begins to turn. Sean takes a quick step away from me as he snickers softly. A moment later, the door opens, and Deklan comes into the hallway with Brian right behind him.

"She's so fucking hot," Brian says. "And she smells so good. I think she must work at McDonald's. Every time I pass her in the hall, I get a craving for a Big Mac."

"You ain't right." Deklan narrows his eyes as he glances between me and Sean, but Sean turns and walks down the hallway without another word, and I let out a long-held breath. Deklan reaches for my arm. "Everything okay, babe?"

"Yes," I say quickly as I press against him. "Can we go home now?"

"Yeah, sure."

"I'll call ya later, Dek. Good to meet you, Kera."

"You, too." I give Brian a brief smile, and Deklan leads me to the front door.

As soon as we're in the car, Deklan's phone rings. He doesn't say much, but I can tell he's talking to Sean. When he hangs up, he reaches over and grips my thigh.

"Did he say something to you?" Deklan asks.

"No." I don't want to lie to Deklan, but I also want to put my encounter with Sean completely out of my head, and recounting it isn't going to help. "Nothing really."

Deklan sighs audibly. I glance over. I can see his chest rising and falling, and his jaw is tense. He takes his hand from my leg to shift gears before running it through his hair.

"I should have told you to wait in the car. Just…just keep your distance from him, okay?"

"Gladly."

Deklan reaches over to stroke my cheek, and I close my eyes, leaning into his touch.

I have no doubt in my mind—Sean Foley is completely insane. I know Deklan said he would protect me, but against his own boss, a man who claims to "own" my husband? Deklan's loyalties are clear, and I'm not sure exactly where I fit on his priority list.

Chapter 11

"I fucking love this thing on you."

I squeal as Deklan grabs me from behind, nearly knocking the spatula right out of my hand. He reaches around and slides his hands under my robe and pulls me against his chest.

"The hash browns are going to burn!" I laugh as he pulls me away from the stove and sucks at my neck, tickling my sides with his long fingers.

"Can't be helped." He turns me around and presses his mouth to mine, and I feel my body melt into his.

Damn the hash browns. I don't care anymore.

I tilt my head back and open my mouth, reveling in the feeling of his hands grasping my ass and pulling me up off the floor so he can better reach my tongue with his. The kiss is too brief, and when he sets my feet back on the floor, I reach up to wrap my arms around his shoulders.

Deklan grins at me and gives me one more swift kiss before turning me back around to face the stove. Breathlessly, I go back to turning potatoes.

"I'm not sure how I'm going to cope with work today," Deklan says. "It's been nice having a few days off."

"I'm not sure what I should do today at all." I finish the cooking and load up our breakfast plates.

Other than the one trip to the Foley residence, Deklan and I have spent the last four days together. He has raved about my cooking and spent a whole lot of time learning every inch of my body, but I still don't feel like I know him well. Every time I ask him to tell me more about himself, he distracts me with his hands and mouth until I can't catch my breath long enough to ask any more questions.

I'm not ready for him to return to work.

"You should relax," Deklan says. "Watch some TV. Read a book. Take a bath."

"I do have a book I need to finish," I tell him. "I'm in a book club."

"Oh yeah?"

"Yes. It's an online club." I look at him pointedly, and he stares back at me for a long moment.

"No phone."

"Yeah, I know."

"I can take you to a place with Wi-Fi whenever you want."

"I guess that will have to do." I consider this for a moment, and another concern comes to me. "What if I need to get hold of you when you're gone?"

"Oh, yeah. I almost forgot." Deklan stands and goes to a drawer in the kitchen. He pulls out a prepaid phone and drops it on the kitchen island next to my plate. "If you need something, just use this. There's only one number programmed into it, and that will go straight to me."

I pick up the phone and turn it on, taking note of the single number in the contacts list before turning it back off. It's a simplistic phone and pretty self-explanatory, so with a smirk I decline Deklan's offer to show me how to use it.

"Only if you really need something," he says. "I'll be working and might not be able to answer right away."

"What if I just miss you?" I look up at him, already feeling alone.

"Then just hold on to that thought, and I'll make up for it when I get home."

I nod. As usual, I don't have much of a choice in the matter.

We finish breakfast, and Deklan kisses me slowly one last time before he leaves. Once he's gone, I stare at the door for a full minute before I turn around and face the empty apartment.

I don't want to watch TV. I don't need a bath, and I'm not much in a reading mood, either. I wander around for a bit, but with only four rooms in the apartment, there isn't much to keep me occupied.

I glance at my phone on the dresser. I'd like to read, but I realize my only book club is electronic, and I don't dare turn the phone on. For all I know, Deklan would know as soon as I did, and I don't want to blatantly disregard his rules. Sure, he's said he wouldn't lay a hand on me, but I'm also sure he has limits as to what he'll tolerate.

I go back to the living room, wishing I had another e-reader. Maybe Deklan would let me get one as long as it couldn't be traced.

Just to pass the time, I take a long shower, clean up the dishes from breakfast, and then give the whole apartment a good once-over. It's already clean, and I'm sitting on the couch, bored off my ass, within an hour.

I literally have nothing to do.

On my phone, there are books, games, social media, and infinite websites to browse. I'm used to physical isolation, but this is a whole new level. I stare at my phone, daring myself to just turn it on despite Deklan's warning, but I can't quite bring myself to do it.

There has to be a nearby place with Wi-Fi.

Deklan didn't tell me I had to stay in the apartment, but he also didn't tell me I could leave. I could call him and ask, but he said to call only in an emergency, and this clearly doesn't fall into that category.

Instinctively, I tap my phone to check the time, but it's off, so the gesture is pointless. I stand up from the couch and go over to the stove to check the time, finding that it's only a little after nine in the morning.

I don't even know what time he'll be home.

"Fuck it." I walk to the bedroom for my purse, toss the burner phone inside, and then grab my jacket from the hook near the door. It isn't until I've shut the door behind me that I realize I don't have a key to the apartment.

The door has locked behind me.

"Shit!"

I jiggle the knob over and over again, like a child pressing the button to make the elevator appear faster. The result is as expected, and I stand in the hallway, staring at the door and trying not to cry.

How was I going to get back inside without a key? Should I call Deklan and tell him what happened? Did this count as an emergency, or would it piss him off to be interrupted?

I consider things Deklan might regard as an emergency and decide this isn't one of them. I am just going to have to wait outside until he gets home, which certainly won't be for many hours. As long as I'm back here by five o'clock, everything should work out fine. It won't even be a big deal if I have to wait a while for him to return.

With a deep breath, I stand up straight and try to pull myself together. There isn't much of a choice now, so I might as well find the nearest coffee house or bookstore.

I walk out onto the street and figure out pretty quickly that I have no idea where I am or what direction I should go. The street in front of the apartment is a fairly busy one, and there are sidewalks leading in either direction but no indication of which way would be the best.

Hoping that I'm far enough away for Deklan's tastes, I turn my phone on and open an app to locate nearby businesses. I'm in luck and find a coffee shop only a few blocks away. I quickly turn the phone off again—just in case—and head that way.

I find myself in a strip mall with a laundromat and what I assume to be the convenience store where Deklan bought my toothbrush during our first night together. The obligatory nail salon and Chinese takeout joint are also present. At the end, I see the coffee shop and head that way. When I get there, I see there are more shops around the corner.

It's actually a nice little area—lots of mom-and-pop boutiques, a small movie theatre, and green space complete with trees and park benches. I spend a few minutes walking up and down the sidewalk, peering into shop windows before returning to the corner.

I head into the coffee shop and buy a mocha latte with the small amount of cash I have on me. One of my Dad's credit cards is also in my purse, but I have no doubt Deklan wouldn't want me to use that. The barista calls out my name and gives me a big smile when he holds out my drink.

"Hope you enjoy it," he says pleasantly. "I gave you a little extra whipped cream."

He winks, and I smile back tentatively. The name tag on his uniform says "Terry." I make a point of taking the coffee from him with my left hand, hoping the giant rock on my finger is noticeable enough to deter him from further conversation. He doesn't say anything else, so I guess it worked.

I find a small table by the window and turn my phone back on. As soon as I start up my favorite chat app, a dozen messages from Kathy appear.

TKbitch: So, did you go through with it?
TKbitch: I want to hear all about this guy!
TKbitch: Helloooooo?

TKbitch: Hey, answer your damn messages! I sent you one on FB, too.

TKbitch: Kera? Kera? Come in, Kera!

TKbitch: Listen here, you bitch—I'm starting to get worried!

TKbitch: ANSWER ME!!!!

And there, two days later, is the final message.

TKbitch: I broke down and called your mom. I really hope everything is okay. Please, please, please call me when you can!

Kathy is the single person I have kept in constant contact with since I started home-schooling. Though she was ahead of me in school, we played together on the playground in elementary school and even had some of the same classes my first year of high school. Despite her moving off to college a few years ago, we talked almost daily, and she was my best friend in the world. I feel instantly guilty for being so preoccupied with Deklan that I hadn't even thought to call her. I quickly type out a reply.

Bookwhore72: I am SO SORRY! Crazy few days and way too much to type. Having coffee now. Call if you can!

My phone rings about twelve seconds later.

"For the love of God, woman!" Kathy screams loud enough that I have to pull the phone away from my ear. "Where the hell have you been? I was about to hire a dude in a fedora to go look for you!"

"I'm so sorry. Really, I am. The past few days have been nuts."

"Spill it! The last I heard, you weren't marrying that Foley guy but some other dude on steroids."

"He's not on steroids." I roll my eyes and sip a bit of my coffee. "He is built like one of those large, earth-moving machines, but I'm pretty sure it's all natural. His name is Deklan."

"And?"

"And, he's…well, he's quite nice." I pause.

"Nice?" Kathy snorts into the phone. "I don't hear from you in almost a week, and all you got is 'nice'?"

"I don't know where to start."

"Try the beginning, bitch."

"Ugh!" I sigh loudly, but I can't stop smiling. I didn't realize how much I'd missed Kathy, and it feels good to hear her voice. "Okay, here's the short version. I didn't even know his last name until the middle of the ceremony. He's got dark hair and blue eyes. He's about a foot taller than I am, and his hands are huge. When he's around other people, he looks like he's four seconds away from literally ripping people's arms off, but at home, he's quite different."

"Different how?"

"He's...sweet. He's gentle. He likes my cooking and draws me baths—candles and everything. I conked myself on the head, and he insisted on taking me to the hospital to get checked out. He's got some strict rules, which is why I didn't message you back, but he says...he says he's going to take care of me. He says he wants to be a good husband."

"Whoa."

"Whoa what?"

"Are you falling for this guy? Already?"

"I don't know if I'm *falling* for him," I say, "but he's a lot better than I thought he would be. I thought things were going to be a lot worse."

I consider telling her about how I thought he was going to kill me but decide to keep that tidbit to myself.

"I'd laugh my ass off otherwise," Kathy says. "All those times you've bitched about 'instalove' in romance books—I'd give you serious shit if it happened to you."

We both laugh.

"So...tell me about the wedding night! Did you go through with it?"

"Yeah." I'm pretty sure she can see my blush through the phone, but Kathy doesn't squeal or cheer or anything. That's not her way, and I love her for it.

"And?" she says simply, prompting me to continue.

"And it was kinda incredible."

"Hold on." I hear a click and realize she's lighting a cigarette.

"Are you at work?"

"Yeah, just taking a break."

"I thought you were going to quit smoking."

"I did. Then I realized I wasn't a quitter."

I roll my eyes and listen to her puff a few times before she starts talking again.

"Now that I have a smoke, give me the deets on 'kinda incredible.'"

"Um…" I look around the coffee shop, wondering if anyone is within earshot. The tables closest to me are empty, and I don't think I'll be overheard. "After I had my usual freak-out moment over the fact that Mom didn't put anything useful in my travel bag, we talked a little. He was kinda pushing to hold off on the whole consummation thing, but I wanted to get it over with."

"'Get it over with?'" I can practically hear Kathy rolling her eyes. "How romantic."

"Hey, I wasn't so sure I was going to live through the night at that point." I cringe when I realize what I've said. I don't want Kathy to sense how serious my fear was, so I laugh it off. "I could have died of embarrassment or something."

"But you didn't, and you did go through with it."

"Yes." I take a sip of coffee and turn toward the wall a little. "He had me get on top. He said it would be easier that way."

"Ride 'em, cowgirl!" Kathy snickers. "What does his cock look like?"

"Kathy!" I laugh and look around me, paranoid that someone might have heard her through the phone, but there isn't anyone close by.

"Hey, I've been waiting for you to lose that cherry for a long-ass time! It's time to compare some notes. How big is it?"

"Um…I think it's pretty big. I don't have anything to compare it with."

"How about comparing it with a damn ruler?"

"Ya know, next time I'll ask. 'Hold on a sec, Dek—let me grab this measuring tape.'"

"Ha! You should at least be able to estimate."

"Geometry was never my strong subject."

"Ugh, Kera! You're killing me here! Could you get your hand around it?"

"Barely."

"Damn!"

"Well, he's not circumcised."

"Really? You married a hood-rat?"

"Hood-rat?" I laugh out loud. "I dare you to say that to his face."

"I've never done a guy who wasn't cut. Does it look like it's wearing a sweater? One of my co-workers is married to a Brit. He's not cut, and she says it looks like a turtle head poking out of the sleeve of a sweater."

"Um…kinda." I laugh again and shake my head. It feels good to talk to Kathy.

"Is it straight? Curved? Does the end bend over into a hook?"

"Enough!" My sides are starting to hurt from laughing. "Tell me how you're doing. How's the new job?"

Kathy finished her nursing degree just a few months ago and was working her first serious job at an OB/GYN office.

"Full of baby goat heads," she says bluntly.

"What the hell is that supposed to mean?"

"Well, you'd think that all women would take care of their hoo-has, wouldn't ya?"

"Um, I suppose so."

"Well, that's a crock of shit. You wouldn't believe some of the things I have seen. I'd send you pictures, but I assume you'll probably want to eat again someday. Just believe me when I say there are women out there who wait way too long to see their doctor."

"What does that have to do with baby goat heads?"

"If someone comes in with some serious weirdness going on down there, you're supposed to take notes in the system for the doctor to see. The problem is, the patients can see the notes. They get all offended when you write 'Moron noticed her labia was producing large, purple growths about six months ago and can no longer pull her pants all the way up. It's occurred to her that maybe that ain't normal.' So we've got a code: baby goat heads. If there's something seriously freaky going on, the doctor gets a little advanced warning, and no one knows what the fuck we're talking about, so they can't really get offended."

"Oh my God! You are not serious!"

"I'm completely serious. That shit happens every week around here. That isn't even the worst of it. There are people who have inserted—"

"Enough!" I yell into the phone. "I don't want any more details!"

Kathy laughs.

"Overall, I really like it. It's pretty much what they told me it would be. I spend more time dealing with bodily fluids than I might prefer, but the people I work with are awesome. Everyone has a sense of humor."

"That's great, Kathy. I'm so happy for you."

"I'll get vacation time after I've been here for ninety days. I might have to come and visit you."

"That would be awesome!"

"I was thinking I'd try to be there around your birthday so we can hit the bars."

"Kathy," I cry with mock indignity, "are you already plotting to get me drunk so you can take advantage? I've only just lost my virginity this past week!"

"Oh, baby, you know it!" We both laugh, but my laughter is cut short.

"Jesus fucking Christ!"

I jump and swivel in my chair to see Deklan standing in the doorway of the coffee shop, glaring at me with piercing eyes.

DEKLAN

Chapter 12

My husband towers over me, jaw tense, hands clenched, and eyes ready to set fire to anything and anyone in his path. My whole body tightens up, and I have to fight the urge to hide under the little round table in front of me, as if that would help.

"Kathy, I gotta go," I say quickly. "Call ya later."

I hang up and turn around to face Deklan's glaring eyes and clenched fists.

"What the ever loving fuck are you doing here?"

"I-I…" I open and close my mouth a few more times, but my voice isn't responding to any commands. The answer to the question is too simple: I'm drinking coffee and talking on the phone. Saying it out loud is not only pointless, but I fear dangerous.

The barista who made my coffee is staring at us. So are some of the other customers. Two women in line lean close to one another, whispering and glancing at me. I'm only vaguely aware of their intruding looks; I'm too focused on the fury in my husband's eyes.

Without another word, Deklan grabs my arm and pulls me out of the coffee shop. His car is right outside, double-parked. He yanks open the passenger side door and tosses me into the seat, slamming the door hard enough to make the car shake. He starts to yell as soon as he gets in the other side.

"I nearly had a heart attack when I got home and you weren't there!"

"I just wanted to make a phone call," I say softly.

"No shit," he says with a growl. "How the fuck do you think I found you?"

"You…you traced it?"

"Yes, I fucking traced it! Who the hell is Kathy Jackson, and why are you talking to a nurse who lives halfway across the country?"

"A friend of mine." I lick my lips, trying not to be completely disturbed that he not only found me this quickly but already knew exactly who I was talking to and where she lives. "We went to school together."

The drive is too short. If it had been longer, maybe Deklan would have calmed down, but he's just as irate as he was when he first found me. He speeds the few blocks back to the apartment, running stop signs and slamming on the brakes with a squeal when he pulls into the garage. He gets out, marches around the car, and pulls me bodily from my seat. I let him drag me down the hall and into the apartment.

I've crossed a line. I didn't know where the line was, but there is no doubt that I leapt right over it. As the door crashes closed behind me, I clear my mind and try to prepare for the worst.

What is the worst?

Deklan had said he wouldn't lay a hand on me in anger, but I've heard similar promises from my father. There's a point where control is lost, and all bets are off. My husband is furious, and I have no idea what he's going to do. However, I do have a notion of what he's capable of doing.

I remember the bloodied shirt, and my eyes burn.

Deklan grabs my face in his hands as he pushes me up against the wall near the door. I squeeze my eyes shut, bracing for the blow to come, but instead of his fist, his lips crash against mine.

His tongue is in my mouth, probing with fierce determination. He groans as he presses his body against mine, pinning me against the wall. Confused, I reach up and wrap my fingers partway around his biceps and hold on as he violates my mouth without mercy.

He pulls away abruptly and glares down at me. His stare is still intense, but his eyes now hold desperation as well as anger.

"Do you have any idea what kind of shit went through my mind when I found you gone? I didn't know if you'd been taken again or if you were hurt somewhere or if"—he takes a breath, sucking the air in through his teeth with a hiss—"or if you had just left me."

"I didn't mean to worry you." My voice is tiny, and I feel a tear fall down my cheek.

Deklan closes his eyes and clenches his teeth. He takes one hand from my face and slams his palm against the wall beside my head, causing me to jump. His breaths are quick and heavy.

"All I could think was that I'd never...I'd never..." He clenches his teeth and looks away for a moment.

Deklan's muscles flex under my hands as he scrapes his fingers over the wall by my head. Without warning, he grabs the top of my jeans and pulls, releasing the button and zipper in one swift movement. He yanks them down one of my legs, along with my panties as I hold my breath, afraid to move. One of my shoes falls off as he drags the leg of my jeans over my foot until my left leg is free. He doesn't bother with the other side, just rights himself and opens his own pants, shoving them down his hips before he picks me up off the floor.

My back slams against the wall as he enters me in a single thrust.

I cry out in surprise, but Deklan says nothing. He just pulls back and starts pumping into me as fast as he possibly can. He has me immobilized against the wall, and I have to squeeze my arms out from between us to wrap them around his shoulders. He moves his hands to my thighs, holding them far apart as he drills into me.

The rhythmic thumps against the wall echo in my ears, and I wonder briefly if there is anyone out in the hallway. I claw at Deklan's shirt and press my temple to his shoulder to keep my head from hitting the wall. He releases my legs, and I wrap them around his waist for balance as I pant against his skin.

I'm getting dizzy, my head swimming from the motion and the intensity. This is not what I was expecting, this dramatic display of want and need. I angered my husband and fully expected to be punished for what I had done, but I certainly wasn't expecting this.

If this is Deklan's idea of punishment, I'm not about to argue.

He's quick and furious with his pace, driving deep as my lower back takes a hit against the wall with each penetration. All I can do is hold on, though he doesn't need my help to keep me pinned exactly where I am. He grinds against me, and I moan loudly as he pulls back and crashes into me again.

I feel sweat collecting on the back of Deklan's shirt as his rhythm continues with me thumping against the wall. He quickens his movement, driving into me with both passion and fury. I wrap my legs tightly around him, trying to get that last bit of pressure I need to send me over the edge.

Deklan stills suddenly, pressing me against the wall as he growls loudly through his teeth. I feel the warm flood of his orgasm deep inside of me as he grunts once more, his breath hot on my shoulder.

He keeps me there for a moment, stroking in and out a few more times as his breathing starts to slow. I keep holding on, afraid to let go, but also pressing up against him, still needing my own release.

"Don't do that again." Deklan slowly pulls out of me and lowers me back to my feet.

"I won't," I whisper. My clit is still throbbing, and my head is still reeling. My back hurts from the pounding he just gave me, but all I can think about is asking him to do it again. And again. And again.

He takes a step away, and the exposed parts of my body are instantly cold. I want to reach out to him and beg him to finish me off, but I don't dare utter a word.

He turns around and starts doing up his pants as he walks into the kitchen and reaches up to one of the higher shelves. He pulls down a bottle of whiskey I hadn't noticed before and pours a small amount into a shot glass. He downs it a second later.

"What the fuck were you thinking?" Deklan mutters.

I'm not entirely sure if the question is rhetorical or not, but I decide to answer anyway.

"I was just going to grab a cup of coffee." My voice is small and timid. I feel like I'm in shock as I slowly pull my jeans back on and try to think of the right words. "I didn't think about a key until I was already outside. I couldn't get back in, so I thought I'd just wait for you. I didn't think you would be back until this evening. I thought I had more time."

"Why didn't you call?"

"You said the phone was only for emergencies. I didn't think locking myself out counted."

Deklan closes his eyes and leans heavily on the kitchen counter, eyes closed.

"I'll have a key made for you," he says, "but you tell me beforehand if you're going to leave the apartment. Don't go anywhere unless I know about it ahead of time."

"Okay."

He turns to me, and most of the anger is gone from his eyes.

"I'm not trying to keep you a prisoner," he says. "I'm not like that, but…"

I wrap my arms around myself and stare at the floor. Deklan takes several deep breaths as he stares at the ceiling.

"Come here," he says softly.

I look at him for a moment, trying to judge his intent. When he leans back against the counter and holds out his arms, I run to him and bury my face against his chest. Deklan runs his hand over my hair and gently kisses the top of my head.

"The Foley's have enemies, Kera. *I* have enemies. Any one of them would jump at the opportunity to use you against me. I can't protect you if I don't know where you are."

He tightens his arms around me, nearly lifting me from the floor again before he relaxes slightly and strokes my back, his lips pressed to my temple.

"I'm sorry I worried you." I reach up and run my fingers through the short hair on the side of his head. "I didn't mean to."

"I know." He stares at me for a moment before turning his head and kissing the side of my hand. "I'm sorry I didn't get you off. I'm going to make up for that later."

I feel heat rise to my face, and I glance away from him, but he turns my head back to meet his gaze.

"I mean it. I should always get you off, but I just…" He inhales deeply and presses his lips together as he stares at the ground. "I just needed to be in you. I needed to come in you." He shakes his head as if he's trying to clear it. "I don't know. I have to go now. Stay here. I'll be back around seven."

"I won't go anywhere. I promise."

Deklan closes his eyes for a second as he nods, kisses me briefly, and heads out the door.

I turn to watch him go before I slowly sink to the tile floor. I'm still throbbing between my legs, and my heart is still pounding quickly, but I don't want to take care of myself. My mind is reeling too fast to even consider it.

Chapter 13

Leaning back against the arm of the couch, I flip through pages of a book on my WiFi disabled e-reader until I find the right chapter. I am nearly done, and my online group is supposed to go over it tomorrow. Deklan promised to take me somewhere to chat with everyone about the ending.

My husband walks out of the bathroom in just a towel, still dripping from his shower. He is running a little behind schedule this morning but seems able to get himself ready for the day in a matter of minutes. Though we've been married nearly a month now, I can't stop myself from staring at his body whenever I get the chance. I watch him from the couch as he shovels a piece of toast down his throat, followed by a cup of coffee.

I still don't have the nerve to ask him about his scars.

"How many languages do you speak?" Deklan asks suddenly.

"Speak? Just three, really. I can get by in a couple more and read a few more than that." I try to brush it off, but Deklan stares at me until I offer more. "English, French, Spanish. I can make polite conversation on specific topics in German, Russian, and Arabic."

"Arabic? Really?"

"Why not?"

"Hardly Latin based."

"Neither is Russian."

He gives me a half nod, conceding the point as he walks over to sit on the other side of the couch. I pull my knees up to give him more room.

"How did you learn?" he asks.

I consider how to answer without sounding snarky. Besides, the whole truth could lead me to a topic I've wanted to discuss with him but hadn't yet built up my nerve.

"After…everything that happened my first year of high school, I studied at home. I didn't go out much. I got bored."

"So you learned more languages?"

"I studied a lot of things."

"Sounds lonely."

"It was." I lick my lips and glance at him through my lashes. "Kind of like now."

"I bore you, do I?"

"Not you, no." I swivel around, discard the e-reader on the coffee table, and place my feet on the floor so I can snuggle closer to him. "But you aren't here all the time."

"I wish I didn't have to leave you all day." Deklan places his hand on my thigh, running it slowly from my knee farther up and under the hem of my robe. "I'd much rather stick around."

I feel his fingers crawling farther up my leg, and I know exactly what that means. Deklan only has about fifteen minutes before he has to leave, and he's not even dressed yet. He'll get me all wound up and then leave with a smirk on his face, but I need to keep my focus.

"I wish I…Oh!" I moan as Deklan's fingers reach their goal. He silences me with his mouth as his fingers circle, and I tilt my hips to press against his hand, rocking slowly.

He kisses down the front of my neck, opening my robe to get to my breasts. He licks my nipples as he keeps working at me with his fingers, and I groan loudly. He moves his mouth back up, licking between my breasts and up over my chin. He kisses me lightly and then stares intently as he slows the rhythm of his fingers and grins.

"Gotta get dressed." He leaves me panting as he heads off to the bedroom. I can hear him going through the closet while my thighs clench and my nipples tingle. A few minutes later, he's back in the living room with his shirt hanging open, and I'm still frustrated.

He grins from the kitchen as he starts to button his shirt.

"Ugh! Why do you do this to me?" I cry as I lean backwards on the couch. My robe opens completely, and I hope it's enough of a temptation to make him chance being late.

Deklan comes up behind me, wraps an arm around my waist as I squeal. He pulls me up until my butt is on the arm of the couch and my back is against his chest. His shirt is still mostly unbuttoned, and I can feel his warm skin on my neck. He reaches under my robe again to stroke me.

"Because I want you to start every day with my fingers right here." He punctuates the words by sliding his fingers inside me, stroking them in and out slowly. He runs his nose along my neck and shoulder, inhaling deeply. "I want you unsatisfied. I want to be the only thing on your mind. I want you hot and wet and so frustrated that all you can think about is my cock throbbing inside of you."

With a quick kiss on my neck, he removes his fingers and lowers me back to the couch. I'm completely unable to speak as he finishes buttoning his shirt, grabs his jacket, and heads for the door.

"Wait for me." Deklan looks at me over his shoulder as he turns the doorknob. "No masturbating today."

I groan, and he winks and snickers as he walks out of the apartment.

"Bastard," I say quietly when he's gone. I shake my head and resist the urge to finish myself off. I'll have to go the cold shower route for now, but I'm going to make him pay for that when he gets home.

I shower and dress. I make the bed and do the breakfast dishes. I try to watch daytime television but quickly get disgusted with every show on every channel and turn it off. I stare at my phone for a long minute, wishing it would magically turn into something that wasn't easily traced so I could use it. I'm actually starting to miss Facebook drama.

Strangely enough, I do not miss my parents—at all. Other than the one nasty text from my father using my mother's phone, I haven't heard a peep from either of them—not that they could have called since my phone is always off, but I wonder if they still think about me.

The day drags.

Every inch of the apartment sparkles. I even polished the shower fixtures. I've done my nails—fingers and toes. Dinner is in the oven and should be done just as Deklan arrives home. The kitchen island is set with dishes and silverware.

Though it had seemed very important to me at the time, I no longer care that I don't live in a huge mansion. Deklan's apartment is simple, and I rather like it this way. Of course, if it were bigger, I'd have more rooms to clean. It would make the time pass more quickly.

I stare out the window that overlooks the street and watch for someone to head down the sidewalk, but the apartment is an out-of-the way place, and there isn't a lot of foot traffic. A few cars pass by, but the angle is wrong for me to see the people inside.

Sighing, I resolve to finish the book. I only have a couple of chapters left, which I want to savor. I settle myself on the couch with the e-reader and a glass of water, wondering if boredom is why housewives turn to wine and vodka.

I browse the previous chapter so I can remember what was going on and lose myself in the story after only a few minutes.

A knock on the door breaks me from my trance. Automatically, I stand and head over to open it when it occurs to me that no one has ever knocked on the door before.

I freeze as Deklan's words about enemies rattle around in my head, making it impossible for me to think rational thoughts. All I know is that I'm not going anywhere near the door. Who could possibly be knocking, and what do they want? Is it someone looking for Deklan? If so, what do I tell them? Do I just ignore the knocking, which is getting louder, or tell whomever it is to go away? What if they try to break down the door?

My arms and legs tense with fight or flight notions, but I don't even know which one to choose. I wrap my arms around myself as I look around the apartment, wondering where I could hide, but there's only the bedroom closet, which is the first place an intruder would check. Maybe Deklan has another gun hidden somewhere, but I don't even know where to look.

"Phone," I whisper to myself and tiptoe over to the kitchen drawer where the burner phone with Deklan's number on it resides. My hands shake as I try to find the right button to turn it on.

The voice from the other side of the door startles me as much as the knocking.

"Kera? Kera! It's Brian."

"Brian?" I grip the phone in my fist and walk softly to the door to look through the peephole. Brian is standing on the other side. He glances down the hall as he hops from one foot to the other. His leg must have healed, because there is no sign of the crutch he was using when I first met him. I lean against the door. "What are you doing here?"

"Dek sent me."

I lick my lips and narrow my eyes at the distorted figure through the hole. It is definitely Brian, but why would Deklan send him here without telling me first? Something is wrong.

"He didn't tell me you were coming."

"You don't have to let me in," Brian says. "He's just gonna be late and didn't want you to worry."

"Where is he?" Deklan has been late plenty of times and never felt the need to notify me before. What's changed?

"Um…" Brian dances on the balls of his feet again. "He um…"

"Out with it, Brian."

"He got hurt."

"Hurt? Hurt how? Where is he?"

"He'll be all right," Brian says. "Just zigged when he should have zagged, I guess. He's in surgery, but they said he'd be f—"

"Surgery?" I grab the doorknob and throw the door open. "Surgery for what?"

"Just a little mishap." His words are obviously meant to soothe, but the lack of real information has the opposite effect.

"What happened to him?"

"He…uh…He got mugged."

"Mugged?" I glare at Brian. No one in their right mind would see Deklan as a viable target for easy mugging. "What kind of bullshit is that?"

"Really," Brian says, "he's fine—cursing and pissy, but fine. Surgery is too strong a word. He just needs a few stitches."

Apparently, I'm not going to get a straight answer out of Brian. Better to get it from the horse's mouth.

"Where is he?"

"County Hospital."

"Take me." I reach over and grab my jacket from the hook and pull it on.

"He didn't say anything about bringing you there." Brian rubs his hand over his mouth and chin as he shakes his head slightly. "I dunno if I should."

"You are going to fucking take me to him right fucking now!"

Brian's eyes go wide, and he wipes the palms of his hands on his jeans. He stares at me with his mouth hanging open, and I can see the debate going on in his head. I take a step forward and point my finger at his nose.

"You are going to take me to the hospital right this fucking second, or I'm going to tell Deklan you made a pass at me."

"I…I didn't! I would never!"

"But I'll tell him you did. Who do you think he'll believe?"

Brian licks his lips, and his shoulders fall slightly.

"Do we have an understanding?" I ask.

"Yes, ma'am."

Chapter 14

The smell of bleach burns my nose as I pace outside the large double doors leading to the operating room. Brian stands off to one side, muttering to himself about how much trouble he's going to be in with Deklan and refusing to give me any details about what happened.

"Mrs. Kearney?"

I flip my head toward the sound of the doctor's voice and head straight over to her.

"I'm Dr. Henry, your husband's surgeon."

"I'm Kera," I tell her. "How is he?"

"He's going to be fine," she says. "It's a serious injury but not life-threatening."

"What happened?"

Dr. Henry narrows her eyes at Brian and then glances back to me. She takes a long breath.

"Your husband was stabbed with a six-inch serrated knife, the kind that's pretty popular with the gangs in the area. Luckily, there isn't any major organ damage, but the knife nicked his lower intestine. It was a small cut, but we had to take care of it or there would be a risk of the contents of his bowels leaking into his body cavity. That can be very dangerous, but we got to it in time."

A tear tries to escape my eyelashes, but I quickly wipe it away.

"When can I see him?"

"He should be in recovery in just a few minutes," the doctor tells me. "I'll have a nurse come get you as soon as he wakes up."

She gives me a reassuring pat on the arm before she walks through the double doors and out of sight. I turn back to Brian with a glare.

"Stitches, huh?"

Brian shrugs and tries to smile. I consider punching him in the face.

"It's not like he was shot or anything," Brian says.

"You are not making me feel better."

"Sorry, Mrs. K."

I sit down on an uncomfortable plastic chair and cross my arms over my chest. Brian sits beside me and leans over with his elbows on his knees.

"If it makes you feel any better," he says, "the guy that did it is in a freezer in the basement of this place."

"It doesn't." I speak the words casually enough, but a cold knot forms in my stomach. Brian hasn't actually said that Deklan killed his attacker, and I don't want to ask. "Who was he?"

"Just some guy on the street." Brian can't even look me in the eye as he says it.

"You're a terrible liar."

"So I've been told."

I glare at the cold, white floor. My stomach is still all twisted up, and there are too many thoughts running through my head. What really happened? Was he going to have a big scar? Would he have to stay in the hospital for a long time to recover, or would he be able to come home?

Above all other questions in my mind, one keeps blaring at me like a military bugle: What if it had been worse? What would happen to me if Deklan were to die?

The automatic doors at the entrance open, and two police officers walk into the waiting area and go up to the nurse at the counter. I can't hear what they say, but they both turn to look at me.

"Mrs. Kearney?" The tall, blond cop walks up to me.

"Yes?"

"I'm Officer Jim Longbow," he says. He motions to the other uniformed man, also blond but slightly shorter. "This is my partner, Allen Sloan."

"Congratulations on the marriage," Officer Sloan says. "I didn't realize Deklan was married."

"Thank you," I say softly. "It was just a month ago."

"We need to ask you a few questions, Mrs. Kearney," Longbow says. "Were you with your husband when he was injured?"

"No," I say with a shake of my head, "I was at home."

"Can you give us an idea of what occurred?"

"I…I don't know what happened. I haven't seen him yet."

"How about you, Brian?" Longbow places his hands on his belt as he turns to my companion.

"I wasn't there," Brian says. He maintains eye contact with the officer with cold, blank eyes. "I don't know anything."

"You brought him to the hospital?"

"Not me. He must've got himself here." Brian leans back in the seat and crosses his arms.

"And how did you know he was here?" the officer asks.

"I'm clairvoyant." Brian continues to stare but refuses to offer any more information.

A nurse emerges from the double doors and heads in my direction.

"Mrs. Kearney, your husband is awake. Would you like to see him?"

"We need to speak with him," Longbow says.

"Family first." The young nurse smiles and leads me away from the police officers. She takes me through the doors and down a hallway to a room shielded with a large curtain. When she pulls the curtain back, I see Deklan lying on the bed with a tube running out of his arm and an oxygen feed in his nose.

Deklan's gaze meets mine. He doesn't smile, not even after the nurse leaves.

"Who brought you here?"

"I was worried about you."

"Brian wasn't supposed to tell you anything, let alone bring you here." Deklan sighs and looks away.

"I made him bring me," I say. I walk over to the side of the bed and pull up a round, rolling chair.

"Held a gun to his head, did you?"

"Figuratively."

Deklan snorts. I reach over and take his hand.

"I was worried. He wouldn't tell me what really happened, and he's a terrible liar."

"It was nothing."

"You just came out of surgery. How, exactly, is that nothing?"

"Just a scratch." He looks down at our hands and twines his fingers around mine. "I'm fine."

"What happened?"

"Misunderstanding."

"That's vague." I squeeze his hand slightly.

"What happened?" I ask again, but Deklan just stares at our hands, ignoring my question. "You aren't going to tell me, are you?"

"No," he says succinctly, "I'm not. I don't want you involved. It's taken care of."

"So I hear."

Deklan turns his head swiftly, his eyes narrowed.

"Tell Brian that he's a dead man."

"Leave him alone."

"Are you giving me orders now?"

"Maybe."

He finally cracks a smile, but it quickly turns to a wince. I reach over with my other hand and stroke his cheek. He leans against me for a moment.

"Go home," Deklan says. "The doc said I can leave in the morning. They just want to watch me overnight."

"I'm not going anywhere, Deklan. If something happened, they wouldn't even be able to reach me."

"God, woman" he shakes his head and closes his eyes, "you are frustrating."

"Well, you left me pretty frustrated this morning. I'm just returning the favor."

"Don't make me laugh anymore." He gives me a half smile, and his eyes soften. He gives my hand a squeeze and closes his eyes briefly. "I hate the way painkillers leave my head feeling."

The curtain moves, and Dr. Henry walks in with a smile.

"How are we doing?" she asks.

"I'll be fine when you get rid of the painkillers in the IV."

"You just came out of surgery," Dr. Henry says. "You're going to need that for a while."

"Bullshit."

She checks his vitals, adjusts the IV, and asks him to rate his pain on a scale from one to ten.

"One," Deklan says. "Ditch the morphine."

"Would you like a bullet to bite on instead?"

"Yes."

Dr. Henry rolls her eyes.

"There are a couple of officers here who want to ask you about the mugging. Are you up for that?"

"No," Deklan says definitively. "I won't be later, either."

"If you aren't in pain, I'm not sure I can refuse them. I don't think they'll leave until they talk to you."

"I don't have anything to say."

"You can tell them that." Dr. Henry gives Deklan a pointed stare before she walks back around the curtain.

"They already asked me about you." I rub my thumb over the edge of his hand and glance at him tentatively.

"What did you tell them?"

"Nothing. I didn't know anything. I still don't know anything."

"And we're going to keep it that way. I don't want them bothering you."

A few minutes later, the curtain rustles and we're facing Longbow and Sloan.

"We need to ask you some questions," Longbow says.

"I got nothing to say, Longbow." Deklan stares at the man, his eyes narrowed.

"Mr. Kearney, a man is dead," Sloan says. "You know we can't just walk out of here without anything from you."

"Oh, did he die?" Deklan shakes his head. "I guess that will save the taxpayers some prison money."

"He was shot in the head." Longbow hooks his thumbs in his belt. "Yeah, he's dead. And we have a recently fired gun registered to you. I have a pretty good idea what ballistics will have to say about it. You have to give me something, Dek."

I'm surprised by the familiarity.

"It's all very simple," Deklan says. "I was walking down the street, and some asshole jumped me and tried to take my wallet. He stabbed me. I shot him. Self-defense."

"Were there any witnesses?"

"I was alone."

"No one on the street?"

"Guess not. It's all one big blur."

"Do you have a name for him?"

"Random mugger number one," Deklan says. "That's what the credits will say when they make a movie about my life."

Sloan snickers, and Longbow glares at him.

"He appears to have also been beaten," Longbow says. "Did you do that before or after you shot him in the temple?"

"No idea what you're talking about," Deklan says. "Maybe it was the guy he mugged before me. Maybe the coroner dropped him."

"Dek…"

"You know what?" Deklan sits up slightly, gritting his teeth. "How about you just take all this up with my attorney? I have nothing else to say to you two."

"If this goes to trial," Longbow says, "it will look better if you cooperate with us now."

"You fuckers know this isn't going to go to trial," Deklan says, "so stop wasting my time."

Deklan refuses to say anything else, and the two officers finally give up and leave, promising to be back in the morning.

"You should go home," Deklan tells me again. "I'm fine, and they're just going to tell me to rest."

"Well, I'll have to stay to make sure that you do." I raise an eyebrow at Deklan when he glares at me. "I'm not going anywhere. Get used to it."

"Stubborn."

"When I need to be."

"Where's Brian?"

"In the waiting room, as far as I know. Do you want me to get him?"

"Just tell him to keep an eye on shit," Deklan says. "I'll talk to him tomorrow."

I deliver Deklan's message to Brian, and Deklan is moved to a private room with a reclining chair so I have somewhere to sleep. Once he's settled in, he asks me to retrieve his phone from his bag of personal effects. I'm surprised to find an actual smartphone inside.

Deklan takes it from me and starts tapping the screen.

"Who are you texting?" I ask.

"Sean."

"I didn't know you had a smartphone."

"I don't use it very much."

He only takes a moment to complete his message. I find it strange that I've never seen this phone before and wonder if he's been intentionally hiding it from me. It's entirely possible. It makes me wonder what else he's hiding—probably quite a bit.

It bothers me. A lot. It reminds me that I know very little about the man I married.

"Can I look through your phone?" I blurt out.

"Why?"

"I want to know what kind of music you like."

"There isn't any music on my phone."

"Why not?"

"I just use it for work."

I narrow my eyes at him. Deklan sighs and holds out his hand, palm up, with the phone lying in the middle of it.

"Go ahead. Look through all of it. I don't text, and there aren't any women's phone numbers in there except Teagan's."

I narrow my eyes at him slightly as I take the phone from his hand. It's not locked, and he was telling the truth about the lack of texts. Aside from the message he sent to Sean, which just says "all good," there are only four of them in the phone's history. All were sent to him. The messages are brief and cryptic, and he only replied to the one from Teagan. The others don't even have a contact associated with them. The only music on the device is some classical piece that probably came with the music app.

I look through the rest of it. It's mostly just the apps that come with a phone though I do find one surprise.

"You have games on here."

"Just a couple."

"Candy Crush? Really?" I laugh.

"Hey, even I get bored at work sometimes."

I don't really believe that, but something about Deklan playing stupid phone games relaxes me.

"Happy now?" he asks as he takes the phone back.

"Not at all."

"Why not?"

I look down at my hands as I search for the right words.

"Because I want to know more about you," I say, "and that didn't help at all."

"Maybe you should just ask."

"You don't usually answer my questions."

"You ask the wrong questions. You ask questions that could get you into trouble, and I'm not going to put my wife at risk."

"So, I can ask you about other things? Personal things?"

"Of course. I can't swear I'll answer them all, but I won't lie to you."

I wonder if the pain medication is altering his judgment but decide it's best to jump on this opportunity. I might not get another one.

"You're really Catholic?"

"Yes."

"Do you believe in all of that stuff? God, Jesus, the Virgin Mary—all that Bible stuff?"

"Yes," Deklan says darkly, "I believe in all that Bible stuff."

"Then how can you reconcile what you do?"

There's a long pause as Deklan stares at me. He takes a couple of deep breaths.

"I go to confession every week."

This is news to me, and I try to picture Deklan cramming himself into a confessional box while a priest listens to him admit to murder and whatever else he's done. The picture in my head looks ridiculous, but he said he wouldn't lie to me.

"I'm tired," Deklan says suddenly. "Can we pick this up another time?"

"Sure." I get up from the chair and turn the lights off.

When I sit back down, Deklan settles back in the bed and reaches for my hand. He rubs my wrist for a moment before he interlocks our fingers and closes his eyes. He's asleep just a few minutes later, but I stay right next to the bed for some time before releasing his hand and situating myself in the recliner.

I can't sleep. The recliner is lumpy, and there is way too much on my mind. I stare over at Deklan's bed in the low lighting.

He's an enigma. He's gentle and protective of me but arrogant and brutal with others. I don't know what to think of it. Either he is two people inside of one body, or one of his personas is a lie.

Which one is the real Deklan Kearney?

Chapter 15

Deklan recovers quickly, and within a couple of weeks, everything is back to status quo. The only evidence of his ordeal is another thin scar on his body, this one on the left side of his abdomen. I have no idea what happened with the police or the man Deklan apparently shot, and he won't tell me any details. He just says it's all been dealt with and not to worry.

I hear that a lot.

I walk slowly to the coffee shop down the street. It's my morning ritual, sanctified by my paranoid husband, and one of the highlights of my day. I can keep my phone on, chat with Kathy on her work break, and get outside for a few minutes.

"How's the housewife life?" Kathy asks.

"About the same." I take my coffee from Terry the barista and ignore his wink as he mentions extra whipped cream—again. He always gives me extra whipped cream although I have never asked for it. His smile is friendly though, so I don't mind the mild flirtation.

"So, the sex is still hot?"

"Oh yes, most certainly. I must be developing some kind of resistance because I'm not nearly as sore as I was in the beginning."

"Your va-jay-jay is getting callouses." Kathy laughs loudly.

"I sure hope not!" I chuckle. "I don't think Deklan would like that much. He does like to leave the house with me horny as hell. I'm going to have to get a vibrator or something."

"Oh, I have just the one for you! It's called Shalimar. I'll send you the link."

"Shalimar?"

"It's purple and sparkles."

"A glittery vibrator? You are not right in the head."

"You'll thank me later."

I shake my head and take a big swig from the coffee cup. It's finally cooled down to the perfect temperature. I lean back in my seat and scan the coffee shop. There are a handful of guys with beards and plaid shirts, a collection of female college students discussing the environment, and one older couple ordering cranberry scones. Near the counter, there's a "Help Wanted" sign written in black Sharpie.

I wonder what sort of experience someone has to have in order to be a barista. I take a closer look at Terry. He smiles broadly at every customer, and his eyes sparkle with genuine affection.

I wonder if I could fake that?

Kathy prattles on about baby goat heads and office gossip, but my focus is drawn to the man in the back of the coffee shop. He's tall and thin, in his mid-thirties with plain brown hair, dull-colored clothing, and an overall nondescript look about him. I hadn't noticed him when I walked in, but he keeps glancing at me, and it's making me nervous.

I've seen him here before. In fact, when I think about it, I realize he's here at the same time I am nearly every day. He holds a newspaper that partially covers his face.

Who actually reads newspapers anymore?

"Are you even listening to me?"

"Sorry, Kathy. I got distracted. I'm listening."

"Some hot guy walk in?"

"No." I laugh. "There is a guy here though. I've seen him before."

"Is he cute?"

"No, not really. He just keeps looking at me."

"I bet that husband of yours has him watching out for you."

"You think?"

"Yep." I hear her take a long drag on her cigarette. "I gotta get back to it. Talk to you tomorrow?"

"Absolutely. Enjoy the rest of your day!" I disconnect the call and toss my cup into the trash before heading out the door. The guy at the back of the coffee shop sets his newspaper aside and starts to get up just after I do.

I wonder if Kathy is right, and this guy really is here at Deklan's request. Would my husband go so far as to have me followed when I leave the apartment?

Yes. Yes, he would.

My suspicions are confirmed when I get back to the apartment building and glance over my shoulder. The same man rounds the corner, sees me looking at him, and quickly crosses the street.

Subtle.

I'm annoyed as I head into the building and down the hall. I don't like the idea of being followed. I consider confronting Deklan about it, but if I did, he'd just find someone else to keep an eye on me. That someone might be more discreet, and I might not notice him. I prefer to know who is watching over me and decide not to mention the man to Dek.

Besides, I have something else I want to discuss with him, and it's best to fight one battle at a time.

For dinner, I make one of Deklan's favorite dishes. I set up a couple of candles on the kitchen island and even acquire a bottle of wine using the sturdy stepstool Deklan bought so I can reach the top shelves. I also change my clothes to tight-fitting leggings, lacy underwear, and a low-cut shirt. I ditch my bra altogether.

I might not have a lot in my arsenal of male seduction methods, but I know how to arm myself with what I have.

I look over the spread, and a thought occurs to me: I'm being far too obvious. Deklan is going to take one look at all of this and know I'm up to something. I need to be more subtle than the guy Deklan has following me, so I put the wine and the candles away.

Hopefully, favorite foods and revealing clothing will be enough.

Just as I'm finishing up the cooking, Deklan arrives home, on time and hungry.

"This"—Deklan uses his fork to point at the half-eaten food on his plate—"is exactly what I needed."

"I'm glad I could help." I smile as I lean up against him. I run my hand over his thigh for good measure, and he turns his head to press his lips to mine. "Did you have a long day?"

"Felt like it." He shovels another forkful into his mouth. "Just too much bullshit and not enough business."

"Who is doing the bullshitting?"

"Doesn't matter." Deklan takes a drink from his glass of water and glances at me sideways. "I shouldn't have brought it up since I'm not going to talk about it. How was your day?"

I'm still frustrated by my husband's refusal to discuss business with me.

"It was fine." I'm not quite ready to spring my question on Deklan, so I lean against him again, my hand still on his leg. I press my cheek to his arm and smile when he looks at me.

"You are very obvious, you know," he says.

"Obvious?"

"You want something. Out with it."

I look away from him and bite my lip. I'm caught off guard, and though I had a wonderful speech all prepared, I can't seem to remember a word of it.

"I, um…I wanted to ask you something."

"Ask away."

"It's about how I've been spending my days."

Deklan's eyes narrow and his shoulders tense. I don't know what he's got going on inside his head, but it must be bad, so I quickly start explaining myself.

"Cleaning this entire place from top to bottom takes about an hour and a half. Doing that every day is pretty much pointless. I can only cook so much for two people. You say it's too dangerous to have internet access, and I can't use my phone here. I'm bored, Deklan, and I don't know what I'm supposed to do!"

"What do you want to do? Go to school or something? There's a community college not far from here."

I sigh heavily.

"You remember I was home-schooled and mostly self-taught, right?"

"Yeah."

"They weren't just high school courses. I have degrees in English, communications, accounting, and philosophy. I know they're all online degrees, and the universities aren't accredited or anything, but I wasn't in any kind of sports, didn't have many friends, and didn't really go out much. I had a lot of time on my hands."

"That *is* a lot," he says.

"Yes, it is."

"So, you're saying you don't want to go to school."

"I do not." I run my hand a little further up his leg. "I need to get out more, Dek. Even when I was with my parents, I had more of a social life than I do now. I didn't get out much, but I did get out and see people sometimes. I need to interact with other people."

"What do you want to do, Kera?"

"I want to get a job."

"You don't need to get a job," Deklan says. "I've got more money than I know what to do with, and you don't seem to be much of a big spender."

"I'm not. Money isn't the issue. I want to get out and be with people. See people. Act like a normal human being."

"What kind of job do you want?"

"The coffee shop is hiring."

"You want to dole out overpriced coffee to a bunch of hipsters?"

"Not just coffee," I say with a smile. "They have scones, too!"

Deklan looks at me out of the corner of his eye.

"I want to get out of this apartment for more than twenty minutes at a time." I sigh and reach for his hand.

Deklan scowls, pulls his hand away, and pushes himself out of the chair. Without a word, he grabs the dishes from the kitchen island and rinses them in the sink.

My body sinks into the chair and my throat tightens. I was so hopeful, but now I can see he isn't going to allow it, and I'm going to be stuck inside this apartment forever.

"I don't like it," he suddenly says. "I can't pretend that I do."

"I don't think I'm cut out to be a housewife."

"I'm getting that idea." Deklan abandons the dishes and returns to me. He swivels me around on the barstool and wraps his arms around me, holding me against his chest. "I worry about you. At least here, I know you are reasonably safe. When you're out and about, I can't stop thinking of how vulnerable you are."

I want to call him out on the man he has following me, but I think better of it. I don't want him to know that I've noticed.

"I worry about you, too," I tell him. "At least I don't end up in the hospital."

142

"You ended up in the hospital before you made it a full twenty-four hours here," he says.

"Touché." I smile grimly. "It's not the same, though. Ever since you were stabbed, I think about Brian coming to the door and telling me something worse has happened."

"I know how to take care of myself."

"I know you do. Shit can still happen." I look at him pointedly, but he can't argue with me on that one and doesn't try.

"And how much shit can happen when you *don't* know how to take care of yourself?" Deklan holds me tighter.

"So, your solution is to keep me in a tall tower? Shouldn't I at least have a handmaiden for company?"

"Don't tempt me." Deklan steps back and places his hands on my cheeks. He stares at me as he inhales deeply. "You're not a prisoner here. I'm not going to say I like it—I don't—but I'm not going to stop you. If you want a job, go get one."

Relief pours through me as I reach out and wrap my arms around his neck.

"Thank you, Deklan! You have no idea how much this means to me!"

"Enough for you to go all out with dinner and wear clothes you know I just want to tear off of you. I'm surprised you didn't try to ply me with wine, too."

I bite my lip to hide my smile.

"There's a condition," Deklan says.

"What's that?"

"I'm teaching you to shoot."

"A gun?"

"No—pool." He laughs. "Yes, a gun. I'll get you a small caliber one, teach you to use it, and you'll keep it with you all the time."

"Do I really need something like that?"

"Hopefully not, but if you are going to be out and about when I'm not around, you're going to have one anyway. How badly do you want that job?"

"Badly."

"Then you'll learn to shoot."

Chapter 16

"Kera, right?"

I look up into the smiling face of Terry, the barista who has made my coffee before.

"That's me!" I give a little wave though I'm the only other person in the shop.

"Welcome to your first day on the job!" Terry smiles at me. He has one of those smiles that dance around in his eyes. It's so genuine, it's impossible not to feel instantly at ease.

"Thanks!" I smile back.

"I'm sure you'll pick up on it all pretty quick," he says. "It ain't rocket science, yeah?"

"Yeah."

He's right. It isn't. Put coffee in the container, add extras, blend, and pour. Not a lot to it, and I figure it out without a lot of trouble. Within an hour, I've served my first customer.

"Once you get used to making the drinks, I'll show you how to run the cash register," Terry says. "You didn't put anything down on your work history. Have you ever run a cash register before?"

"Never," I tell him. "This is my first job, really."

"Whaa?" Terry places his hands on his cheeks and makes a face like the kid in the *Home Alone* movie. "I thought you were like, twenty or something."

"I am."

"And this is your first job?"

"I've been in school."

"Ah, that makes sense. Well, no worries. You're the only one who applied." He snickers. "No cash register experience, but you don't appear to be an idiot, and I'm going to take a wild guess and say you have a smartphone, yes?"

"I do."

"Well, the cash register is just an app on an iPad. The owner likes to think he's very high tech, but really, he figured out how much cheaper this was than replacing the old machine when it broke."

"I suppose that's important."

"He thinks so." Terry laughs. It's a big laugh that matches his smile.

Within a couple of days, Terry and I fall into a comfortable working rhythm, alternating customers and splitting the tips at the end of the shift. It feels good to make my own money although Deklan says we don't need it.

I wonder how much money Deklan actually has.

"How long have you worked here?" I ask.

"Let's see"—he taps his finger against his chin—"about eight months, I guess. I moved here last summer. Worked at one of those mini gas station kiosk places for a month before a tornado flattened it."

"Seriously? Were you in it?"

"Nah, I wasn't working at the time. The dude who was working that night was okay—just a few scratches. He was lucky."

"I guess so."

"I like it here better anyway. People who come in to buy cigarettes at gas stations tend to be very grumpy people, in my experience. People are happy when they get their coffee, especially when they get extra whipped cream."

I glance over at him and raise an eyebrow when he winks at me.

"You do realize I'm married, right?"

"Whaa? No way!"

"I am." Apparently, flashing my ring at him when I picked up my coffee had been ineffective.

"You're too young," he says. He turns his smile back to a woman ordering a caramel macchiato. "I take it you have a kid or two, then?"

"No, no kids."

"Why did you get married so young?"

I glare at him, wanting to be angry at the intrusive question, but his expression reveals nothing but genuine curiosity.

"It just worked out that way."

He looks like he wants to ask more, but a bunch of customers come in all at once, and we are both busy for the next couple of hours. By the time we get a moment to breathe, Terry seems to have forgotten the topic.

"Ah, hells." Terry stands up from where he was crouched in front of a refrigerator. "Out of Half and Half up here. I need to grab more from the back, and it's buried behind four hundred bottles of vanilla flavoring. Do you think you're okay up here by yourself for a few minutes?"

"I think so."

"I'll be quick." Terry jogs through the door to the kitchen, and I'm left alone up front.

Thankfully, the next two orders are easy, and then the line goes dead for a bit. I clean some dirty cups off of tables and rinse out the mixers before the next person comes to the counter.

"Hello there, former betrothed."

I jump at the sound of the voice—I hadn't heard anyone come in. It's Sean, and he's smiling. His smile is nothing like Terry's; Sean's smile is full of lightning and poison.

"Hi." I don't know what else I should say, and I end up just staring at the counter.

"Well, are you going to take my order?" He places his hands on the counter and leans forward. "This is a coffee house, isn't it?"

"Yes, um, what would you like?"

"A nice, wet pussy." Sean crosses his arms and leans even further across the counter—far enough that I take a step back. "Doesn't seem to be on the menu, so I guess I'll just have something else hot and creamy. What would you recommend?"

All the hairs on my neck are standing at attention. I can barely breathe, let alone look him in the eye and make polite suggestions about what kind of coffee he might want to drink.

"Do you think I have an infinite amount of time to spend with you?" Sean asks. "If I did, you would definitely be horizontal. Since you're standing on your feet, my time must be limited."

I have to come up with something, so I say the first thing that comes to mind.

"Um…a latte?"

"Well, wouldn't that be positively decadent!" He slams his palm against the counter, and I jump again. "Make me a fucking black coffee without any crap in it."

I turn around and quickly grab a large cup. He didn't specify size, and I don't even care at this point. My hand shakes as I write his name on the side of the cup. I'm not sure why I'm bothering, since I already know exactly who he is, but it's part of my training, and I seem to be on automatic.

"Here you go, sir."

"Ooh—sir. I like that." Sean reaches out to take his cup but grabs my wrist instead. He squeezes just hard enough to make me freeze. "I kinda like this whole idea of you servicing me."

"It's just coffee." My eyes are starting to burn. I glance around the shop for the guy Deklan has following me, but he is surprisingly absent.

"For the moment." He takes the coffee with his other hand, still holding tightly to my wrist. He turns my hand palm down. "I bought this ring, you know. Gave it to Dek when he asked what to do about it. Had to get a different one for him, of course. The one made for me barely fit on his little finger."

I want to call Sean a liar, but I have the feeling what he's saying is true. Deklan wouldn't have had time to pick out a ring for me. He had even less notice than I did.

"Please let go of me," I say softly. "I have work to do."

"There's no one else in line," Sean says. "I'm the only one here who needs your assistance. Do you think you can assist me?"

"What else do you need?"

"I think I need to find out exactly what I missed," Sean says. He tightens his fingers around my wrist painfully. "I need to feel those lips wrapped around my cock."

I gasp, and a single tear escapes from my eye. For a moment, I smell dead fish and hear the lapping of water against wet wood. My stomach churns, and I startle at a noise behind me.

"Woo hoo!" Terry appears from the kitchen with two bottles of half and half—one in each hand—and a big smile. "Found it! That stuff was really buried back there!"

Sean releases me and takes a step back. He tilts the coffee cup slightly to read his name scrawled on the side. He sneers when he drops the full cup in the trash as he walks out.

"Who was that?" Terry asks. "Not happy with his coffee?"

"I guess not. He didn't actually say anything about the coffee."

"Did he ask for his money back?" Terry asks. "If he did, there's this form—"

"He didn't pay for it." My stomach cramps up again. I can't get the smell of dank, wet wood out of my head. Why is Sean doing this? He gave me up. He said he didn't want to marry me, so why is he doing this now?

"Kera, you know you have to ring it up before…"

Terry's words fade. I'm not sure if he's still speaking or not. I feel a hand on my arm, and I cry out, pulling away and backing myself up against the coffee machines behind me.

"Hey, are you all right? What did that dude say to you?"

"It's nothing." I can't keep my voice from shaking. "I just need a second—a bathroom break, I mean. I'll be right back."

I slip through the kitchen door and into the back hall where the employee's restroom is located and lock the door behind me. I splash cold water on my face, but it doesn't help—I'm still shaking. It takes several minutes before I even begin to calm down.

I don't understand why Sean is doing this. My first thought is to tell Deklan what happened, but I fear that will make matters even worse. Sean is Dek's boss. If Deklan gets angry and confronts Sean, what might happen to him?

I remember how he looked in that hospital bed, and my mind immediately conjures up a much worse version: Deklan unconscious with tubes running out of him and Dr. Henry telling me he's not going to make it.

Sean would do it, too.

"Kera? Are you all right?"

"I'm fine, Terry."

"Are you sure? I shouldn't really leave the counter, but you've been in here a while. Are you sick?"

"I'll be out in just a minute."

"Okay."

I hear him walk away, splash more water on my face, and stare into the mirror. My eyes look hollow and red. Had I been crying? I can't remember. I wish I had brought my purse in with me so I could at least fix my makeup.

My purse.

My purse has a small, .22-caliber pistol in it. Deklan insists I keep it with me anytime I leave the apartment. Both of them are in the employee break area, inside a locker. Maybe I should keep it on me, but I have a feeling management would frown on an armed barista. Besides, what would I have done with it? Threatened Sean Foley? Shot him?

I shake my head to rid myself of such ridiculous thoughts, take several deep breaths, and return to my station.

Several people are already in line, and I manage to throw myself into making mochas and lattes. I focus on the ratios of coffee to cream to various flavorings and push thoughts of Sean Foley out of my head completely. By the time business slows down, and Terry asks me how I'm doing, I am able to smile sweetly and tell him everything is fine.

That evening, Deklan is harder to convince.

After dinner, we sit on the couch with the television turned on to the news. The reporter is talking about increased violence on the east side of town and possible connections to organized crime. I sit with my e-reader in my lap, but I can't focus on the words long enough to actually read.

"What's on your mind?" Deklan suddenly asks.

"What?" I glance up from the screen. "Nothing."

"You have been staring at that same page for a half hour. You obviously aren't reading."

I shrug. Anything I say will just remind me of my encounter with Sean Foley, so I say nothing. As Deklan continues to ask questions, my muscles tense, and I clench my teeth. He wants to know everything I did all day long, but he never tells me anything about what he's done all day. He never tells me anything about himself at all.

"Tell me about your day at work," he says.

"I made a lot of coffee."

"Come on, Kera." Deklan turns toward me and takes my chin between his fingers. "You're obviously upset about something. Apartment life bores you, so it has to be something at work. Is one of your coworkers giving you shit?"

"No, Terry is fine."

"Terry?"

"My coworker."

"What is it, then?"

"Nothing."

"Dammit! Will you stop saying that? You've barely uttered ten words since I got home. Tell me what's going on!"

"Why don't you tell me what you did today?" I stare at him pointedly. "How's business?"

"You know I'm not going to talk about that. I'm not putting you at risk."

"Well, the coffee business can be pretty risky, too." I toss my e-reader on the coffee table and lean back, crossing my legs in front of me with my arms across my chest. "You never know when you're going to run out of Half and Half."

"What the fuck has gotten into you today?"

I'm being pissy, and none of this is Deklan's fault. Guilt washes over me, but I know I need to come up with something else, or he's just going to keep pressuring me. Dad always said the best way to lie was to give it an element of truth, so I go with something else that has bothered me.

"I'm just…annoyed."

"About?"

"It's just…just…"

"Just what? Jesus, Kera! Out with it already!"

"I don't know anything about you!" I pull my knees up to my chest and put my chin on my knees. I glance sideways at Deklan.

He pauses and his eyes darken. Pushing himself from the couch, he stalks out of the living area and into the kitchen. He leans heavily against the counter for a moment before pulling a bottle of whiskey from the cabinet. He takes a long pull from the bottle before he puts it on the counter with a loud clunk that echoes around the room.

"What do you want from me, Kera?" he asks. "Do I need to tell you my life's story or something?"

"Yes."

"Fine."

DEKLAN

Chapter 17

"I never talk about this," Deklan says as he pours whiskey into a glass and returns to the couch.

I can see that he's nervous, but all I feel is excitement. Deklan never talks about himself, and I know almost nothing of his background. He's turned off the television, and the silence is too much for me.

"I just want to know you better," I say softly. I reach out and place my hand on his arm. "Most people find out all this stuff before the marriage, not after."

"Yeah, we aren't exactly conventional."

"We aren't." Deklan reaches for my hand and pulls it into his lap. "We're okay though, aren't we? I mean, this might not be what we had planned, but it's worked out okay. At least, it has for me."

Deklan stares into my eyes, and I see a rare vulnerability in his gaze.

"For me, too," I say softly. I touch the side of his face with my free hand. "I'm glad I married you, Dek."

"I'm glad, too." He squeezes my hand and leans his face against my palm for a moment and then looks away. "I admit it, Kera...I'm afraid to tell you shit. I'm afraid that if I tell you too much—tell you the wrong things—that you'll change your mind. I'm afraid you won't want to be with me if you know the truth."

"I know what you do." I can't meet his eyes as I say the words.

"No," Deklan says, "you really don't. I hope you never do. I'm not going to tell you any of that, but I will tell you how I got here—how I started working for Fergus Foley."

Deklan reaches over and pulls me close to him, his lips brushing over mine as he closes his eyes and hugs me tightly. After a moment, he releases me completely and reaches for his whiskey. I settle back against the couch and wait as patiently as I can for him to begin.

"I just barely remember my birth parents," Deklan says. He takes a long breath as he stares into the liquid of his glass, swirling it around as he speaks. "When I was four, there was a break-in at our house." He pauses and takes another long breath. When he speaks again, his voice is shaking slightly. "I was upstairs with my mother—I remember that part clearly—but I don't know where my sister was. My mother had just put me into my pajamas and was reading me a book when we heard the front door slam open. There was a lot of shouting, and then I heard the loudest sound ever. My mother shoved me into the back of my closet and threw a blanket over me. She told me not to move or make a sound. I don't know how long I was there. I heard more shouting, and I heard more loud bangs. A while after that, someone walked into my room. When the closet door opened, I closed my eyes and tried not to breathe. A couple minutes later, I heard footsteps going out of the room."

Deklan drains his glass.

"I don't know how long it was before the police showed up. Maybe a few minutes. Maybe an hour. I don't know. I never moved from that spot until they showed up. They took me out of the closet and out of the house. We had to go through the living room to get outside, and I saw blankets lying over lumps on the floor and a lot of red. At the time, I didn't realize they were my parents' bodies.

"I was taken to a house where a woman and three other children lived. I remember the swimming pool in the back yard. It felt like a vacation to me, but when I asked about my parents, no one would tell me anything. It was weeks before I really understood everything that had happened, and even then, I only understood as much as a four-year-old could. My parents and my sister were gone, and they weren't coming back.

"There wasn't any extended family for me to go live with, so I got shuffled around in the system. Five different foster homes the first two years. Once I started school, I was never in the same place for more than a semester, never made any friends or anything. When I was nine, I was put in a more permanent home. That's when I started really looking into what happened to my family.

"It was years before I knew the whole story. No one would ever give me any information when I asked. My foster mom would take me to Mass, and the priest would tell me my family was with God and that they were happy now. I tried to focus on that, but I needed to know what happened. It ate at me. When I was ten, I figured out how to get ahold of court documents, and I found the police reports of the break-in. A neighbor had called the police when he heard gunshots, and he saw three men leaving the house before the police got there. He didn't get a good look at them and couldn't ID them or anything like that. When the police arrived, they found three bodies in the living room and one four-year-old boy hiding in the closet. My sister had been…had been raped before they killed her."

"Oh my God." I reach for Deklan's leg, but he doesn't look at me. He drains the glass and continues.

"No one was ever charged with the crime. I might have dug into it more then, but that's about the time my foster father died of a heart attack, and my foster mother went nuts."

"What did she do?"

"She was convinced my foster father died because the rest of us—herself, me, and another boy in the foster care system—had sinned against God, and we were all being punished. She was convinced that she was going to die as well unless we all atoned."

"Atoned?"

"The other boy was Brian. He only had to put up with it for a couple of months before he was moved to another family. I was left there to take the brunt of it."

"Brian? As in the guy who took me to see you at the hospital? You were in foster care together?"

"Yeah, that's him."

I ponder this for a moment. In essence, this makes Brian Dek's brother, and I see him in a slightly different light now.

"What did your foster mom do?"

"I was a sinner," Deklan says quietly. "I had to pay for my sins. It's not like I ever did anything—she was just a nut, ya know? But I had to pay for whatever she thought I'd done. At this point, I figure I still have a few more sins to commit before I catch up to the punishments."

"How did she punish you?"

He looks at me with dark, narrowed eyes. There's a long pause before he answers.

"Whipped us with a belt. Made us stand with our arms out, holding up Bibles, boiled water for the bathtub. That was the worst of it."

"She put you in boiling water? Oh my God." I gasp as I place my hand over my mouth. My thoughts spin around in my head as I put it all together. "The scars on your leg…"

"I guess the neighbors heard me screaming," Deklan says. "Had to have skin grafts because the burns were so bad. That's when they took me away from her for good. I never saw her after that. She died of an overdose a couple years later."

"I was twelve then and was placed in a group home. I ran away and was caught and placed in another group home. That was the trend over the next couple of years until I figured out how not to get caught.

"I lived on the streets for about six months, just doing whatever I could to survive. Not long into it, I came across Brian, and we helped each other out sometimes, finding odd jobs, mostly quick manual labor stuff at restaurants or loading docks. I was big for my age and pretty strong even then. People seemed okay with giving obviously underage kids a few bucks to haul boxes around.

"I met Fergus Foley at a loading dock. I'd made a bit of cash there earlier in the day, and it was raining that night, so I stayed in the shipyard and was going to sleep in one of the containers. Sometime in the middle of the night, Mr. Foley caught sight of me, questioned me, and then put me to work. He offered to buy me a steak dinner and give me a place to sleep for the effort."

"I kept loading containers for Mr. Foley for a few weeks after that. After a while, Brian joined me. Fergus and I talked more, and he found out what happened to my family. One day, he came in and told me he knew who had killed them."

"I'd never felt such rage before. When he offered to help me locate them…I didn't even consider consequences. I wanted revenge, pure and simple. Fergus Foley helped me get that."

Deklan glances at me before giving me a wry grin.

"I'll spare you the details, but believe me, they paid for what they'd done."

"You killed them." It's not a question, but I still need the confirmation. He doesn't answer me in any case; he just stares at the bottom of his empty glass.

"So that's how I started working for Mr. Foley full-time. He set me up in this apartment so I would be close to him, got me a car to get around in, and paid me a shit-ton of money. He gave me a job, a purpose, and helped me get my revenge. He gave Brian a job, too, which got him off the streets. I owe the Foley family everything."

I stare at my hands as I take in everything Deklan just told me. All thoughts of my encounter with Sean are gone. All I can think about now is Deklan and what a horrible childhood he had. I try to imagine Deklan as a child, hiding under a blanket in a closet as his family is murdered, but the image that comes to my head is too horrible. I think about him as a teenager, loading cargo containers for Fergus Foley, and that's a much more relatable picture.

"So that's me," Deklan says as he sits up a little straighter on the couch. "You now know more about me than anyone alive does."

I swallow hard as I look at my husband's blank expression. Despite his efforts to remain emotionless, I can see the tension in his jaw and the tightness in his shoulders. I pull myself up on my knees and crawl into his lap, wrapping my arms around his neck and laying my head against his shoulder.

"I'm so sorry, Deklan. I'm sorry that happened to you and your family. You were so young. No one should have to go through all that."

Deklan doesn't speak. He coils his arms around me and holds me to his chest and rests his head on top of mine.

"It feels weird," he says, "telling someone all of that."

"I'm glad you did."

"I'm not sure." Deklan sighs. "I don't think you need to be burdened with my past. You've got your own trauma."

"I don't remember it," I say with a shrug. "My therapist said I blocked it all out. Sometimes I dream about it, but I can't recall the details."

"I didn't know you had a therapist." Deklan runs his thumb back and forth along my wrist, and I relax with the touch.

"I haven't seen her since we got married."

"Do you want to see her?"

"I haven't given it much thought," I say. "I used to see her regularly, but I didn't think I was getting a lot out of it, and Dad bitched about the cost."

"Maybe...maybe if you talked to her now, you would remember something."

"Why would I want to remember any of that?" I press against him, inhaling his scent. "It's over and done with. Remembering it doesn't make any difference."

"Maybe it would," Deklan says softly. "Maybe if you remembered it, things would be different."

"I'm okay with how things are now."

"Are you?"

"Yes." I tilt my head up to kiss his cheek. "I like being here with you."

"I like it, too. I thought it would be difficult learning to live with someone after being on my own for so long, but it's nice having someone to come home to."

"You just like my cooking." I giggle.

"I do like your cooking, and that's no joke." He brushes his lips over mine. "I also like taking you to my bed at night. I like watching your eyes roll back in your head when you come."

"They do not!"

"Oh yeah," he says, "they do. That's how I know I got just the right spot."

I glare at him, and he kisses me gently.

"It's more than the cooking and the sex," he says softly as he runs his hand from my shoulder to my wrist. He wraps his fingers around my arm and rubs the skin with his thumb. "I like you just...just being here. I like talking to you."

"I like being around you, too."

Deklan stares at me for a long moment before he speaks again.

"I don't remember my parents well, but they were good people. They were good to me, and I loved them. They loved each other. I want to remember what that was like, so that I can give that to you, too."

Chapter 18

"Think you've got it?" Terry asks as I poke at the iPad screen to navigate the cash register app.

"It's pretty straightforward."

Terry watches as I ring up the next customer.

"Nice!" he says. "Now we can alternate. One of us does the register while the other makes the drinks until we get tired of what we're doing. Then we can switch. Or we can alternate customers—whatever you prefer."

"Let's alternate customers," I say. "That way I can remember what I'm making."

"Deal!" Terry gives me a big smile, and I return it. I've decided his smiles are contagious.

We fall into a smooth rhythm for a while. Around ten o'clock, the man who is always following me around comes in. He lets a woman go in front of him, and I'm pretty sure it's so he ends up with Terry taking his order and not me.

He can think he's subtle, but he's not. In fact, he's as obvious as he could possibly be. I do take note of the name Terry writes on his cup—Charlie. I wonder if it's even his real name. He goes to the back table with his newspaper and coffee.

"Has he always been a regular?" I ask Terry.

"The weird guy?" Terry winks.

"Yeah, the one who always sits in the back and reads the paper."

"Who reads newspapers anymore?"

"Right?" We both laugh.

"I guess he's been coming in here regularly for the last few weeks. I'm pretty good about remembering customers."

"About the time I first started coming here?"

"Hmm…maybe." Terry tilts his head and looks at the ceiling. "A week after, I think. Why?"

"Just curious."

"Do you know him?"

"No, but I've seen him around."

My shift ends in the afternoon, and as soon as I head out the door, I see "Charlie" across the street on a bench near the bus stop. I watch him out of the corner of my eye as he stands and follows me down the street at a distance.

I am already sure he's following me, and this just adds to my evidence. If I ever decide to ask Deklan about it, he won't be able to deny it. There are just too many coincidences.

Surprisingly, Deklan is home when I get there.

"Do you want the good news or the bad news?" he asks as soon as I walk in.

I hesitate. I'm not sure if I want to hear either one.

"Good?" I hang my jacket up on the hook and walk over to the kitchen.

"I'm taking the rest of today off," Deklan says as he wraps his arms around me. He kisses me gently before letting go.

"What's the bad news?"

"I need to make some preparations," he says. "In the morning, I have to leave for a couple of days."

I frown.

"Do you have to?" It's a stupid question, but I ask anyway.

"Yeah, I do."

"The whole weekend?"

"I should be back Sunday night. I guess it's a good thing you got that job, or you'd be stuck here all weekend on your own."

"I requested the weekend off."

"Why did you do that?"

"It's my birthday weekend."

"What?" Deklan's eyes go wide. "Are you serious? Fuck, Kera—I had no idea. I never…well, shit. I never even asked you when your birthday was."

"Saturday," I say with a shrug. "It's no big deal. I can occupy myself for a couple of days."

"I'm so sorry, babe. I'll make it up to you. We can go out tonight or when I get back—wherever you want. Dinner, movie…anything."

"It's okay." It's not, but I'm trying not to get angry. I never mentioned my birthday, so I can hardly blame Dek for not knowing it was so soon. "We can do something when you get back. Where are you going?"

"Chicago."

"Why?"

"Don't ask too many questions, babe. You know I'm not going to give you the details. I will make it up to you though—promise."

He pulls me close to him again, kissing me gently and stroking my cheek.

"Let me make you dinner for a change," he says. "I don't cook as well as you do, but I didn't starve before you were here, either."

"You wouldn't poison a girl before she's even legal to drink, would you?"

"Nah." Deklan grins and kisses me again. "Maybe I'll even give you a glass of wine before I lure you to my bed. You young ones are easy to manipulate."

I struggle playfully in his grasp, calling him a jerk as he wrestles me against the counter and shoves his hand down the front of my leggings. My muscles rebel against me when his fingers reach the right spot, and he slowly circles as he holds me upright.

"You're already wet," he says. "Have you been thinking about me on the way home?"

"Always," I say, breathless. "You always leave me wanting you."

"I try." He captures my mouth with his, kissing me deeply as his fingers slide inside my body. He twists and turns them until I moan into his mouth.

"Forget dinner," I say as I push against his chest. "Let's just go to bed."

Deklan grins as he swoops down and lifts me up off the floor. He tosses me over his shoulder as I squeal and then hauls me to the bedroom.

I don't even know what happens to my clothes. They just seem to fall to the ground along with Deklan's as his mouth and tongue demand all my attention. He throws me backward onto the bed, and is immediately on top of me, pushing my legs apart and entering me swiftly as I cry out and grasp his shoulders. He grabs my wrists and holds them above his head, immobilizing me.

I let my head drop back against the mattress and just let myself feel for a moment. My skin tingles everywhere he touches me. I arch up when he runs his tongue over my nipples and then blows cool air across them and pull my knees up, allowing him better access as he drives into me in a slow, comfortable rhythm.

My heart pounds. My breathing is labored, and my muscles are tight. I'm already close when he suddenly pulls out.

"Aargh!" I cry in protest. "Don't stop."

"Roll over." Deklan releases my wrists and grins down at me.

He leans back on his heels, grabs me by the hips, and pulls me over until I'm on my stomach. He snakes a hand under me and pulls me up on my hands and knees.

"Spread those legs for me. There you go…" Deklan runs his hands over my thighs, pushing my legs a little farther apart. He grips my hips and pulls me back against his hard cock, rubbing it between my legs. Sliding his hands up my sides and around to the front, he pulls lightly at my nipples, and I moan. "You like that, baby?"

"So far." I don't know how I feel about being in this position. We've always faced each other before—either him or me on top, but never like this. I feel vulnerable as I look over my shoulder.

Deklan's eyes shine in the dim light of the bedroom. He reaches to my shoulders and massages them, and I relax a little.

"If you decide you don't like it, just tell me." Deklan gathers my hair up in one hand and kisses the back of my neck. "I can stop any time."

He releases my hair, allowing it to fall over my shoulder, and then trails his fingers down the center of my back. I feel him grip my hip with one hand before he presses the tip of his cock against me and slides forward.

I gasp. The angle in this position makes everything feel different. A deep groan comes from Deklan's throat as he leans over my back, rubbing my shoulders and arms.

"Do you like that?" I feel his hot breath on the back of my neck.

"It feels different."

"Good kind of different?"

"Yes." I adjust my knees against the mattress and push back against him a bit, and Deklan grunts as he buries himself deeper.

He moves back and forth slowly a few times, then a little faster. He reaches around and grips my breasts, pinches my nipples, and kisses between my shoulder blades before he sits back up, changing the angle again, and starts moving with long, hard trusts.

"Oh, God!" I cry out. I reach forward and dig my fingers into the sheets as I try to match his pace, pushing back to meet each stroke.

"Do you know how perfect you look with your ass in the air and my cock sliding in and out of you?"

"Fuck...Deklan...ugh!"

"Sweet Jesus, that feels good."

He moves faster and harder, and each thrust feels like it's going deeper than the last. He grips my hips hard and pulls me back against him as he moves.

"I want you to feel this," Deklan says, punctuating each word with a thrust, "every moment I'm gone. I want you so sore, you can't walk without thinking about me."

He continues his relentless pounding until I can no longer hold myself up on my arms. With my face pressed against the mattress, I give up trying to match his pace, and just let him take me as he wants.

"Give me your hand," he says as he slows down for a moment.

I reach my hand down toward his knees, and he takes it, moving it to my center.

"Touch yourself," he says. "Make yourself come on my cock."

I can barely make my muscles obey my commands, but I do as he says, rubbing my fingers back and forth and then in a circle around my clit. Deklan pulls back and then slams into me.

"Ahh!"

"Shush!" He smacks my ass but only lightly. It surprises me but doesn't hurt. "Play with that pussy. I want to feel you tighten up around me."

He pulls back and slams home again and again. I cry out with each deep thrust, matching the furiousness of his movements with my fingers until the tidal wave builds, crests, and crashes all around me.

"Sweet Jesus, yes…" Deklan moans as I fall apart from the inside out. My muscles give up on me, and Deklan has to hold my hips to keep me upright as he leans over, grabs my arms tightly, and starts pounding quickly. "Oh, God! Kera! Kera!"

With a long groan, Deklan thrusts hard and holds himself against me as I feel warmth spread deep inside. He keeps himself there for a few seconds before he collapses on my back and rolls us both to our sides.

As we fall against the bed, he slips out of me with another grunt and then places a hand against my stomach, pressing my body to his. I curl up with my back to his chest, thoughts of dinner completely gone from my head. He wraps both arms around me and kisses my shoulder as he runs his thumb back and forth across my wrist.

"If I'm going to get that every time you travel," I say, "you should travel more often."

"You can have that every day when I'm here, as far as I'm concerned. Three times on the weekends."

"I'm already sore."

"Good."

I snicker and snuggle closer, suddenly exhausted.

The next morning, Deklan is up early. He's showered and dressed before I even awaken. I roll over and place my feet on the floor with a grunt. My body resists every movement as I force myself to stand.

He's definitely left me sore. When I look at myself in the bathroom mirror, I see bruises on my arms and legs. I don't remember him holding me that tightly at the time, but I was rather caught up in it all. I'll definitely be thinking about him every time I take a step today, which was certainly his intention. I can tell by the smirk on his face when he sees me waddle from the bathroom to the kitchen.

"Coffee?" Deklan holds out a cup.

"Yes, please." I take the steaming cup and walk over to the couch.

Deklan butters his toast and wolfs it down as he pokes around in the suitcase by his feet. He must have packed before I woke up.

"Are you flying or driving?" I ask.

"Driving," he says, "but not my car. I'll leave you the keys in case you need to go somewhere."

"Who's going with you?"

Deklan's only answer is a quick glance and a raised eyebrow. I give up on the questions and just watch him finish shoving things into the suitcase and draining his coffee cup.

"Stop looking at me like that," Deklan says. "I feel guilty enough as it is."

"Sorry." I'm pouty. I don't want to be alone on my birthday, and it makes me feel like a petulant child to be mad at Dek about it. I take a deep breath and force myself to smile. "What if I want to talk to you?"

"Emergencies, babe." Deklan hauls the suitcase to the door and then walks over to me. He kneels in front of the couch and takes my face in his hands. "I'll be working. Text if you really need something. Call if there's an emergency."

"An emergency, like I'm horny and I need birthday phone sex?"

"Wish I could." Deklan grins at me as he shakes his head slowly. "I'm sorry I'm leaving right before your birthday."

"It's all right." I wrap my arms around his neck and stand on my toes to reach him better. "It's my own fault for not telling you when it is. Um, speaking of such, when is your birthday?"

"Christmas Eve." Deklan gives me a half smile. "I always ended up with combined birthday/Christmas presents as a kid. It sucked."

"I suppose it did." I chuckle and hug him tightly.

Deklan leans back, stares into my eyes for a moment, and then presses his mouth to mine. I try to hold on, but he breaks the kiss and smiles down at me as he stands. A moment later, he's out the door and gone.

My stomach sinks moments after he's left. Tomorrow is my twenty-first birthday, and I have no plans at all. I could waste some time taking a shower, but at the moment, I still smell like Deklan, and I don't want to wash him off of me just yet. I stare into my cup of coffee, now gone cold, and sigh.

"Self-pity doesn't suit you," I say out loud.

Though I don't have to work today, I decide to take a little walk to the coffee shop instead of warming my existing coffee in the microwave. It would be nice to talk to Kathy for a bit. The weather is finally turning warm, so I leave my jacket behind. The sun is bright, and I squint as I let it warm my face. It mellows my foul mood a bit but not enough.

As soon as I get down the street and turn my phone on, I already have a voicemail from Kathy telling me to call her immediately or face the gravest of punishments. I snicker as I find her contact info and press the call button.

"Yo, bitch!" she screams into the phone as soon as she answers. "I sure hope you don't have any plans for the day!"

"Why?"

"Because I'm in the airport, and I'll be there in a few hours."

"Whaa?" I put my hand over my mouth, realizing I'd picked up one of Terry's expressions. "What are you talking about?"

"There's a nursing conference Monday and Tuesday, and it's just a half hour from you. I'm coming early to spend the weekend!"

"Are you shitting me?"

"No shitting," Kathy says. "Well, probably some shitting—I'm human last time I checked. Also some drinking, which can lead to shitting…"

I laugh loudly, my mood instantly lifted.

Deklan is going to be gone for two days, so the timing is perfect. I mean, what the hell else am I going to do around the apartment?

"Are you going to stay with me?"

"The clinic is putting me up at a hotel," Kathy says. "I figured you could stay with me! That way we can be plastered and hung over together."

"What time does your flight land?"

"Ten thirty," Kathy says, "but there is all that taxiing around on the runways, collecting baggage and crap. There's an Asian fusion sort of place about a half mile from the airport. It'll be faster for me to just take a cab and meet you there for lunch about 11:30."

"That works perfectly! I can't wait!"

I feel a bit like jumping up and down as I forget all about going to the coffee shop, turn on my heel, and practically run back to the apartment. Once inside, I race to the bathroom and get myself a shower. I feel a little sad that I won't smell like Deklan the whole time he's gone, but it's probably not a scent Kathy would appreciate as much as I do. I scrub down and gather up my overnight bag.

It's way too early to go, but I have nothing else to do, so I decide to head to the restaurant now. I grab the keys Deklan left on the counter and head to the parking garage. I've only driven Deklan's car once, but it's easy to drive. I just have to be careful not to speed.

I jump in the car and make my way to the fusion place. They have a coffee bar and a bunch of noodle dishes, including noodles wrapped in a tortilla. There's a hostess near the door, but instead of leading me to one of the empty tables, she just hands me a menu.

"When you've made your selection, you can order right over there!" She points to a row of cash registers.

Apparently, I need to order and pay up front. I'm not completely sure how my food is going to find me, but the cashier gives me a little blinking box that will alert them to where I've chosen to sit. I feel completely lost and confused, but I follow directions and find an empty table to sit and wait for Kathy.

As I wait, I look around at the décor and the clientele. Many of the patrons have luggage with them, so this must be a popular place to pick people up from the airport. As I glance around, I see a familiar face, newspaper and all.

I glare down at the top of the table. I'm really not surprised. Deklan probably plans to have me followed all weekend.

"Fuck it," I mumble. I refuse to let Dek's paranoia ruin my weekend. If it comes down to it, Kathy and I can hit a dance club, and I'll ask the guy to dance.

Thinking about what my stalker's face would look like if I extended that sort of invitation amuses me, and I lean back in the booth with a self-satisfied smirk, waiting for my friend.

Chapter 19

"I've fucking had it!" Kathy throws her arms in the air and starts in before she even says hello.

Ranting is actually my favorite thing about Kathy. Once she gets going, there is no stopping her. It doesn't matter what the topic might be though I've never heard her go on about politics. But she'll rant about everything else, from the organization of the fruit in the produce section at the supermarket to the amount of space someone leaves between their parked car and a stop sign.

Today's rant: tipping.

"With what?" I stand up briefly to give her a welcoming hug before I sit back down and sip at my coffee, trying to hide my smile. To an outside observer, it might appear that Kathy is about to strangle the most convenient person available, but I know she's harmless.

Mostly.

"What the hell is up with tipping anyway?"

"Tipping? What about it?"

"It's out of control." Kathy shoves her carry-on luggage against the side of the table, tosses her purse and coat in the booth, and then slides in next to the pile.

We haven't seen each other for over a year, but that has never mattered with us. As soon as we are together again, it's as if we had spent the last few days in each other's constant company. It's just how we are, and there is no need for pleasant "How are you?" or "Great to see you again" jabber.

"We are never coming here again." Kathy places her elbows on the table and reaches toward me with her pinky finger extended. I grasp it with mine though I have no idea why we're pinky-swearing over a restaurant.

"Why not?"

"I don't know what to do about the tip."

"I paid in cash," I tell her. "I was going to just leave a tip on the table."

Deklan had left me a thousand dollars in cash on the kitchen counter before he left, telling me to treat myself to some birthday shopping. I had told him it was an insane amount of money, but he just shrugged, suggested jewelry, and promised to bring me something back from the Windy City.

"I paid by credit card," Kathy says. "It makes all the expense reporting easier when I get back, but that's not the point."

"What is the point?"

"Tipping is supposed to be for your server, right? Not the owner or the guy who rings up the bill or whatever. Tip the server for really good service. I'm great with that. But if I'm paying the bill up front, before I even get my food, what the hell am I supposed to tip? Five percent? Ten? The default comes up at eighteen when you swipe your card. Cheeky bastards."

She's on a roll and not about to stop now.

"When I bought some peanuts on the plane—and don't even get me started on buying plane peanuts—it came up asking what percentage I wanted to tip. Since when do you tip a flight attendant? Or does the attendant hand it over to the pilot? If the pilot crashes the plane and I live, can I get my tip back? Does the dude who loads the plane up with fuel get a cut? Where does it end?"

176

I tilt my head to one side and consider what she's saying. I haven't flown recently, and I think she's got a pretty good point. Working at the coffee shop isn't something I do for money, so I've never paid much attention to the tips.

"I always thought tipping was made up for mom and pop restaurants where the kids were the servers," I say. "The parents couldn't afford to pay their kids, so the customers did instead."

"Where did you hear that?" Kathy narrows her eyes at me.

"I don't know if I heard it anywhere," I say with a shrug. "It's just what I've always thought."

"It kinda makes sense," Kathy says with a nod. "I'll check."

On her phone, Kathy starts to google the origin of tipping but then is distracted by her food being placed in front of her. The guy who brings it doesn't say a word, and when Kathy asks him where her drink is, he points out a self-service beverage dispenser.

"You see what I mean? I want my damn tip back." She gets up from the table to retrieve her drink, and I try to keep my giggles in check.

When she returns with her iced tea, she's still at it.

"And when did tipping become something everyone gets just for doing their jobs? I tip the hairdresser, the massage therapist, and now the flight attendants. I mean, who do I need to start tipping next? My gynecologist? Oh wow, your hands are nice and warm today! And the way you handle that speculum! I'm impressed! Here's an extra twenty bucks!"

I can't help it—I laugh out loud this time.

"Isn't your gynecologist also your boss?"

"Irrelevant. Besides, I work for the clinic, not the doctor herself though she is my supervisor. You're getting me off topic!"

"Tipping…warm speculums…I'm keeping up!"

"I told you about the peanuts, right?"

"Yep."

It's refreshing to be with Kathy. I'm not anxious, waiting to say or do something wrong. Even when it's just me and Deklan, I sometimes still feel a little on edge. Everything is still so new, and it's hard to have a conversation with a man who won't talk about his work.

I feel like myself, and I'm completely relaxed for the first time since the marriage.

"Let's go to the hotel," Kath says as she finishes up her food. "There has to be a bar at the hotel."

"It's barely noon."

"Then we shouldn't have to deal with a crowd!"

"True."

We have to bus our own table, which sends Kathy on another tipping rant that lasts for the entire ride to the hotel. Once we get there and check in, we dump our stuff in the room and head straight for the far end of the bar.

"I'll need some ID," the bartender says.

Shit.

"Um…" I look over at Kathy, not sure what I should do, but she's already digging in her own purse. Then a thought occurs to me, and I quickly reach for my wallet. Next to my real driver's license is the license Deklan used that time he took me to the hospital—the one with the name Kera Malone on it. It has my birthday as three months earlier than it is. "Here you go."

The bartender gives the ID half a glance before handing it back to me.

"What would you ladies like this afternoon?"

Kathy looks at me sideways but doesn't say anything until after the bartender takes our orders.

"Let me see that." She grabs the license from me and snickers. "You with a fake ID. Who woulda thunk it?"

"Hush, you!" I grab the ID out of her hand and shove it back in my wallet. "It's for emergencies."

"Vodka is an emergency." Kathy nods seriously.

The bartender brings us our drinks, and we clink them together. Being underage and rather sheltered, I've rarely had any alcoholic drinks, and by the time we are halfway through the second vodka-cranberry, I'm already feeling it.

"So, you don't even know what he's doing on this trip to Chicago?" Kathy drains her glass and orders another one.

"No clue," I say. "He doesn't tell me anything. I'm just glad he left me the car, or I would have been looking for an Uber to come meet you."

"I'm sorry I don't get to meet him," Kathy says. "I was kinda looking forward to that. Then again, a girls' weekend is better. Now, show me how big his dick is with your hands."

"No!" I laugh and feel my face getting warm. "It's big enough."

"But he's tall, right?"

"About six foot four."

"So, is it proportional?"

"Kathy! I am not talking about my husband's cock!"

"Yeah, you will." Kathy raises her hand and beckons the bartender. "My friend here needs more alcohol. I need her to give me some information regarding her husband's penis, and she is thus far refusing my inquiries."

The bartender grins and hands me another drink.

"I'm not even done with this one!"

"Catch up." Kathy leans back in against the barstool and grins. "I need deets."

I shake my head, finish my second drink, and move on to the third. I need to get her ranting about something so she'll forget about Deklan's dick.

"How was the flight?" I ask.

"Bumpy." Kathy rolls her eyes. "And the airport—ugh! What is it Douglas Adams said? Airports are ugly."

"Profound." I down the rest of my drink and nibble at the basket of pretzels on the bar.

"He said they were *really* ugly."

"Uh huh." I roll my eyes.

"Context!" Kathy slams the palm of her hand on the bar. "You're just going to have to read the book."

"Which book?"

"I don't remember."

"Ugh!"

We both laugh, and Kathy downs the rest of her drink and practically inhales a basket of pretzels sitting on the bar.

"Any screaming babies?"

"Of course," she says. "One of them was in the seat across from me. Honestly, screaming babies don't bother me. I don't have to deal with them, and I kinda feel sorry for the parents. Teenagers on a plane—they are the really obnoxious ones. They're always leaning over the aisles, sprawling out in their seats, and fucking around with the window shades. The chick in front of me, who was airsick before we even took off—she was all kinds of fun."

I try to pace myself on the drinks. I can't keep up with Kathy—she has obviously had a lot of practice since I last saw her. I hoard the pretzels and, when the time comes, order something carb-filled for dinner.

We laugh. We cry a bit. We hug a lot. We drink more. At the end of the evening, we have to hold each other up as we get off the elevator, laughing and stumbling our way down the hall. It takes both of us to use the simple keycard to open the door, and we practically fall into the room.

"I miss you so much," I say as I fall onto the bed.

"Aww, I miss you too!" Kathy flops down on the other side, rolls over and hugs me. "I wish I was a lesbian so I could show you how much I love you."

I laugh. The room is spinning, so I close my eyes. Kathy pokes my shoulder.

"Kera?"

"Hmm?"

"How big is it?"

I hold my hands up, eyes still closed.

"Holy shit. That's big!"

"It's sooo big!"

The fits of giggles continue until we both fall asleep.

DEKLAN

Chapter 20

Room service breakfast-in-bed makes a morning almost perfect.

"Happy birthday!" Kathy starts to sing as she places the tray across my lap, but I quickly silence her with a piece of toast.

The eggs are nice and greasy, soaking up the alcohol from the previous day. There's a ton of butter for the toast, too. Strawberry jam gives it just the right amount of sweetness.

"I can't believe I don't have a headache," I say as I munch.

"Remember all that water I kept making the bartender refill?" Kathy asks. "That's the trick, you know—hydration. Constant hydration. You learn these things when you get drunk in nursing school."

She turns on the morning news, which we ignore almost completely in favor of the food and conversation."

"Seems like this Deklan guy has surprised you."

"He has." I nod as I finish chewing. "He's really very sweet though a bit paranoid and overprotective. He's very much a 'my way or the highway' kind of guy, but if I choose my timing just right—like I did about getting a job—he can be reasonable about most things."

"You haven't shown me a picture of this guy," Kathy says. "You said he was attractive."

"You know, I don't have any. Deklan's very opposed the use of phones in general, and I've never taken a picture of the two of us. There wasn't a photographer or anything at the wedding. I think Sean's sister might have taken a couple of candids. Maybe I can ask her sometime."

"But he's hot?"

"I think so." I laugh. "He's definitely built."

"So, what about the guy you were supposed to marry?"

My skin goes cold even thinking about Sean.

"I'm really glad I'm not with him."

"Deklan is that good, huh?"

"Sean is that bad."

"You seemed to be into him before." She leans back against the pillows and waits for me to explain.

I know with Kathy there is no judgment. She knows more about me than anyone else in the world, and she's always taken the time to understand my position.

"I was, I suppose." I take a deep breath. "I didn't really know him, of course, but there's more to it than that. He's different than the times I met him before."

"How so?"

"He's crazy. I'm not just saying that, either—I think he's one hundred percent nuts."

I tell her the details of the day Sean said I was going to marry Deklan, the things he said to me during the reception, and his comments to me afterward—both at the Foley house and in the coffee shop.

"Damn, girl." Kathy lets out a long whistle. "You really dodged a bullet there."

"Yeah, funny you should put it that way. Deklan is making me carry a gun whenever I go out, but it didn't even occur to me to get it when Sean came into the coffee shop."

"A gun? Really?"

I go to my purse and pull out the .22. Kathy looks it over and whistles again.

"I went out with a guy who was into guns," she says. "He took me out to the range a few times, but I've never owned one."

"It feels weird having it in my purse," I say. "I don't think I'd ever actually pull it out."

"You never know." Kathy hands the pistol back to me, and I shove it deep inside my purse. "Someday, you might not have a choice."

"Let's hope it never comes to that."

"It proves my point, though," Kathy says. "Deklan is obviously very into you if he's worried about your safety. Does Deklan know about Sean coming to your work?"

"No," I say with a shake of my head. "I honestly don't know what he would do if I told him. He's very loyal to the Foley family. I don't want to come between that."

"You're afraid he'd choose them over you." Kathy's words are not a question.

"I don't know…maybe."

"You are."

"What if he did?" I feel tears burning behind my eyes. "What if I told him, and he told me that Sean was his boss, and I just needed to shut up and deal with it? What if he tells Sean to just take me back?"

"Do you think he would?"

"I have no idea."

"Really?" Kathy sits up and crosses her legs. "From everything you have told me, Deklan is seriously into you. Yeah, it wasn't what he was expecting, and he didn't ask for it, but he's way into you now."

"You think?"

"I know. There's no way he'd take Sean's side, not if he found out what Sean was saying to you. I think he'd be pissed—*really* pissed."

"I'm not sure that would be better," I say. "I mean, if he and Sean get into it, what happens next? He's always worked for the Foley family. What if he got fired? What if he got something worse than being fired?"

"It's always the unknown that scares you the most," Kathy says. "At some point, the here and now gets scarier. You'll have to tell him then."

Kathy scoots over and hugs me, and I hug her back tightly. I let a few tears escape as I hang on.

"I'm so glad you came to see me." I sniff as we part, reaching over to grab a tissue from the nightstand.

"Me too."

We go back to breakfast, both of us silently contemplating as we chew. Kathy finishes first and gets up to rifle through her luggage.

"What's the plan for today?" I ask.

"I don't know about you," Kathy says, "but I'm thinking more of the same. Are there any clubs around where we can drink and dance, and I can flirt with a hot bartender?"

"I'm sure there are."

"Then that's the plan!" Kathy goes to her suitcase and pulls out a headband, sparkling with rhinestones. "But first, we need to find you an outfit that goes with this."

"What the hell is that?"

"Your birthday tiara! Every woman needs a birthday tiara!"

"Deklan did leave me some money for shopping."

"Then let's go!"

We get ourselves cleaned up and ready to go before we head down to the lobby to get the car from the valet. After a trip to the mall, we return to the hotel with several packages, including a sequined shirt to match the tiara. Kathy makes me wear it the whole time we are shopping, which brings far more attention than I usually prefer.

I grin and bear it, though, even when the valet makes a comment, and Kathy announces my birthday quite loudly.

"I'll plan on getting you a cab instead of giving you the keys back," he says with a wink.

"Hold on!" Kathy says. "We need to get the stuff out of the trunk!"

I open the trunk and grab the packages. One is shoved way in the back, and Kathy leans inside to grab it while the valet checks out her ass. I roll my eyes at him, and he winks again.

"What the fuck is all this?" Kathy asks.

I tilt my head to the side as she pulls out a brown sack I don't remember seeing before. Inside is a strange assortment of items, including zip ties, latex gloves, and an electric blanket.

"I have no clue," I say. I don't want to think about why Deklan would have those things in the back of his car. "Must be Dek's."

I shove the bag back inside and slam the trunk closed.

Kathy and I go to the room to change. Then we hit the hotel bar for a quick drink. I'm all paranoid that the bartender is going to realize the ID I used last night is a fake, and Kathy notices my nervousness.

"Let's bail and go to the bar across the street," she says. "You need better drinks. Make sure you use your real ID this time—people love to get a newly of-age chick drunk. You'll be drinking for free all night!"

"Martinis, here we come!"

Kathy was right about one thing—newly twenty-one-year-olds get a lot of free drinks. We catch Ubers to different bars around town, and every bartender makes sure I get my fill. At some point, we end up at a biker bar.

The bar is L-shaped, dark, and in a secluded area off the main strip. I didn't even notice it from across the road, but the Uber driver said we could have a good time here. There's a sign in the window, but it doesn't light up to tell you the name of the place or anything like that. Inside, a long bar occupies the long side of the L, whereas the short side is lined with booths.

I follow Kathy to the closest bar stools, and she orders cosmos for both of us. The bartender looks at us quizzically, shakes his head slightly, and then starts poking around to see if he can find martini glasses somewhere. He can't and ends up pouring the drinks into highball glasses instead.

"We should go jewelry shopping."

"Jewelry shopping? Didn't we already shop enough?"

"Not actually shopping for actual jewelry." Kathy snickers and leans in close. "It's code."

"Code for what?"

"Code for going around and trying to figure out which guys are pierced where. Start with that one. I bet he has a Prince Albert."

The guy she points out sits at one of the booths. He's covered in tattoos and has several visible piercings. He slams back a beer at the urging of his buddies.

Kathy has already forgotten about the guy as she announces my birthday to the bartender, and a shot magically appears in front of me. Then another. And another.

"What is this stuff?" I laugh as I slam back another one. "It tastes like Big Red gum."

"Fireball," Kathy replies. "It's good shit."

"I think I'm drunk." I laugh again.

"You were drunk before we got here. Drink this!"

Kathy shoves a glass of ice water toward me and strikes up a conversation with the guys sitting next to us. She begins to babble on about tipping, gynecologists, and warm hands, but I no longer hear exactly what she's saying. My attention is drawn to the booth behind the pierced beer-guzzler and a tall, shadowy form I know all too well.

Deklan is sitting in the very last booth with his back to me. If it weren't for his size, no one would be able to see him at all. In fact, I think he's sitting there alone until I see a hand attached to a tattooed arm reach across the table and take a piece of paper from Deklan's fingers.

What is he doing here?

Who is with him?

I can't tell from this angle if the person he's with is a man or a woman, and I slip for a moment into jealous mode. I shove myself off the bar and take a step closer.

"Kera? What is it?" Kathy asks as I start to walk away.

"I'm not sure yet." I stand up and head straight to the table where Deklan sits across from the unknown person accompanying him. All I can see is that they're leaning close to talk to one another. Deklan's body blocks my view of his companion.

I take a few steps down the row of booths and finally get a better look at the person with Deklan. Now that I'm closer, I can see that the tattooed arm is definitely masculine. The tattoos aren't familiar though, and I don't think it's someone from the Foley crew.

Even though Deklan isn't sitting with another woman, my anger has built up. I have no idea what he's doing here or who he is with instead of me. He isn't even supposed to be in town. I grit my teeth and walk straight up to the table.

I stumble before I reach my destination, and I have to adjust my tiara before it falls off.

Deklan glances up, and his eyes go wide.

"What are you doing here?" He gets the words out before I manage to speak.

"I was going to ask you the same thing." I try to put my hands on my hips, but I miss. "You aren't even supposed to be in town."

Deklan glances across the table at the man sitting there, eying us both. I glance at the man's face and pause.

He's one of the most physically attractive men I have ever seen in my life. High cheekbones, broad shoulders, and well-built.

He's not huge like Deklan but definitely muscled. His hair is light brown and cut in a short, military skin-fade. His piercing eyes meet mine, and I immediately wish I had never come to the table.

In his eyes, there is nothing but the cold, calculating desire to kill.

"What the fuck is this?" the man mutters.

"Apologies," Deklan says softly as he glares at me. "She's leaving. Now."

He gives me a slight nod, but I don't speak or return the gesture.

"I thought you were in Chicago," I say softly. All the anger is gone from my voice. Just looking at this guy is giving me the creeps and making me want to back away slowly.

"Chicago came here instead." He stares at me, and his look dares me to ask anything else. "I'll be back late tonight. Don't wait up."

His words are clearly a brush off, and my ire returns. He's sitting here having a drink with some dude I've never seen before instead of being with me on my birthday.

I forget about the man across from him as the alcohol begins to talk.

"You know, if you just didn't want to see me this weekend, you could have said so."

The man across from Deklan smirks and raises an eyebrow. Deklan doesn't smile in the slightest. In fact, his eyes have gone almost as cold as his companion's. He stands abruptly, grabbing my arm.

"Give me a sec," he says as he drags me away from the table and out the front door.

I'm mad.

I'm so mad, I don't watch where I'm going and trip on the small step at the door. Though Deklan has me by the arm, he doesn't have me in a tight enough grip to keep me from falling, and I skin my knees on the pavement before he can get me upright again.

"Jesus Christ, Kera. You're drunk."

"So?" I try to wheel around to face him, and he has to catch me again. "It's my fucking birthday, and I'm having a fucking drink or two!"

"Or ten, it seems." He grabs both my arms despite my protesting and hauls me away from the door. He stops near the end of the building and turns my back to the concrete wall, holding me in place so I don't fall. "What the fuck are you doing in a place like this?"

"Shots." I glare at him.

Deklan's eyes narrow, and I realize I might have crossed a line.

"Even drunk, I would think you'd know better than to interrupt me when I'm on business," Deklan says. "Jesus Christ, he's seen your face. He may try to find out who you are. This shit is dangerous, Kera! Don't you understand that?"

"Who is he?"

"No one you need to think about. I certainly don't want him thinking about you."

"I don't like him."

"Good. You shouldn't. What the fuck were you thinking, coming up to me in there?"

"You aren't even supposed to be here!" I yell back. My anger peaks. "What am I supposed to think when you've obviously lied to me? Now you won't even tell me why you're here or who the hell you're with!"

"He'll be on his way back to Chicago soon," Deklan says. "I don't think we'll end up working with him. Not now, anyway."

"Am I supposed to believe that?" I try to take a step forward and immediately lose my balance again. Deklan grabs me by both arms and holds me up against the wall.

"I am not discussing this shit with you." Deklan stands tall and glares down at me. "You are getting into a fucking cab and going home. Now."

"I'm out with my friend for my birthday," I yell back into his face. "I'm not even going home tonight!"

"What the everloving fuck, Kera?"

"Get your hands off her!" I startle and look to my left. Kathy is approaching quickly with something in her hands. She raises an arm and points it in Deklan's direction.

In my inebriated state, I can't quite make sense of what's happening. I recognize the .22-caliber pistol in Kathy's hands as mine, but I don't understand where she got it or why she is pointing it at my husband.

Deklan understands before I do, and I see him reaching into his jacket for his own gun. I realize he intends to point it at Kathy and quickly grab his arm.

"Deklan, no!"

He looks down at me and then to Kathy. I hold tightly to his arm with both hands, and he keeps his hand low, the gun pointed at the ground as I glance back at Kathy. She looks confused as she lowers the gun slightly.

"This is Deklan?" she says. "What the fuck—"

A loud crack deafens me.

My ears start to ring as Deklan shoves me against the side of the building and shields me with his body. I can't even see around him at first, and I can't comprehend either the sound or why he's holding me so tightly.

I pull my head away from his chest, knocking it against the concrete wall and twisting until I can see under his arm. I blink several times at the sight of Kathy lying on the sidewalk just a few feet away from me.

"Arden, get the fuck out of here," Deklan says over his shoulder.

I turn my head to the side and see Deklan's business partner standing in the shadows at the edge of the building, gun drawn. He gives Dek a quick nod before disappearing. I look back in the other direction as slow comprehension creeps over my skin and lodges deep in my brain.

Then I start screaming.

Chapter 21

Flashing blue and red lights invade my eyes. I know people are trying to talk to me—ask me questions—but I can't answer. Dozens of people in black leather and chains are milling around, muttering to each other and pointing at me. I can't take my eyes off the lump on the sidewalk that is now covered by a black blanket.

My throat is raw from screaming.

"If you'd just check the damn gun, you can see it hasn't been fired."

My husband's voice brings me out of my trance. I blink a few times as I see three police officers surrounding him. One of them is putting him in handcuffs.

"We still have to take you in, Mr. Kearney. Your gun matches the type that killed our victim."

Victim.

I stare back at the lump on the ground.

"Ma'am, please. We really need you to come over here so the EMT can check you out."

I glance at the face of the woman next to me. I see her put her hand on my arm, but I can't feel it. I look from the woman to the lump and then back again.

"Is she okay?" I ask. My chin starts to quiver, and tears begin to pour down my face.

This is a dream. A nightmare. This isn't happening.

"Kera. Kera!" I look up at the sound of Deklan's voice and see him being pulled away by the officers. "I'm gonna get this worked out. It's all gonna be okay, babe. Just hang in there."

"All okay," I whisper. I can't focus, and I'm starting to feel sick.

"She's quite intoxicated. She's got some scrapes and bruises and is showing some signs of shock. We better take her in."

Multiple hands lift me off the ground and onto my feet. I can't seem to make my feet work, and I'm half dragged to an awaiting ambulance. Someone shines a flashlight in my eyes and touches the palm of my hand.

"She's cold. Let's get her inside."

I'm lifted again and end up on my back inside the ambulance. There's an EMT on either side of me, and they strap me onto the gurney before the ambulance takes off.

"Ma'am? Can you tell me how you got hurt?"

"Hurt?"

"There are bruises on your arms and legs, and your knees are scraped."

"My husband…" The ambulance turns quickly, and my head spins with the motion. I can't complete my sentence.

"Is he the one they took into custody?" he asks as he looks toward his coworker.

"Yeah, I think so."

"Asshole. Did he shoot that girl?"

"I heard they found a gun on him."

Another swift turn from the ambulance, and I roll my head to the side, vomiting on the floor before the EMT manages to get a container below my head. I hurl again before I pass out.

When I come to, I'm in a dim hospital room with a tube running into my arm. My lips are dry and cracked. My head is pounding, and I can't make sense of my surroundings. I blink a few times, and a nurse comes into the room to check on me.

"Hello, Mrs. Kearney," she says. "How are you feeling?"

"What happened?" My throat burns.

"Just relax now." She holds a cup of water with a straw to my mouth. "Have a little water, but don't try to talk just yet."

"Don't try to talk. You've been through a trying ordeal, but you're safe now."

I push the water away and try to sit up, but the nurse pushes me down by the shoulders and tells me to lie still.

"Not safe," I mutter as I squeeze my eyes shut. "Where's Kathy? Where's Deklan?"

"Just relax…"

"I don't want to relax!" I yell back at her, and the tears start to fall. "Oh my God! Oh my God! She's dead, isn't she? She's dead!"

My throat hurts, but I can't stop screaming as the nurse holds me. A moment later, another nurse comes in and injects something into my IV, and I feel my muscles give out as I drop back down and close my eyes.

*****

My temples pound as I sit up on the hospital bed with my arms wrapped around my knees. Every time I swallow, my throat aches and my eyes burn. I'm acutely aware of every sound around me, from the beeping of monitors at the nurses' station outside my door to the shuffling of visitors' feet across the floor. I hear every keystroke on the computers and the ring of every phone. I focus on the benign noises, trying to make sense of it all.

Nothing feels real.

When I close my eyes, I see blue and red flashes and a blanket on the ground, so I keep them open. I stare down at the mattress through the gap between my thighs and take careful note of every wrinkle in the sheet.

Gentle rocking contrasts with the painful position I'm lying in. The smell of mold and dead fish permeates my nostrils and leaves me feeling sick. My hip and shoulder hurt, and I can't move enough to adjust my position. Something holds my mouth open.

The sound of laughter invades my ears. I can't see. The smell of sweat and fish makes me feel sick. There's a bitter taste in the back of my throat, and I can't breathe. My wrists burn from the tight ropes.

I jerk out of my memories and squeeze my eyes shut. I need to find another thought to focus my attention, but no suitable replacements are within my grasp. I keep hearing the blast of a gunshot, and my ears start ringing all over again. I have no idea how much time has passed. I don't want to know.

A nurse comes in. Behind her is another woman who smiles gently as she says hello and pulls up a rolling chair to the side of the hospital bed.

"My name is Elizabeth," she says. "I'm a counselor here at the hospital. How are you feeling, Kera?"

I don't answer or look up. I find the question ridiculous.

"I've talked to your doctor," Elizabeth says as the nurse finishes checking me out and walks out of the room. "Seems like you are ready to be discharged soon."

I find this news to be irrelevant. It changes nothing.

"Before you go, I'd like to ask you about these." She points to the small bruises on my upper arm. "Did you get those last night?"

I glance at my arm, recalling the small marks reflected in the bathroom mirror. I didn't even remember Deklan holding me that tightly.

"Kera? Can you hear me?"

"Yeah." I glance at her and then stare at the hairs on my arms.

"Last night, you told the EMT that your husband was responsible for them. Do you remember saying that?"

"No." I narrow my eyes at her. I barely remember anything about the ambulance except for puking on the floor.

"Can you tell me how you got them?"

"It's nothing," I say.

"I'd still like to know."

"It doesn't matter."

"It does to me."

My shoulders tense as I squeeze my hands into fists.

"Look, it doesn't fucking matter, okay? Just a little...exuberant sex. I didn't get them last night."

"Exuberant?"

"Yeah." I glare at her. I don't like the way she's looking at me as if I'm an idiot. I know what she's implying. "I'm fine. Deklan's not hitting me; he's not like that."

"I didn't say that he was." She leans forward a little. "Why did you bring it up?"

Manipulative bitch.

"Could you tell me what happened last night?"

I shake my head.

"There are a couple of police officers outside. They'd like to talk to you. It might be easier if you and I talk first."

"No."

"What do you remember, Kera? Can you describe the men who took you? Tell us how you got to the hospital. Do you remember how long you traveled in the van?"

"I don't remember! I don't remember! Just leave me alone!"

"You're going to have to talk to someone, Kera," Elizabeth says, pulling me out of my daydreaming. "I can see there's a lot going on inside your head right now. I have a call in to Dr. Jolly. I understand you have worked with her before."

I don't want to see my previous therapist, and I don't want to talk at all. However, this woman obviously won't take no for an answer. What I need right now is for her to go away.

"I'd like to wait and talk to her," I say quietly. "Would that be all right?"

"Of course," she says. "I'm afraid I can't speak for the officers outside though."

She pats me on the hand before standing and heading to the door. I don't watch her leave. It's too late. I've already retreated. I'm back inside my head.

"If you don't allow yourself to remember what happened to you, how do you think you will ever begin to heal?" Jennifer Jolly tapped her pen against a legal pad.

"How is remembering going to help with that?" I didn't look up from my hands. I didn't want to see her look of disappointment again. "I'm fine. I keep telling you I'm fine."

"But you aren't."

"Mrs. Kearney?"

I don't look up as a man and a woman in uniform approach my bed. I remember them trying to come in earlier, but the doctor had sent them away.

"Mrs. Kearney, I'm Detective Warren," the man says. "We need to ask you some questions about what happened last night."

Last night. Was it just last night? If I went back in time just a fraction of a day, could I fix it all? Could I stop myself from going up to Deklan's table? Could I tell the Uber driver to take Kathy and me to a different bar? Could I go back to morning and breakfast in bed, opting for a day in instead of a night out?

"We have several witness statements, but we'd like to hear things from your side. Can you tell me what you remember?"

The events of the evening run through an alcohol-fugue filter in my head. Breakfast, tiara, shopping, martinis, shots, Deklan...

"Mrs. Kearney"—Warren moves to the side of the bed, closer to me—"we really need to know what happened."

"Where's Deklan?" I ask. "Where's my husband?"

"He's in custody," Warren says.

"Why?"

"You're bruised, Mrs. Kearney, and witnesses say there was an argument between you and your husband."

I look up at the woman speaking, trying to remember if she had mentioned her name. She's young. I wonder if it's her first day on the job.

"Deklan didn't hurt me." I stare back down at the mattress. "It's a misunderstanding."

"And the gun found on him?"

"What about it?"

"A young woman is dead, Mrs. Kearney." Detective Warren looks at me, his jaw set and his forehead creased. "I understand she was a friend of yours. The person who did this needs to be brought to justice before he does it again." He crouches down until he's eye level with me. "Kera, don't you want justice for your friend?"

"Deklan didn't shoot her."

"Can you tell me who did?" Warren asks.

"I don't know."

"Can you tell me why Miss Jackson was holding a gun or where she might have gotten it?"

My stomach tightens up. I have no idea what I should do. Deklan didn't do anything to Kathy, but she must have thought he was going to do something, or she wouldn't have brought out the gun. I don't even know whose name the gun is registered under or if it's registered at all. Anything I might say sounds wrong, and I don't want to say anything.

"Kera?" Right on cue, Deklan is suddenly standing in the doorway.

I stare at him. There's rough stubble on his face, and he's wearing the same clothes he had on last night. Our gazes lock, but I can't understand the unfamiliar look in his eyes. Fear? Sadness? Panic? I can't tell.

"I need to speak with my wife," Deklan says with authority as he walks into the room and moves between the detective and the bed.

"We still have some questions."

"They said you were in jail," I say quietly.

"They let me out." Deklan reaches forward tentatively and places his hand on my arm. "It's all right, babe. Everything will be all right."

I shake my head slowly.

"It's not okay, Dek." My voice breaks. "It's not okay! It's not!"

Deklan sits beside me and wraps his arms around me. I want to resist. I want to scream that it's all his fault for being there with that…that man. But it's not his fault. I know it isn't.

It's my fault.

"It's all my fault!" I scream. "She…she only came early because it was my birthday. She didn't have to be here. She just came here for me…"

Deklan holds me tightly. I want to push him away, but his grip is unyielding, warm and familiar. I lean against him and sob into his shirt as he faces the detective.

"Look, my wife obviously isn't up for this now, and you guys need to go."

"We need some answers, Mr. Kearney." Warren squares his shoulders and tries to stand tall, but Deklan stands as well, towering over him. "I can always issue a subpoena, but it would be a lot easier if you both cooperate."

"Well, I'll bring her to the station with our attorney when she's feeling better. For now, you need to get out."

I don't look up, but I hear grumbling and footsteps walking away. Deklan sits back down beside me, enveloping me once again.

"It's not your fault, babe. You know it isn't."

"It is!"

"Hush." Deklan strokes my hair and rubs my back, and I cling to his shirt. "You didn't do anything wrong. You couldn't have known. It's not your fault."

"Why were you there, Dek? You were supposed to be out of town!"

"I was," he says softly. "I was in Chicago but had to return early. There were details that had to be discussed with Sean in person. I really can't say any more than that."

I barely hear his words as my mind replays what happened. Arguing with Deklan. Kathy appearing out of nowhere with my gun pointed at my husband. Grabbing his arm. The insanely loud crack that echoed through the street. The man in the shadows.

"Arden, get the fuck out of here."

"It's *his* fault." I tighten my fingers around the fabric of Deklan's shirt. "He's the one responsible."

Deklan tightens his grip around me.

"*He* did this. He killed Kathy!" I begin to shake. I have to clench my teeth to keep them from chattering, and the pain in my head increases as I pull back from Deklan's chest and stare him in the face.

"You have to kill him, Deklan. You have to kill him for me."

Chapter 22

Deklan stares at me with wide eyes and a slightly open mouth.

"Kera," he finally whispers, "you don't know what you're saying."

"I do," I reply through gritted teeth. "I want him dead, Dek. I want him *gone!*"

Deklan glances quickly over his shoulder, staring at the open door and the nurses' station beyond.

"Don't say anything else about it," he says quietly. "I talked to the doctor, and he said you can be released shortly. We'll talk at home."

I'm left alone while Deklan goes to find my doctor so I can get out of here. As I sit on the bed, I see the face of Kathy's killer in my mind. His eyes are cold and calculating. He's a monster.

Deklan returns with the doctor and shows me where to sign the discharge papers. A nurse walks in behind them with a plastic bag full of my clothing. I pull out the sequined shirt I had been wearing, and tears well up in my eyes. When I see the tiara at the bottom of the bag, I lose it completely.

I cradle the headpiece in my arms as Deklan picks me up like a child, tells the nurse with the wheelchair to fuck off, and carries me out to a black sedan. He slides me into the passenger seat and then walks around the front of the car to get in.

"Whose car is this?"

"Rental," Deklan says. "At some point, you'll have to tell me where my Viper is."

"The Hyatt downtown."

"I'll have Brian pick it up." He reaches over and takes my hand. With his thumb, he slowly massages the top of my wrist as I stare out the window at the traffic.

Once we get home, Deklan takes me straight to bed. He brings me water and a sandwich, which I don't touch, and then lies down beside me. I move closer, wrap my arm around his chest, and place my head on his shoulder.

Deklan cradles my head and runs his hand down my arm until he reaches my wrist.

"You have to kill him, Dek," I whisper.

"Oh, baby." He takes in a deep breath and exhales audibly. "It's not that simple."

"It is. It's what you do for a living, isn't it?"

His body tenses, and for a moment, he stops rubbing my wrist.

"The night we were married," he says, "I made a promise to you. I told you that if there was ever anything you wanted that I could get for you, I would."

He stops for a long moment, breathing slowly.

"And you never ask me for anything. You were expecting a life of extravagance with Sean, and I figured you'd demand a big house, a lot of clothing and jewelry—that kind of stuff. But you never asked for anything. You seemed perfectly happy, living the way I do. The only thing you've ever really asked for was to get a job."

I glance at his face. His eyes are closed and his jaw is tight.

"And now…now you're asking me for something, and I can't give it to you."

"Why not?" I glare up at him. "Because you're in business with the guy? Whatever he does for Sean is more important than me? More important than...than Kathy's life?"

Tears flow.

"No, Kera." Deklan shakes his head and hugs me against him. "If that were it, I wouldn't hesitate to give you what you want. I'm not saying that I *won't* do this for you. Kera...I *can't*."

"I don't understand. Did they arrest him?"

"No. He was long gone before anyone got there."

"Then why did they let you go if they didn't have him?"

"I didn't do anything," he says softly. "Witnesses said as much, and my gun hadn't been fired. They had to release me."

Deklan stops talking for a few minutes as he looks down at my hand and rubs his thumb across my wrist.

"Kera, did I hurt you? I mean, when I held you against the wall? I was only trying to keep you from falling over."

"No, you didn't hurt me. I knocked my head on the wall, but that was me, not you."

"They kept accusing me of beating you. They said you were hurt while we were fighting, and that you were all bruised up."

"Oh." I stare at the buttons on Dek's shirt.

"Kera? Where did the bruises come from?"

"The other night."

"What other night?"

"The night before you left, um, when we were in bed. I didn't even notice them until morning, but the ones on my arm kinda look like fingerprints."

Deklan turns my arm over for a better look.

"Did you get these when we were having sex? Is that what you're saying?"

"Yeah."

"Shit, Kera," Deklan mumbles. "I didn't know I grabbed you that tight."

"Neither did I." I press my cheek against his shirt. "They don't hurt."

"I'm sorry."

"It's okay," I say as I look back up at him. "Now, will you please go back to the subject at hand? I don't understand why you can't do anything about that man."

"I know you don't." Deklan sighs. "You don't know who he is."

"Then tell me."

"He's the king of hitmen, and probably one of the deadliest men in the world. There's always a bounty on his head, and he's probably had a hundred attempts on his life. Do you know what happened to every one of them? They're dead, Kera. Every fucking one of them is dead. This guy—he's the real deal, Kera. I...I brought him here because Sean wants something done that's out of my league, and Arden is a vicious killer with no qualms about what he does."

"And you have qualms?"

"Yeah, Kera, a lot of them," Deklan says. I can feel the tension in his muscles, everywhere we touch. "I'm successful in my job because of how I look. I have size and what is a somewhat undeserved reputation. More times than not, a simple threat is all that's needed. I rarely have to resort to actual violence."

"But you have." I remember the bloody shirt in the bathroom. "You can if you need to. You could go after him."

"Arden works with one of the most powerful organizations in Chicago. Crossing them is suicide, and he practically runs the damn place. They are far larger than the Foley operation. They have informants everywhere, and if he got wind that I was looking for him, I'd have a bullet in my head without ever knowing where it came from."

"You'd just have to shoot first," I say, but my stomach is knotting up. I have no idea what I'm talking about, and we both know it.

"It's not that easy, Kera," Deklan says. "I would never get close enough to him. I'd never get a shot off. I'd be dead, and where would that leave you? He might very well decide to take you out as well, just for good measure. How am I supposed to protect you if I'm gone?"

"We witnessed what he did," I say. "What if he's already planning to get rid of us?"

"He's not."

"How do you know?"

"Because"—Deklan huffs through his nose—"because I've talked to him."

This is news to me, and I'm not happy about it. Kathy is gone, and Deklan is conversing with the man who killed her. I grit my teeth.

"When?" The word leaves my mouth sounding like snarl.

"As soon as I was released. I wanted to know what the hell he was thinking, and when he explained…" As Deklan's voice trails off, he hugs me and kisses the top of my head before he continues. "He thought she was going to shoot me. He didn't know who either of you were and reacted only to what he saw. He thought…well, he thought he had my back. His intent was to protect me, showing me that he could do the job we need him to do."

"Is that supposed to make me feel better?"

"No, I know it doesn't." Deklan shifts his position and takes my face in his hands. "I'd do anything for you, Kera—really, I would—but I have to balance that with your safety. Going after Arden is beyond risky, and I can't risk you."

I pull my face from his hands and lay back down on his chest. I want to yell and scream at him—tell him I'll leave him if he doesn't do what I want—but it's futile. My position hasn't changed. Though I don't believe that Deklan would hurt me, I still have nowhere to go. Besides, nothing he does will bring Kathy back.

My head is still pounding, so I focus on the pain. I just want to be numb. I want my mind to go blank, but it's not cooperating.

Deklan leans back against the pillow and holds me as he starts stroking my wrist again. I get an odd sense of déjà vu, but it only lasts a second. As he rubs, and I relax against him, I'm reminded of the other times he's done this, starting with our wedding.

"Why do you do that?" I ask.

"What?"

"Rub my wrist. You always rub my wrist."

"Do you want me to stop?" His voice is so quiet, I can barely hear him.

"No, but why do you do it?"

I close my eyes and wait for his response, but he's gone quiet. My head feels heavy, and the warmth of near-sleep starts to fill my limbs. By the time he answers my question, I barely remember what it was I had asked.

"Because"—Deklan pauses for several seconds before continuing—"because it's what I did the first night I met you."

"You mean at the wedding?"

"No, before then."

I glance at Deklan for a moment, trying to remember a previous time when he had touched me. It wasn't the day before the wedding—I remember that clearly. When had I been in Deklan's presence before that? When would he have been close enough to touch me at all, let alone so intimately?

I feel strong arms as they wrap around my shoulders and under my knees, lifting me from the deck of the boat. I can smell leather and gunpowder as my head is cradled against his shoulder. The stale odors from the boat are replaced with fresh rain as I'm carried outside. He tears the blindfold from my eyes, and as I look up into the face of my rescuer, I am in awe of him.

"Deklan?" I sit up and pull my hand away from him. He stares at me for a moment before he looks away. I blink several times as I hear a now familiar voice in my head.

"It's all right," he says. "You're all right now. They can't hurt you."

The voice in my head belongs to Deklan. I blink again, trying to make sense of it. How could I be hearing the voice of my husband in a memory of my kidnapping?

I remember the feeling of the arms around me and how my rescuer picked me up and mentally compare it with the feeling of Deklan carrying me out of the hospital. The sensation is the same.

"It was you," I whisper.

Deklan nods but says nothing.

"You rescued me."

Deklan closes his eyes and grits his teeth before pushing himself off the bed and walking out of the room. I jump up to follow him into the kitchen, fully awake now. I stand off to the side as Deklan pours himself a drink, confused at the vague memory that keeps replaying itself in my head.

"Sit down." Deklan points to the couch in the living room, and I comply. I watch him get another glass from the cabinet and fill it with water.

"I didn't know who you were." Deklan hands me the water and sits beside me on the couch. "I was just doing a job. Mr. Foley told me to go to the marina and get the girl who was being held on a boat there, so I did."

"You killed the men who took me."

Deklan doesn't respond.

"You saved me from them."

He nods again, remaining silent.

"Why didn't you tell me before?"

"I thought...I thought you remembered. That day before the wedding, I thought that's why you said you were okay with it when Sean told you to marry me instead. It wasn't until you told me later that you didn't remember any of it—that you didn't *want* to remember any of it—that I realized you didn't know who I was. I was afraid if I said anything, it would bring back memories you didn't want to recall."

"Did…did the Foleys have me kidnapped? Is that how you knew where I was?"

"No," Deklan says with a shake of his head.

"Who did?"

"I have no idea. I was just sent to get you. I'd never seen the men who were holding you before that night."

"So, my dad asked for help from the Foleys; Fergus Foley found out where I was and sent you to get me?"

"There's more to it than that," Deklan says quietly. "A lot more."

"Tell me."

"You sure you want the whole story? It might make you remember."

"Yes," I say. "All of it."

Chapter 23

Deklan makes himself another drink before rejoining me on the couch. He turns sideways with his back against the arm and his foot up on the cushion and reaches out to me. My chest is tight, and my stomach feels as if a nest of bees is having a party inside of it, but I go to him, resting by back against his chest as he wraps his arms around me.

"I'd heard about the kidnapping," Deklan says. "It wasn't on the nightly news, but this business has its own networks for such information. I hadn't really paid much attention to it before your father asked for a meeting, and Fergus sat him down in the office."

"He went to ask the Foleys for the ransom money," I say.

"Yes. He didn't have enough, and he was already in debt to Fergus. He said he had no one else to turn to, and he was afraid you would be killed if he didn't meet the deadline."

Deklan hugs me close for a moment before he continues.

"I've never thought much of your father. I think you've probably figured that out. He was always on the fringes of the organization, never in the fold, so to speak, and he wanted to get closer. He knew that if he was laundering the Foley's money, he'd be set for life even with his gambling habit. Fergus never wanted to do business with him, not on that scale. He was too unreliable and desperate.

"Even when he was there, begging for your life to be saved, I got the impression it wasn't concern for you in his heart but concern for his reputation if he were to let something happen to you. It annoyed me. To me, Cormick O'Conner had everything— a wife, a kid, a bunch of successful businesses—and he squandered it all. He blew it on fucking poker, and I figured it was probably his bookie that had his kid.

"When your dad offered Fergus anything in the world to get the money for his kid, Fergus saw an opportunity. He'd been having problems with Sean. He wasn't falling in step the way his father wanted him to, and he was close to his eighteenth birthday. Fergus was looking for a way to get him to wise up and take some responsibility.

"Your dad was thrilled with the idea. Marrying his kid to the Foley heir would bring him that much closer to the organization, which was exactly what he wanted. It absolved him of his debt to the Foleys, and he didn't have to worry about coming up with ransom money at all. He was all smiles when he walked out, and I just kept thinking, 'How can this dude be happy when he has no idea what his kid is going through right now?' As soon as he was gone, Fergus called me over. He handed me the picture your father had given to him along with a piece of paper.

"'That's the address where she's being held,' he told me. 'Take the rest of the day off. Wait sixteen hours and then go pick her up. If you go too soon, it will look suspicious.'"

"He already knew where I was?"

"Yeah."

"How?"

"I have no idea. I never asked. Fergus had a dozen informants all over the city. He usually knew everything that was going on, especially if someone was operating in his territory."

Deklan reaches over to the coffee table and takes a quick drink from his whiskey glass.

"When I left, I got in my car and put your picture up on the dashboard where I could see it. It was a school picture, I think. You were wearing a green dress, and your hair was curled. You looked bored against the blue background that didn't go well with your hair."

"I remember that picture," I say. "It was from the eighth grade."

"You were just a kid," Deklan says softly, "and I was still pissed about your father's attitude. Every time I looked at the picture, I wondered what was happening to you right then. I wondered what you were thinking and how scared you must be. You were the same age my sister was when she was killed. When I got home, I couldn't stop thinking about you. I checked the address and saw it was a slip at the main dock at the lake. You were only about a half an hour away. Then I started thinking about how long a half hour must feel like to the girl in the picture."

"It didn't sit right with me, not at all. I couldn't stand the thought of some kid being in that position for something her father did. For the first time since he took me in, I went against what Fergus Foley told me to do. I didn't wait sixteen hours to go pick you up. I grabbed my gun and my car keys and headed to the lake.

"It was late, dark, and raining. There wasn't anyone around when I got to the lake—only one car with out-of-state plates. I parked next to the dock and made my way to the slip that matched the one on the paper Fergus gave me. There was a small cargo boat there, but no one was on deck. When I went on board, I could hear two men talking."

"What were they saying?" I ask when Deklan pauses.

"Nothing pleasant," he replies. "I could tell by the conversation that I had the right place."

"So you shot them?"

Deklan nods and takes another drink.

"I headed down the stairs to the cabin. I killed the first one before either of them saw me enter. The other one panicked and went for a gun, but it was close quarters. I grabbed it away from him, put my gun to his head, and asked him where you were. He told me you were in the cargo hold. I...incapacitated him before I went to find you."

"Incapacitated?" I turn my head so I can see Deklan's face, but he keeps staring at his whiskey. "What did you do?"

"I blew off his kneecaps," Deklan finally says after a deep breath. He glances at me briefly before looking away again.

His jaw is set, and I'm not sure if he just doesn't want me to know the details or if he's embarrassed by them. Inside my head, I hear two blasts and screaming, but the memory fades quickly. It occurs to me that this is the first time he's actually admitted to me that he's killed someone, and I shudder.

"I needed to make sure you were really there," Deklan says, continuing with the story. "If he lied, and they had moved you, I wouldn't have anyone to ask."

"You let him live?"

"Not after I saw you. You were in the hold, right where he said you would be. You were blindfolded, hogtied, and crying. As soon as I found you, I finished him off and went back down to the hold. You were shaking all over when I came up to you, and you tried to scream. You were...well, you were a mess. I just wanted to get you out of there, so I picked you up and carried you off the boat."

My jaw is cramped. I hear footsteps on the stairs and struggle against the ropes. The footsteps retreat, and I hear another loud blast. Then another. The footsteps return, and I feel a hand on the side of my face. Fingers reach into my mouth, removing the gag before I feel myself being lifted from the floor...

"Once I had you on the dock, I took off the blindfold and untied you. You tried to fight me, and I kept telling you it was going to be all right—that I was there to help you. I don't know if you finally believed me or just gave up, but you stopped struggling. I tried to lead you back to my car, but you couldn't even walk, so I carried you to the car and got you out of there."

"Was Fergus mad that you went early?"

"He never found out."

"You didn't take me to him?"

"Not right away."

"Where did we go?"

"Back here." Deklan stills as he says the words. "You were going back and forth from comatose to hysterical. It was almost daybreak by then, and I couldn't risk someone seeing you like that, so I brought you here."

I glance around the apartment, trying to remember, but it doesn't trigger anything. I've been here long enough to have seen every inch of the place. If I was going to remember something, I would have already.

"Wait a minute," I say. "What does all this have to do with you rubbing my wrist?"

Deklan runs his fingers down my arm, stopping at my wrist. He slowly begins to massage the skin there, and I reflexively melt into him.

"When I brought you here, you were exhausted. You'd stopped screaming, but you were still crying. I laid you down in the bed, but you latched onto my arm and wouldn't let go, so I lay down with you. There were red marks from the ropes around your wrists. They...well, they looked painful. I started rubbing the marks, hoping it would make your wrists feel better. That's when you finally started to calm down."

"Did we stay there the whole time? Sixteen hours?"

"By the time I got us back here, it was more like fourteen, but yes. Once you calmed down, you slept for a long time. When you woke up, you started to panic. I don't think you knew where you were. I rubbed your wrist again, and you relaxed. I got you to drink water and eat something, but then you went right back to sleep. I waited until dusk before I moved you. I didn't want anyone to see me."

"Did you take me to the Foley's?"

"No, I took you to the hospital. I put a note in your pocket with your father's phone number on it and left you in the emergency room. You slept the whole way over there, and you were still pretty groggy when I left. I waited in the parking lot where I could see you through the window. Once one of the nurses came over to you, I left. Your father came back the next day to thank us for delivering you safely. He said your mother finally stopped her bitching."

Deklan shifts his legs and grabs my waist, moving me to sit beside him as he turns and glares at his glass. I try to process everything he's revealed to me. From the few flashes of memory I do have, his story fits.

"So you knew who I was the day before the wedding. You knew I was the one you rescued when I came there, thinking I was going to marry Sean."

"Yes, I knew who you were. I'd seen you a few times over the years, but you never really looked at me. While you were here, I told you a few times that I was going to take you home but that you couldn't tell anyone about me. I told you to forget all about it."

"I guess I listened to you." I let out a short, humorless laugh.

"I hadn't thought about it that way," Deklan says. "I guess you did."

I watch as Deklan drains his second glass of whiskey.

"I've never seen you have a second drink," I say.

"I rarely drink at all." He glances in my direction. "I wasn't sure how you were going to react to all of this, especially after…after last night." Deklan furrows his brow and looks down at the empty glass in his hands for a long moment. "I was afraid you would blame me for what happened."

"To Kathy or when I was a kid?"

"Either. Both."

"Why would I blame you if you're the one who rescued me?"

"You might think I was responsible for having you kidnapped."

"Were you? Was Foley?"

"God, no." Deklan turns to face me. "I didn't even know your name before your father came to ask for Fergus's help. Kidnapping kids…that isn't something I would ever do. It's a fucked up organization I'm in, but Fergus never would have sanctioned something like that."

"Would Sean?" I ask quietly, and Deklan snorts.

"Then? No." He shakes his head and places the glass back on the coffee table. "Now…well, I wouldn't put anything past him now."

Deklan closes his eyes. His face looks relaxed, but his shoulders are tense as if he's waiting for the other shoe to drop. I realize that is exactly what he is doing and reach out to touch his arm.

"I don't blame you for Kathy," I say softly.

He turns his head toward me, and the light hits his eyes in such a way that it looks like he is ready to cry, but I'm sure I see it wrong.

"I shouldn't have argued with you," he says.

"I was drunk," I say. "If anyone started anything, it was me."

He closes his eyes and opens his arms, and I crawl into his lap. Wrapped up in his strength, I let the tears flow again.

"I'm so sorry, Kera. I'm sorry all this happened."

I cry into his shirt with my fingers digging into his shoulders, and he just holds me there. Memories of Kathy flash through my mind—everything from the playground in grade school to our room service breakfast in bed.

Eventually, my cries turn to sniffles, but I don't let go. Deklan just keeps holding me and occasionally kissing my head. I've probably ruined his shirt, but he doesn't seem to care. He strokes my hair and rubs my wrists until I pull back and look up at him, studying his face.

"I can't believe I didn't realize it was you," I say.

"You've blocked it out," Deklan replies with a shrug. "It makes sense you wouldn't remember my part in it."

"But I don't even remember being here for more than half a day."

"You slept most of that time."

"Still…" I place my head back on his shoulder, but I can't form any words to go with my thoughts.

"I was going to tell you," Deklan says, "several times, actually. It just never seemed to be the right time. I was shocked when I realized you didn't remember, and after that…well, it's not exactly a topic that just comes up in normal conversation."

"I'm glad it was you." I wrap my arms around my husband's neck and press my cheek to his.

"Glad it was me who rescued you or glad it was me you married?"

"Both."

Deklan grins and presses his mouth to mine. He kisses me slowly and gently before wiping the tears from my cheeks.

"So am I," he says. He wipes more tears away and stares at me intently. "Do you remember any of it? I mean, now that I told you my side of things? Did that make you remember?"

"Not really," I say. "There are a few flashes. I remember the gun shots and you picking me up. I remember that it was raining. Everything that happened before that is blank."

"Maybe that's best," Deklan says quietly. "Maybe you don't need to know any more."

I'm about to agree with him, but something is still bothering me.

"So, you have no idea who was responsible for me being kidnapped in the first place?"

"None."

"But...but what if you didn't get them all?"

"What do you mean?" Deklan asks.

"What if it wasn't just those two guys? What if there was someone else involved?"

"Whoever it was has had plenty of time to come after you again if they wanted to," Deklan says. His rationale makes sense but doesn't help the sinking feeling in my stomach.

"But they haven't, Dek." I shift in his lap to face him better. "Since I got out of the hospital, I've almost never been alone. I was homeschooled until I married you. Even now, there's always someone with me. I'm surprised he didn't tell you we were at the same bar."

Deklan tilts his head and looks at me with slightly narrowed eyes and creases in his brow.

"Who is 'he'?"

"That guy." I give Deklan a half smile. "The creepy dude you have following me that keeps tabs on whatever I do."

Deklan is silent as I grin at him. I've caught him off guard with my declaration, and catching him off guard is a rare thing.

"Kera..." Deklan takes several deep breaths, but his entire body remains tense. He speaks his words very slowly. "What 'creepy guy' is following you?"

Apparently, my husband is going to try to deny all knowledge of this, but I don't want to let him off the hook.

"You know who he is. The guy with the newspaper. Who reads actual newspapers anymore?"

When I laugh, Deklan's face remains tense.

"Kera," he says, still speaking very slowly, "I have no idea who you are talking about."

Chapter 24

"It's okay, Dek." I smile and stroke his cheek. "I understand you're a little paranoid. I don't mind that much."

Deklan's eyes go dark and he stares at me—hard.

"Kera, let me be perfectly, *crystal* clear," he says. He's so tense, his arms are starting to shake. "I am *not* having you followed, and I have *no idea* who this guy is."

His fingers dig into my arms for a second. He's definitely shaking now.

"Get off of me," he says with a growl. "Now!"

I scoot sideways off his lap, landing beside him on the couch. Deklan leaps up and starts stalking the room, hands clenched. I pull my knees up to my chest and stare at him, mouth open, as he grabs the whiskey glass and smashes it against the wall.

"Why the fuck haven't you told me about this before?" he roars. "Who is he, huh? How long has he been following you?"

"I...I don't know!" The panic inside my chest is tightening around me, making it hard to breathe. I thought I'd seen Deklan angry, but he's never acted like this.

Deklan stalks into the kitchen, grumbling under his breath. He grabs the edge of the counter and leans against it for a second, breathing heavily. All of a sudden, he hauls back and punches the refrigerator, leaving a dent in the stainless steel.

"Who the fuck is following you?" he screams.

"I don't know! I thought you told him to!"

"Jesus fucking Christ, Kera! Why would I do that?"

I don't have an answer. I'd always assumed his paranoia made him hire the guy, and now I'm embarrassed to admit it.

Deklan closes his eyes and leans against the counter again. I watch his shoulders rise and fall as he breathes slowly and deeply. After a full minute, he steps back and faces me. He clenches his hands a few times as he walks slowly back to the couch and drops to one knee in front of me.

I flinch and press my back to the couch cushion.

"Kera," Deklan says softly as he holds both of my hands, "I'm sorry I lost it there. The thought of someone threatening you is"—he takes another long breath—"Please, just tell me everything. Start with the first time you noticed this man."

"He was just always there, in the back of the coffee shop." I try to keep my voice soft as I answer. "That's where I saw him first. I noticed he was looking at me, but when I looked at him, he'd stick his nose in the newspaper."

"Describe him."

"He's just a normal looking guy. He's six foot or so, skinny, with brown hair, maybe brown eyes—very plain. He always waits until I'm busy making someone else's coffee, so Terry takes his order, but I saw the name Charlie on his cup."

"Who's Terry?"

"The assistant manager at the coffee shop."

Deklan nods as he takes another breath. He runs his thumbs over the back of my hands as he looks at me, his eyes still intense.

"Is that all he's done?" he asks. "Just watch you?"

"He's followed me back here."

Deklan squeezes my hands for a second as he grits his teeth.

"He followed you here? Into the building?"

"Not inside," I say. "He usually stops at the corner or crosses the street."

"Where else have you seen him?"

"Mostly just at the coffee shop, but I thought I saw him twice when I was out with Kathy. I'm not sure though."

"You were drunk." Deklan closes his eyes and shakes his head before glaring back at me. "Drunk, and some creep is following you. This is fucking fabulous."

He releases my hands and leans back on his heels.

"You think his name is Charlie?"

"I don't really know," I say. "That's the name he gives for his orders, but it's not like we check IDs."

Deklan stares into space for a moment. I wonder if he's trying to come up with anyone he knows named Charlie or Charles.

"When have you seen him at the coffee shop?" he asks. "What time of day?"

"Around ten o'clock when I'm not working. Earlier when I am."

"It's after noon now." Deklan glances down at his watch.

"But it's Sunday. You're usually with me on Sundays."

"Do you work tomorrow?"

"No, not until Wednesday."

"Time?"

"Nine."

"When you go to work Wednesday, you are going to text me as soon as he gets there."

"What are you going to do?"

"Depends on who he is. I know one thing: you will not be out of my sight between now and then."

I nod quickly as I reach for him. I don't want to be out of his sight—not now. The images flash through my head from each time I have seen the creepy guy, but I now see him in a different context, and it terrifies me. Who would have me followed? Sean? Whoever kidnapped me before? I have no idea, and I grip Deklan's shoulders as tightly as I can.

"I'm sorry I got angry," Deklan says. "I didn't mean to scare you. I can't believe you didn't tell me about this before."

"I really thought you knew," I say again. "With all the phone restrictions and making me carry a gun...I just thought you had him watching me to make sure I was okay, especially after the first time I went to the shop, and you didn't know where I was."

"For future reference," Deklan says with a sigh, "I'll tell you if I do something like that."

"Okay."

He pulls away a bit to look me in the face but doesn't let go of me.

"Is there anything else you've been keeping from me?"

My thoughts turn immediately to Sean. I've never divulged the things he's said to me, and all his lewd and obnoxious comments invade my head at once. Deklan must notice something in my expression, and he places his hands on the side of my head.

"What is it, Kera? Do not hold anything else back from me."

I can't say anything about Sean—I just can't. Deklan is completely loyal to the Foley family, and Sean is his boss. Anything I say about Sean's behavior has the potential to get Deklan in trouble. What if he gets angry again like he just did? And that was just over a guy watching me. What would his reaction be if he knew what Sean has said to me? What would happen if Deklan confronted his boss?

This time, I need to protect my husband.

"There is one thing," I say seriously.

"What?"

"You know that shepherd's pie you like so much?"

Deklan narrows his eyes at me.

"The biscuit crust...it's not homemade. I use a mix." I hang my head in mock shame.

Deklan rolls his eyes, and we both laugh. He presses his lips against mine for a moment before pulling away and standing up.

"I need to call Brian," Deklan says. "Why don't you jump in the shower? Take your time and try to relax a little. I'll make you something to eat while you're in there."

"I'm not really hungry."

"Well, you haven't eaten anything, and there is probably still alcohol flowing through your veins, so you're gonna eat."

"Ugh! Fine!"

I head off to the bathroom. Deklan is right—the shower feels good, and I stand there and let the heat of the water seep into my skin. Staring at the blank wall of the shower, thoughts of Kathy flood through my mind, but I seem to be out of tears.

Deklan is still on the phone when I'm finished.

"You can't expect him to just lie back and take it," Deklan says. "Tell her she needs to be patient. We'll work something out."

I smile at Deklan when he looks up at me, and he points to a pot of macaroni and cheese on the stove. He places his hand over the phone's mouthpiece for a moment.

"Eat," he says softly.

I roll my eyes and scoop some of the macaroni onto a plate.

"You want some?" I ask.

Deklan shakes his head and goes back to his conversation, and I sit at the kitchen island and try to eat.

"She's dealt with it this long," he says. "She can hang on a bit longer. I'll see you in a little while."

Deklan hangs up and comes up behind me.

"Eat more," he says as he wraps his arms around me from the back. He kisses me lightly on the side of my neck. "Brian is bringing my Viper back and returning the sedan."

I eat about half of what's on my plate but can't stomach any more than that. Deklan grumbles but accepts the amount I've had.

"You should take a nap," he says.

"I'm not sure I can sleep."

"At least try."

"You've gone through so much in the last twenty-four hours," he says. "You need time to recuperate, and you need time to grieve."

Deklan takes me to the bedroom, strips me of my jeans, and tucks me under the blankets.

"Sleep," he says. "I'll be right in the next room, and I'll come check on you."

"All right."

I've barely fallen asleep when there's a loud knock at the door. I jolt awake, my muscles tensing with the unique sensation of falling from a great height. I gather my senses as I hear the door open.

"Will you shut the fuck up?" Deklan says with a low snarl. "Kera's sleeping!"

"I'm in trouble, Dek. Big trouble!" It's Brian's voice.

I hear the door close and footsteps in the kitchen.

"Slow down," Deklan says, his voice still quiet. "What are you talking about?"

"I called her right after I talked to you, but she already did it. She told him off and everything. He'll kill her, Dek!"

"Jesus Christ, Brian. Keep your voice down."

I can still hear mumbled words, but I can't make anything out. I push the blankets off and slide out of bed. Slowly, I walk toward the door of the bedroom. Through the opening, I can see both of them in the kitchen. Deklan has his hand on Brian's shoulder, and he leans down to speak softly.

"I am going to help you, all right? But you have to calm down."

"Okay, Dek." Brian nods and takes several breaths.

Deklan stands, goes to a drawer in the kitchen, and pulls out a box of latex gloves and a cloth. He tosses the gloves to Brian.

"What are these for?" Brian asks but gets no response.

Deklan moves out of my view, closer to the sink. I shift my position in the hallway just enough to see them. Deklan opens the cabinet under the sink and kneels down. He reaches all the way in, and I hear the sound of tape being ripped as he pulls out a handgun. Taking the cloth, he wipes the gun carefully and then holds it in his hand, finger on the trigger and barrel pointed toward the floor. He grips it for a moment.

"Put those gloves on," Deklan says.

Brian slides a pair of gloves over his hands, and Deklan hands him the gun.

"Don't touch that without the gloves," Deklan says.

"But Dek, it's got your—"

"Just do what I tell you."

They move back into the living room and out of my view. I can't see them unless I reveal myself, so I strain to listen instead. Deklan speaks softly in mumbled words I can't make out. After a few minutes, I hear them both stand and go to the door.

"I don't know if I can do this, Dek."

"You can," Deklan says. "You will."

"What if I fuck it up?"

"Then she's screwed, and I'll get the chair. You don't want that, do you?"

"No." Brian's voice is soft.

"You just do exactly what I told you to do," Deklan says. "Make sure the timing is right. I'll take care of everything else."

"I'm sorry to drag you into this, bro."

"Yeah, like I don't have enough shit going on. Get the fuck out of here so I can take care of my wife."

"Say hi to Mrs. K for me."

"Yeah, sure."

I listen to the door open and close again. Deklan lets out a sigh, and I quickly scuttle back to the bed. I draw the sheets up to my chin just before he comes back in the room.

"Everything okay?" I ask as Deklan crawls in beside me.

"Yeah, babe. All's good."

"Was that Brian?"

"Yeah. He says hi."

"He sounded upset. Is the car okay?"

"It's fine," Deklan says as he leans over and kisses my cheek. "He just needed a little advice. Woman shit, you know?"

"Right."

"Go back to sleep," Deklan says. "I'll be right here with you. When you're up for it, we'll go out for a nice dinner. I still owe you that."

Chapter 25

"Come on, babe. It's time to wake up."

I feel Deklan's warm mouth on my throat as he softly shakes me awake. I'm still groggy as he pulls me to a seated position.

"You've slept all day, babe," Deklan informs me. "You also barely ate yesterday, so I'm going to make sure you have a proper dinner. Besides, I promised you a night out for your birthday."

"Hmm?" I rub my eyes and try to focus.

"Dinner. Out. You. Me. Get yourself ready."

Birthday dinner.

Slowly, everything starts coming back to me, and it feels as if someone has put anvils on my shoulders. It has been almost three days since Kathy was killed. I've napped constantly, and I still feel this way every time I wake up. I glance up at Dek, and he smiles gently and runs his hand over my cheek.

"It will help keep your mind off things for a little while," he says. "I'm going to insist, so please don't argue with me. Just do whatever you need to do to get ready. No need to dress up; this place is casual."

"What place?" I push myself out of bed and grab some clean clothes from the closet.

"A nice little steakhouse I've heard about but never tried. It's supposed to be great."

Deklan walks out of the bedroom as I head into the bathroom. I take a quick shower, fix my hair, and put on some makeup, hoping Deklan was serious about the place being casual. I'm not up for a dress and heels.

When I come out of the bathroom, Deklan is sitting on the couch and making a phone call.

"Yes, I'd like to report a theft." There's a pause for a moment before Deklan continues. "My Beretta appears to have been stolen. Yes, ma'am, that kind of Beretta. Well, the car was parked with the valet at the Hyatt, and I assume they keep everything locked up. I honestly don't know when it might have happened. I just noticed a little while ago that it was missing. I kinda assume someone broke in over the weekend. Yes, ma'am, it is."

I stare at Deklan open-mouthed as he gives all his personal information to the woman on the phone.

"I don't know off the top of my head, but I should have it in my files somewhere. Would it be all right if I brought that by the station in the next day or two? Oh yeah? Well, I guess it makes sense you would have access to that. Yes, ma'am. That would be great. Just let me know if you find it."

Deklan hangs up and smiles at me.

"What was all that about?"

"Nothing." He stands and walks over to me. "You're gorgeous, you know. Even in jeans and a T-shirt."

"Were you talking to the police? What was taken from the car?"

"Nothing too important," he says. "Just don't worry about it, okay?"

"Deklan, what the hell is going on?"

"Have you ever heard the expression that the best lie is one anchored in the truth?"

232

"I suppose so. Something like that anyway."

"Well, just know that if anyone asks you about our evening, you can be one hundred percent truthful, okay?"

"Who would ask?"

Deklan responds with a shrug. He's obviously not going to tell me anything, so I don't bother to ask again.

"Are you ready?" he asks as he checks his watch. He grabs my coat from the hook near the door and holds it out for me.

"I really don't need a birthday dinner at this point." I let him put the coat around my shoulders. I know arguing with him is useless, and he doesn't even reply to my comment.

He leads me to the parking garage and helps me into the car. It's a bit of a drive to the restaurant, and Deklan checks his watch at least five times along the way. I want to ask him about it, but he keeps me occupied with chatter about the weather, traffic, and basketball scores. In fact, he talks so much, I can hardly get a word in.

It's probably best. I'm more in a mood for listening than talking.

"It will be about thirty minutes before I can seat you, Mr. Kearney," the hostess says when we arrive at the restaurant. "Would you like to have a seat at the bar while you wait?"

"That would be perfect," Deklan says as he glances at his watch again.

Deklan places his hand on the small of my back and leads me to the middle of the bar. There are several seats at the end, but he goes straight for the two seats surrounded by other patrons.

"Are these seats taken?" he asks the couple next to us.

"Not at all," the man says. "Please."

Deklan shakes his hand and thanks him profusely. It's over the top, and I narrow my eyes at my husband as he pulls my seat out for me.

"It's the wife's birthday," he says to the man as he points at me. "I'm hoping the steaks here live up to their reputation!"

"They're wonderful," the man says. He looks at me and smiles. "Happy birthday!"

"Thank you."

The bartender comes over, wiping his hands with a bar towel.

"My name is Keith," he says. "What can I get you?"

"Good to meet you, Keith!" Again, Deklan is overly friendly. "I'm Deklan, and I'd love a bourbon. What would you like, Kera?"

He smiles at me as I quietly order a glass of wine. When the bartender comes back with our drinks, Deklan places a hundred dollar bill on the bar and tells him to keep the change.

"Thank you very much, sir! Let me know if there's anything else I can get you!"

"That was generous," I say after the bartender walks away.

"I like to get to know my bartenders," Deklan says quietly. "Big tippers are remembered. That way, I always get good service."

I'm not buying his explanation even though it's a reasonable one.

Once we are seated in the dining room, Deklan introduces himself to the server, Rachel, and tells her it's my birthday. She congratulates me and promises to bring out a cake after we eat. When she leaves with our orders, I glare at Deklan but say nothing.

When dinner is delivered, I have to admit that the steaks are fabulous, and I am far hungrier than I thought I would be. Deklan seems very pleased with himself and even tells the people at the next table that it's my birthday. They sing along when the cake is brought out.

"Embarrassed?" Deklan asks as he leads me back to the car. He's grinning from ear to ear.

"Confused." I narrow my eyes at him. I don't understand whatever game he's playing. He is obviously up to something, but I can't fathom what it might be.

"I'm sorry about all that." He chuckles softly, negating the apology. "I just wanted to, you know, keep you occupied."

"I realize that." I have the distinct feeling that there is more to this little outing than Deklan is telling me, but I don't let on. It *was* a nice dinner.

"How about a movie?"

I let out a sigh. I'm tired, and I'd rather just go back home and go to bed, but Deklan is insistent. I'm not even sure of the movie title when we walk into the huge theatre with large sodas and popcorn.

As soon as the previews start, Deklan spills the popcorn all over the guy next to him.

"What the fuck?" The guy stands up and popcorn flies everywhere.

"Dude!" Deklan jumps up as well. "I am so sorry. Totally my bad. Here"—Deklan pulls a card from his pocket—"this is my card. Give me a call tomorrow, and I'll pay for your cleaning. Hell, I'll buy you a whole new outfit. It was completely my fault."

I shake my head as Deklan sits back down. He does seem to have placated the man beside him, who grumbles as he shoves Deklan's card in his wallet.

"What does the card say on it?" I ask quietly.

"Deklan Kearney and a phone number."

"That's it?"

"Yep."

"Whose number?"

"Mine."

"For the phone you never have turned on?"

"It's on now."

I shake my head, thoroughly confused. As the movie plays, I keep looking over toward my husband, but he just stares at the screen with an odd, distant look on his face. Every so often, he looks down at his watch.

It's late when we finally get home, and I'm exhausted. For the first time since our wedding night, I'm hoping Deklan will let me just go to sleep without any hanky-panky beforehand. I'm about to say as much as I hang up my coat, but he's disappeared into the bedroom already.

When I join him, he's already stripped down to his boxer briefs. Strangely enough, he also has laid out a pair of pajamas he bought for me on our first shopping trip, though I've never worn them.

Since the very first night we were together, we've always slept naked.

"Why are those out?" I ask.

Without a word, Deklan comes over and starts helping me out of my clothes and into the PJs.

"Deklan, what has gotten into you?"

"Nothing," he says. He doesn't keep eye contact with me.

"I've never worn those," I say, as if he's forgotten.

"You're tired," he says, "and I want you to be warm and get a good night's sleep. You need it."

He pulls the pajama shirt over my head.

"You always keep me warm." I raise an eyebrow at him, and he smiles but still doesn't look me in the eye.

"Why are you acting so weird?"

"Weird?"

"Yes, weird."

"I'm not."

"You most certainly are." I put my hands on my hips and glare at him. "What is up with you?"

For a brief second, frustrated anger crosses his face, but he quickly reins it in.

"I'm just…not so good at the whole birthday thing," he finally says.

I stare at him and he stares at the floor. Is that why he's been acting so strange? Because of my birthday?

"Dinner was great," I say quietly. "The cake was a bit much, but it was nice."

"Was it?" Deklan turns his back to me and starts rummaging through one of his dresser drawers.

"Yes." I sit down on the edge of the bed. When I look back at Deklan, he's staring at the floor with his hands behind his back and a weird expression on his face.

"Kera?" Deklan tilts his head sideways and looks at me.

"Yes?"

Deklan glances down at the floor again and then back up to me.

"What is it?"

"I have something for you." He brings his hand from behind his back and holds out a small box wrapped in silver paper and a light blue bow. "I know it's late, but I've been trying to figure out a good time to give it to you."

I recognize the box as one from an expensive jewelry store and wonder what Deklan might have picked out for me. I take it from his hand and slowly open the box, revealing a silver medallion on a chain. In the center of the piece is a raised figure of a man with a staff and a halo around his head. A small shamrock decorates the bottom.

"It's Saint Patrick," Deklan says. "He built the first Irish church."

"It's beautiful." I turn the medallion over and read the inscription. "'Christ in hearts of all that love me.'"

"Like I do."

Deklan's words are so soft, I barely hear them. I definitely don't infer his meaning.

"Like you do what?" I ask as I rub my finger over the metal.

"Like I love you."

I stop fingering the metal and look up.

Deklan is standing near the edge of the bed, running the palms of his hands over his thighs like he's looking for pockets in his underwear.

Did he just say what I think he said?

He stops moving his hands and looks away from me. The light in the bedroom is dim, but I think his cheeks are a little red.

"When all this started...when you first..." Deklan stops and takes a long breath. "When we were first married, I hoped maybe...maybe we'd at least like each other, but I didn't dare think...or hope...Fuck! I suck at this."

He turns away and closes his eyes.

"No, you don't," I say softly. My heart is pounding hard enough I can feel it in my ears. I watch as Deklan slowly looks back at me.

"I love you, Kera," he says again. "I don't know how or when it happened, but I do. I just thought I should tell you that."

I stare up into his eyes, and I can feel his words dive deep down inside of me. They twist around my heart and through my body, entangling my insides with their meaning. The words hold me close, and I feel utterly and completely safe.

I blink a few times before I find my feet and manage to stand. I take two steps forward and reach up to lock my fingers behind Deklan's neck.

"I don't know how or when either," I say as a tear slips down my cheek, "but I love you, too."

Deklan closes his eyes and lets out a long, sharp breath as he pulls me to him. He hugs me so tightly, I can hardly breathe, but I don't tell him to stop. Instead, I try to hug him just as tightly. We stand silent for a moment before Deklan pulls back and kisses me, molding our mouths together as he whispers the words against my lips.

"I love you. I love you."

"I love you," I reply over and over again, entrusting the words to my lips as I commit the deeper meaning in my head and heart.

"Sweet Jesus," Deklan whispers. He pulls back. "How did this happen?"

"I don't know, but I'm glad."

Deklan grins and reaches for the medallion. I turn so he can clasp it around my neck and then hold it out so I can see it. I turn it over, trying to read the words upside down.

"I want you so bad right now," Deklan says.

"I'm not stopping you."

"No." Deklan shakes his head slowly. "I meant what I said about you needing sleep."

Contradicting his own words, he picks me up and carries me to the bed. He climbs in beside me and holds me against his chest.

"The next time I take you to this bed," he says, "I'm going to make love to you like we never have before. I swear it, Kera."

"You won't have to take me very far," I say with a grin. "I'll be right here in the morning."

Deklan glances away from me, focusing for a second on the wall clock.

"Sleep now," he says softly. "I love you, my wife."

DEKLAN

Chapter 26

At four in the morning, I'm awakened by pounding at the door. It's so loud, I startle awake with a jerk and a slight scream. I quickly cover with my mouth.

"Wait here," Deklan says, but before he can even get out of the bed, the door bursts open, and uniformed police officers invade the apartment.

They file in with guns drawn, screaming commands about keeping our hands up and not moving. Detective Warren, the man who questioned me at the hospital, is in the lead.

"What the fuck, Warren?" Deklan yells as he jumps up with his hands raised. "You better have a fucking warrant!"

"I certainly do, Kearney," Detective Warren says. "This one is for your arrest."

"What is going on?" I cry as two officers grab Deklan's arms and pull them behind him, but no one pays any attention to me.

"For what?" Deklan glares at the officers but doesn't resist as they place him in handcuffs.

"The murder of Michael Hardy."

"Who the fuck is that?" Deklan asks.

"You probably know him better as Crackers."

"Can't say that I do."

241

"Crackers, the pimp," Warren says.

"Someone pops a lowlife pimp, and you think it's me?" Deklan laughs.

"Yes, I do."

"I'm married, asshole. I don't need a hooker."

"Yeah, but you'd still kill a pimp if your boss told you to," Warren says as he holds up the warrant for Deklan to read.

"I was with my wife all night, boys," Deklan says after glancing at the paper. "You aren't pinning this on me."

"Sure you were." The cop sneers and tightens the cuffs around Deklan's wrists until he grimaces.

"Do you mind if I put on my fucking pants first?" Deklan nods toward a pair of sweatpants neatly folded on the top of the dresser. "It's kinda cold out there."

"You got sloppy, Kearney," Warren says. He nods at one of the cops to grab the sweatpants. "Used your own gun and dumped it way too close to the crime scene. You aren't getting out of this one."

"Deklan, what's happening? What are they talking about?"

"Your husband is a criminal," one of the cops says, "and he is finally going to get what's coming to him."

"It's all right, Kera." Deklan ignores the cop and looks right at me. "It's all going to be fine. Just some kind of mistake. Don't worry, babe."

"Search everywhere," Warren says. "There's no telling what we'll find."

I follow as Deklan is hauled out of the bedroom and into the living room. More officers come in from the hallway outside the apartment door and start going through drawers and cabinets in the kitchen.

"Dek?" I stare into my husband's apologetic eyes, too confused and scared to make sense of what is happening.

"It's all right," he says again. He lifts his foot so a cop can pull the pants up his leg. "Can you grab my shoes? Once they leave, just call Brian. He'll take care of everything."

"I don't know his number."

"It's in your phone."

A cop follows me into the bedroom and makes me stand off to the side while he gets Dek's shoes. He keeps warning me to keep my hands where he can see them and not to make any sudden moves.

"Question her, too," Warren says when we come back out with the shoes.

Tears run down my face as Deklan is hauled away, and one of the cops sits me down on the couch. I watch helplessly as the apartment is ransacked.

"Can you tell me where you were yesterday evening?"

I stare at him for a moment, not even understanding the question. I realize it's the same officer who talked to me after I conked my head—Longbow.

"Mrs. Kearney?" Longbow sits on the coffee table and looks me in the eye.

"We went out for dinner," I say.

"Where did you go?"

"A steakhouse. I don't remember the name of the place."

"What time did you arrive?"

As I go over the entire evening, cops go in and out of the apartment, digging through every drawer and closet. I keep waiting for them to come up with one of Deklan's guns or a large stack of cash, but they don't seem to find anything of interest.

"Her purse has about seven hundred in cash," I hear a cop tell Detective Warren. "No guns, no ammo. There isn't even a joint in this place."

"He's moved whatever was here," Warren says. "Check for storage lockers, and go through his car."

"The car isn't in the parking garage. There's a rental in his assigned spot."

"Dammit!"

I look up at the officer, confused by his words. When did Deklan change cars? We had taken his to dinner last night, so where did the rental come from? For that matter, why were the pants he wears to the gym lying out on the dresser?

I know one thing—I'm glad I'm actually wearing pajamas. Otherwise, I would have been completely naked when they got here.

Did Deklan know they were coming? Is that why he insisted I wear something to bed?

"What time was the movie?" Longbow asks.

"Around eight," I say. "The ticket is in my purse."

Longbow finishes his questions and goes over to Warren.

"If her story checks out, and the ME's time of death is verified, we're going to have a problem."

"It was him," Warren says with a shake of his head. "I know it was. His gun. His prints. We have him this time."

"I'm not so sure," Longbow replies.

"She's not a reliable witness," Warren says. "We can't go on her testimony. Bring her to the station. I want to question her myself."

Longbow comes back over and sits next to me.

"Detective Warren would like you to come answer a few more questions," he says. He glances up at the detective, who is rooting through some paperwork on the kitchen island and mumbling to himself. Longbow leans close and speaks softly to me. "You're not obligated to come. He can't make you without a subpoena."

I look at him for a moment as his words sink in.

"I need to make some phone calls," I tell him. "I also need to get dressed. I'll come by later."

Longbow nods and pats my hand before he goes back to Warren. Warren looks over his shoulder and glares at me but says nothing else. The cops gather up a few items and leave without closing the door behind them.

In a daze, I shut the apartment door and retrieve my phone from the nightstand where it is charging. When I look in my contacts, I find Brian's number in my favorites and touch the number on the screen.

"Yeah?"

"Brian? It's Kera. Deklan's been arrested."

"Hang tight," Brian says. "I'll be there shortly."

He disconnects the call, and I stare around at the disaster that is our apartment. Everything that was in a drawer is now out. There are papers everywhere. When I go to the bedroom to get dressed, I find all my clothes have been tossed on the bed.

Brian arrives ten minutes later.

"Aw, Mrs. K," he says as soon as he sees me, "don't cry. Lucas is going to meet us at the station. Dek won't be arraigned until tomorrow, but he'll be back right after. They got nothing to hold him on."

"You seem to know more about what's going on than I do." I fold my arms across my chest.

"Trust me," he says. "It's better that way. Did you tell them the details of your date night?"

"Yes. Do you know where Dek's car is?"

"I've got the Viper." Brian whistles low. "Damn, I love driving that thing."

He smiles at me, but I don't return it.

"Really, Mrs. K—everything is fine. He's got his alibi, and they won't be able to tie him to any of it."

"Are you going to tell me what all this is about? Who the hell is Crackers?"

"A dumb-ass pimp on the lower east side. Apparently, someone killed him last night. Wasn't Dek though, was it? You two were eating cake about that time."

He winks at me, and suddenly, all of Deklan's strange behavior from last night begins to make sense—all that time he spent chatting with the bartender and the man sitting near us, making a point of telling people it was my birthday and ordering cake, even spilling popcorn on that guy—it was all to establish an alibi.

And Brian…Brian had Deklan's gun. Deklan gave it to him a few days ago. He even made sure his prints were on it.

Brian drives me down to the station where Lucas is already pointing his finger at Detective Warren.

"Arraignment is a waste of taxpayer's money," he says. "I've got statements from six witnesses establishing Mr. Kearney's whereabouts throughout the evening. There's a report filed regarding the theft of the weapon in question. You need to release my client immediately."

"Not until the medical examiner verifies the time of death." Warren glares at Lucas. "The timestamp on the report is only preliminary. You will have to wait until the autopsy is complete, and that's going to take all day. Arraignment is at ten tomorrow morning, and your client can just sit his ass in that cell until then."

Despite Lucas's arguments, that's exactly what happens.

Early the next morning, I sit next to Brian in the courtroom, and Deklan is brought out in an orange jumpsuit. The prosecutor speaks to Lucas before they both go into a room behind the bench. A few minutes after that, they return with the judge, who bangs his gavel and releases Deklan due to lack of evidence.

"I told ya not to worry, Mrs. K." Brian pats my arm, and we return to the waiting area to wait for Deklan. A short time later, Lucas and Deklan, now dressed in his sweatpants and shoes, come out of the hallway and approach.

Brian rushes up and hands Deklan a T-shirt.

"Thanks, bro." Deklan reaches for me, and I hug him tightly. "No worries, babe. I told you everything was fine. You did great."

"How do you know that?"

"I have my sources." He winks and kisses me on the cheek before turning back to Lucas. "Any chance of me getting my Beretta back?"

"None whatsoever," Lucas says.

"I guess it's time to go shopping, then." They both laugh, but I'm not finding anything funny about this.

"Someone want to explain this shit to me?"

I'm startled by Sean's voice as he comes up behind me. I press tightly to Deklan's side. Apparently, Sean isn't finding this amusing either.

"Nothing to be concerned about, boss," Deklan says.

"Dek's gun and prints, but his alibi is airtight," Lucas says. "The judge didn't even want to hear any more after I handed him all the witness statements."

Sean nods as he looks back and forth between Deklan, Lucas, and Brian. He never looks at me—not once.

"I didn't sanction any action on Crackers." His voice is low. "Someone want to explain?"

"No, sir," Deklan replies, and Sean glares at him.

"How did this killer get your weapon?" he asks.

"I reported it stolen a few days ago," Deklan says. "Anyone could have used it."

"You had a gun stolen?" Sean tilts his head as he questions Deklan.

"Yeah, the registered Beretta."

"How the hell did someone steal a gun from you?"

"Well, if I knew that, I'd probably know who stole it." Deklan keeps his unwavering gaze on Sean. "The last I knew, it was in the glove compartment of my car. Then it wasn't there anymore. I rarely lock the car, so I guess anyone could have gone through it."

I tense, surprised that Deklan is lying to his boss. Maybe it's just the location that has him sticking to his story. There are cops all over the place.

"You never mentioned it." Sean glares at Brian for a moment.

"I've been spending time with my grieving wife," Deklan says. "Didn't really think it was worth mentioning. I've got others without registrations. I just bought that one on a whim because I liked it. I can always get another one."

"Well, considering it's now evidence, I don't think you'll be getting it back—not with Longbow gone."

"Longbow is gone?"

"Suspended. Something about mishandling evidence. Lucas, I'll need you to find him a good attorney."

"Sure, boss."

Sean steps closer and points a finger right at Deklan's nose.

"I expect you to keep better track of your weapons, Dek. I don't like to hear about people stealing from my employees."

"Won't happen again, boss," Deklan says. "I guess if they find the shooter, I'll know who stole my gun."

"We are going to talk about this later." It's clear that Sean isn't satisfied with Deklan's explanation. "Lucas, any other paperwork that needs done?"

"No, boss. It's all good."

"Fine. At my office in a half hour." Sean glares at Brian again. "All of you."

Chapter 27

"Just stay in the car," Deklan says as we arrive at the Foley place. "This shouldn't take long."

"I was supposed to be at work this morning. Is it okay for me to call Terry from here?"

"Sure." Deklan heads into the house, and I turn on my phone.

"Claire's Coffee Creations, this is Terry. How may I help you today?"

"Terry, it's Kera."

"Kera! Where the heck are ya, girl?"

"I am so sorry. This week has been…insane. I can't even begin to explain everything over the phone."

"I was kinda surprised you didn't show up this morning. I figured it was something important. Business is light today. I can cover for you."

"Thank you so much! I'll be in early tomorrow."

"No problem, Kera. Hope everything is okay!"

"Hey, Terry?"

"Yeah?"

"You know that weird guy who always comes in and reads the newspaper for hours at a time? I think his name is Charlie."

"Yeah, I know who you mean."

"Is he there now?"

"Actually, no. He was in earlier, but he left without buying anything."

"Oh. Okay. Well, I'll see you tomorrow."

"See ya then!"

I lean the car seat back and pull my knees up to my chest. The sun is shining brightly through the windows, and the car is nicely warm. I pull up a game on my phone and poke around at it for a while. About thirty minutes later, Deklan returns.

"Well, Sean is pissed." He starts the car and pulls away from the house.

"He didn't know what you and Brian planned."

Deklan looks at me out of the corner of his eye but doesn't reply.

"Did you tell Sean?" I ask.

"Yeah."

"Are you going to tell me?"

"No."

I glare at him, but he doesn't look back at me. He reaches toward the dash to turn on the radio, and I grab his hand.

"Do you think I'm okay with being woken up in the middle of the night to watch you get arrested? And don't you dare say you didn't know it was going to happen. Insisting on me wearing pajamas for the first time ever was a bit of a giveaway."

"I didn't know for sure," Deklan mumbles as he gives up on the radio. "I didn't want them walking in on you naked."

"Bullshit. You knew they were coming."

"I had an idea."

"Then tell me what the hell is going on! That scared the shit out of me, and you knew exactly what was happening before it even started. You have to let me in on this."

"No, I don't."

"Dammit, Deklan!"

He ignores my outburst and just stares at the road ahead while I fume quietly in my seat. He reaches for my hand, but I pull it away. I don't want his comfort right now. I want to wallow in my anger.

"Kera, please don't do that."

I peek at his face from the corner of my eye. He looks devastated, and I'm tempted to give in, but if I do, this kind of behavior will never end.

"I've had enough of the secrets, Dek. You aren't protecting me—you're protecting yourself."

"Don't hold back." Deklan stares hard at the road ahead of him.

"I'm tired of it." I turn toward him and try to catch his eye, but he won't look at me. "Refusing to tell me anything is not helping."

"I don't want you to have to lie for me," Deklan says with a sigh as he stops for a red light and finally looks at me.

"I'd rather lie than be in the dark all the time."

"It's for your own good, Kera."

"How is that? Did it protect me from all that shit last night? Did it protect me from that creepy guy at the coffee shop? The only reason you didn't know about him before is because I assumed you'd hired him. If it weren't for the secrets, I might have told you about him sooner."

Deklan lets out a giant breath that ends up sounding more like a growl. He grips the gearshift until his knuckles go white.

"You really want to know?"

"Yes."

"Brian fell in love with this chick that lives in the apartment down the hall from him. He thought she worked at the fast food place down the street, but as it turns out, she's a hooker. She wanted to get out of it, but her pimp wouldn't let her. He had a bit of a reputation for getting nasty with his girls when they wanted to break ties, and Brian didn't want to see that happen to her, so we got rid of him."

"You killed him."

"I didn't," Deklan says. "Brian did."

"Using your gun."

"Yes."

"And you timed it so you would have an alibi even though it's got your prints on it."

"I didn't need to tell you anything. You already figured it out. That worries me."

"Why?"

"Because if you figured it out, Warren might, too. Doesn't change the fact that I have an alibi, but accessory to murder still gets me time."

"Will they be able to connect you and Brian?"

"Easily," Deklan says. "Connecting me to Brian to a chick he likes to her pimp, that's something else. I've never met the guy, and the Foleys don't do business with him. All the evidence would be circumstantial at best, and it's hard to convict on that alone."

"This isn't over then. They could come back and arrest you if they figure it out."

"Unlikely. It would never be enough for a conviction. Sean has police and prosecutors on the payroll, and it would never even get to court. Those guys know who they're dealing with."

"Whom."

"What?"

"It's whom, not who."

"Whom they're dealing with? That sounds weird."

"Grammatically, it would be 'with whom they are dealing.'"

"Whatever. I didn't have your schooling."

Deklan clenches and unclenches his hand a few times. He's gone from angry to upset, and I feel bad about being so pissy.

"Sorry," I mumble. "It's been a long day already."

This time when he reaches over, I take his hand. He interlocks our fingers and pulls my knuckles to his lips, kissing them gently.

"I'm sorry, too. Don't worry though, okay? It will all be fine."

I consider his words before relaxing back into the passenger seat. Deklan's jaw is tight when he releases my hand to change gears, and he's still gripping the knob too tightly, but I'm relieved to finally get some information out of him.

"I'm glad you told me."

"I'm not sure how I feel about it," Deklan says. "I'm afraid anything I tell you just puts you in danger."

"I think I'm already in danger, Dek."

"Your stalker."

"Yes, him."

"Did you get ahold of your manager?"

"Yeah, I called. Terry said I was covered. I need to be in first thing in the morning though."

"Good. I don't want that guy following you anymore." Deklan reaches over and squeezes my hand. "I told Sean I needed to take care of some other business over the next couple of days, so I can focus on that. I don't want you scared."

"I need a shower," Deklan says as soon as we get back to our apartment.

"Shall I join you?" I smile sweetly as I reach up to wrap my arms around his neck.

Deklan places his hands on my hips but keeps his head up and out of my reach for kissing.

"No." Deklan runs his hands from my hips up my sides and down again. "I need a few minutes to myself. You are going to get undressed, lie in the center of that bed with your legs spread, and wait for me."

"I am?"

"Yes, you are. I'm still annoyed with you for pestering me and making compelling arguments against my better judgment. You're going to lie there and think of what I'm going to do with you when I come out. You are not going to touch yourself."

I bite down on my lip. I have a dozen retorts, including suggesting that I get myself off if he takes too long, but the look in his eyes silences me. Instead, I nod.

"Good girl. Now get in there." He smacks me on the ass to get me moving.

I squeal and scuttle down the hall. As I hear the shower start up, I quickly undress and climb into bed on top of the duvet.

Checking left and right, I try to place myself in the exact center. I lie back and spread my legs apart. I place my palms against the duvet and stare at the ceiling.

As I listen to the water pelting the shower tiles, I can feel my heart rate increasing. I pull my knees up and spread my legs a little wider. Glancing down, I check myself over, wondering how Deklan will view me when he gets out of the bathroom. I imagine the look on his face and the way he'll runs his hands over my skin and realize I'm biting my lip almost hard enough to break the skin.

I take a deep breath through my mouth. My nipples are getting hard. I'm tingling everywhere, and my clit is beginning to throb.

He hasn't even entered the room yet.

I lick my lips, adjust my position slightly, and look over to the bedroom doorway. There's still no sign on Deklan.

I really, *really* want to touch myself.

I consider the consequences of getting caught in the act. I've read enough mommy porn to know some of the various options, and none of them sound all that bad—not if the punishments were dealt out by Deklan. However, he might decide to just leave me squirming and sleep on the couch, and I can't risk that.

I need his warmth.

Deklan comes into the bedroom wearing absolutely nothing. He moves to the head of the bed on my left but doesn't join me. Instead, he starts to walk around the bed. Actually, he doesn't walk—he stalks. He looks like a large African cat going after an antelope or, in my case, a compliant deer. His gaze drifts up and down my body until I can practically feel invisible fingers stroking me everywhere his eyes roam.

"Put your hands up over your head," he says softly. He nods when I comply. "There you go."

He reaches with a single finger to stroke the palm of my hand, then my wrist, and then down my arm. I squirm a little when he reaches my armpit—it tickles—and he grins at me before running his fingertip down my side, over my hip, and all the way down my leg.

When he reaches my ankle, he switches sides and goes all the way back up to my wrist.

My nipples are pointing straight at the ceiling. It's becoming more and more difficult to keep my legs spread. I want friction so badly, I can feel sweat collecting at the hairline around the back of my neck.

Thankfully, Deklan moves to the end of the bed and crawls on top of the duvet, right between my legs. I'm familiar with this move—he'll now run his hands over me as he crawls the rest of the way up, kiss me hard, and then slowly push inside of me.

I look down at him, waiting for him to continue crawling over me so I can kiss him, but he stops. With his gaze locked with mine, he leans over and kisses my stomach—just his lips at first, and then open-mouthed. He circles my navel with his tongue and then moves lower, still staring right at me.

Deklan licks his lips and then tilts his head to kiss the inside of my thigh. He glances down before sliding both arms under my legs and angling my hips up until he's staring right between my legs.

"Deklan…" My voice is nothing but a breathy whisper.

He looks back at me with dark, eager eyes. He pauses, and I wonder if he's waiting for me to protest. I say nothing. I just stare at him wide-eyed and apprehensive. He grips my thighs, holding my legs apart and my hips firmly against the mattress.

Without breaking our stare, Deklan leans forward, reaches out with his tongue, and licks my folds from bottom to top. I gasp at the warm, wet sensation. The pressure against my clit as Deklan circles it with the tip of his tongue sends flutters up my spine. I try to sit up, but he pushes me back to the bed.

"Be still." Deklan looks up at me with a wicked grin. "I'm just getting started, and I won't stop until you come all over my face."

"Ugh!" I can't even attempt any kind of verbal answer. I let him hold me down with one hand placed between my breasts and the other one still wrapped around my leg.

He starts slowly, exploring every bit of me with the flat of his tongue, then doing it all again with the tip. Flicking his tongue against my clit makes me shudder every time, and I find myself biting my lip again just to keep from screaming.

Deklan moves faster, repeating a pattern of circling my clit, moving down, then back up to circle again. He holds my leg down with his arm and reaches for my clit with his thumb. I feel his tongue entering me, then pressing against the walls of my pussy. I can hardly stand it.

"Deklan! Please!" I don't even know what I'm begging for, but Deklan continues until there are tears running out of the corners of my eyes. I try to twist and turn, my body moving of its own accord. Deklan holds on tightly, forcing me to stay still as his tongue lays siege to my most intimate parts. He licks, sucks, and kisses until I can't take any more.

Short, high-pitched sounds come from my throat. My whole body tightens so much that it's shaking. With a final shudder, the tension releases, and it's as if everything inside of me has turned to mush. I simply melt against the bed, sweat running down my neck, and my breath coming in quick pants.

But my husband isn't done with me yet.

He sits up, still holding on to my legs, and moves backward off the edge of the bed, dragging my body with him. He positions my ass right at the edge while he stands between my thighs. Deklan then grabs my leg just behind my knee and hauls it up and over his shoulder. Positioning himself at my opening, he moves forward slowly.

Usually, it takes a little while for Deklan to get completely inside of me. He always goes slowly and carefully, stretching me and waiting until I'm ready to take all of him. This time is different. This time, he slides into me easily with the first penetration.

"Oh, yeah..." Deklan's moans cause me to clench all over. "So fucking wet. You loved having my tongue all over you, didn't you, Kera?"

He leans forward, impaling me as I cry out again. I try to respond in some coherent way, but I only manage to mumble the word "yes" a couple of times. Deklan smiles and starts moving faster, pulling nearly all the way out before diving back in again.

I stare at his form, silhouetted by the light from the hallway. His shoulders and arms flex as he holds me right where he wants me. Sweat collects on his forehead as he clenches his teeth and rams into me repeatedly.

I extend my hand toward him, but I can't reach him at the edge of the bed. I whimper, and Deklan pulls out suddenly, leans over, and slides me back up the bed. He positions himself again, pressing his lips hard against mine as his cock throbs inside of me.

I press my heels to the bed, lifting upward as he thrusts downward. I can barely keep up with his pace. With my arms around his neck, I hold his mouth to mine, stroking his tongue as his cock strokes inside of me.

He breaks the kiss and leans his forehead against my shoulder. He slows down, making every thrust long and deep. His quick, audible breaths tell me he's close.

"Sweet Jesus, Kera…" Deklan's words are hot against my skin. He pulls back and slams forward two more times before he lets out a final, growling grunt, and I feel him empty inside of me.

Deklan collapses on top of me, nearly knocking my breath away. I wrap my arms around his shoulders and hold him tightly, welcoming the sensation of his weight on me even though it's difficult to breathe. I can feel his heart beating, and I close my eyes as I concentrate on the rhythm. As it slows, Deklan nuzzles his nose against my neck and lets out a long, deep breath.

I feel his weight shift, and instinctively inhale deeply now that I can again. My husband leans slightly to one side, holding his weight up on his elbow as he uses his other hand to stroke the side of my face.

"I have no idea what I ever did to deserve you," he says. "I wish I knew. At some point in my life, I must have done something pretty awesome."

"Maybe it was just the act of saving me from marrying Sean," I say, and Deklan nods once.

"Maybe." He strokes my face again. "I love you, Kera."

"I love you too, Deklan."

"I will take care of all of this," he says. "I will keep you safe. Whoever the creepy stalker guy is, I will find him, and he will never bother you again."

For a moment, I consider asking him what he would do if Sean were the threat, but I think better of it. I'm afraid I might not like the answer.

Chapter 28

"When he gets there, do not talk to him. Take the burner phone. Text me as soon as he comes in."

"We've been over this ten times, Dek," I say with a sigh. "I've got it, okay?"

"I just want you safe, babe."

For once, my walk to the coffee shop does not bring me joy. My legs are shaking, and with every step, I check all around to see if I catch sight of the creeper. Once I get to the shop, I smile at Terry when he waves and head to the employees' lockers.

It's early, but people want their coffee early, so there is already a line when I get back out. Terry asks me how I'm doing, but there is—thankfully—no time to talk about it. I get lost in making lattes and mochas for a while before we get a bit of a break.

"That was quite a morning rush!" Terry blows out a breath and rinses one of the blenders. "Glad that didn't happen yesterday. What happened to you anyway?"

"I don't even know where to start." I shake my head. "A friend of mine…well, she was killed over the weekend."

"Oh, shit! I'm sorry!" Terry sets the blender down and comes over to hug me.

"Thanks." I give him a quick hug back. "As if that wasn't enough, my husband got arrested, and I was in court when I should have been here."

"Damn! What did he do?"

"Nothing." The lie comes quite easily to me. "It was just a mistake. They released him, but it still took all morning. I swear—I didn't even realize what day it was until right before I called you. I'm glad you didn't fire me!"

"Nah." Terry makes an exaggerated wave with his hand. "Not for a first time thing. You've always been reliable, and you have a pretty good excuse. Just remember to call if there's ever another emergency."

"Sorry to leave you in the lurch."

"It's only coffee." Terry shrugs and gives me a reassuring smile. "I'm just glad you're okay, and I'm really sorry about your friend. If you ever want to talk, I'm here for ya."

We both go back to cleaning up until a couple more people come in. I take the order and start making the coffee while Terry deals with the next couple.

"That's the guy you were talking about, right?" Terry says quietly as he slips past me for the milk. "The one in the dark coat?"

I glance up and see Charlie the Creeper walking through the doorway. He glances at me and then quickly looks back at the menu.

"That's the one."

"Why were you asking about him?"

"He's been following me," I say. "I'll tell you more later. Can you take his order?"

"Sure."

Terry heads to the cash register while I head to the back room to text Deklan. When I return, Terry is handing the guy his coffee. He heads to the back of the shop, just like he always does, and shoves his nose inside his newspaper.

I go back to taking orders and pouring flavored caffeine. Only a couple of minutes pass before Deklan is at the door of the shop. He scans the room as he enters, pausing as he sees Charlie the Creeper in the back. Dek glances at me, and I confirm with a nod toward the creeper.

"Who is that?" Terry asks quietly.

"My husband. That guy has been following me around."

With long, purposeful strides, Deklan walks up to the guy.

Charlie sees him and immediately drops the paper. He starts to stand, but Deklan sits him back down with a hand on his shoulder. He leans over and stares the guy in the face, speaking softly. I can't hear what he's saying, and I'm suddenly terrified he's going to shoot him right here at my workplace.

"Shit! What's he going to do?" Terry asks.

"I honestly don't know."

Other patrons are taking note of the exchange between Deklan and Charlie. One of the hipster regulars pokes his friend in the arm and gestures toward them. Another customer looks over to Terry—as if he could do something about it.

Deklan stands up straight, and Charlie the Creeper stands as well. His face is completely white. Neither of them looks in my direction as Deklan grips Charlie's arm tightly and leads him out of the shop.

"Dude, your hubby is huge!" Terry lets out a long whistle.

For a moment, I feel a deep sense of pride.

Yeah—that's my man.

"He looks like he's gonna kill that guy!" Terry laughs nervously.

All my smugness dissipates as I realize Terry might be right.

"I think I should go after him," I say. "The line is gone. Are you good for a few minutes?"

"Sure," Terry says. "Don't be too long."

"I won't."

I toss my apron on the counter and rush out of the shop. I look around but see no sign of Deklan or the creeper. I head around the corner in the direction of the apartment and spot Deklan's Viper parked near the entrance to the alley. I approach slowly and hear voices.

"You have about four seconds to give me a better answer," Deklan says, "or I'm going to rip your balls off."

I peer around the corner and into the alley. The dumpster used by the coffee shop is up against the brick wall, and behind it, I see my husband. With him are two men I recognize from our wedding though I never got their names. They're holding Charlie the Creeper up against the bricks as Deklan slams a fist into the guy's face.

Blood spatters as the guy's nose cracks, and he cries out.

"I don't know what you're talking about!"

Deklan shakes his head slowly.

"Wrong answer."

The two other men grip Charlie tighter as Deklan grabs him by the hem of his pants and rips them down. He begins to scream as Deklan reaches down. I can't quite see what he's doing with the dumpster in the way, but I have a pretty good idea.

"No! Don't! Don't! I'll tell you! I'll tell you everything!"

"That's better." Deklan nods and takes a step back as the two men release Charlie.

Charlie drops to the ground on his knees, grabbing at his pants and trying to pull them up as he falls.

"I was hired, okay? I wasn't going to do anything to her—just watch and report."

"Report to who?" Deklan circles around and kicks him in his bare ass, sending him sprawling on the concrete.

I have to step back to avoid being seen and to fight against correcting Deklan's grammar.

"I don't know! I just call a phone number and leave a message."

He starts to scream again, and I peek around the corner to see Deklan dragging him by the hair to a puddle near the wall. He shoves his face into it and holds him there for a moment.

"Care to revise that statement?" Deklan says calmly as he hauls the guy back to his knees.

One of the men with Deklan leans back against the wall and lights a cigarette. He puffs on it a couple of times before handing it to Deklan. He holds the lit end up close the Charlie's eye.

"No! Please!"

"Give me a name. Give me a name right now, or so help me God, I'm going to burn out your eyes, blow a hole in your head, and let Mac over here skull-fuck you."

The guy who lit the cigarette snickers and rubs the front of his pants.

Charlie stares at them both wide-eyed until Deklan slams his head into the puddle again.

"Give me a fucking name!"

Charlie coughs and sputters. He chokes out a sound, but I can't tell what he's said; I can only see Deklan's reaction. He goes completely still for a moment. Then his shoulders flex as he pulls Charlie's face close to his. I can tell they are talking but hear nothing. I strain my ears and take a half step closer, but I'm afraid of being seen.

"Motherfucker," Deklan mutters as he stands up, drops Charlie to the ground, and pulls out his gun.

"No! No, please! There's more! I can tell you more!"

"Start talking fast." Mac hands a cylindrical object to Deklan, and he attaches it to the end of his weapon before pointing it at Charlie's head.

I gasp, and Deklan turns his head to see me.

"Goddammit!" He passes the weapon over to Mac and stalks out of the alley. He grabs me by the arm and pulls me over to the car, checking left and right to make sure no one is watching us. "What do you think you're doing?"

"I wanted to know what was happening."

"Tell me how much of that you saw." Deklan's voice is soft and calm, but his eyes aren't.

"Most of it," I whisper.

"Jesus Christ, Kera." Dek closes his eyes for a second before he pulls me against his chest. "I never wanted you to see anything like that."

"Who hired him?"

"Later." Deklan holds me at arm length. "I've got to…to finish up here. You are not going back to work. In fact, you're going to quit."

"Quit?" I stare up at him, hoping he doesn't mean what he's saying. "I don't want to quit!"

"Not until you're safe," Deklan says, "and you're not."

"Who is he, Dek? Why is he following me?"

"I said *later*." Dek takes a deep breath, closes his eyes, and then leans close to me. "Don't push me on this, Kera. Not now. We'll talk later, but do *not* cross me here. Go back to the coffee place, and tell that guy it's your last day. Mac will stay close by and walk you home. I'll try to explain then."

My shoulders sag as I nod. I don't want to quit, but I'm not going to fight about it now. Something is still going on, and I'm not going to get any answers unless I do as Deklan says.

Terry is shocked when I tell him I'm not coming back to work. He tries to get more information out of me, but I really don't even know what to tell him. I finish my shift in silence, and Mac meets me at the door when it's time to head home. When I get there, Deklan is on the phone. He covers the mouthpiece and tosses a suitcase at me.

"Pack," he says.

"Pack what?"

"Everything. We're moving."

"Moving where?"

"Elsewhere." He goes back to his call. "No, not there…Because it's too close to the railroad tracks. I'll figure it out. Mac just got here. I want you and him to go pick up the stuff we moved last week. I'll let you know where to bring it tomorrow."

Deklan looks over at me, sees I'm not doing anything, and then points from the suitcase to the bedroom. I cross my arms and tap my foot but don't move. He rolls his eyes and disconnects the call.

"Pack," he says again.

"Deklan, why are we moving?"

"Too many people know where we live," he says. "The cops have been here. That guy has followed you here. Mac has been here now, too. It's not safe for you. We're moving."

"And you think I can get all my stuff in this thing?" I point at the carryon-sized luggage.

"Get what you need for now. I'll get the rest after I find a place." He drops down on one knee and grabs another suitcase from the back of the closet before turning to Mac. "Go find Brian. I'll call you later."

"Sure, boss," Mac says.

"Stop calling me that." Deklan glares at him.

Mac just grins and heads out the door as Deklan heads to the bedroom and starts loading the suitcase with clothes.

"What did you do with that guy?" I ask as I follow him. "You said you would explain later."

"I will," Deklan says. "Later. Pack!"

"Ugh!" I grab the suitcase and toss some clothes in it, still grumbling, but I can see Deklan is a man on a mission. There is no point arguing with him now.

As soon as our necessities are in the suitcases, we leave the apartment. I'm overwhelmed and feeling pissy about having to quit the coffee shop, so I say nothing as Deklan drives us to a motel just out of town. He books a room for the night, and I flop down on the bed and glare up at him.

"I'm sorry about all of this," Deklan says with a sigh. "I wish it didn't have to be this way, but I swear it's temporary. I'll find a place tomorrow. I'll find a really nice one—there are a lot available. I just need to find the right one."

"I could help."

"I really don't even want you out and about by yourself."

"And I really just wish you'd tell me what the fuck is going on!"

Deklan puts his hands over his face and rubs his eyes. He hauls our suitcases over to the chest of drawers and leans against it for a moment, running his hand through his hair. He stares at me before he sits on the bed, still tugging at the hair on the top of his head.

He needs a haircut.

"Have you remembered anything else about your kidnapping?"

"No, not really." I consider accusing him of changing the subject, but I fear he hasn't. "I've thought about it, and I remember a bit more about you taking me away from the boat, but that's about it."

"Do you remember seeing the creeper guy at all?"

"He was involved, wasn't he?" The look on Deklan's face confirms my suspicions. "Who hired him, Dek? You have to tell me, and don't you dare say 'later!'"

"I'm pretty sure he was," Deklan says. "Exactly how, I haven't figured out yet. I was hoping you might remember something else—something I could use against him—but I don't want to push you."

"Miss Jolly said she could help me remember if I wanted to."

"That therapist?" Deklan wrinkles his nose at the idea. "I don't want her in our business."

"But she said if she hypnotized me, I might remember it."

"Seriously?" Deklan shakes his head. "What a crock of shit."

"It might work, Dek." I sit up and place my hand on his leg. "I might remember him. I might remember all kinds of stuff."

"That's what I'm afraid of," Deklan mumbles. "You don't want to remember. You've said that many times."

"Maybe it's different now."

"What's different? What could possibly make you want to remember it now when you have kept that shit out of your head for years?"

I think carefully before I answer.

"I kept it out because I didn't want it to interfere with my life. I didn't want to dwell on bad memories. Remembering doesn't change anything that happened, and not knowing the details might save me some grief. But now...now it's interfering with my life anyway. I'm getting escorted around by some goon; you're worried, and I can't even go to work. If I remembered, maybe I would know who else was involved, and you wouldn't have to worry about me."

I refrain from saying why Deklan wouldn't need to worry. Pointing out that I know he's going to kill anyone involved isn't going to make me feel better about remembering.

"If you aren't worried, maybe I can keep my job." I look up at him pleadingly. "I *like* my job, Dek. I know it's mundane and kind of silly, but I like it. I don't want to quit."

"Even if that means remembering the other shit?" he asks quietly. "Maybe shit you don't want to know?"

I think about it for a long moment, but my mind is already made up. I just want him to know that I'm considering everything before I answer.

"I want to remember, Dek. I want to remember it all."

Chapter 29

"Correct me if I'm wrong, but this isn't the man you told me you were going to marry."

Jennifer Jolly has been my therapist since I was released from the hospital after the kidnapping. Though she has heard much of my innermost secrets over the years, she doesn't know about my family's business, and I've never told Miss Jolly about the deal my father made with the Foleys. I had told her about my plans to marry Sean, and Deklan's appearance at my therapy session has surprised her.

"He isn't," I say with a slightly embarrassed smile. "Deklan works for Sean. Sean"—I struggle for a moment to come up with the wording—"well, Sean dumped me, and Deklan and I just hit it off."

Miss Jolly raises an eyebrow and purses her lips but chooses not to question my lame explanation.

"Well, however this came about, I'm glad to hear you finally want to try to recover your memories. It sounds like Deklan has helped you come to this decision."

"He has." I reach for Deklan's hand. "He already helped me remember a little. You see, Deklan is the man who found me on that boat and took me to the hospital."

He doesn't say anything. We'd discussed the story we would relate to my therapist and had enough detail to keep her from asking further questions. I get the idea he's not completely comfortable being in a room with a therapist, but he insisted on coming along.

"Really?" Miss Jolly tilts her head and looks at Dek more closely. "How did that happen?"

"I had a fishing boat on the dock." Deklan's voice is monotone. "I was about to go out on the boat when I heard two guys talking about a girl. I listened in, figured out they had someone tied up in the bottom of the boat, and chased them off. She was pretty out of it, so I took her to the hospital."

"There was no report of who brought her in," Miss Jolly says.

"Yeah, I guess not though I don't know why. I brought her in, told the nurse I found her, and then I left. I guess no one ever reported it. They didn't take my name."

"Interesting." I've spent enough time with Miss Jolly to know she's not buying it, but again, she doesn't push. "We've talked about hypnotherapy before. You know it isn't always one hundred percent, but considering the dreams you've had since that time, I think we have a good chance at being successful."

Miss Jolly has me lie back in a reclining chair while Deklan sits off to one side. She instructs him to remain quiet as she closes the blinds and dims the lights.

"Close your eyes," she says. "Do you hear the clock ticking on the wall?"

"Yes." I hadn't even noticed the large clock before or heard the ticking of the second hand, but now that the room is quiet and the sound has been brought to my attention, it's very loud.

"Focus on the clock's ticking. Relax into the rhythm and breathe slowly—in through your nose, out through your mouth. Take yourself back to that day."

I do as she says. I remember going to school and being worried about an English test, but it ended up being pretty easy. We had a pep rally that day, so the last bell was cut off early.

"Picture yourself leaving school." The ticking of the clock fades, and Miss Jolly's soft voice is the only thing I hear. "Remember getting on the school bus. Think about who is around you, what you see and smell."

"The bus is mostly empty," I say as the image comes into my head. "We are the second to last stop. Heather is with me, and she's going on about some guy she likes. I'm glad when we get to our corner because I can't stand the guy she's head over heels about."

"What happens when you leave the bus stop?"

"I wave at Heather, and she goes off down the street. I'm walking home, listening to a new playlist."

"What song?"

"'In One Ear' by Cage the Elephant." The song plays through my head.

"There's a man standing against the wall near the alley."

"Do you know him?"

"I don't know his name, but I've seen him before."

"Where?" Deklan's voice startles me.

"Please, Mr. Kearney, try not to speak. Go on, Kera. Tell me where you have seen the man before."

"He's been to our house. He didn't come inside, but he was out on the porch when my father was talking to one of his clients. He kept puffing on one of those e-cigarette vaporizer things. He has it with him now."

"Can you describe him?"

"His hair is blond, and he has high cheekbones. No, his cheeks and eyes are sunken; it just makes him look like his cheekbones are high. His teeth are really yellow."

"That's good, Kera. Keep going."

"He says hello when I walk past, but I ignore him. He calls to me again, and I tell him to leave me alone, or I'll tell my father he was bothering me. That's when the van pulls out of the alley. The door opens, and another guy jumps out."

My breaths become short and sharp, and I start feeling dizzy.

"What's happening, Kera?"

"The first guy blocks my way, and the other one grabs my arms. I drop my book bag and try to turn to kick him, but he's holding too tight. The other guy grabs my leg, and they push me into the van. Something's placed over my eyes. I can't see!"

"That's all right, Kera. What do you hear? What do you smell?"

"The engine of the van is loud. It's clicking like it needs an oil change. The van smells like grease. I scream, but I get punched in the head. It hurts and makes my ears ring. I get hit again..."

"What's happening, Kera?"

"I...I don't know. I think I got knocked unconscious."

"When you wake up, what do you hear?"

"Water. It sounds like water washing up against something—boats or maybe the shore. I can't tell. I'm being carried, and I can hear their footsteps. We stop, and I'm pushed down on my knees. The floor is wood. It smells bad."

"What does it smell like?"

"Like dead fish and mold. Everything feels damp. Someone's standing over me, tying my hands behind my back. I can't move!"

"Take a deep breath. Can you hear anyone talking?"

"Yes."

"What are they saying?"

"I...I don't know!"

"Relax, Kera. You're safe here. Focus on what they're saying."

"They're…they're talking about my dad. One of them says he's finally going to get his payment and that this is a great plan, but the other one's not sure. He thinks my father will double-cross them, and they won't get paid."

"Do they say anything else?"

"I…I can't hear them. They moved away, and I'm alone. I try to scream, but my mouth feels so dry…there's something tied around my head and in my mouth. I…I think it's a bandana. They leave me alone for a long time."

"What happens when they come back?"

"Someone takes out the gag. He tells me not to scream, then gives me water. He shoves something else in my mouth— bread with peanut butter on it. It smells nasty, and I spit it out. He smacks my face."

"Do you know if it's the same man? The one you saw at your parents' house?"

"I don't know. He never takes off the blindfold."

My limbs are tense, and my chest feels tight. I can feel the thrumming of my heartbeat in my neck and temples.

"Remember that you're safe now, Kera. Take a deep breath…There you go. Can you tell me what happens next?"

"I'm…I'm alone again. I can't see, and no one comes close to me. I don't know how long. I keep trying to sleep, but my shoulders hurt so badly, I can't get comfortable enough. Someone comes in and gives me more water and a piece of a sandwich. I'm too hungry to spit it out this time. I try to talk to him, but he doesn't answer me."

"Can you tell me what you feel?"

"It's cold," I say. "I can tell when it's daytime because it gets a little warmer but not much. I try to remember how many times that's happened, but I'm not sure. I don't know how long I was knocked out. I'm so hungry and thirsty, and I'm just waiting for someone to bring me food and water again."

A shiver runs through my body.

"They're talking about me," I whisper. "They're saying it's past the deadline my father was supposed to pay the ransom. I think…I think they're going to kill me. When I hear footsteps on the stairs, I try to struggle against the ropes, but it doesn't help. They say they're going to…going to…"

I choke back a sob. I can't say the words.

"He…he's holding my mouth open and shoving something inside. I…I can't close my mouth. Oh, God! He's…he's…"

"Kera! Kera, listen to my voice. You aren't there. You are not on that boat. You are safe, here in my office. Do you understand? Come back here now."

"Yes." Tears are streaming down my face when I open my eyes. The room is still dim, but even the small amount of light hurts my eyes. "They raped me, didn't they?"

I sit up and look at Deklan. His hands are clenched into fists against his thighs, and his jaw is clenched. My heart beats in my chest as I wait for him to explode, but he doesn't. Something isn't right about his reaction. I can see his anger, but I expect more from such a revelation.

"You already knew about it."

Deklan drops his gaze to the floor and nods.

"When I found you, there was a ring gag in your mouth," he says quietly. "There really isn't any other reason to gag you like that."

My heart is pounding too fast. I can't catch my breath, and I'm starting to feel dizzy.

"Kera?" I hear Miss Jolly, but I can't respond.

What did they do to me? How many of them? What else did they do that I still don't remember?

"Kera!" Deklan's voice and his hands on my arms pull me from my thoughts. "Kera, listen to me! They didn't do it. You hear me? They didn't."

I stare at him and try to comprehend what he's saying. Deklan doesn't take his eyes off mine as he addresses Miss Jolly.

"I need a minute with my wife."

Miss Jolly nods and leaves the room, closing the door behind her. Deklan immediately takes my face in his hands.

"They did *not* rape you," he says as he stares deep into my eyes. "They were going to. They were *about* to, but I got there first."

"You didn't tell me that."

"I didn't want you to think about it. I still don't want you to think about it."

I close my eyes for a moment, and it all floods back.

The hands on my head, holding my face tightly as the gag is shoved in my mouth. The sound of laughter and then a loud burst of gunfire. Laughter turns to screams. I have no idea what's happening as I'm left alone again. I hear scuffling above me, screams, and more shots.

I begin to understand the rest of the story that Deklan didn't want me to remember.

"What did you do?" I whisper.

Deklan is silent for a long time. He grits his teeth, and his eyes flash with a fury I have never seen before. When he finally speaks, each word is slow and deadly.

"I made them suffer."

I swallow hard. He's right—I don't want to know any more.

Miss Jolly comes back in. She and Deklan talk softly, but I don't listen to them. I'm trying to remember with more clarity.

"It's past the deadline. He ain't gonna make it."

"What now?"

"Kill her, that's what."

"We ain't gonna kill her. Not yet, anyway. This is his deal, and we're gonna get our money. Just be patient."

"Fuck being patient. If we're stuck waiting on O'Conner, we should at least have a little fun with her."

"Gotta keep her a virgin. That's part of the deal."

"So? Her mouth works, don't it?"

I feel pressure against my face, and my mouth is forced open. Whatever he's put inside keeps me from closing it again. I smell sweat and hear chuckling. Tears are pouring out of my eyes, soaking the blindfold. I wait for it to happen, but I hear the gunshots first.

Deklan did get there in time. If he had obeyed Fergus Foley's orders, he wouldn't have. If he had waited, it would have been too late. They would have raped me, and I might have ended up dead.

I grip Deklan's fingers tightly, and he reaches over to rub at the back of my wrist. I place my head against his shoulder, suddenly exhausted though it can't be much past noon.

"I think she's had enough for one day," Miss Jolly says.

"Agreed."

"Make sure she gets some rest. She should eat and drink plenty of water, too. It will help."

"I'll make sure."

Miss Jolly gives me a quick hug and says she'll call with an appointment time in a couple of days. Deklan shakes her hand, and we head for the door.

"Deklan?"

He stops and turns to face Miss Jolly.

"I've seen the reports," she says. "The police found the boat where they suspect Kera was held. I've heard about what was found there."

"And?"

Miss Jolly's eyes narrow. She sets her jaw and stares intently at my husband for a long moment. They seem to be having a conversation with their eyes, and I don't know what to make of it.

"And," she finally says, "I have no problem with what I've heard."

"Good." Deklan takes my arm and leads me out the door.

I toy with the idea of asking him what that was all about, but I consider that there are some details I don't really want to hear. Deklan's explanation is plenty for me at this point. Besides, there is something else I want to address with my husband.

"You knew the whole time." I turn toward him as he drives us out of the parking lot and back toward the motel.

"The new apartment should be ready tomorrow morning," Deklan says casually.

"Do *not* do that!" I can't help but snap at him. "Do not change the subject—not after I just went through all that!"

Deklan presses his lips together and grips the steering wheel.

"You've never asked me for oral sex," I say. "You've never even hinted at it. That didn't even occur to me until just now."

"I never will, either." He looks over at me, but I can't understand the expression in his eyes.

"Don't you like it?"

"Not the point." His stare is intense.

I want to press the issue, but I have no idea what I want to communicate. The thought of even trying it brings the taste of bile into the back of my throat. Maybe I should let this one go.

"I didn't remember anything about the creepy guy—Charlie." It's not a complete change of subject, but Deklan's eyes soften a little. "Maybe he wasn't a part of it."

"He was." The assuredness of Deklan's words brings goosebumps to my skin.

"You still aren't telling me something."

"That shrink said you've had enough for one day," he says, but he doesn't deny it. "It can wait until later."

"No," I tell him. "I said before—I want to remember everything. I also want to know everything that you know. You can't hold back on me, Deklan, not when it comes to this."

He taps a finger against the steering wheel as he ponders. After glancing at me several times, he finally agrees.

"After we get to the motel, and you have had a full meal, I'll tell you what I've figured out."

True to his word, as soon as I'd finished the last bite of takeout, Deklan sat down beside me on the bed, took my hands in his, and told me what he knew.

"Last night after you fell asleep, I had Brian come watch over you while I went out."

"And?" I glare at him, not pleased to find out he'd been sneaking out, but he refuses to look at me.

"And I had a little talk with Charles Grange."

"He's alive?" I bite down on my lip, but I can't hide the shock from this revelation. Deklan glances at me briefly and nods. "He was involved, wasn't he?"

"Yes, he was. I don't know that he was ever on the boat, so there might not be anything about him you could remember, but he was definitely involved."

Deklan pauses. I know there's more, but he's reluctant to continue. I try to wait him out, but when he doesn't speak for some time, I prompt him.

"He wasn't the one behind it, was he?"

"No. Charles Grange was involved, but it wasn't his idea."

"Whose?" I wait for an answer, but Deklan has gone silent again. I grip his fingers until he looks at me. "Whose idea was it, Dek?"

"Honestly, Kera," Deklan says as he closes his eyes for a moment, "I have no idea how to tell you."

"But you know who was behind it all."

"Yeah, I do."

"Just say it."

Deklan takes a long breath, swallows hard, and speaks the words.

"Kera—it was your father. Cormick O'Conner orchestrated the whole thing."

DEKLAN

Chapter 30

I sit on the motel bed and try to figure out exactly what Deklan had just said. The words bounce around inside my head, but they don't make sense.

"I think I must have heard you wrong," I finally say.

"I wish you had."

"My...my *father* had me kidnapped?" I stare at Deklan with my mouth hanging open. "That doesn't even make sense! There was a ransom demand. How does he demand ransom from himself?"

"Think, Kera." Deklan holds up a finger for each point he makes. "Your father had no money, was in all kinds of debt to the Foleys and at least one other organization, and had no way to pay anyone back. His debts were out of control. He had nothing to bargain with except you. If he could get Fergus to buy into it, he'd not only have the debt relieved, but he'd walk off with the ransom money as well."

I want to scream at Deklan. My father would never do such a thing! He'd never endanger me for the sake of money, but it would be a lie, and Deklan knows it. Nothing is more important to my father than gambling, and that requires money.

I wonder how many others he was indebted to besides the Foleys when he decided to concoct such a plan and if the ransom was just enough to pay everyone off.

"My father had me kidnapped." I let the words roll out of my mouth in a monotone—a hollow echo that takes residence in my heart.

"He planned it all." Deklan's voice is soft, but I find nothing about it reassuring. "Sean had been in trouble for a while, and your father found out about it. Charlie Grange was feeding your father information that he was getting from someone in the Foley outfit. He knew that Fergus wanted Sean to settle down and take responsibility. All he needed was the right girl to pair up with Sean, and you fit perfectly."

"Quite the plan." I want to cry, but no tears come out.

"Kidnap you and beg Fergus to save you in exchange for marrying Sean." Deklan abruptly pushes himself off the bed and begins to stalk around the room. "I should have seen it. I should have put two and two together when the topic came up—it was as if pairing you and Sean had already been discussed between Fergus and Cormick. I should have realized right then and there when your father was so happy about the arrangement they made. He was too happy. He wasn't worried about you at all. I'm not sure he even cared what you were going through. He was going to have his debt paid to the Foley family and get a pile of ransom money, to boot."

"But the ransom wasn't paid."

"No, it wasn't."

"Because you rescued me instead."

"Yes."

"So how did Fergus Foley know where I was?"

Deklan stops pacing and looks over to me, shaking his head slowly.

"I'm not sure yet. There's a connection, but I don't know where. Charles Grange had to have been passing information between someone in the Foley organization and your father, but I can't figure out who that is, and he's not saying."

"So, he's really is still alive?"

"Yeah." Deklan doesn't elaborate, and I wonder if Charles Grange might be wishing he were dead right now. "Whoever his contact is, they must be holding something big over his head. He won't talk to save his life, but I'm not going to stop until I know who he's been talking to in Foley's outfit."

"What if…what if it's Sean?" I can't look at Deklan when I say the words. I don't want to see his reaction. Instead, I stare at my hands and wait.

"I know Sean can be a little…trying," Deklan says, "but he was only a kid when this started and far more interested in tallying up as many notches on his bedpost as possible. Willing girls were plentiful. I can't see him bothering to take the time to kidnap you, and he can't stand your father. He wouldn't have done business with him, not even back then."

I can't argue with Deklan's logic.

"It has to be someone close in the organization," Deklan says. "There really aren't that many of us. I'm having a hard time coming up with any of them that would consider having my wife followed. I didn't think any of them would dare."

"But one of them is working with my dad," I say quietly. I'm still trying to wrap my head around it all, and it's causing my temples to throb.

I don't want to think about any of this.

"He's getting information from one of them," Deklan says. "Maybe not directly. Maybe he's paying someone to get information from someone else. I don't know. I'm going to have to have Mac look into it."

"What if it's him?"

"Can't be Mac…" Deklan cuts himself off and grimaces. He looks at me grimly. "All right, Brian then. He's someone I know I can trust."

"He's like a brother."

"Very much so."

"Lucky for you, he's not like a father." I can't stop the venom in my voice.

Deklan reaches over and pulls me against his chest. I press my cheek against his shirt and inhale, trying to concentrate on his smell instead of all the revelations in my head.

"You will never see him again," Deklan says softly.

A cold feeling starts at the back of my head, creeps over my shoulders and down my spine. I don't have to ask Deklan what he means by that statement—I know exactly what he's planning.

My initial reaction is to tell him not to do it. I can't sit back while he says "I'll be back in a few minutes" and goes off to kill my father.

Can I?

"What about my mom?"

"What about her?"

"If...if Dad is gone, what's going to happen to my mother?"

"If she had anything to do with it or even knows about it, I don't give a fuck."

I swallow hard. I don't want Mom dragged into any of this. She was never a great parent, but she was a victim of her circumstances, just like I was. She had to go along with whatever Dad wanted her to do.

My phone rings, and the sound startles me. I didn't realize I'd left it on after leaving Miss Jolly's office. Deklan glares at me, and I shrug apologetically as I check to see who is calling.

"It's the coffee shop," I say as I stare at the screen quizzically. I answer before Deklan can tell me not to. "Hello?"

"Kera? It's Terry."

"Hey, Terry. What's up?"

"I just…well, I thought you should know that the police showed up here. They were asking about you and your husband. It's Deklan, right?"

"Yeah."

"Well, some detective named Warren was here asking a lot of questions. He wanted to know where you live and about a guy named Charles Grange. They say he's missing. Is that the weird guy who kept coming in here? I told them I hadn't seen him for a couple of days."

"Um, wow, Terry," I say as I glance at Deklan. "That's really strange. Why would the police be asking about my husband?"

Dek glares at the phone.

"I guess someone called about an argument here," Terry says. "They said something about a fight in the alley, but I don't know what they were talking about."

"I don't know either. Thanks for keeping me in the loop though."

I disconnect the call and relate Terry's message to Deklan. He immediately calls Brian and finds out the police were at our old apartment earlier in the day.

"It's a good thing we left," I say. "Did you know they would be showing up?"

"I didn't know for sure," he says. "I had a feeling though. Grange has some ties to the police department. I had a feeling he was going to be missed."

"Are you going to let him go?"

"I don't know. I might have to, but I don't like the idea."

"Where is he now?"

"With Brian."

"Vague." I fold my arms and give him a hard look, but I get no information regarding Grange's whereabouts. Instead, I get a subject change.

"Want to go see the new place?"

"Is it ready?" Maybe if I can get him distracted with the new apartment, he'll decide to talk some more.

"Let's go find out."

The new apartment is much bigger than the old one— newer, too. It smells like fresh paint, and all the appliances are shiny. I find a brand new Jacuzzi tub in the bathroom.

"That's going to be fun," Deklan says as he wraps his arms around me from behind and kisses my neck. "I can think of all kinds of things I can do to you in there."

"It's big enough, you might actually be able to lie down!"

"That would be nice. We'll have to save it for later though. Brian is on his way over with the stuff from the other apartment."

Brian shows up with a trailer full of boxes from our old place. While I unpack a couple of boxes of kitchen supplies, Brian takes Deklan aside. I have to listen closely to hear their conversation.

"I had to ditch the cops on the way here," Brian says.

"They were following you?"

"Yeah—they were at your old place. Do you know how hard it is to ditch cops when you've got a trailer?"

"Did they question you?"

"Nah. They were definitely looking for you, not me."

"Are you sure you ditched them?" Deklan asks.

"Positive," Brian says. "I got on the freeway and kept close to a couple semis. I got off on an exit, and they kept going. I still drove around for a bit before heading this way, just in case."

"Good deal."

"Warren has got it out for you, boss."

"I get that idea." Deklan scowls at Brian. "And what's with the 'boss' shit? You been hanging around Mac too much, and he needs to cut that out."

"He don't trust Sean," Brian says with a shrug. "You earned your rep."

"Dissension is never a good thing. Don't call me that, or you're gonna slip up and say it in front of Sean. How do you think he'll take that?"

"Point." Brian rolls his eyes. "I gotta get that trailer returned, but after that, you want me to take the Viper for the night and leave you with the rental? You know they'll be on the lookout for your car."

"Yeah, that's a good idea."

"Sweet!"

"Don't wreck my car."

"I won't drive over ninety—I swear." Brian gives him a big smile.

"Sure you won't. The tank better be full when you bring it back."

Brian waves at me as he heads out, and Deklan starts opening boxes and putting things away. By the time Brian returns to exchange cars, I've had enough of unpacking.

"Want me to get some carryout?" Deklan asks.

"Ugh, not again." I bat my eyes at him. "Can't we go somewhere? I can't stand looking at boxes anymore."

"I would prefer that you stay out of sight."

"You can't keep me locked up in here, Dek."

"Don't tempt me."

"I'll be with you," I say. "I can't think of anyone better suited to keep me safe."

"We do need to pick up some groceries." He reaches over and takes my chin between his fingers. "How about a compromise? We'll go get what we need, and then I'll make a nice dinner back here, okay?"

"Yeah, that's okay." I check around the kitchen. "I just hope we can find the silverware."

"We'll get plastic," he says. "We can even get some wine and try out the new tub."

Deklan winks at me.

"Deal!"

Deklan has barely cooked anything aside from toast and soup since we've been married, and I'm surprised when he whips up a rather tasty lasagna and a fresh salad to go with it. While sitting on the floor of the living room, we eat off paper plates and drink wine from plastic cups. As he eats and drinks, Deklan starts talking more than usual.

"What are you going to do about that detective?" I ask, assuming I'll get the usual brush-off.

"Warren is looking for anything to use against me at this point," Deklan says as he shovels another plastic forkful of lasagna into his mouth. "I'm gonna have to be a little more careful. I can't have Grange turning up dead now."

"Can't you just…just get rid of the body?"

"It's not that easy." Deklan eyes me with a grim half smile. "Eventually, they get found, and there's always some kind of trace evidence if you know where to look. It's better to have the body found and have an alibi or someone else to blame it on. Now that people have identified us as having an argument, I'll be the prime suspect."

"Like with Brian and the pimp," I say. "You left the evidence but made sure you had an alibi."

"Exactly. Once they have evidence to point toward one person, they have a hard time looking past that. Even if they find something that links another person, getting a conviction becomes impossible, even with an attorney who sucks. All you have to do is point out the inconsistent evidence, and you got your reasonable doubt."

"So will you plan something like that again?" It feels strange to be talking about such things so casually.

"Depends on him," Deklan says with a shrug. "If he talks, and the information checks out, he could be more useful alive. I don't know at this point. If I find out he was planning on hurting you…"

Deklan grits his teeth. A moment later, the plastic fork snaps in half, and I fetch him another one.

"I shouldn't be telling you all of this," Deklan mumbles.

"I'm glad you are." I reach over and touch the back of his hand. "I need to know, Deklan. It's keeping me in the dark that makes everything dangerous."

"You scare the shit out of me." Deklan shakes his head slowly as he tosses the fork onto the plate and leans back. "Do you know that?"

"I don't think I'm that big of a threat to you."

"Oh, how wrong you are. You are the biggest threat I've ever had in my life."

"Why do you say that?"

"The job is the only thing I've cared about since I was a teenager. I've worked for the Foley family, done a lot of their dirty work, and made sure they were protected. Nothing else mattered to me...not until you."

"And that's bad?"

"If anyone understood how I feel about you, they could use it against me." Deklan turns his hand over and interlocks our fingers. "It makes me vulnerable."

"Because someone could get to you through me."

"That's part of it, yes."

"What else?"

Deklan pauses and stares down at his empty plate. After a moment, he pushes himself off the floor and starts to pace.

"I've never had to...had to *balance* before." Deklan runs his fingers through his hair. "Anything and everything I did had a single focus—Fergus Foley. Now, everything is different."

"Because of me."

"Not entirely," Deklan says, "but yeah, it's mostly you."

I look away from him as my chest tightens. I can feel pressure behind my eyes, and I take a few deep breaths to make it stop.

Deklan turns on his heel and quickly makes his way to me. He shoves the paper plates out of the way, drops to his knees front of me, and takes my hands in his.

"And I wouldn't trade that for anything," he says. "It just means I have some adjustments to make in my thinking."

"What kind of adjustments?"

"I can usually think calmly about things," Deklan says. "I can rationalize and figure out the best course of action without a lot of emotion, but when it comes to you...well, I just can't think clearly."

I stare into his eyes, trying to read his expression. He's not angry—I can see that—but he doesn't seem happy, either.

"Is that such a bad thing?" I ask. "Aren't you supposed to be emotional when it comes to your wife?"

"It has the potential to be bad," he says. He grabs my chin when I try to look away from him. "Being emotional about you isn't bad, but it could turn into something dangerous for us both."

"I can be used against you."

"I'm confident I can keep you safe from that."

"Then what has you so worried?"

"I'm worried that I might do something stupid."

I need a better explanation, and he knows it. I keep staring at him until he clarifies.

"Do you know how bad I want to go after Arden for you? Even though I know I wouldn't stand a chance, I want to do it just so you can have closure. Rationally, it's an idiotic thing to do and would likely get us both killed, but I've considered taking the risk more than once."

"I don't want you to risk yourself," I tell him. "I never meant for you to do that. When...when I saw Kathy lying there and...and..."

"I know." Deklan strokes the side of my face.

"I never should have asked you to do that."

"You were in so much pain, it hurt just to look at you. I wanted to fix it. I wanted to take that pain away. I still do."

"I don't want you to put yourself in danger."

"But I would," Deklan says quietly. "Don't you see? I'd do anything for you, and that's what scares me."

Chapter 31

"Um...okay, boss. I'll get it done." Brian closes his burner phone and looks over at me warily.

"What is it?" I stop hauling kitchen towels out of a box and look over at him.

After two weeks of Deklan's delving into who knew about my kidnapping, he's been surly and quick-tempered. I wasn't very upset when he said he was going away for a couple of days and that Brian would be around if I needed anything. I was ready for a break.

"It's Sean," Brian says. "He needs me to go do something, and he wants it done now."

"So, go do it."

"I gotta get ahold of Deklan. I'm not supposed to leave you."

"I can survive a little while on my own. Can't you have Mac or someone stop by?"

"No one else knows about this place," Brian says. "That's how Dek wants it. No one knows, not even Mac."

Brian tries for a good ten minutes but can't reach my husband.

"Shit," he mumbles.

"Just go," I say. "Really—I'll be fine. I could use a little alone time anyway."

"Sorry, Mrs. K. I don't mean to be in the way."

"I know you don't. But I can hear your snoring from the bedroom."

Brian is tense and uncertain about leaving but finally goes to do Sean's bidding, and I got back to my unpacking and organizing. I want to get it all done tonight so I don't have to think about it anymore.

The noise from the television is my only company as I move the plates and bowls from one cabinet to another—again. I can't seem to find the perfect place for them in the new kitchen. It's much bigger than the one in the old apartment, and there are too many choices of location. There is even a second bedroom that's completely empty, and I have no idea what we'll do with it. Maybe we can turn it into a guest room for Brian. With an actual bed to sleep in, maybe he wouldn't snore as much.

I'm actually starting to miss Brian's presence a bit. As much as I thought I wanted some alone time, I miss having someone else around.

All the boxes are unpacked, and all the furniture is in place. There isn't a coffee shop in walking distance of the new apartment, but Deklan said we would talk about getting me my own car when he returned.

I'm not sure how I'm going to approach getting my old job back. It's hardly convenient now, and Deklan's paranoia hasn't waned. Nothing has changed about my feelings on the subject—I need somewhere to go, something to do, and somebody to see. I hope I don't have to convince my husband of that fact all over again.

I yawn and glance at the clock. It's much later than I realized. I look up into the cabinet once more, decide the dishes are as organized as they are going to get, and close the cabinet door.

I hear a beep from the burner phone on the counter. It's a message from Brian saying Deklan has been delayed and won't be returning until tomorrow. As I'm reading it, the phone actually rings.

"Hello?"

"Hey, Mrs. K. It's Brian."

"Hey, Brian."

"I was about to head back your way, but the boss wants me to do one more thing for him. I should be back late tonight, but I don't wanna wake you. I'll just park outside and watch the place from the car."

"That's fine."

"I figured." Brian laughs. "I know you didn't like me sleeping on the couch."

"You were fine."

"Uh huh." He makes an exaggerated snoring sound, and we both laugh. "I'll see ya in the morning, Mrs. K."

"See ya then."

I head to the bathroom for a shower. The bathroom in the new place is awesome all around, but my favorite part is the huge rainfall showerhead. I can stand under it for an hour and just let it pour over me. The stall is also big enough for both Deklan and me to shower together, and the ceiling is high enough that Deklan doesn't have to duck to keep from hitting the showerhead.

The lavender scented soap makes me even sleepier than I was before. I stumble out of the bathroom with a towel wrapped around me and crawl straight into bed. Once I'm under the sheets, I pull the towel off and toss it in the general direction of the bathroom. I'll pick it up tomorrow.

I shiver, suddenly wishing I'd kept hold of the towel. The bed is insanely big without Deklan in it. The sheets are cold, too. All I can think about is how much I want to feel his body next to mine and envelop myself in the heat.

Yes, I had welcomed a little break from Deklan and his sour mood, but I miss him now. In fact, I feel very alone and vulnerable at the moment. Brian was right—I wasn't happy about him sleeping on the couch while Deklan was gone—but now I wish I could hear his snoring.

Mostly, I want my husband back.

Tears fall as I grab Deklan's pillow and hold it to my chest. I wish it smelled more like him, but laundry had been done the day before he left, and the pillowcase just smells like detergent. I stare into the darkness until the tears dry up, and exhaustion takes over.

At some point in the night, I wake, freezing.

I'm still gripping Dek's pillow, but the blankets are all on the floor. I've never kicked them off like that before, and I wonder what I had been dreaming about. I shiver as I climb out of bed to retrieve the blankets.

A soft click from the other room captures all my attention.

"Brian?" I call out softly but get no answer.

My heart begins to pound. I call his name a little louder, but there is no reply. I grab the end of the sheet and hold it to my chest as I tiptoe to the nightstand and grab the gun concealed inside. I check the barrel, just like Deklan taught me, to make sure there's a round in the chamber. I peer around the edge of the door, but I don't see or hear anything.

Stepping out into the kitchen, I can see there is no one else is in the apartment, but I can feel another presence. I sniff the air, almost positive there is a hint of cologne, but neither Deklan nor Brian wears any. Maybe no one is here now, but I'm sure someone was. I check the apartment door and find the deadbolt unlocked.

I turn it quickly as my heart pounds in my chest. I'm pretty sure I locked it before I went to bed. Then again, it's a new place, and I'm not comfortable here yet. Maybe I did forget. Maybe the noise I heard was the refrigerator or the furnace.

I consider calling Deklan, but I'm not even sure what I'd say to him, and I don't want to give him something else to worry about. I could call Brian, but if I did, he would tell Deklan all about it. If he told Dek, Brian would be in trouble for sleeping in the car. For all I know, it was Brian who stopped in to grab something he forgot, and that was the noise I heard.

What about the cologne smell?

I swallow hard. I glance at the gun to make sure my finger isn't on the trigger. My hands are shaking, and I'm going to end up shooting the refrigerator if I'm not careful. I sniff the air again, but the scent is not as noticeable as it was just a minute ago. Maybe I imagined it. Maybe it was just something left over from whatever nightmare I was having. Regardless, if I call anyone, I would just sound needy and paranoid.

I shake my head, return to the bedroom, and drag the blankets back onto the bed. Instead of lying back down, I sit in the center of the bed with the gun still in my hands, listening carefully.

An hour passes. I hear nothing and feel ridiculous. After placing the gun on top of the nightstand, I lie back down and pull the covers up to my chin. I stare at the doorway, but it's too dark to see much.

I grab the gun and jump out of the bed, quickly running to the bathroom and turning the light on so it floods the hallway. I rush back to the bed and sit, holding the gun again.

You are being ridiculous.

Everything that has happened has me so worked up, I'm not thinking straight. Kathy being killed, finding out about my father and the creepy stalker—it's all been too much. I'm on overload, and I need to get this shit out of my head.

I take several deep breaths until my heart finally stops racing. I slowly place the gun back in the nightstand drawer and force myself to lie down and close my eyes.

Sleep doesn't come quickly.

Chapter 32

"I want my job back."

Deklan refuses to look at me. He turns his back as he grabs his watch from the top of the dresser and clasps it to his wrist. He holsters his gun and walks out of the bedroom without a word.

I follow.

"I really can't take sitting around here anymore." I cross my arms over my chest and hope I look determined enough that my stubborn husband will give in to my demands. "We talked about this before. I can't just hang out here in the apartment, bored off my ass, while you are gone all day."

"It is not safe for you to go back to that coffee shop," Deklan says. He grabs a waffle out of the toaster and shoves half of it into his mouth. He still doesn't look at me.

"Terry said he would hire me back."

"Absolutely not."

"You can't stop me." As soon as the words are out of my mouth, I know I made a mistake.

Deklan stops chewing, tosses the remaining bit of waffle into the trash, and then leans heavily against the counter. I can see the tightness in his jaw, and I take a step back when he turns toward me. It's not far enough, and all Deklan has to do is reach out with his hand to grab my wrist and bring me close to him.

"Kera," he says in a calm but cold voice, "do not think that because I have allowed that to happen before, I will allow it again. Don't make the mistake of believing this is a marriage of equality. It isn't."

My shoulders slump, and it feels as if all my organs have dropped into my stomach. This isn't news to me—I know my station in my life and this marriage—but Deklan has always been lenient, and to have it spelled out for me is a painful reminder of reality.

I feel his hand on my cheek, but when he tilts my head up, I look off to the side.

"I love you," he says, "but you will do as I tell you. Once all this is sorted out and I know you are safe, we can talk about you getting another job. In the meantime, you will stay here, and Brian will be here when I'm not. You are just going to have to trust me on this."

"It's not like you trust me." I swallow past the lump in my throat, willing myself not to shed any tears of anger.

"I do trust you." Deklan narrows his eyes.

"Oh sure," I say as I pull out of his grasp and toss my hands up in the air. "As long as you have someone watching over me twenty-four hours a day, you trust me completely!"

"That has nothing to do with me trusting *you*. I don't trust anyone else. Don't fight me on this, Kera. I'm not going to budge when it comes to your safety. I'm sorry if that upsets you, but that's not going to change my mind."

I slump down on a kitchen chair and stare at my hands in my lap. I'm running out of arguments, and I really need to find a way to win this one.

"I don't like being left here alone," I tell him. "I even had a nightmare the other night that had me so paranoid, I thought someone else was in the apartment. I barely slept at all."

"You didn't tell me about that."

"It was just a dream."

300

"Where was Brian?"

Shit. I hadn't meant to rat Brian out. I try to brush it off, but Deklan grabs my chin and glares at me until I answer.

"He….he had to step out. Sean called him, and Brian said he would just stay in the car outside and watch over the place from there."

"Motherfucker," Deklan mumbles.

"Please, don't be mad at him. It was my fault. He knows I don't like him sleeping on the couch."

"Mad?" Deklan lets out a hollow laugh as he releases my chin. "I'm a little beyond that."

"He tried to call you."

"He knows I don't want you left alone—ever."

"Well, what is he supposed to do if the boss tells him to do something, and he can't reach you?"

Deklan doesn't have an answer to that one. He leans against the counter again and scowls at the floor.

"How long?" I finally ask. "How long will it be this way?"

"I don't know," Deklan says. "I need to figure out if there was anyone else involved in your kidnapping aside from your father and Grange. There are still a couple of missing pieces."

"Maybe I could help with that."

"I don't want you involved."

"I'm already involved, Dek." I stand up and move in front of him, wrapping my arms around his neck. "I don't want to fight about this."

"I don't want to fight with you either." He places his hands on my hips and kisses my forehead.

"Maybe we can compromise?" I tilt my head and watch him carefully as he narrows his eyes, and an idea forms in my head.

"What kind of compromise?"

"Well, how about I come work with you?"

"Fuck no."

"Deklan—"

He pushes me away and heads for the coatrack.

"Completely out of the question, Kera! There is no way I'd allow that!"

"I don't mean doing...what *you* do." I go after him and grab onto his hand before he can put on his jacket. "But I could still do something. I could translate like I did that one time or maybe help Teagan with the books or something. You could keep an eye on me yourself and not have to rely on anyone else."

I can see by Deklan's expression that I've made a good point. I look up at him hopefully.

"I don't know." Deklan shakes his head slowly, and I know I need to pounce quickly before he changes his mind.

"You know I could be useful," I tell him, "and you wouldn't have to worry about me—I'd always be close by."

He takes in a deep breath, stares into the distance for a moment, and then looks back to me.

"I'll talk to Sean about it," Deklan finally says, "but I'm not making any promises."

I smile broadly and stand on my toes to plant a big kiss on his lips. He kisses me back, then glares down at me again.

"Frustrating woman," he says. "You can come with me today. You are the topic of conversation for the morning anyway, so you might as well be a part of it."

"I am?"

"Yeah."

"About my father and the kidnapping?"

"Yeah. Now get yourself ready so we're not late. I'll tell Brian to meet us at the house."

Deklan takes a roundabout way to the Foley mansion, constantly checking his rearview mirror for anyone following us. I glance back a few times myself, but I never see anything. Deklan is obviously tense, and I'm afraid to ask why. I have the feeling he might decide to turn around and take me back to the apartment if I say anything.

Brian is getting out of his car as we pull up. Deklan slams on the parking brake and jumps out of the car, heading straight for him. As Brian starts to greet him, Deklan hauls back and punches him in the face. Brian falls to the ground, grabbing his mouth as a trickle of blood runs out between his fingers.

"Don't you ever leave my wife alone again!"

"I'm sorry, Dek! Sean told me to—"

"I don't give a shit what Sean tells you!" Deklan reaches down and hauls Brian to his feet by his collar. "You tell him I said you can't leave, and I will deal with the consequences. You get me?"

"I…I got you, Dek. I swear!"

"You better." Deklan grabs my hand and starts to haul me up the front steps. I look back at Brian and mouth an apology to him. He shrugs as he gently rubs his chin, and I get the idea this isn't the first time Deklan has punched him. Brian pokes at his busted lip as he follows behind us.

"What's she doing here?" Sean asks as we walk into the study.

"This concerns her," Deklan says. "Besides, I think she can help out. She already has once before."

"What? We got a translator now?" Sean laughs. "What's next? A sous chef?"

"She can help Teagan out, too."

"You good with computers?" Teagan asks me.

"I know my way around."

"I could use the help."

"What the fuck?" Sean rolls his eyes and tosses his hands in the air. "Whatever. She can at least hang around and be eye candy. Sit, sweetheart. We'll work out the details later."

Once we sit down, it's all business. Sean sits in his wingback chair. Teagan leans against the desk and taps on her phone, and Brian and I sit on the couch in front of Sean. Deklan takes his place standing next to Sean. No one mentions Brian's bleeding lip as Deklan explains to Sean and Teagan what he found out about my father's involvement with the kidnapping.

"Let me get this straight," Sean says as he leans back in his chair. "You are telling me that Cormick O'Conner—Kera's own father—arranged her kidnapping just to fuck with me?"

"I'm not sure he saw it that way," Deklan says. "He did it for the money. He did it to get out of debt with your father and hoped to walk away with the ransom money too. I'm sure he saw a lot of opportunities opening up with the thought of Kera marrying into the Foley family as well."

"And you got all this from that Grange dude?"

"Yes, sir."

"Is he dead?"

"Not yet, sir." Deklan pauses and glances at me before continuing. "I still don't know who he is working with now."

"How much of this did you know about?" Sean says as he turns toward me. "Were you in on it the whole time?"

"She was tied up in the hold of a fishing boat, Sean," Deklan says. "I don't think anyone does that to themselves. Besides, she was only fourteen."

"I don't know." Sean stands up and crouches in front of me. His eyes dance with lightning as he gazes at me, and my stomach churns. "How badly did you want me, baby?"

"I was just a kid," I whisper. I can't look him in the face, and he's blocking my view of Deklan. "I had no idea what was happening."

"But you knew this Grange guy was involved?"

"I don't remember him being there. The first time I saw him was at the coffee shop."

Sean raises an eyebrow at me before looking at Deklan.

"But you think he has a contact here in my organization."

"I think he must have," Deklan says to Sean. "How else would your father have known where to send me to pick her up?"

"That is a damn fine question!" Sean leaps up from where he's squatting in front of me and turns to Deklan. "And who the fuck is that, huh?"

"Well, Neil told Dad where she was held," Teagan says, glancing up from her phone.

"What? How do you know that?" Sean takes a step toward his sister. "You were still in high school back then."

"I was there," Teagan says with a shrug. "I was working on the books when Dad and Neil were talking about O'Conner coming over here. Neil gave Dad a piece of paper with an address on it, which Dad gave to Dek after O'Conner left."

"Call him," Sean says to his sister. "Call him right now, and tell him to get his ass over here."

Teagan lets out a long sigh before calling their cousin and informing him that he was needed immediately.

"Why didn't you tell me about this before?" Sean asks when she's off the phone.

"You never asked," Teagan replies. "Neil always got information for Dad. I didn't think anything about it."

Sean grabs the phone from Teagan's hand and throws it across the room. It hits a lamp on a side table, causing the light to topple to the floor and shatter.

Teagan doesn't move, and her expression doesn't change.

"From now on," Sean says as he points his finger at her nose, "you tell me fucking everything. I don't care if you think it's relevant or not."

"Shall I start with the time I ate the last cookie out of the cookie jar and lied about it?" she asks.

"Don't be a bitch," he replies.

They stare at each other for a long moment. No one else moves or speaks. When I look at Deklan, he's staring straight ahead with his hands clasped in front of him.

"Did you fix that shit with Longbow?" Sean finally asks.

"Well, he's no longer suspended, but the whole promotion thing fell through," Tegan replies, and the tension is abruptly lifted. "Warren blocked it."

"How the fuck is he supposed to get shit done for me if he ends up sitting at a desk?"

I recall Officer Longbow from my previous encounters with him. From the way Deklan had spoken to him, I'd had the impression he was on the Foleys' payroll. It's good to feel like I'm in the loop for once. I sit up a little straighter and listen intently to everyone's words, trying to take in as much as possible without asking any questions.

"It's manipulating evidence against us that got him stuck at that desk," Tegan says. "He'll figure something out. He is quite aware of the consequences if he fucks up."

"I think Longbow has outlived his usefulness."

"He already 'lost' Dek's Beretta out of evidence," Teagan says, "not to mention he got it done while he was on suspension. I'm not sure what else you think he's supposed to do at this point. All the charges were dropped."

"Maybe if you did your job right, this wouldn't have happened."

"Sean, don't be ridiculous." Teagan sighs. I get the idea she's had enough of her brother's ranting. "I can't control who the cops decide to hire and fire."

"You hacked the system."

"For the information, which I got. It's not like I can plant a computer virus that will change who they decide to promote. Humans still do some of the work, you know."

Sean looks like he's going to continue the argument, but Neil walks into the room with Lucas trailing behind him.

"What's up?" Neil asks. He saunters over to the globe-shaped bar and pours himself a drink.

Lucas walks over to a free chair and sits down, opening his briefcase across his lap before he begins to shuffle through the papers inside.

"Have a seat, Neil." Sean gestures to the open spot on the couch next to me as he sits back down in his chair. He leans back with his hands on the arms of the chair and looks around the room. I wonder if he thinks he's on a throne, which leads me to imagine Deklan dressed in a knight's armor, holding a sword.

The image in my head is pretty hot. I lick my lips and cross my legs as Deklan glances at me, his expression confused. I quickly look away before I start to blush.

Neil looks at Sean and then Teagan. He tentatively walks around Sean's chair and sits beside me with his glass clasped between his hands.

"Neil, I have a question for you." Sean tilts his head to the side.

"Yeah?" Neil replies with narrowed eyes. "I got a couple of questions myself—starting with where the hell Dek's hiding Charlie Grange."

"So you know the guy?"

"Yes, I know him. I've known him for years. He worked for your dad, and he still works for me."

"So, you're fucking him," Sean says simply.

Neil doesn't respond. He just lets out a long, exasperated sigh.

"You've been keeping information from me, Neil," Sean says. "You know I can't just look past that. Not only are you withholding information, but apparently, you're acting on it. Having poor Kera here followed? That's not cool, Neil."

"That's not new, either," Neil replies with a snort.

Deklan glares at Neil, and I can see my husband's fingers clenching. Sean squares his shoulders and stares directly at his cousin. From Sean's reaction, he doesn't know anything about this.

"Here's a thought," Sean says, "why don't you fucking explain yourself?"

Neil rubs his chin and looks over to me. I pull back, and my shoulder presses against Brian's for a moment. I wonder if I can change seats without being noticed, but of course, that's impossible. I try to shift away from Neil as much as I can while reminding myself that I asked to be here.

"Your father asked me to keep tabs on her from the beginning," Neil says.

"My father," Sean says with a growl, "is dead. I don't give a fuck what he asked you to do years ago. You fucking work for *me*, not him!"

Neil looks nervous as he glances between Sean and Deklan. Deklan stands motionless and expressionless, but I can still see the tension in his shoulders and arms.

"I thought it might be important," he says slowly. "She's O'Conner's daughter, and he's a problem."

"Oh really?" Sean leans forward in his chair. "O'Conner is a problem, is he? He's a fucking gambling addict who ran out of funds and friends years ago, and you think that makes him a problem for me? Seriously?"

"You know she had to be in on it, too," Neil says with a sneer. "Who has his own daughter kidnapped?"

"You knew about that?" Deklan breaks his silence and nearly loses his composure.

"Of course I did!" Neil stands and points at Deklan. "I am the information man, am I not? I know everything, and that asshole has been trying to play us from the beginning! And now his daughter is sitting here like one of the family. Do you really think that's a coincidence? You think he didn't plan that from the beginning?"

"Don't you fucking accuse my wife of anything." Deklan's voice is soft and calm, but there's a cold, deadly undertone that sends a chill through my bones.

"I'll say whatever the fuck I please." Neil's words are strong, but his tone lacks conviction. "This concerns *my* family, and you're just the hired help."

Deklan takes a half step forward, and Brian stiffens next to me.

"Hold on," Sean says as he holds his hand out, effectively stopping Deklan. "I need to know one more thing."

Sean stands and then crouches in front of Neil much like he had in front of me just minutes ago. He reaches forward and puts his hand on Neil's knee before speaking.

"Neil, I don't care much for spies. I certainly don't care much for spies I know nothing about. Now, this Grange guy is tied up in the warehouse, and I need to know just how far you'll take this shit."

"What do you mean?" Neil presses his back against the couch cushion.

"I mean, Deklan is going to drive you over there, and you're going to put a bullet in your fuck buddy's head."

"Fuck you!" Neil yells. "He's a valuable informant, and we're not just going to off him!"

Sean smiles, and my skin goes cold.

"Are you saying, dear cousin," Sean says slowly, making each word count, "that you are refusing my request to kill your lover?"

"Yeah," Neil says as he folds his arms across his chest. "I'm not doing it, and you're not having that fuckhead over there do it, either. I'm getting a little tired of you making the decisions all the time. Uncle Fergus always asked for everyone's input, and you've been going off half-cocked since he died. This is a family decision and not just yours."

Neil settles back with a smug expression as Sean nods with that disturbing smile still on his face. He stands, walks over to Deklan, and puts his hand on his shoulder.

"Dek?"

"Yeah, boss."

"I need you to perform your job."

Lucas looks up from his papers, quickly closes his briefcase, and exits the room without a word. Teagan stands up a little straighter, tight-lipped and eyeing her brother, and Brian shifts nervously beside me on the couch. I sit completely still and try not to make eye contact with anyone, completely regretting my insistence on coming along.

I'm about to see my husband kill someone. I've known it, but I've never witnessed it. I've never even allowed myself to imagine it.

I'm not prepared for this.

"Boss?" Deklan looks at Sean through narrowed eyes.

"There is a completely and totally useless member of my team. There's no software for hiring and firing. In fact, there's only one way to get out of this business, and my cousin over there is getting out of it right now."

"Sean, be reasonable for once," Neil says with a sneer. "You aren't going to kill me. I'm a member of this family, and I haven't done anything wrong. You rely on the information I gather for you, and Charlie is a part of my network."

"Charlie is your whore," Sean replies. "Apparently, you tell your whore as much as he tells you."

"I only tell him what he needs to know to do his job." Neil glances at me out of the corner of his eye.

"You refused an order," Sean says. "I'm pretty sure that's a court martial offense in the military. I'm pretty sure the sentence is execution. In fact, I'm positive it is."

"This isn't the fucking army." Neil is doing a good job of keeping his voice firm, but his hands are starting to shake.

"Sean, what the hell are you talking about?" Teagan takes a step forward. "Neil's right—he's family. Dad apparently knew what was going on, and it's not like you ended up marrying her anyway, so what difference does it make? We need to move on."

"We are moving on," Sean says. "Neil just isn't moving on with us."

"Boss, are you sure about this?" Deklan asks.

Sean replies by stomping over to Deklan and punching him in the face. I gasp and quickly cover my mouth, but Dek takes the blow without a word.

"Are you going to fucking kill him or not?"

Deklan stands completely still for a moment before slowly nodding.

"Kera," he says, "go into the back office."

My knees shake as I start to stand.

"Sit the fuck down!" Sean yells, and I fall back into the seat as if the words had pushed me square in the chest. Sean turns back to Deklan. "You want her to be a part of this? Well, she is now. Do your fucking job."

"She doesn't need to see this."

"Yeah, I think she does. This is her revenge too, isn't it? If it weren't for all this fuckery, she would be in college now, banging some frat boy, and not stuck with your ass."

"I'm not stuck with—" I'm cut off before I realize I'm speaking.

"Shut up!" they both yell at once.

"Sean, you can't be serious." Neil sets his drink on the table beside the couch and stands up. "This is all ancient history, and you know you need me. There's more going on that you don't know about, and I'm the only one who can tell you."

"Deklan, do it."

My husband looks at me. I know he's trying to convey some meaning with his gaze, but I can't fathom what it is. Leave anyway, despite Sean's words? Close my eyes? Forgive him for what I'm about to see?

Deklan swallows and breaks his gaze with me.

"Boss, I—"

"Fuck it." In a flash, Sean shoves Deklan as he reaches inside his jacket and grabs his gun from the holster. Sean turns, takes two steps forward, and points it at Neil's head. "Bye."

The sound is deafening.

I bite my lip hard enough to taste blood, but it's the only way to stop myself from screaming. Brian grabs me and pulls me against him, but I can feel blood and bits of Neil's head on my arm and shoulder.

"Don't move," I hear Brian whisper.

I can't make my muscles respond anyway. I want to close my eyes, but I can't. Teagan has her hand over her mouth, and her eyes are staring blankly at the mess next to me. Deklan seems frozen in place as Sean turns toward him.

"Deklan Kearney," Sean says slowly as he stares at Deklan's face, "my father might have thought of you as a son, but you need to remember what your last name is. You are hired by the Foleys, not one of them. You work for me, and when I tell you to do something, you fucking do it without hesitation. You got that?"

"Yeah, boss," Dek says. "I got it."

Sean smiles, pats Deklan's shoulder, and sits back in his chair. He looks around the room, making eye contact with each of us as his eyes dance in his skull.

"As you can see," he says to no one in particular, "being family doesn't negate your wrongdoings."

Chapter 33

"Shh, baby. It'll be okay."

I can't stop crying. My nose is stuffed up, and I can't breathe. Deklan holds me tightly in his lap as he sits on a toilet somewhere in the Foley mansion, but I'm only barely aware of my surroundings. I keep hearing the gun blast in my ear, and I keep feeling the wet spatter of blood on my arm even though I know Deklan's washed it all off of me.

Neil's body is probably still in Sean's study, but I'm not crying for him. I'm not even crying because chunks of his brain ended up all over me. I'm crying because I keep seeing Kathy lying on the sidewalk outside a noisy, dark bar. I tighten my arms around Deklan's neck, but I can't get close enough to him to push the memories from my head.

"I never should have brought you here," Deklan mumbles. "I don't know what I was thinking."

He hands me another tissue, and I wipe my nose and eyes. I take several deep breaths and try to get my shit together again.

"I need to be here," I say softly. "Deklan, I *need* it. I can't be kept in the dark anymore. That's why Kathy died—because I didn't know what was going on."

Deklan stares at me as he holds my face in his hands. He looks like he's about to say something when there is a knock at the door.

It's Teagan.

"Dek?" She opens the door a crack and looks back and forth between us.

"Yeah?"

"Sean wants to talk to you." Teagan stares at Deklan, her face expressionless.

"Has Andrew been by?"

"Yeah, he just left with Brian."

They look at each other for a moment without speaking, and then Deklan glances at me.

"I don't want her alone."

"I'm going to show Kera how to run the numbers for the legal books," Teagan says. "Sean wants me to start networking with Neil's associates to start gathering information. He also wants Grange released."

I feel Deklan tense around me.

"Why?" he asks.

Teagan glances over her shoulder, staring out into the hallway for a few seconds before responding.

"We're going to need to talk privately," she says softly.

Deklan nods.

"Kera," Teagan says, "come on with me. I'll show you how to get to the spreadsheets."

I follow her back into the study. The tension in my shoulder releases slightly when I see that everything has been cleaned up. Neil's body is gone, and there is a brand new couch in the room. Sean is still in his chair, leaning back and grinning as if he's on an iron throne.

"Deklan, we need to have us a little conversation," Sean says.

"Sure, boss."

"In the back room." Sean stands and Deklan follows him to a small door in the back of the study while Teagan and I sit at the desk, and she starts to show me a bunch of spreadsheets full of numbers.

"These are the legal books," she says. "You're going to start with those. Once you get the hang of it, I'll show you the real ones."

"Okay."

"I'll also show you the reporting features within the database. You can run monthly reports for the accountant and Lucas."

Teagan shows me how to navigate the spreadsheets and gives me a few simple tasks so I can get used to using the software before excusing herself and leaving me alone in the study.

Deklan and Sean haven't returned from the other room, and I feel a little weird being here by myself, especially after what was going on here just a couple of hours ago. I close my eyes, breathe deeply for a few seconds, and then try to focus on the work.

Teagan's spreadsheet is complicated, and it's taking me a while to figure it all out. I get through three rows of calculations before I glance at the door to the back room and wonder what's taking them so long.

I strain my ears, but all I hear is muffled sounds coming from the room. I can't help myself—I slowly and quietly get up from my chair and tiptoe over to the door. As I get close, I can hear Sean's voice.

"She was supposed to be mine anyway," he says. "You know that."

"You made the decision to change that, Sean." Deklan's words are slow and steady. "You made that choice, not me. You were right about it, too. Doesn't make sense for you to marry O'Conner's kid. I was the better choice, and you saw that. You helped him save face, too, so we can keep doing business with him."

"And you ended up with a hot piece of ass. I could have given her to Lucas."

"But you didn't. We've been over this before. You made the right decision, boss."

"Why? Because you've fallen for her?" Sean laughs. "You have! You have fallen for her! You fucking idiot."

Whatever Deklan says in response is too low for me to hear. I shuffle closer to the door so I can press my ear to the wood. Deklan's words become clearer.

"Whatever happened to get us here, she's my wife now. You said so. We stood out there, and the state made it legal in their eyes and God's. We can't forget our roots, Sean. We're still Catholic, and the church doesn't sanction divorce or adultery."

"So, what are you saying Dek? You aren't fucking anyone else?"

"Why would I?"

"Why indeed?"

"Sean, don't you think we should get back to the actual business at hand?"

"No, I don't." I hear Sean let out a big sigh. "What I want is for you to admit that your wife wishes she had married me instead."

"I don't see that it's relevant." Deklan still sounds calm, but there's a tightening of his voice. "What's done is done."

"She'd drop on her knees and suck my cock if I told her to."

If Deklan replies, I can't hear it.

"Where are your loyalties, Dek? With me or with her?"

"Both," Deklan finally says. "We should make sure we all stay in alignment so neither ever comes into question."

There is a long moment of silence before Sean replies.

"It's a good thing I'm feeling kinda generous today, Dek. I'll let this slide for now, but I'm going to expect some compensation."

I hear footsteps heading for the door, and I quickly run back to my seat at the desk and start tapping the keyboard and moving the mouse around.

"Time to go," Deklan says. He grabs our coats from the rack and practically pulls me out of my seat to help me get my coat on.

"I haven't finished what Teagan asked me to do."

"Later. I've got stuff to do." He doesn't say another word as we leave the house and wait for John to bring the Viper around to the front door. Deklan puts the car in gear, and we speed away from the house.

"Are you all right?" I ask quietly. I'm tempted to tell him what I overheard, but I'm not sure what his reaction might be.

Deklan ignores my question and tightens his grip on the steering wheel until his knuckles go white. I don't want to keep secrets from him. I want to tell him what I heard, but he is obviously in no mood to talk.

His phone buzzes in the console between us, but he ignores it.

I sit and silently look out the window at the buildings speeding by and force thoughts and images of the day from my head.

The phone buzzes again, and the sound puts me on edge. The third time it buzzes, I grab it to look at the screen. The contact name is Teagan, and the text message just says "WH."

"Deklan? There's a message from Teagan on your phone."

Deklan takes the phone from my hand and glances at the screen.

"What does it mean?" I ask.

"She wants to meet with me."

"Now?"

"Yeah."

"I'm going with you."

"I'm not leaving you alone," Deklan says, "so yeah, you are."

Deklan glances over his shoulder and then makes a quick U-turn. He guns the engine and speeds around a couple of cars in his way as I hold onto the door handle and try not to freak out over his driving.

"Where are we going?"

"There's a warehouse near the dock," Deklan says. "That's where Teagan is."

"What do you think she wants to tell you?"

"I don't know."

"What should I do while you're talking to her?" I ask quietly.

"I don't want you by yourself," Deklan says. "I guess you're coming with me."

"What's Teagan going to think about that?"

"Right now, I don't care."

We park the car in an empty, gravel parking lot. I follow Deklan as he stomps through narrow rows of storage containers to a large, windowless building behind the storage area. It looks like there is street access from the other side, but there aren't any cars parked in front.

Deklan pulls out his keys and uses one to open a padlock on the door and then leads me inside. Teagan is in a dimly lit office near the door, and she looks up with raised eyebrows at Deklan when we enter.

"Is this a bad time?"

"Yes."

"Sorry. Gotta talk anyway." Teagan looks over at me. "You might want to send her out."

"Don't you dare," I say quietly to Deklan. "No more secrets."

"Out with it, Teagan."

Teagan raises an eyebrow at Deklan.

"Sorry," Deklan mutters. "Please, just say what you came to say."

"I knew Grange was working with Neil. I knew he was passing info to O'Conner, too. My dad was aware of what was going on, and he wanted to see how it would all play out. He thought it would be best for Sean."

"I got the idea."

"There's more." Teagan leans against the desk and tilts her head. "Sean knew as well. I don't know why he was playing dumb back there. He knew about Neil and Grange. In fact, Sean was the one who told Grange to keep tabs on Kera."

"Then why the fuck did he shoot him?"

Teagan just stares at him, expressionless and silent.

"Because he's a fucking lunatic," Deklan finally says softly.

"It can't keep going on like this," Teagan says. "We are going to have to do something."

"Yeah," Deklan says, "like what? He's the head of the family now, Teag. What exactly do you think we should do?"

"He won't listen to me at all," she says. "You might have a better chance."

"If you heard our last conversation," Deklan mumbles, "you wouldn't think that."

"Then we have to consider other options."

Deklan shakes his head slowly.

"He's still...trying to get his bearings. He's exerting his authority—trying to make a place for himself. He needs time to figure out how to do it all."

"He wants her." Teagan nods over to me.

"He's testing me," Deklan says. "He wants to know I am as loyal to him as I was to his father. This is his way of doing it. If he wanted Kera, he could have married her in the first place, and he didn't. It's God asking Abraham to sacrifice his son. Sean is testing my faith."

"How long do you think it will be before he makes a demand for her? He's talked about it before."

"He doesn't really mean it." Deklan shakes his head.

"He sounded like he meant it," I say quietly.

"What?" Deklan turns his head sharply in my direction.

"I overheard you," I finally say, "when you and Sean were talking about me."

"Jesus Christ."

"What did he say?" Teagan asks.

"He wants me on loan," I say with a snort. My chest feels tight, and I can't take a deep breath.

"It doesn't matter," Deklan says before I can give any details. "He's just talking shit."

"He's losing it, Dek. I used to think he at least had a game plan, but now I think he's just winging it."

"He's figuring everything out." Deklan stares at his hands and nods once. "He needs some time to adjust—we all do. He hasn't been the same since your father died."

"It started before then," Teagan says, correcting him. "You know it did. It started with Marie."

"Who's Marie?" I ask.

"A hooker," Teagan says.

Deklan glares at her.

"She was." Teagan shrugs at him before she looks back at me. "He'd been seeing her regularly, but then she turned up dead. Overdose."

"She was just a junkie hooker," Deklan says.

"You know he was behind it. He practically bragged about it."

"I need time," Deklan says. "I need time to think. I can't…I just can't quite deal with all this at once."

"Don't take too long," Teagan says. "I have the feeling I'll be the next one on the chopping block, and then you'll be on your own."

"He'd never do that." Deklan glares at her. "You're his sister."

Teagan raises an eyebrow.

"How long are you going to keep those blinders on, Dek?"

DEKLAN

Chapter 34

We get into the car, and Deklan places his hands on the wheel and stares out the windshield without starting the engine.

"You know I'd never let him touch you," he says.

"He's your boss."

"You're my wife."

"He obviously thought you were going to tell him it was all right, or he would have just said that in front of me."

"He wouldn't say it in front of you."

I glance over at my husband, wondering if he's really that blind when it comes to Sean. I remember what Teagan said about the hooker, and I ask Deklan to tell me more about it.

"She was just a hooker," he says. "She didn't mean anything to him. After she overdosed, he went a little off the deep end."

"Why would he go off the deep end if she didn't mean anything to him?"

Deklan glances at me, furrowing his brow. I suddenly realize how right Teagan is and how blind to Sean's behavior Deklan has become. When he doesn't come up with an answer, I ask another question.

"What did Sean do after she died?"

"Fought with his father, mostly. Sean went on a lot about how he would run the business better than anyone else ever had. They had one big argument over a supplier, and Sean took it upon himself to blow up the delivery van."

"He blew up a shipment?"

"Yeah." Deklan shakes his head. "He was a kid blowing off steam and arguing with his father. I don't think it was all that abnormal."

"Blowing up a van is normal teenage angst to you?"

Deklan chuckles, but I don't find anything funny.

"Well, not in a normal family, I guess. For the Foleys, maybe it is."

"So, Fergus Foley probably did the same sort of thing when he was a kid?"

"Fergus? No, he was always very levelheaded. Sean's mother was a trip, from what I've heard."

"I don't know anything about her," I say. "Is she gone?"

"Gone, not dead." Deklan finally starts the car and pulls out of the lot. "She's in an institution somewhere upstate."

"A mental hospital?"

"Yeah. She's schizophrenic or something like that. Some kind of personality disorder, maybe. I don't remember. Fergus hated doing it, but he had to have her committed. She wouldn't keep up with her meds, and he couldn't run the business and deal with her at the same time."

"Do you think Sean might be the same way? I mean, is he like his mom?"

"I don't know." Deklan sighs. "I didn't have a lot of contact with her before Fergus sent her away."

"Maybe that's what's wrong with him," I say quietly and then bite at my lip, wondering if I should just keep my mouth shut.

"He's the boss, Kera," Deklan says. "I swore loyalty to the Foley family when I was a teenager, and Sean is the head of the Foley family. Without them, I don't know what might have happened to me. I would probably be dead, and Brian would be, too."

"But that was Fergus, not Sean."

"That doesn't change my loyalty to the family."

I watch Deklan out of the corner of my eye, wondering why he can't see reality. Sean is insane and needs to occupy the room next to his mother's, but Deklan won't admit it. Even Sean's own sister sees it, but my husband can't. He can't see past his loyalty to Sean's father.

Where does that leave me?

"You really would do anything for them, wouldn't you?"

"I would. I *have*."

"You've killed people for them. For *him*."

Deklan stares straight ahead, ignoring my question. Maybe he thinks it's rhetorical. Maybe he realizes there is another question that comes afterward. It was the same question Sean asked him in the back room.

Would Deklan let Sean have me if Sean insisted on it? What if he told Deklan to kill me? If it came down to his loyalty to the Foley family and his loyalty to me, which one would he choose?

Do I want to know the answer?

I'm silent the rest of the way home. It seems like this day has gone on forever, and all I want to do is go to sleep and forget about all of it. When we get back to the apartment, Deklan asks what we should make for dinner, but I just shrug. I'm not hungry.

"Kera, what's wrong?"

"Nothing. I'm fine." I walk over to the couch and turn on the television. I don't even bother to change the channel, I just stare at whatever show pops up until Deklan grabs the remote and turns the TV off.

"I hate that you know," he says.

"What?"

"You saying everything is fine when it's obviously not." He sits next to me and reaches for my hand. "Is this about what you overheard?"

I think about all the obnoxious and borderline threatening things Sean has said to me. I've managed to ignore them for long enough, so why is what he said to Deklan so much worse? Is it because Deklan heard it but isn't going to do anything about it? Or is it because Sean is that much closer to making good on his threats?

There are too many reasons, and they are weighing me down. I can't think straight. When Deklan starts rubbing at my wrist, I realize the last thing I want right now is his comfort.

I pull my hand away from him and stand up. My whole body is tight, and my eyes are starting to burn. I turn away from Deklan and walk swiftly to the bathroom, locking the door behind me.

"Seriously, Kera? Are you really locking yourself in the bathroom instead of talking to me?"

I don't answer. I have no idea what to say, and I want to just forget it all—pretend it never happened. Something inside my head made me forget the kidnapping for years. Why can't I do that at will?

I drop onto the closed toilet, and my phone falls out of my pocket and onto the floor. It's still on, but Kathy is gone, and I have no one to call. I depress the power switch, and tears fall as the phone turns off.

"Are you going to make me break this door down?"

I wonder if he would really do it and decide he probably would. I don't want to deal with a broken door reminding me of this day, so I wipe the tears off my face and open it. I don't look at Deklan as I move past him and into the bedroom.

He follows me.

"Are you going to talk to me?" he asks.

"No." I reach into a dresser drawer and pull out pajamas. I start to head back to the bathroom when Deklan grabs my arm.

"Is that how you cope with shit?" he asks. "Just ignore it?

I look down at Deklan's fingers wrapped around my arm. For a moment, I feel other hands grabbing at me. I see the inside of a windowless van before things go dark inside my head, and my focus is back on my husband's grip.

"Well, I'm married to a murderer," I say simply, "so what else am I supposed to do?"

Deklan goes still for a moment, but I just keep staring at his hand on my arm.

"Don't you dare judge what I do." Deklan's voice is quiet and almost monotone, but I can hear the anger behind it.

For once, I don't care.

I shake my arm out of his grasp and turn toward him, throw the pajamas on the floor, and face him with my hands on my hips. I have to tilt my head to glare into his eyes.

"Then don't you dare judge how I choose to cope!"

His eyes widen, and he takes a step back as if my words punched him in the gut. I back away from him, my voice rising.

"You'll take his side over mine, won't you?"

"Whose side?" Deklan shakes his head in confusion. "Sean's?"

"Who else?" I step closer to him but not close enough to touch. "Are you going to do it, Dek? Are you going to give me to him?"

"Kera, he's not serious about that."

"He is. He's told me as much."

"What?"

I don't reply.

"Kera, you're my wife..." Deklan starts to reach for me but stops before making contact.

"So? I'm only your wife because he told you to marry me. It's his ring I have on my finger, so I suppose he can have me whenever he wants!"

Deklan stills and stares at me for a moment.

"What do you mean, 'it's his ring'?"

"He told me. One of the times he was harassing me, he told me he bought this ring for me, not you."

Deklan closes the gap between us and grabs both of my hands. He leans down a little and looks into my eyes as he speaks.

"What has he said to you? When have you even seen him when I wasn't around?"

"It doesn't matter." I shake my head and try to push away, but Deklan holds fast.

"Kera, do not make me ask again. What has Sean said to you before?"

"Just…a lot of similar, suggestive stuff."

"When?"

"A few times."

"I swear to God, if you don't stop being so vague, I'm going to end up punching a hole in the wall."

"I don't know where to start!" I finally say. "The first time was at the wedding reception. Then he came into the coffee shop. A couple of times at his house. Whenever I'm around him and you're not, he says something."

"He came to the coffee shop?"

"Yeah, when I first started working there."

"How did he even know you had a job there?"

"I thought you must have told him."

"I didn't. What did he say to you at the coffee shop?"

"He just…scared me."

"How? What did he say about the ring? Give me the damn details, Kera!"

"He grabbed my arm, and he said he bought my wedding ring. He said that he picked it out for me."

"Motherfucker."

"I figured that was true. I understand. It's not like you had time to go shopping. I would have figured it out myself eventually."

"He still shouldn't have told you that."

"There are a lot of things he shouldn't have said to me."

"Come here." Deklan pulls me close to him before leading me to the edge of the bed. We both sit, and he strokes the side of my face. "I would never let him touch you—you have to know that. I love you, and I wouldn't let anyone hurt you, not even Sean."

I want to believe him, but I'm not sure I can trust his words. When it comes right down to it, if Deklan has to make a choice, I'm not sure which way he will go.

"Please, Kera." "I'll keep you away from him," Deklan says. "I swear I will. You will always be at my side, and you will never be alone with him again."

"Do you think that will stop him?"

"Yes, I do." He hugs me to his chest. "If it doesn't, and he says something to you in front of me, I'll take care of it."

"What does that mean?"

"I will make it clear that I won't put up with that."

"He might not listen."

"Let me worry about that if the time comes."

"Maybe I should just stay away from the Foley place completely."

"No, it will be easier for me if you are close by. Working for the family is a good thing for you, and Teagan approves. That's important. Besides, you were right about needing a job. I can't keep you locked up here under twenty-four hour guard even though it is tempting sometimes."

I press my head to Deklan's chest, finally letting myself be comforted by him. I want to believe everything he says. I need to believe it all. If I don't, I'll go as mad as Sean already is.

"Please don't be angry with me." Deklan runs his hand over my back.

"I'm not," I say quietly. "Not really."

"You're scared."

"Yes."

"I am, too."

I'm startled by this admission, and I lean back to look into his eyes. He is scared. I can see it all over his face as he strokes my cheek, but I don't know if he's scared for me or for himself—maybe both.

"I need you," Deklan says. "Everything's falling apart around me, and you're the only thing I have left to hold onto that makes any sense."

Chapter 35

Gentle rain patters on the pavement as Deklan and I enter the Foley mansion, wipe our feet, and head to the study. Teagan is waiting for me. She's going to show me the rest of the accounting software today. As we work, Deklan, Sean, and Brian talk quietly off in the corner. I can't hear them, and Deklan didn't give me any idea why they are meeting today.

"The numbers here update another spreadsheet," Teagan says. "I know it seems complicated, but once you figure out how they tie together, it will all make sense. It's actually pretty easy to run the numbers when you need to."

"It seems pretty straightforward," I say. I flip from one spreadsheet to another. "I'd like to get a look at the backend database. I think I could learn faster if I did."

"You fancy yourself a database girl?" Teagan smiles. She obviously loves her tech, and I think she appreciates having another technical person around. "I'll give you access, but it will be read-only so you don't have to worry about fucking it up."

"Cool. I just want to look at the structure and relationships."

Teagan shows me the database and then joins her brother and the rest of the guys. Deklan comes over a few minutes later.

"We've got some business," he says. He doesn't make eye contact with me, and I'm not about to ask him where he's going or what he's going to do. "I don't like the idea of leaving you here, but Sean will be with me, and Teagan is in the house if you need anything. Are you going to be all right?"

"I'll be fine. I'm still learning the system, and I need alone time with the computer to get the hang of it."

"I don't know how long we'll be gone. It might be a while."

"I'm fine, Deklan, really." I am, too. As long as Sean is with Deklan, he can't bother me. "I've got plenty of work to keep me busy."

"Okay." Deklan takes my chin between his fingers and kisses me lightly. "I'll be back as soon as I can."

I glance over and see Sean watching us with narrowed eyes. I shiver slightly. Deklan glances over his shoulder and then looks back at me.

"Love you, babe," he says loud enough for anyone in the room to hear.

"I love you, too." My voice isn't as loud but probably still audible enough. Deklan smiles and kisses me once more.

All the men leave. Teagan heads into another part of the house, and I go back to my work. Teagan comes into the room once or twice to answer questions, but for the most part, I am on my own for the afternoon. I'm finally getting the hang of the spreadsheets and how they interconnect, and it's nice to have something to focus on for a while.

I'm also getting an interesting view of the Foley family enterprise. Between racing and stud services, the horses are a major source of legitimate income as are the investment firms and a chain of delicatessens. Interestingly enough, I see funds set aside to buy out a list of car wash facilities, one of which is owned by my father.

Out of curiosity, I look at the plans for future business acquisitions and notice that most of my father's businesses are on the lists of places to be purchased. In fact, some of them have already transferred ownership.

Is this my Dad's way of getting into the family?

I remember Deklan's response to my father's involvement in my kidnapping, and I'm sure he wouldn't allow my father to profit from business sales. I check the numbers, but I don't know if the offers are high or low.

I shake my head. I don't want to think about my father.

As early evening approaches, it starts to rain harder. Thunder rattles the windows, and the lights flicker before going off altogether. The power outage only lasts a couple of minutes, and I'm grateful for the laptop's battery. I've lost my connection to the database, but at least I haven't lost any work.

When the lights come back on, I can't get the damn laptop to connect to the Wi-Fi and eventually give up. Before the power went out, I was really close to being done with the last task Teagan gave me for the day, and I want to finish. I know there has to be another computer around here, so I head into the room behind the office where Deklan and Sean hold their conferences.

I see a laptop on a desk facing the far wall. The computer is still illuminated from whoever might have used it last. I'm surprised to find that it's not password protected, and I wonder if I will even be able to access the server.

There's a thick cable coming from the floor under the desk, and I see the laptop has a wired connection to the server, which is perfect. It's not at all secure, and I make a mental note to talk to Teagan about security in general.

I look at the icons on the desktop, hoping to find the software I need, but the icon isn't there. I start to browse through the files to find the right program but stop when I see a folder with my name on it.

I can't help it—I double-click the folder to open it.

There are pictures inside. Nothing too interesting—mostly pictures of me working at the coffee shop and a few from the wedding reception. Still, a creepy feeling runs up my arms as if I've just walked through a spider's web. I assume these are pictures that Charlie Grange took while he was spying on me. Looking at them leaves a bad taste in my mouth.

I'm about to close the folder when I see that one of the files is a video. The preview image is dark, and I can't make out what's in the frame.

Only one way to find out.

My hand shakes as I press the play button.

The video has obviously been taken on someone's phone. I recognize the hallway immediately—it's the one leading up to the apartment where Deklan and I live. The video jumps around to the rhythm of soft footsteps before it stops at the door to our apartment. A man's hand reaches out and fits a key into the locks—first the deadbolt and then the doorknob.

Inside, the apartment is dark. The video shifts to the kitchen and then the hallway to the bedroom. A moment later, I see myself lying on the bed with my arms wrapped around Deklan's pillow. The image focuses on my sleeping face and bare shoulders for a moment before the hand returns, grips the top of the sheet and blanket, and slowly pulls it away from my nude body.

"Oh, God," I whisper. I know instantly when the video was taken. I remember waking up in the middle of the night, blankets on the floor, and hearing the front door shut. "It was him."

"Kera, Kera, Kera." I recognize Sean's voice on the video. "So fucking gorgeous."

The image pans back and forth over my body as my heart begins to pound. I watch Sean's hand reach out again. He touches my shoulder lightly with his fingertip and then moves lower, circling one of my nipples. It hardens as he touches it, and a wave of nausea hits me hard.

"Should I just fuck you right now? Have you wake up with my cock buried inside of you? Would you cry? I'd fucking love it if you cried."

I can taste bile in my throat, and I have to swallow hard.

"Deklan won't like the idea of sharing. Someday, though—someday he's going to screw up. He'll beg for my forgiveness and offer you up to me. Then I'm going to make him watch."

I cover my mouth with my hand as my stomach turns. I swallow again and again just to keep from throwing up. My head starts to pound along with my heart as I stare at the screen.

He's touching me. He's touching me. He's touching me.

"What the everloving fuck is that?"

I startle, nearly scream, and swivel in the chair to see Deklan standing over my shoulder, staring at the screen with wide eyes and his hands balled into fists. He turns his glare at me, but as soon as he sees my face, he closes his eyes. He turns his head away for a moment, gritting his teeth and flexing his arms.

He takes in a long breath before he looks at me softly. He reaches out and brushes a tear from my cheek.

"Show it to me," Deklan says quietly.

"What?"

"Go back." Deklan turns the chair so I'm facing the computer again and then places his hand on my shoulder, rubbing gently. "Go back to the beginning. I want to see it all."

I swallow hard before I drag the cursor over the screen to bring the video back to the beginning. It starts up again, and the nausea comes back. I can't watch, so I look down at the keyboard instead. I can still hear Sean's words though, and they echo in my head even after the video ends.

Deklan turns the chair until I'm facing him again. He drops to one knee and takes my face in his hands.

"You said you had a dream. You said you woke up and thought someone was there, but you thought it was just a dream."

"I thought it was."

"He…he was there, in our apartment." I'm not sure if he's asking a question or not. Deklan closes his eyes and shifts his head away. "You never knew?"

"I didn't know." Tears continue to fall down my cheeks, and Deklan wipes them away with his thumb. "How could I have known?"

Deklan closes his eyes and grits his teeth again.

"Teagan was right," he whispers. "I have been blind to all this. I've been blind to *him*. Other than Brian, he is the only other person who knows about the new place. He has a key, too."

Deklan takes out his phone. His hand is shaking as he punches in a number.

"Brian?" he says. "Gather everyone together—Teagan and Mac, too. Everyone but Sean. I'll meet you in an hour."

Deklan shoves the phone back in his pocket, rubs his eyes with his hand, and then turns to me. He leans over and takes my face in his hands and speaks his words slowly.

"This ends now."

Chapter 36

At the warehouse, everyone has gathered. Teagan sits on top of the desk, configuring her new phone. Brian and Mac sit next to one another at a folding card table, mumbling too quietly for me to catch their words. They go quiet as Deklan and I take our seats across from them. Lucas is the last one to arrive. When he takes a seat at the table, they all look at Deklan.

"We have a problem," he says.

"We've had one for a while now," Teagan replies. "I'm glad to see you're finally willing to recognize it."

"Well, I had a bit of an eye-opener." Deklan watches me closely as he tells everyone about the video I found on Sean's laptop.

I glance at Brian as Deklan relates the details of the video. His face has gone completely white, and it's clear he knows exactly what night this occurred. He glances up at me for a second, and it looks as though he's about to cry.

"It's my fault," he says. He clears his throat and then looks at Deklan, repeating the words louder. "It's all my fault, Dek. I never should have—"

"It's Sean's fault," Deklan says. He looks sternly at Brian. "He's violated my wife, and it's not going to happen again."

Brian leans forward with his arms across his knees. He looks like he's about to vomit.

"Let me be clear to all of you, but especially you, Teagan. This family has been my life for a long time. Kera is now a part of that, and any affront to her is an affront to the family. I don't claim the Foley name, but—"

"Dek, I've never given a shit about what your last name is." Tegan scowls at him.

"I know." Deklan nods and gives her a quick smile. "I just want to be clear that this isn't all about me or my wife. Sean killed his own flesh and blood. Most of you were there when he did it."

"You're talking treason, boss," Mac says quietly. "Are we really going there?"

"I'm open to suggestions," Teagan says, "but I don't know what other choice we have."

"Teagan is on our side, and Neil is dead," Deklan says. "Sean is the only other Foley left, and my loyalty to him is broken. One thing Sean is right about—no one just walks away from this."

"He killed a member of the family." Teagan's usually stoic face goes pale for a moment, and her lips press together. "Neil was our cousin. No matter what else has happened, we don't kill one of our own."

I feel the color drain from my own face as I recall Sean's words at our wedding reception.

"I'd say next time he'll know better than to drink anything I've mixed for him, but it's kinda late for that."

"Deklan?" I whisper as I touch his arm. "I need to tell you something."

"What is it?"

I bite down on my lip. I don't want to cry in front of all of these people, but tears threaten to fall anyway. I should have told Deklan about this a long time ago, and I have no idea how he will react when he hears what I have to say.

"Something Sean said to me." I swallow hard, trying to figure out the right words to say. "Right after we were married, Sean came up to me. He said he never had any intention of marrying me, and that his father was just trying to control him."

I pause and glance around the room at all the faces staring back at me. Deklan grips my hand for a moment.

"He...he told me that he made a drink for his father right before he died."

"Kera, what are you trying to say?" Deklan tilts his head toward me. "Sean made drinks all the time."

"It was the way he said it." I'm not making my point, but I don't want to just come out and say it. Even as the words form in my head, I realize it's all speculation. "I...I think he meant he poisoned him."

"Oh, fuck." Teagan sucks in a breath, and Deklan turns toward her. "He was asking about poisons just a month before then. He specifically asked about ones that could be mixed into drinks without detection."

The room goes silent as everyone looks around for everyone else's reactions. Teagan squares her shoulders, and her expression goes blank as she focuses on my husband. Deklan abruptly shoves himself out of the chair and heads straight for the warehouse door. He slams it behind him as he leaves.

"Should I go after him?" Brian asks.

"No, Kera should." Teagan looks at me. "We can't delay this any longer."

I stand on wobbly legs and follow Deklan's path out the door and into the aisle between the storage containers. Deklan is leaning against one of them, vomiting on the ground.

"Dek?" I approach slowly and place my hand on his shoulder.

"He...he killed Fergus. Oh, God! How could he...?" He doubles over with his eyes squeezed shut but doesn't throw up again. "Why didn't you tell me before?"

"I swear, Deklan—I didn't really put it all together. I suspected, but it seems like so long ago, and so much has happened since then. I'm sorry. I should have told you."

Deklan stands up straight and leans his back against the side of the storage container. He stares up at the sky and blinks a few times before wiping his mouth on his sleeve and looking back to me.

"No more," Deklan says. "No more secrets. We tell each other everything. Everything!"

I nod, and Deklan's brow furrows as he speaks.

"Your father is dead," he tells me. "I killed him myself while you were working earlier today. I'm going to take care of your mother though. She didn't know anything about your kidnapping. She'll retain ownership of two of the legitimate businesses, and that should be enough to keep her going. You don't have to worry about her."

I take in this information and try to run it through my head, waiting for myself to react, but I only feel numb. I should feel something. I *want* to feel something, but I don't.

"What did you do with him?"

"Do you really want that level of detail? I'll tell you if you really want to know."

I shake my head as various options run through my head. He's right—I don't want to know the specifics. Knowing he is dead is enough for me.

"I'm glad my mom will be okay," I finally say.

"Grange is still alive. Once we figure out what happens next, we'll decide what to do with him."

I nod, and we walk together back into the warehouse to sit back down with the group. Teagan and Brian both watch Deklan carefully as he settles himself down, takes a few breaths, and then starts talking.

"Sean has to go."

Teagan closes her eyes and nods.

"He killed Fergus," Deklan says. "He betrayed Neil, set him up, and then killed him for it. He broke into my apartment and took video of my wife sleeping. The Foley family has been everything to me, and it still is, but that doesn't change the facts. Sean is unstable, and he's now a threat to the business and all of us."

"You know I'm behind ya, Dek," Brian says. "Whatever needs to be done, I'm with ya."

"What are you saying, boss?" Mac asks. "I mean, what are you really saying here?"

"This has to end," Teagan says as she looks at Mac. "We are out of options. Sean dies. The only remaining question is how to do it."

"Hold on a sec," Lucas says as he closes his briefcase and stands. "I can't hear any more of this. I still need some aspect of plausible deniability."

"Bullshit," Deklan says as he glares at the attorney. "Attorney-client privilege, and as of right now, you work for Teagan. You aren't going anywhere."

Lucas licks his lips as he glances between Deklan and Teagan. Mac comes up behind him, and Lucas sits back down slowly.

"He killed my father," Teagan says quietly. "Would any of you have me forgive him for that? In my mind, he's already dead. The rest is a formality."

"Are we in agreement then?" Dek asks the group.

No one makes eye contact, but everyone nods.

"Who's gonna do it?" Brian asks.

All eyes turn to Deklan.

"It can't be you, Deklan," Teagan says. "Some of the older families still hold on to that code. If you kill your boss, they'll never let you take over."

"Who says I'm taking over?"

"Do you think I'm going to do it?" Teagan raises an eyebrow. "I'm just a bookkeeper. I don't want to run shit. Never have. Besides, this is about the most chauvinistic profession around. I would never be taken seriously. It has to be you."

"You're the only Foley left, Teagan. It's your family." Deklan shakes his head.

"And you will always follow a Foley," Teagan replies. "I don't care what Sean said—you're family. You've been around since I was a kid, and you were more of a brother to me than he ever was. If you want, we can go get your name changed."

Deklan stares at her for a long moment.

"Is this really what you want?" he asks. "I'm not asking for it. You do understand that."

Teagan nods.

"Our family is in trouble, Dek." Teagan reaches over and places her hand on his. "I need you to step up and take over the business when Sean is gone."

"Yeah, you're already the boss as far as I'm concerned," Brian says. "You know Mac agrees."

"Do I need to do it?" Mac asks. "I'll do it if you ask me to, Dek."

"If one of us takes him out, there will be no end to it," Brian says.

"It can't be either of you," Teagan says. "It can't look like treason, or the other families will rebel. We have to find someone else."

"No," Deklan says. He leans forward and presses his fingers into his eye sockets. "I won't chance this on an outsider."

"I have an idea," Teagan says. "You might not like—"

"I'll take care of it," Deklan says quietly. He doesn't take his hand away from his eyes.

"Not you, Dek," Teagan says. "You can't—"

"I said, I'll take care of it!" Deklan drops his hand and stares at her hard. "You want to put me in charge? Fine, but you'll live by my decisions."

Teagan takes a half step back and then smiles.

"Whatever you say, boss."

Deklan rolls his eyes and pushes himself away from the table.

"I'm going to need to think about this for a while. Let's meet back here in the morning."

Lucas, who hasn't said a word throughout any of this, starts to stand.

"Where are you going?" Deklan asks.

"I was going to go back to my office," Lucas says.

"Not on your own." Deklan looks over to Mac. "I want you with him until this is over."

"Sure, boss."

"Whatever for?" Lucas asks.

"It's for your own protection," Deklan says.

"Protection from whom?" Lucas narrows his eyes. "Do you think Sean will be after me next? I can assure you that he would not do that."

"No," Deklan says, "it's protection from me, because if I find out you talked to Sean and told him what we were planning, I'd have to make sure you suffer. Mac will make sure that doesn't happen. Now you sit tight until I've had a word with him.

Deklan takes Mac aside as Lucas sits back down. I can see the tension in his jaw as he stares straight at the briefcase on the table.

As Deklan has his conversation with Mac, I glance over at Teagan and Brian. They have also moved off to the side and are speaking quietly to one another. Brian nods slowly as he listens closely to Teagan's words. Curious, I get up from my chair and move toward them.

"Take this," Teagan says as she slips a piece of paper to Brian. "Call him. Get it all arranged. We're going to need the backup, and I don't care what he charges."

"You got it."

I narrow my eyes at her as I step closer. Teagan gives Brian a little push on the shoulder and tells him to get going. As he heads toward the door, he glances back at me over his shoulder with an indiscernible expression.

"What was that all about?" I ask.

Teagan pauses for a moment before answering.

"It's always good to have a Plan B."

Chapter 37

I'm pressed up against the kitchen counter. We've been in the apartment about nine seconds, but Deklan's hands and lips are all over me.

"I need you." His words warm my ear, but his pleading tone and frantic hands set me on edge. "Please, Kera."

"Yes," I whisper.

He yanks my shirt up over my head and then kisses from my neck to my shoulder as he pulls at the button on my jeans. I place my hands on his shoulders for support as he yanks my jeans down my legs.

He's been like this before—a sudden, overwhelming need to be inside of me consumes him, and all I can do is give myself to him completely.

Leaving my clothing on the floor in the kitchen, Deklan hauls me into the bedroom and throws me on the mattress as he nearly tears his shirt and pants off. He's on top of me a moment later and inside of me a moment after that. I gasp and tighten my fingers on his arms as he enters—I'm not quite ready to take him in. He leans his forehead against my shoulder and stills himself. His light kisses against my skin apologize for the roughness of his strokes.

His breaths are labored and accompanied by rhythmic grunts that match my own. I'm bouncing wildly on the bed, and I can't steady myself enough to get my legs around him to hold on better. I give up, lay back, and just let him fuck me.

He needs it. I need it. It's the only way to stop thinking about everything else that's happening.

I try to relax, but he's going so deep, it almost hurts. It's a good hurt—a deep and overwhelming feeling of being wanted, needed, desired. I feel my stomach quiver, and it sends a shockwave through my legs. I press my thighs against his hips as the cascade of sensation hits me, and I cry out.

He slows for a moment, adjusts his hand on my hip, and begins to pull me to him with each thrust. With a loud cry, he buries himself and fills me.

Deklan's hands and arms tremble, and he collapses on top of me. I take the weight and wrap my arms around him, holding his head to my shoulder. After a moment, he rolls off, and I gasp again as his cock slips from me. I'm going to be sore tomorrow.

He lies on his back with one arm under his head, staring at the ceiling. His breathing has returned to normal, but his jaw is still tight.

"Are you all right?" I ask softly. I lay my head against his shoulder and look at his face, but he doesn't turn toward me.

"No," Deklan says, "not really."

"I'm sorry."

"It's not your fault." Deklan slides his arm under my shoulders and pulls me closer. His chest rises as he takes in a deep breath. "Teag is right—I've been blind to Sean's behavior. I didn't want to see it and acknowledge it for what it is. I kept thinking he was just...just...I don't know. Getting his bearings, I guess. Learning to run the family business. I feel like an idiot, and I put you in danger. I'm not sure I can forgive myself for that."

"I don't blame you." I snuggle against his chest and wrap my arm around his waist. "I should have told you what he said to me before now."

"Fergus was fine the day before he went into the hospital," Deklan says. "Even when he said he was going to see the doctor, he told me he thought the clams he'd had the night before must have been off and that he'd be fine. The next thing I knew, he was gone. I should have seen it. He had always been in peak health. I should have realized something wasn't right."

"How old was he?"

"Sixty-four. Too young."

We lie together quietly as the room darkens with the setting sun. I can tell Deklan isn't sleeping, but he doesn't seem to want to talk, and I'm all right with that. I don't know what to say.

After an hour of just lying there, Deklan pulls his arm out from under me and gets out of bed. I watch him walk out the bedroom door, assuming he's going to pee, but he bypasses the bathroom and disappears down the hallway. After a few minutes, I follow.

Deklan's standing on the small balcony of the apartment, leaning against the rail and staring at the street below. The sliding door is still open, so I walk up quietly, slip my arms around his waist, and rest the side of my head against his back.

"I wish I had some weed." Deklan chuckles through his nose.

"You smoke weed?"

"Not for a while, but I have." He glances at me briefly before looking back down at the street. "Usually being with you is enough, but right now, I could use something else to relax me."

"I'm sorry."

"Don't apologize." He turns and wraps his arms around me. "I'm grateful you put up with me when I'm like that. I don't mean to take my frustration out on you, but you take it anyway even when I'm a little too rough."

"I don't mind." I smile up at him. "I kinda like it, really."

"Do you now?" Deklan raises an eyebrow.

"Yes." I can feel myself blushing. I look away and off to the buildings in the distance.

"I owe you a nice, long bath," he says. "I'll even throw in bubbles."

"I'd like that, too."

"It will be all about you," he says as he places his hand on my cheek and turns my head to face him. "Warm water, massage, and at least three orgasms."

"You'll have to warm up the water a few times if you are going to keep me in there that long." I giggle.

"Done." He kisses me softly and strokes his finger across my cheek. "I really don't know if I could cope with all of this if you weren't here."

"It probably wouldn't be happening if it weren't for me."

"Not true." Deklan shakes his head. "I'm finally seeing that. You are the excuse, but not the reason. Sean's crazy, and he would have made this happen with or without you. He would have found a reason to kill his father and take over the business early even if you were never part of the equation. I don't know if he's hungry for the power, the money, or if he's just plain nuts, but don't ever blame yourself."

I nod and try to believe his words. It's difficult not to feel responsible, but I also agree with him. Sean is crazy. He will always find a reason to justify whatever he does.

"Are you really going to take over the Foley business?" I ask.

"It's what Teagan wants," Deklan says with a shrug. "I never had any plans to do this, but if this is what she wants, I'll do it. If she ever changes her mind, I'll give it back. I want to do what Fergus would have wanted, and I think he'd want it to go to her."

"It sounds like he thought of you as a son as well."

"I don't know. Teagan might think of me as a brother, but I only worked for her father."

"You were important to him."

"I got the job done."

"From what Teagan said, it seems like it was more than that."

Deklan licks his lips and stares up at the sky. It's a clear night, and though there is a lot of light pollution, a few stars can be seen, and the moon is full and bright. Deklan focuses on the moon for a moment before he speaks.

"I barely remember my own father," he says quietly. "The only picture I have is the one used in the article about the break-in and murders. Sometimes, when I can't remember my dad's face, I have to look at that article."

"Can I see it?"

Deklan looks at me for a long moment before nodding. We go back inside, and Deklan pulls a small box from the top of the bedroom closet. Inside the box is the faded newsprint article about the Kearney family deaths.

I swallow hard as I look at the picture under the headline. It must have been taken for a Christmas card—everyone is dressed up. Four-year-old Deklan is in a tiny suit and bowtie, and he smiles up at the camera like the world is full of puppies and rainbows.

"Don't cry," Deklan says softly.

"I can't help it." I wipe the tears from my eyes and sniff as I hand the article back to him. "You look so happy."

"I remember *being* happy." Dek places the article back in the box and the box back on the shelf in the closet. "All those memories are pretty vague now though. I think the next time I felt happy was when Fergus asked me to work for him."

"And he became your surrogate father."

"I suppose so."

"You loved him." I tilt my head and watch his expression. He closes his eyes for a moment and presses his lips together.

"Yeah," he finally says, "I did."

"And you are going to take care of the person who killed him, regardless of who it is, and you're going to take care of his business as he would have wanted you to."

Deklan looks at me, blinks a few times, and then smiles.

"You're right," he says. "That's exactly what I'm going to do."

Chapter 38

"No." Deklan's tone is low, but he slams his palm against the table. "Kera isn't going to be anywhere near this."

"She won't still be there when it goes down," Teagan says. "Mac will drive Sean to make sure they're far enough behind us. We cross paths at the intersection and switch passengers—Kera will be with me, and Brian will be with you. Mac and Sean follow you to the secondary warehouse. Sean won't even know she's not with you anymore."

"We'll have about thirty seconds," Brian says.

"That's not much time."

Teagan glances at Brian, and he nods very slightly.

"It's enough time," Teagan says. "If Lucas did his job right, Sean is focused on all the acquisition stuff right now, which is a good distraction.

"He is," Lucas says with a scowl.

"Yeah, Lucas gave him a whole stack of papers," Mac says. "It's enough to keep him occupied until Christmas."

"We don't need that long." Deklan says. "We also don't need Kera there at all."

"She's supposed to be there, Dek." Teagan sighs and reaches across the table to touch Deklan's arm. "She sets Sean off just by being in the room. If she's not there, he might not take the bait. With her in the room, there is no chance he will back down. He has to show his authority over you in front of her—he can't help himself. That's what we need."

Deklan closes his eyes and presses his lips together, but he knows what Teagan is saying makes sense.

"It's all right, Dek," I tell him. "I'll be fine."

"Going to deal with Grange at the last minute will take him by surprise," Mac says. "He'll be pissed off that it wasn't already done, and that should keep him focused."

"I don't like it." Deklan leans back in the chair and folds his arms over his chest.

"I think it's the best option," Teagan says. "Sean will insist on going when Grange is released. He doesn't trust you not to kill the guy."

Deklan glances over at me and narrows his eyes. I nod at him. I'm okay with the plan Teagan and Brian have concocted even if I do have to go back to that house and be near the man who broke into my apartment and videotaped me sleeping naked. By the time it's all over, Sean will be dead, and I'll never have to worry about him again.

"Are you sure?" Deklan asks me.

"Yes." I nod more emphatically. "Whatever risk there is, it will be worth it."

Deklan rubs his chin with his hand before he looks back at Teagan.

"Let's go over it all again from the top," he says. "I want to make sure everyone gets it right."

*****

"I'm gonna go release Grange."

Despite how calmly Deklan says the words, I can't help how my body tenses. I bite my lip and look up from the computer screen on the desk toward Sean. He's seated on the opposite side of the room at the larger, grander desk. Mac is on the couch, twirling a toothpick between his fingers.

Deklan's words are supposed to set everything off.

"What?" Sean tilts his head and glares in Deklan's direction. "I told you to do that days ago."

"I haven't gotten around to it," Deklan says with a shrug. "It's okay—Brian has been feeding him. Come on, Kera."

I close out the spreadsheet and stand slowly, watching Sean's every move as he continues to glare at the back of Deklan's head. As I glance between them, I can see the vein in Sean's temple starting to pulse just before he slams his fists down on the desk and stands.

"When I tell you to do something, you fucking do it!" he yells.

Deklan looks over his shoulder at Sean in mock surprise.

"Sorry, boss," he says. "I didn't realize you wanted it done right away. I figured it would be good for him to stay locked up a while longer—teach him a lesson. Hell, he could probably use a few more days of it."

Sean stalks over and looks up into Deklan's face, apparently unfazed by my husband's size. Sean points his finger at Deklan's nose.

"You do what I say when I say to do it," Sean says with a growl. "The hired help doesn't get to assume anything!"

Deklan takes a slow, calculated breath.

"I'll do it today," he says.

"You'll do it now."

"Kera and I have dinner reservations," Deklan says. "He can wait a little longer."

"Am I somehow not being clear?" Sean leans back on his heels as his eyes sparkle with fake charm. "Gee, I'm sorry about that. I guess I'm not making my point."

Deklan doesn't move or say anything, but his shoulders and chest are tensed as if he's waiting for a blow.

"You're going to do it now," Sean says, still smiling. "In fact, I'm going to go with you just to make sure you don't fuck it up."

"That isn't necessary," Deklan says. "I'll take care of it now. I just need to run Kera home first."

"Fuck that." Sean turns his syrupy smile on me. "Kera can go with us."

"I'm going to take care of it for you, boss," Deklan says again. "There isn't much of a back seat in the Viper."

"I'm going, and so is she," Sean says again. "I didn't ask you to give me suggestions."

"I can drive ya, boss," Mac says. "That way everyone's comfortable."

"There ya go," Sean says with another smile. "No more bullshit excuses. We leave now."

I'm doing my best not to tremble as I follow the three of them out of the office and to the front door. Deklan and I head outside to the Viper, and Mac heads toward the driver's side of Sean's BMW with Sean close behind.

I can't believe how well this has worked so far. Sean is behaving exactly as Teagan said he would, and the plan is in full swing. Now I just need to make it to the intersection where Brian and I will switch places. Once Brian and Deklan get to the secondary warehouse where Grange is being held, Deklan will take out Sean.

We slip into Deklan's car, and I realize that within an hour, it could all be over.

"Fuck you!" From Deklan's open window, I hear Sean yelling at Mac. "I'm driving."

Mac looks up at Deklan with wide eyes as Sean takes the keys out of his hand and shoves him toward the passenger side of the car. Deklan gives him a slow nod, and Mac drops into the passenger seat.

"What do we do now?" I ask softly.

"It'll work out," Deklan says, but he's not convincing. "You might just have to move a little faster if he stays close to me."

We pull around the circular driveway with Sean driving Mac's car directly behind us. As we get to the end of the drive and turn onto the street, Sean isn't just following behind us; he's right on Deklan's bumper.

Deklan reaches into his pocket and slowly pulls out his phone.

"Keep the phone in your lap and text Teagan. Tell her Sean's driving."

"Okay." I do as I'm told. A few second later, Teagan replies, and I read her message out loud to Deklan. "She says, 'Two choices—lose him or we meet you there.'"

"If I try to lose him, he's going to go apeshit. Any element of surprise will be lost."

"Should I tell her to meet us there?"

"Not sure we have a choice."

I type the message. Teagan doesn't respond, but I assume she understands. Deklan increases his speed a little, but Sean is still right up behind us.

Deklan reaches over and gives my hand a squeeze. His expression is grave.

"Stay close to me," he says. "When possible, make sure I am between you and Sean. If that's not possible, get behind Brian. Understood?"

"Yes."

We arrive at the intersection where we were supposed to exchange passengers. I glance in the side mirror and see Mac's car, with Sean driving, looming close behind. As I read the words on the glass—"Objects in mirror are closer than they appear"—I'm reminded of that dinosaur movie from years ago. An image of the Tyrannosaurus Rex chasing the characters as they try to drive away fills my head, and I swallow hard.

"Where is this place?" I ask.

"Not far from here," Deklan says. "It's a basement warehouse off an alley. It's below a restaurant the Foley family owns. Since it's centrally located, we only use it when timing is important. It's in the middle of the city, and there are often people around. It's not as secure as the other place."

"Just stay in the car," Deklan says as he pulls up in front of a Thai restaurant and engages the parking break. "I'll be back before you know it, and we can—"

Deklan is interrupted by my door opening and Sean pulling me out of the car by my arm. I let out a surprised squeal, and Sean growls at me to shut up.

"Move!" Sean grips my arm and shoves me toward the alley.

I glance from Sean to the wide alley and the tall buildings of the city skyline beyond. A stench comes from the nearby dumpsters used by the restaurant, and I'm not sure if my stomach is rebelling at the smell or the man who has me by the arm.

I can hear Deklan's car door opening and closing, but the alley is full of potholes, and I'm being dragged too quickly to look back at him without tripping over one of them. Sean finally stops in the middle of the alley and stands near a set of large metal doors leading down to the basement of the restaurant. The doors are enclosed by an iron gate on either side and locked with a padlock and a thick chain.

Deklan stops only a few feet away, and Mac walks cautiously past him until he's closer to Sean's side. At the end of the alley, near the street, Brian appears from around the corner and heads in our direction.

"Sean," Deklan says in his calm, deadly voice, "let go of my wife."

"Fuck you!" Sean spits at the ground near Deklan's feet. "You know what, Kearney? I've had enough of your shit. I'm sick of you not obeying your orders and walking around like this is your business when it's not. You aren't a Foley—I am! It's time you understood that."

"I never claimed to be a Foley," Dek replies, his voice still calm, but his right hand is balled into a fist, "but Kera has nothing to do with any of this. Let her go."

"Yeah, boss," Brian says as he comes up behind Deklan, "Mrs. K doesn't need to be here."

"Shut the fuck up," Sean says. His grip on my arm tightens, and I grimace. "You think I don't know you're on his side?"

"Boss," Brian says as he takes a step forward, "I'm with ya all the way, but Mrs. K should go. I can call Teagan to come and get her if you like."

"I do *not* 'like,'" Sean says. He takes a step backward, pulling me roughly to his side as he moves. "This little bitch needs a lesson as much as you do, Kearney."

"Sean," Deklan says, his voice starting to reflect the look in his eyes, "let go of my wife right now."

Deklan steps forward and then stops suddenly, his eyes widening as I hear a sharp click near my ear.

I glance down. Sean has a large, black handgun pressed against the side of my head. Brian stops his advance and looks quickly between Deklan, Mac, and Sean. Mac takes a step away as Sean waves the gun at all three of them. I stumble as Sean moves us both away from the group and points the gun at my side.

I brace myself for the shot, but nothing happens. I want to run or fight, but I can't move—I'm completely paralyzed as tears start to fall down my cheeks.

"Please, Sean," I whisper, but he ignores me.

"Open the fucking door," Sean says to Deklan.

Deklan nods, holds his hands up passively, and then locates a key on his key ring. He crouches at the basement door and unlocks the padlock. He loops the lock over the iron gate and then pulls the chain from around the door handles before standing up and backing away again.

He stares into my eyes, but I don't understand the look in them. Does he want me to stay calm or to fight? What am I supposed to do now? Though there was talk of a couple alternative scenarios, this wasn't covered in the briefing with Teagan.

"Mac," Sean says, "go get Charlie."

Mac glances quickly at Deklan. Deklan gives him a quick nod, and Mac pulls open the doors and carefully navigates the stairs into the darkness below.

"Now, let me tell you how this is going to play out," Sean says with a wicked grin. "Charlie is going to come out here, and he's going to take your place as my bodyguard."

"That don't make no sense, boss," Brian says. "You know Dek's the best, and with everything we got coming up, you're going to need him."

Brian tilts his head and smiles at Sean, but I can see his hand slowly creeping towards his waist.

"I don't need him," Sean says. "In fact—I don't need you, either."

I see the flash before I feel Sean's arm jerk and hear the blast. Brian's eyes go wide. He looks at the gun in Sean's hand before glancing at Deklan. Brian opens his mouth to say something, but Sean levels the gun and shoots two more times, blowing holes in Brian's jacket and sending him flying backward and onto the ground. Sean turns the gun on Deklan, but Deklan is moving to Brian's side when the shot is fired.

I scream as Deklan crumples to the ground, grabbing his shoulder and landing just a few feet from Brian. Sean shoves me forward until we're right next to both men, and then he pushes me by the shoulder until I'm on my knees.

I cover my mouth with my hand as my gaze focuses on the blood seeping through Deklan's jacket. The shot must have gone through, since there's more blood on the back of his jacket than the front.

I shake my head in disbelief. This wasn't supposed to happen, and it's all happening too quickly for me to wrap my head around it. I have no idea what I should do.

Sean stands right next to me and points the barrel of the gun at Deklan head.

"I was his son!" Sean yells. "I was his only son, but you are the one he looked to. You are the one he talked about. You are the one he wanted to be his flesh and blood. You took everything from me, even the woman that was supposed to be my wife!"

Deklan's eyes go wide.

"You wanna kill me, boss?" Deklan rises up on his knees and tries to get between me and Sean, but Sean uses his foot to shove him backward. Deklan rights himself and looks back at Sean. "Fucking kill me if you want, but leave Kera out of it."

"Leave her out of it?" Sean laughs and looks up to the sky as his eyes dance in the sunlight. "This is all because of her! Don't you see that? She's the reason for everything! She's why Fergus had to die! She's why Neil had to die! She is the catalyst to everything that has happened to you!"

"You wanted this, boss," Deklan says. "Remember? You wanted me to marry her. This was your idea, and you're the one in charge. That's why I did it. I'm loyal to you, and so is Kera. You don't have to do this."

"No you aren't, and it's all her fault." Sean giggles for a moment, the sound reminding me of a schoolgirl. "She's your downfall, Deklan Kearney. Love killed you both."

He takes the gun and places it against my temple. I close my eyes, wishing I could somehow reach out and hold Deklan's hand when all of this comes to an end.

"Open your fucking eyes, bitch!" Sean screams.

I startle and bite down on my lip, drawing blood. I slowly open my eyes and look up to Sean's wild eyes as they sparkle with lightning and fire. I remember at one point, back when I was a teenager, how I stared at his picture on my nightstand and dreamed of the day I would be married to him.

How did we get here?

I stare up at that maniacal grin as the end of the gun presses into my skin, and the asphalt presses into my knees.

"How does it feel, Dek?" Sean asks slowly. "How does it feel to lose everything?"

Chapter 39

Sean laughs once more, still sounding like a young girl as he looks down at me, and his expression changes into a sneer. I watch the muscles in his shoulder and arm tense, and imagine the neurons firing from his brain, down his arm, and to his trigger finger.

Sean suddenly stops.

He stops speaking. He stops moving.

Blood begins to run out of his ear. I watch as the lightning storm in his eyes suddenly dims when he drops to the ground beside me.

A split-second later, there is a distant popping sound.

"Jesus." Deklan's breathy voice reaches my ears at the same time his left hand grabs me by my arm. He pulls me against his chest like a ragdoll. "Are you all right?"

I can't answer. I can barely keep from pissing myself as I stare at Sean's open, dead eyes. My stomach clenches and threatens to send my lunch all over the alley. I don't understand what my eyes are showing me. Am I dead? Did I miss the part where I got shot in the head? How is Sean lying lifeless on the ground before me?

Deklan shifts with a grunt and moves his hand to my face. He turns my head until I'm looking him in the eyes. I can see his mouth moving, but his words aren't making sense. Mac appears from the basement doors, gun drawn, and looks all around. He calls out to Deklan, and they both stare up into the city skyline. I follow Deklan's gaze, but there is nothing to be seen—just buildings.

"Dek?" I say as I finally find my voice. "What just happened?"

Before he can answer, there's a groan from beside us.

"Holy fuck!" Brian says as he rolls to his side. "That shit hurts!"

"Brian!" I reach out as I watch him blink up toward the sky.

"It's okay," Brian says with a smile. "I'm wearing a vest."

"Motherfucker," Deklan says with a grumble. "Who the hell gave you a vest?"

"Teagan." Brian looks up at the skyline above us and chuckles.

"Did she…?" Deklan shakes his head and glances upward again.

Brian grins at Deklan as he gets back on his feet and rubs his chest, still staring up at the buildings. Deklan helps me to my feet, and his eyes widen as he follows Brian's gaze. I do the same, but I see nothing. When I look back to my husband, there is understanding in his expression.

"You have some explaining to do later," Deklan says to Brian and then to Mac. "Both of you."

"I have no idea what's going on," Mac says. "I was trying to get a lock on him, but he was blocked by her, and I couldn't see. Where the hell did that shot come from?"

"There wasn't time to tell you about it before." Brian grins. "We ran out of options, and he's the only one who could do it."

I look back and forth, trying to understand what just happened.

"That dude is one hell of a shot!" Brian whistles. "I never even heard it! I wonder how far away he is."

"I don't know," Deklan mumbles as he glances at me. He only meets my eyes for a moment before he looks back at the ground.

Suddenly, I understand.

"It's that man, isn't it?" I glare at Deklan until he finally makes eye contact with me again. "The man who killed Kathy."

"Arden," Deklan says as he nods slowly. "In case it isn't clear, I wasn't consulted on this."

"Teagan swore she'd take the heat," Brian says with a shrug. "She's waiting over by the car."

Mac and Brian lead Deklan and me away from the body in the alley and back to the quiet street. Aside from a couple of homeless guys on the other side of the restaurant doors, no one is around, and no one seems to have noticed what just happened in the alley. If anyone did hear, they didn't care.

"I knew you couldn't do it, Dek," Teagan says as she leans against the Viper and gives Deklan a half smile. "I know you wanted to, and if it came down to Sean or your wife, you were going to choose your wife, but if you pulled the trigger on Fergus Foley's son, you'd never forgive yourself."

"You hired Arden? You and Brian?"

"Yes. After that kerfuffle with Kera's friend, you weren't going to consider him, but he was the best option. Besides, he offered. I don't think he cared much for Sean after the first time they met."

Deklan wraps his good arm around my shoulders and pulls me close to his side.

"I'm going to have to be consulted on this shit if I'm going to be in charge," Deklan says gruffly but then smiles. "Still, I'm glad to know you have my back."

"Always." Teagan looks at Deklan stoically. "My father meant the world to me, just as he did to you. Sean was right—he loved you more. He was your father, too."

Deklan takes a long breath and stares at the ground for a moment with closed eyes. He licks his lips, shifts his weight from one foot to the other, and then squeezes his eyes shut as he grunts in pain.

"We should get you to the hospital," Brian says as he moves closer and checks out Deklan's shoulder.

"No hospital," Deklan says. "It will just raise questions."

"The vet, then," Brian says. "You need stitches."

"Vet?" I ask.

"Yeah, there's a guy on the west side of town," Brian says to me. "He can do stitches."

"The bullet went clear through," Dek replies as he looks at Teagan. "It's not even bleeding that much. I can wait."

Brian opens up the trunk of the Viper and pulls out a first aid kit. Inside, there is rubbing alcohol and gauze for Deklan's shoulder.

"We need to get Arden his money," Teagan says. "He's waiting at the main warehouse. We can all get in your car, and Mac can use mine to clean up. It's got the trunk space."

"I'll call Andrew and the cleaning crew," Mac says. He pulls out his phone and walks back into the alley.

"I can't shift with my shoulder like this," Deklan says.

"I'm happy to make the sacrifice of driving your car for ya," Brian says with a big smile. He hands me the first aid stuff. "Kera can patch you up a bit on the way."

Deklan and I climb into the small back seats of the Viper—it's not easy considering Deklan's size and wound—and Teagan takes shotgun. While Brian drives, I do my best to use the gauze to stop the rest of the bleeding, which is minimal. I put some tape over the gauze to hold it in place, and Deklan pulls his jacket back on.

Brian pulls in near the warehouse. On the far side of the lot is a sleek, classic Camaro. As we get closer, I see a bumper sticker that once must have read Soccer Mom but is now partially ripped off.

"It will look better if *you* pay him off," Teagan says as she tosses a thick paper envelope into the backseat. "Start of a new relationship and all."

"I'm not doing business with him again." Deklan picks up the envelope and holds it in the palm of his hand, testing the weight. "How much?"

"Seventy-five."

Deklan shakes his head as he shoves the envelope into his pocket.

"We are going to need all the allies we can get." Teagan says. "Chicago is going to be a big part of that."

"She's right, boss." Brian turns around in his seat and looks back at Deklan.

"Let me out," Dek says with a heavy sigh.

Brian jumps out of the Viper and pulls the seat up so Deklan can exit. Deklan grunts as Brian grabs Deklan's good arm and helps him out. Teagan gets out of the car as well, angling the seat up for me.

"Come on, Kera," Deklan says when I don't move.

"You want me to go with you? I have nothing to say to him."

"He did save our asses, Mrs. K." Brian leans against the car, peers in at me, and grins. "Ya gotta give him that."

"Fuck him."

"Come on anyway." Deklan moves around the Viper and grabs my hand to haul me outside the car.

Brian and Teagan are close behind us as Deklan holds my hand and leads me across the empty lot. When we get close, Arden gets out of the Camaro and nods at us.

"Expectations met?" he asks simply.

"I'm still standing, and he isn't," Deklan says. "I would say expectations were exceeded."

Arden nods in acknowledgement.

"Holy shit, man!" Brian reaches out and shakes the bastard's hand. "I've never even heard of someone shooting like that! How far were you?"

"About seven hundred meters. Sky is clear and there isn't any wind today, which makes everything easier."

"Day-um!" Brian leans over a little to peer into the back of the Camaro. I can see a large black bag in the back, presumably concealing a rifle.

I fold my arms across my chest. I don't care if he did save our lives—I don't want to stand here and compliment Kathy's killer on his marksmanship.

Deklan hands the large envelope over to Arden.

"It's all there," Deklan says as Arden looks through the envelope. "Seventy-five large."

"Yeah, it's here." Arden looks at me for the first time.

"We all good then?" Deklan asks.

"Can I have a sec with your wife?"

Deklan looks at me.

"Sure." Deklan motions to Brian and Teagan. "Let's go. Kera, just come to the car when you're done."

I watch dumbfounded as the others walk back toward the Viper, leaving me alone with Evan Arden. I glare at him. I have nothing to say to this man.

"I'm not much for apologies," he says. "Not sure I've ever apologized for anything, really. I just wanted you to know that I misread the situation, and I'm sorry about that. I wouldn't have shot that girl if I'd known. I didn't even know Kearney was married."

"If you're looking for forgiveness, you aren't going to get it." I keep glaring.

"That's okay." He shrugs. It doesn't matter to him.

"Did Deklan put you up to this? Does he want me to play nice with you now so he can keep doing business with you?"

"Our business is done," Arden says. "I'll be back in Chicago before morning. And no, I didn't even ask him if I could talk to you beforehand. I know there's nothing I can say that could change what happened, but I want you to know I'd take it back if I could."

"You're right," I say. "This doesn't change anything."

I place my hands on my hips. I'm being a complete bitch, and I don't care. I don't want his apologies. Nothing he says will take away the image in my head of Kathy lying on the sidewalk.

Arden nods slowly as he runs his hand over his short, cropped hair.

"I'm fucked up." He stares at me with those piercing eyes and taps himself on the temple. "Something in here is broken, maybe always has been. I don't know. I tried the whole relationship thing for a bit, but I sucked at it."

I narrow my eyes at him. I have no idea why he's saying such a thing, and again—I don't care.

"What did you do, kill her?" I regret the words as soon as they're out of my mouth.

"One of them." He glances away for a second.

A shiver runs down my spine as I realize he means what he says—he has actually killed a woman he was in a relationship with. I swallow hard and glance back toward the Viper. Deklan is leaning against the hood, watching closely.

I look back at Arden, and he's still staring at me intently. He takes a deep breath before he speaks again.

"This kinda business—this kinda *life*—isn't an easy one to navigate. We all get here by different roads. Those of us who weren't born to it, maybe we had a choice and maybe we didn't. Some people think we stay because of fear, but that's not it. It's loyalty that keeps us here."

He tilts his head to one side and furrows his brow.

"Do you know what it takes to come between that?" he asks. "To wedge yourself between a man like that and the family? To strip away that which he holds so closely to his soul that he always thought they were one and the same?"

I stare at him, unsure if the question is rhetorical and unable to answer regardless.

"That guy there," Arden says as he tilts his head in Deklan's direction, "he's a good guy. He really loves you, and I think he'd do anything for you. He's not like me."

"I know he isn't."

"Good." Arden nods. He takes a step forward, closing the gap between us. I start to step back, but he grabs my arm and shoves the envelope full of cash into my hand. "Open up a scholarship in her name or something. I don't want it."

Without another word, he drops into the driver's seat of the Camaro, guns the engine, and pulls away.

Chapter 40

I'm still overwhelmed, in shock, and not completely sure what's happening around me. Sean has been gone nearly a month, and it seems we haven't stopped to take a breath since that afternoon.

Business, business, business.

At first, it was all about letting the other organizations know that Deklan was in charge. Apparently, this was a relief to many of the local crime lords who had dealt with Sean. Everyone seems glad he is gone, and more opportunities keep coming out of the woodwork on a daily basis.

We relocated to the Foley mansion.

Deklan was hesitant, but Teagan can be even more stubborn than my husband. He caved when Teagan threatened to sell the place, and we moved in the next day. The bedroom is larger than our apartment, and there's a fireplace in it. I had gotten so used to living simply; I'm not sure what to do with the extravagance all around me.

I suppose I got used to life without it, and I'll get used to living with it as well. All in good time.

Brian married Lauren, the former prostitute whose pimp was mysteriously murdered months ago. They're still on their honeymoon in Las Vegas, which I thought was pretty appropriate.

Deklan paid for the expenses and gave Brian a bonus to go blow on blackjack tables.

It has been hectic, to say the least, and I'm not sure if I can cope with one more thing as I sit in the ginormous master bathroom and stare at a small white stick with a seemingly large pink plus sign on its display.

I swallow hard. I don't know if I should laugh or cry.

"Babe? You ready?"

"Just a sec!" I call back to my husband, who is already dressed and ready for dinner. It's our six-month anniversary, and I can't believe everything that has happened in such a short time.

I have no idea how he's going to take my little bombshell.

"What's going on in your head?" Deklan asks quietly as he leans across the restaurant table and takes my hand in his. "You seem rather distracted."

I shrug, unable to meet his gaze. If I look at him, I'm sure he'll know. I don't know how he will know, but he will. I decide on a subject change instead.

"What ever happened to Charlie Grange?" I ask. "I never saw him after...after that day."

"That's what's on your mind?" Deklan leans back and scowls. "He's never going to bother you again, that's for sure. Did you really think I would let him just walk after all that?"

"So, he's dead?" I ask quietly. Deklan's blank stare tells me that he is.

"That's not really what's bothering you," Deklan says. He leans forward again and sips from his wine glass. "Out with it."

I glance at him through my lashes. He has that ominous stare on his face which means he's not going to let me distract him. I could probably offer to let him fuck me in the bathroom of the expensive restaurant, and he would still demand an answer first.

"I took a test before we left," I say quietly.

"A test? What are you doing, learning another language?" He chuckles.

"No, I, um…" I stop and look away for a moment, hoping to catch the server's eye to refill my water glass or order dessert or something, but he's nowhere to be found. Deklan is still staring at me intently, impatiently waiting for my answer. "I took a different kind of test. It was a, um, a pregnancy test."

Deklan's hand seems to freeze in midair with the wine glass halfway up to his open mouth. He blinks a few times, clears his throat, and sets the wine glass back on the table.

"You're pregnant?" he says in a nearly inaudible whisper.

I suck my lower lip behind my teeth and nod.

"Like, with a baby?"

"Is there another kind of pregnant I should know about?" I can't help it—I giggle. "Yes, with a baby."

"That's why you haven't touched your wine."

"Yeah."

"Shit!" Deklan's eyes go wide as he pushes his own wine glass away from himself, nearly toppling it onto the white linen tablecloth. "I shouldn't be drinking either! Alcohol can do shit to your sperm!"

He looks positively horrified, and I can't stop my giggles from turning into a loud laugh.

"It's too late to worry about that, you dork! It's already done!"

"Oh, yeah." Deklan blows out a huge sigh of relief and shakes his head to clear it. "Good, because I really need another glass now."

"Are you mad?" He seems so shocked, I really can't tell.

"Mad? Jesus, no!" His eyes sparkle as he says the words, and he gives me a goofy grin. "I'm fucking ecstatic!"

"Oh, good!" I smile, and Deklan reaches over the table again to squeeze my hand.

"When?" he asks. "I mean, how far along are you?"

"I'm not sure," I say. "I think maybe two or three months. With everything else that's been going on, I haven't really kept track. I'll have to go see a doctor to find out."

"But you're sure?"

"Positive." I giggle again. "I can show you the plus sign on the test if you like."

"Well, shit," Deklan says. "That trumps my plan."

"What plan?"

"There was something I wanted to ask you." He looks me in the eye with that silly grin still on his face.

"What's that?"

Deklan gets quiet for a moment, and the grin disappears. His shoulders rise and fall with a deep breath before he looks at me again.

"You told me I should do this," Deklan says softly. "You said I should take over the business at Teagan's request and lead this organization. I never wanted it, though I will do it, but Kera—I can't do it alone."

"You won't be alone," I say. "Teagan and Brian are behind you one hundred percent."

"I don't mean them, Kera. I want you to be a part of it, too."

"I'm doing the books." I'm confused, and I'm not sure what he's getting at.

"I want you to be a bigger part of it," Deklan says. "You're awesome with the books, but we can hire someone to do that. I need you at my side, helping me make the right decisions. I need you to run this organization with me, babe. I promise you'll never be bored again."

I stare at my husband and think about his words. Did I want to help him lead an entire crime organization, whatever that might entail? Did I want to know all the gritty details of what, before, has always happened outside of my earshot? Could I handle what Deklan does when I'm not looking?

I think about the bloody shirt I found in the bathroom trash shortly after we were married and about everything that has happened since that day. I think about how I feel when Deklan goes off without me and how much more comfortable I am in his presence, no matter what is being discussed. Could I do this? Did I want to?

Yes. Yes, I can, and I do.

"Yes, Deklan," I say with confidence. "I'll help you."

"Good." Deklan's smile returns, and I swear he blushes slightly as he looks away from me. "I have something for you."

He reaches into his pants pocket and pulls something out. He holds whatever it is between his hands so I can't see it.

"Ever since you brought up that bit about Sean buying that ring, I haven't been able to get it out of my mind. We didn't start this right, and I want to fix it."

I gasp as Deklan moves one hand and opens a small, blue box containing a platinum and diamond ring. It looks nothing like the one Sean picked out. It is absolutely beautiful.

"I want a real Catholic wedding in a church with a priest. I want you to wear the ring I picked out for you. I want to marry you because I love you, and I want you to agree because you love me and because you want it, not because you are forced into it. I want to put how all of this started behind us and begin all over again."

"No more secrets. No more lies. We work together— always." I look at him as I repeat what has become our mantra.

Deklan stands up from the table and moves in front of me. He drops down on one knee and holds the box out as he squares his shoulders. He reaches for my hand, and for a moment, he stares down at my wrist as he rubs his thumb against it.

"Will you marry me again, Kera?" Deklan looks up at me in earnest. "Please?"

My eyes burn as I reach out and touch his hand. By the time I answer, tears are streaming down my face.

"Yes, Deklan. I will most certainly marry you again."

He slips the other ring off my finger and replaces it with the one he bought. I can't stop crying as I wrap my arms around his neck, and he nearly pulls me out of my chair as he returns the embrace.

Everyone in the restaurant begins to cheer.

Epilogue

"I'm fat." I turn back and forth, gazing at myself in the mirror. The bulge in my midsection isn't huge, but I can definitely tell the difference.

"You're pregnant." Teagan reaches up and adjusts the tiara on my head.

I'm not sure where the tiara fits in the list of old, new, borrowed, or blue, but I'm wearing it anyway. It makes me feel like Kathy is here with me and that she approves.

"People will know."

"All the people who care already know."

"They know I'm fat?"

"Ugh!" Teagan smacks my shoulder and then moves to straighten out the train of the dress. "Just shut it. It's about that time."

A knock takes my attention from my bulging stomach, and Teagan goes to open the door.

"You ready, kid?" Brian grins from the doorway. "If we don't go soon, I think Deklan might take off for the bar. I'm never seen him so nervous!"

"What's he got to be nervous about?" Teagan asks with a snort. "It's not like he hasn't already done this once."

"I don't think it's quite the same for him," Brian says. "He's all about being in God's house and all that. This one means a lot to him."

"It does." I smile at Brian as I take his arm, and he leads me to the doors of the sanctuary. Teagan sneaks around to the side door, and a couple of minutes later, the "Wedding March" begins to play.

"I think that's our cue," Brian says quietly.

He pushes open the door, and I stare down the long, candlelit aisle of the church.

A church. We're getting married in an actual church, and there's a priest standing at the altar, wearing a long robe and a purple sash. I can't help but compare everything around me to our first wedding, held in an office with a madman at Deklan's side.

Most of the guests are the same ones who were at the first wedding, minus my late father, of course, and the addition of Brian's wife, Lauren. The biggest difference is that my mom is in the front row, smiling instead of bawling. We haven't actually reconnected since the last ceremony, but I want to try. With my father gone, she is going to need me.

Teagan stands as my maid of honor—again—and Mac is standing up for Deklan since Brian offered to give me away.

Deklan.

As I walk down the aisle getting closer and closer to him, I see him in such a remarkably different light. I feel no fear, only hope for what the future might bring to us and our growing family. I'm captivated by the love in his eyes as Brian puts my hand in Deklan's, and the priest starts speaking.

Much like the first time, I barely hear any of the words, but for a much difference reason. All my focus is on the man next to me.

When he held my hand the first time, I was terrified of the huge, imposing figure I was about to marry. I was sure my wedding night was going to end in blood and that I was being given to my executioner.

Now, I know who Deklan really is. Strong, without a doubt, but also the gentlest and kindest man I have ever known. He's thoughtful, caring, and willing to take my feelings into consideration despite his own propensity for stubbornness.

And he loves me.

We say traditional Catholic vows, exchange rings, and listen to the priest as he reads scripture, and we hold hands and stare at each other as if there is no one else in the room. When we're pronounced husband and wife and told to kiss, Deklan places his hand on the back of my head, and I stand up on my toes so I can reach him better.

His lips are warm and soft against mine. I close my eyes, and my skin tingles down to my toes. As we part, he grins and hugs me to his chest.

"I'm going to take care of you," Deklan whispers in my ear, and my heart swells at the words and the true meaning behind them.

"I'll take care of you, too," I whisper back as our lips meet again. "Always."

"Always," he repeats. "Forever. I love you, Kera."

"I love you too, Deklan."

As we turn to face the small gathering, everyone begins to cheer. When I glance at Teagan, I swear her usually expressionless eyes look a little misty. Rice is thrown at us as we exit the church, and a limo waits outside to take us to the reception at the restaurant where Deklan proposed to me.

Inside the back of the limo, Deklan hugs me against his side and places his hand against my stomach.

"How are ya, little guy?" he asks. "Did you like the ceremony?"

"You don't know if it's a he yet." I tilt my head to the side and smile. Deklan started talking to my belly a week ago, and now he's acting like a junkie getting a fix.

"Just a guess." He strokes the fabric covering my stomach. "I got a fifty percent chance of being right. That's better odds than Brian gets in Vegas."

He finally looks up from my stomach and kisses me again.

"Thank you for indulging me in all this." Deklan blinks a couple times and swallows hard. "It really meant a lot to me."

"I'm glad we did it." I touch the side of his face, kiss him again, and let myself get lost in the sensation of his lips on mine.

This is the way it was meant to be, with smiles, happy tears, and an unstoppable love.

~~THE END~~

Author's Notes

This book has taken longer to write than any other book I've released since I started doing this fulltime author gig. Thanks so much for being patient with me, and I hope getting to know Deklan and Kera is worth the wait! If you are an Evan Arden fan, I hope you enjoyed a little glimpse into his dealings outside of Chicago. If you don't know him and want to delve into the mind of a hitman, check out Evan's six-book series!

I definitely have more books planned for the rest of the year, so make sure you are following me on social media so you know what's coming up next!

Until then, keep reading!

Shay Savage

DEKLAN

More Books by Shay Savage

Stand Alone Novels:

Transcendence

Offside

Worth

Alarm

Win Some, Lose Some

Surviving the Storm Series:

Surviving Raine

Bastian's Storm

Evan Arden Series:

Otherwise Alone

Otherwise Occupied

Uncockblockable (a Nick Wolfe story)

Otherwise Unharmed

Isolated

Irrevocable

Unexpected Circumstances Series

The Handmaid

The Seduction

The Consummation

The Shortcoming

The Concubine

The Apprehension

The Devastation

Novella Collection:

Savaged

Caged Trilogy:

Caged: Takedown Teague

Trapped

Released

DEKLAN

About the Author

Shay Savage is an independent author from Cincinnati, Ohio, where she lives with her family and a variety of household pets. She is an accomplished public speaker and holds the rank of Distinguished Toastmaster from Toastmasters International. Her hobbies include off-roading in her big, yellow Jeep, science fiction in all forms, and soccer. Savage holds a degree in psychology, and she brings a lot of that knowledge into the characters within her stories.

From the author: "It's my job to make you FEEL. That doesn't always mean you'll feel good, but I want my readers to be connected enough to my characters to care."

Savage's books many books span a wide variety of topics and sub-genres with deeply flawed characters. From cavemen to addicts to hitmen, you'll find yourself falling for these seemingly irredeemable characters!

Made in the USA
Middletown, DE
02 July 2017